THE RUINS OF ISIS

MARION ZIMMER BRADLEY

PUBLISHED BY POCKET BOOKS NEW YORK

**POCKET BOOKS, a Simon & Schuster division of
GULF & WESTERN CORPORATION**
1230 Avenue of the Americas, New York, N.Y. 10020

Copyright © 1978 by Marion Zimmer Bradley

Published by arrangement with The Donning Company/Publishers
Library of Congress Catalog Card Number: 78-14268

ISBN: 0-671-82819-3

First Pocket Books printing August, 1979

10 9 8 7 6 5 4 3 2 1

Trademarks registered in the United States and other countries.

Printed in the U.S.A.

I am only a man
And I have no part in Paradise.
Twice have I tasted bliss
And twice have I been driven forth;
Once when I left my mother's womb
And again when I was driven forth
From my Mother's house.

When I am done with life
Will the Goddess take me, perhaps
To her loving breasts?

*Song of
the Men's House
of Ariadne*

chapter one

THE PILOT OF THE SHUTTLE SHIP WAS A WOMAN. CENDRI
had been prepared for this—intellectually—but the
reality was a shock. A small, hard-bodied woman, hair
clipped short, a band of metallic cloth around her
breasts, another, wider, around her hips, low magnet-
ized shoes, and a small crimson badge pinned on her
shoulder-band. The observer in Cendri, the anthropologist she had been trained to be, asked automatically,
*uniform? Badge of office? I didn't think they had a space
service of any kind, they have so little contact with the
Unity.*

She wanted to clutch at Dal's hand, all the time
knowing perfectly well that this was the one thing, here
at the very entrance—officially—to the Matriarchate of
Isis/Cinderella, that she must *not* do.

The Pilot was waiting, with raised eyebrows.

"Scholar Dame Malocq?"

Cendri gathered herself together. Fortunately the
pilot took it for granted that the brief disorientation of
the transittube from the Unity ship had simply left
Cendri dizzy and, for a moment, unable to speak.
Cendri knew that the moment of truth was on her—
truth? The moment when the impersonation must
begin. She said, steeling herself for the lie:

"I am the Scholar Dame Malocq."

1

The pilot, gravely and unsmiling, made the formal gesture—hands clasped before the face—which, on the planets of the Unity, was the universal greeting and mark of respect. Cendri wondered who had coached her.

"Welcome to the Matriarchate of Isis, Scholar Dame." Again, with detachment, Cendri took mental notes. *They don't use the name Cinderella.* She hadn't really expected them to, though the name was still carried double, Isis/Cinderella, in the Unity records, and on University.

"And this—" the look the pilot gave Dal was cold, clinical, impersonal; he might have been another suitcase or travelpak, "—this is the Scholar Dame's consort and Companion?"

Cendri nodded in acknowledgement. She and Dal had made jokes about this; it had sounded like a light-hearted imposture, a formality, a technicality. They had laughed together about the rigid laws of Isis/Cinderella, the Matriarchate. But before the unsmiling, uninterested eyes of the young woman pilot, it had suddenly ceased to be funny; and Dal was standing behind her where she could not catch his eyes, even for the momentary reassurance of the shared joke. She said "Yes. His name is—"

But the pilot was not listening. "The Scholar Dame is aware that the import of offworld males is technically an infringement of the laws of the Matriarchate. Concessions have, as the Scholar Dame knows, been made to the respected status of the Scholar from University; but certain formalities may not be waived. I am required to fill out a declaration in the name of the Scholar Dame." She whipped out a form and some kind of writing instrument. "Does it have a property tattoo?"

"Does it have—*what?*"

The pilot repeated, with well-concealed impatience, "A property tattoo or brand, an unremovable mark signifying permanent ownership and responsibility. Is my command of the Scholar Dame's language insufficient? Would the Scholar Dame wish me to summon an Official Translator?"

"No, thank you," Cendri said weakly, "the—the term was unfamiliar, that is all. No, Dal is not—not tattooed or branded. It is not—not our custom to disfigure males."

The young pilot's shoulders lifted in a faint shrug, without interest. "As I told the Scholar Dame, concessions have been made to her respected status; this requirement has been waived by special action of the Pro-Matriarch, as a diplomatic courtesy." Somehow she managed to convey, without the faintest change in her inexpressive, courteous tone, that she felt this concession had been a mistake. Cendri wondered if she was being hypersensitive. She clasped her hands formally before her face and murmured that she was appreciative of the courtesy of the Pro-Matriarch, wondering who the Pro-Matriarch was.

"Nevertheless, as the Scholar Dame certainly understands, the formal declaration of responsibility, and some form of permanent identification cannot be waived, even for diplomatic purposes," the young pilot said. "If you wish, we can be met immediately upon landing by a malesurgeon, and arrange to have it branded or tattooed upon the spot. The process is quite quick and extremely humane, and the marking can be either inconspicuous or ornamental, as the Scholar Dame desires."

Cendri blinked, looked helplessly at Dal, but—as he had been carefully briefed to do—he was staring straight ahead and pretending not to hear. The one thing she could not do was to consult him. She had not been prepared for this. She swallowed, and said, with a firmness she was far from feeling, "We were not advised of this requirement, and we cannot accede to it. Since we are not intending to take up permanent residence on Isis/Cinderella, it would not be suitable to have him branded or tattooed."

What will I do if they insist? Bluff it out, threaten to turn around and go back to University?

The pilot raised her eyebrows again, and Cendri realized she had made two mistakes in one sentence. She had used the name under which the planet was still carried on the rolls at University, *Cinderella*. Even more serious, she had made a mistake in language against which she had been especially, and repeatedly warned; she had referred to Dal as *him*, instead of by the special neuter pronoun used for males except in a specifically sexual context. The pilot was actually blushing; and to apologize for the indecency was to compound it. Better to let the pilot think Cendri ignorant than vulgar.

The young pilot struggled with a nervous giggle as she said "In that case, the Scholar Dame must arrange for a temporary marking of some sort. It can be marked—" she very faintly emphasized *it*—"with an earclamp or collar tag, but the most effective method is for a subcutaneous electronic implant in one testicle. This is an excellent training and disciplinary device for a male not accustomed to civilized restraints, as it can be located and controlled at any moment."

The implications of that swept Cendri with shock and horror; but she managed, somehow, to keep her face and voice calm.

"No, I think not; that would be quite excessive."

"I compliment the Scholar Dame upon her confidence," said the pilot indifferently. "If she is willing to be content with an ear clamp or collar tag—"

"A collar tag, I think, will be quite sufficient," Cendri said, and didn't dare look at Dal. Not for the first time, she found herself admiring her husband's courage, and the scientific curiosity which had prompted him to accept this subordinate position.

"—in that case, we can dispense with the attendance of a malesurgeon," the pilot said, "I am licensed to install an earclamp myself; I have done it many times, and I assure you it would cause the male only temporary distress, if the Scholar Dame wishes for the added security." Cendri shook her head, and the pilot, although she looked doubtful, nodded in compliance.

She said, "I am also equipped with a diplomatic collar-tag," whipped it out of a kind of utility pouch at her belt, and locked it, on a narrow metal chain, around Dal's neck; marked a number on it with a carbide pencil. She said, "The Scholar Dame is, of course, legally responsible for any damage caused by her property; does the Scholar Dame fully understand that it is liable to be summarily destroyed if it should attack any citizen of the Matriarchate?"

Cendri, in a daze, was wondering; *how did we get ourselves into this?* But it was too late, now, to retreat. The idea was ludicrous—that Dal was a dangerous animal, likely to attack a citizen, and to be summarily destroyed for it! The pilot's voice was pleasant, neutral, but it seemed to Cendri to hold sinister menace. "Will the Scholar Dame sign a form of legal responsibility?"

"Certainly," Cendri said, trying hard to steady her voice, and scrawled her name on the form held out to her. One part of her noted the ancient custom preserved—on University she would simply have presented her Scholar's identity number for registration. But she was light-years away from University, and a good way outside the Unity itself.

Formalities concluded, the pilot favored her at last with a smile. "We can get under way now, Scholar Dame. I will signal the Unity Ship for breaking orbit in minutes." Efficiently, she was stowing Cendri's luggage in special compartments, carefully indicating a padded seat, belts, restrainers. Cendri hesitated before getting into it, looking anxiously at Dal, and the pilot shrugged. "If the Scholar Dame is worried about her Companion—you can put it in the seat over there, and wedge it in with blankets. But I wouldn't worry. A few bumps and bruises don't hurt them, you know. They really don't feel things the way that we do. That is a scientifically established fact, Scholar Dame, and we have quite careful humane regulations to avoid accidental harm to males."

Cendri gulped and wedged Dal carefully into the indicated extra seat. She said in an undertone, "I'm afraid it's going to be a rough ride." This kind of shuttle ship was not very smooth even with proper restrainer seats. Without them, she didn't like to think about the surge away from the Unity ship, the long deceleration down into the atmosphere of Isis/Cinderella.

Dal smiled, and the smile heartened her. He said, in a voice low enough not to be heard by the pilot, who was getting into her own acceleration couch, "Relax, love, we had this all out before we agreed to come here. So far, I can cope with it. The shuttles on Pioneer weren't very smooth, either, remember; it was only when women started going offworld that we even bothered with couches in the shuttles." He chuckled softly, and the pilot gave him, over her bare shoulder, an irritable glance.

Just as if, Cendri thought, the noise of a barking dog had distracted her.

Yes, just exactly like that. . . .

Cendri got into her own couch, carefully fastening the restrainer straps and pads. What Dal said was right, of course. He had grown up on Pioneer, and among the men of Pioneer, endurance of hardships of this kind were regarded as a test of courage and manhood. He was used to this kind of thing.

But he's not used to it now. . . .

She told herself, firmly, to stop fretting. Dal had assured her he would be all right. The pilot turned briefly to check on her passenger, then spoke into an intercom of some kind, evidently getting clearance from the Unity ship and the port on Isis. Then she said, "Brace yourself, Scholar Dame; the first surge is powerful. After that, the braking rockets will fire on a count of three, after which we will spend approximately four minutes in free orbit before we begin to decelerate for landing. In slightly less than fourteen minutes we will be landing in the city of Ariadne."

As she had warned, the acceleration surge away from the Unity ship was forceful. Cendri, tense with anxiety about Dal on his restrainer-free couch, felt the surge of violent nausea as the violent reversing sensations turned her dizzy, then sick with the weightless feel of free orbit. The pilot, seemingly oblivious, whistled an odd little tune as she concentrated on her work.

Cendri clamped her teeth in her lip, and thought, not for the first time, *I'll never be able to handle this. Not even with Dal's help. Never.*

Maybe the Unity is right, not to give assignments like this to women. I know I'm going to make a mess of this one!

It's going to be rough on Dal if I fail at this—and maybe worse if I succeed. Women on Pioneer are never Scholars; there hasn't been a Scholar Dame from Pioneer in the history of University!

Cendri and Dal had met on University, the scholar's world, where all the knowledge of the known planets of the Unity was gathered in a single central location. Cendri had been already a Scholar, then, while Dal was still only a Student. At first—she knew it—the very difference had intrigued the young man from Pioneer. Cendri's own world did not regard scholarship in a woman as anything so very surprising, and there had been a few—though not many—Scholar Dames from her home planet, Beta Capella; mostly in education and linguistics, but it was not really unusual for women to excel in the social sciences.

She had found it intriguing when he had courted and flattered her. She knew that she herself had been the first woman he had ever known who was genuinely his intellectual equal. She was flattered that he had turned to her, rather than to one of the men, for help in finding his way around the bewildering new world of University. And also, at first, she had been flattered that he had tried to meet her on an intellectual level, as a fellow Scholar, rather than as a man meets a woman. Later it had seemed almost a slight, and when he had begun to court her in earnest, she had felt relieved, as if, in some way, he had confirmed the quality of her womanhood. Soon sexuality had begun to shadow and compete with their shared interests and tastes; and before very long they were spending so much time together that it had seemed logical to marry instead of maintaining separate quarters.

They had been married, now, just over a year. Dal had been preparing for his examination as Master Scholar, and Cendri knew he was already regarded as the most promising Scholar in the Department of Alien Archaeology and Artifacts. He had chosen to do his thesis and graduate research on the very few remaining extant ruins of the mysterious, and still hypothetical, race known as the Builders. He had applied for, and been accepted, as Research Assistant to the Scholar Dame Lurianna di Velo.

The Scholar Dame di Velo was a woman of considerable age, powerful, important, author of many controversial, but impeccably scholarly, works on Archaeology. She was considered *the* foremost authority on alien artifacts; but she was notorious because she adhered, publicly, to the controversial theory that the entire Galaxy had, at one time, been seeded, or colonized, by a single race of beings which had been given the name of Builders. Master Scholars and Dames all over the Galaxy attacked her thesis; but they could not fault her scholarship or her respectable credentials; the theory had acquired respectability largely because of her defense of it. It had previously been considered questionable, if not completely crackpot.

Cendri herself should have applied, two seasons before, for a Scholar Dame's grant. But on her marriage, she had applied for a season's leave of absence, and had been granted it. Afterward, she had delayed. Cendri's own field, the Department of Xeno-anthropology and Comparative Culture, still insisted that all research theses be done as fieldwork, and Cendri did not want to be parted so quickly from Dal. She was hoping that Dal's first assignment with the Scholar Dame, while he qualified for his own credentials as Master Scholar, would take them together to a planet where Cendri could do her own thesis work at the same time.

And then she had begun to wonder, hesitate about doing it at all. After all, Dal was from Pioneer; he had come a long way in one generation, but culturally imposed social attitudes were not changed overnight. Considering that, perhaps one advanced degree was enough in a family. There was always interesting work to be done for a Scholar; she had no particular ambition, now, to be a Dame. And she was not sure it would please Dal if she became a Dame.

Dal liked the Scholar Dame di Velo and respected her work. But it was clear that he found it hard to accept the notion that a woman could be his superior in position and status; she knew he was chafing until his own Master Scholar qualifications would make him the Scholar Dame's equal. He said often, as a joke—but he said it once or twice too often for a joke—*what would they think of me on Pioneer, taking orders from a she-Scholar?*

Then everything had happened quickly. The Scholar Dame di Velo had been requested, by the Matriarchate of Isis/Cinderella, to come and examine the ancient ruins on their world, which might, or might not, be of Builder origin. The Scholar Dame di Velo had regarded this as a vindication of a long campaign; Dal had been considerably less enthusiastic.

"The Matriarchate on Cinderella!" Dal had been halfway between despair and disgust. Cendri, feeling the lurch and sway as the shuttle ship shuddered out of free orbit into deceleration, remembered the dismay with which Dal had spoken of the Matriarchate.

"A society run entirely by women! *Sharrioz!*" He had scowled and stormed for hours about this assignment. "There won't be any chance at all for me to do independent research, not in the Matriarchate! I'll just be there to fetch and carry for the di Velo woman!" he raged, "and here I was thinking I could get my Master's quals before I went—"

Angry as Dal had been, Cendri could not help being excited.

"The Matriarchate! Oh, Dal, if we could go

together—if I could get a grant to do my research *there*—there are almost *no* records of study actually *within* a matriarchal society—"

"That's because there aren't any in the civilized worlds," Dal had grumbled, "and I already asked the Scholar Dame." His injured tone had said clearly, *see, I'm always thinking about you,* and Cendri had cringed even while she was grateful to him. "The Matriarchate refuses to allow any anthropological research on Cinderella, something about being a working society, not a freak to be studied—so you can't go openly as an anthropologist. But the Scholar Dame said you can go along; she's going to invent some minor job for you, so you can be with me, and maybe you can take notes enough to expand them into some kind of research work. There's so little information about any working Matriarchy that even a *little* information about them ought to be valuable." And Cendri had been grateful for even that crumb, until he had added gloomily, "If I go at all, that is. I ought to throw up this job and get a Research Assistantship with some good, qualified man."

But there had been really no choice. The Scholar Dame di Velo was the only Scholar of repute working on the Builders at all, and only her reputation had made work on the Builders remotely acceptable. Dal had to stick with the Scholar Dame, or do the last two seasons of his research over again on something else—not to mention that if he deserted the Scholar Dame di Velo on such flimsy grounds, he would never again get a decent Research Assistantship.

The pilot glanced over her bare shoulder at Cendri and said, "We will now be descending into atmosphere, Scholar Dame. In a few minutes you will be seeing the shoreline of Ariadne." Cendri, fighting the growing tug of gravity—unaccustomed after so long in the Unity ship—winced again at the undeserved title. Obsessively, she went back to remembering, as if she had to get it all straight before they landed.

There had been all the preparations for departure to Cinderella, which the Matriarchate had renamed Isis. Taped lessons in the language, in what little was known of their culture. Cendri remembered that, and remembered, more clearly, Dal's increasing distress and disquiet at the assignment, so that Cendri felt guilty about her own growing eagerness. How could she be so happy when Dal was so wretched?

She had discussed the project with her own Research Mentor, and he had agreed to give her tentative approval—subject to review on her return, and the amount of research she could actually complete on Isis/Cinderella—to use this as her Research fieldwork.

And then the accident, which had so completely altered their plans. The Scholar Dame Lurianna di Vclo was, at present, in an amniotic tank on University Medical Center, growing a new hand and a new eye, and regenerating assorted internal organs. At her age, that was a complicated and lengthy business. It had looked as if the Isis/Cinderella project would have to be abandoned; and Cendri had not known whether she was glad or sorry. The Matriarchate had been duly notified of the accident; and after certain delays, an answer had come. It had told them that in lieu of the Scholar Dame di Velo, the Matriarchate would gladly accept the presence of her assistant, the Scholar Dame Malocq.

Cendri was, like most Scholars, a passable linguist; but she had not been extensively trained in semantics, and had not, at first, understood the implications of this. On her own world, a married woman did not take her husband's name at all, and Cendri still thought of herself as Cendri Owain; Scholar Owain. But it *was* the custom on Pioneer, and it had seemed very important to Dal; so she had applied for, and received, identification in Dal's name. Cendri Malocq.

"Don't you see," Dal said, "in *their* language, there is no special word differentiating *Master Scholar* from *Scholar Dame*. The word for a higher degree would translate something like *Extra-Scholar,* but it is translated *Scholar Dame* because on Isis/Cinderella *all* honorifics are feminine. It didn't occur to them that a famous woman scholar—and they *did* know that di Velo was a woman, they had made sure of it—would not have a woman assistant. So in sending a message accepting the Dame di Velo's assistant, they naturally used the feminine honorific."

"But why should they assume—?"

"I thought you had studied the Matriarchate. One of their basic assumptions is that all worlds in the Unity are completely dominated by men, and that no woman intelligent enough to be a Scholar would risk this domination. So they believe di Velo's assistant, Scholar Malocq, would *of course* be a woman—"

"But you aren't—" she said, not quite seeing what he was driving at, and he had said, "But you are. Don't you understand? There is a Scholar Malocq, with credentials. Isn't it lucky that you took my name? Now you can go in the Scholar Dame's place—"

"Dal, I can't," she protested, panicked, "I don't know *anything* about Archaeology—"

"But I do," he had said, in excitement. "I can give you tapes, educator crash courses, hypno-learning sets—enough to give you the patter, enough to get by! And I'll be right at your elbow all the time as *your* Research Assistant—don't you see? I'll be doing the work, and getting my quals, and you'll be fronting for me! And you'll be able to do your *own* research, too, you can observe everything because they'll take you everywhere as a visiting dignitary—can't you see, Cendri, what a wonderful chance this is, for both of us?"

She had still protested. It wouldn't be honest, it wasn't fair to the Matriarchate. But her protests had been half-hearted. A chance to study the Matriarchate at first hand, an assignment where she could get qualification as a Scholar Dame and which would not separate her from Dal! The authorities on University

had been all too willing to go along with the deception.
It was, after all, the first time anyone with anthropologist's credentials had been allowed inside the Matriarchy. Anyway, it wouldn't have been easy to find a
replacement for the maverick di Velo; she was the only
Scholar of repute who would seriously investigate the
possibility of Builder ruins on Isis.

And so Cendri had been qualified; hastily, and
provisionally, as Acting Dame for the term of her stay
on Isis/Cinderella; and here she was.

The young pilot spoke into her intercom, meaningless technical phrases to Cendri, then said, "We are
now flying at an altitude of six thousand Universal
Meters over the shoreline of Ariadne, Scholar Dame, if
you would care to see an aerial view of the harbors and
coastlines. There is a viewport directly at the side of
your couch; the latch releases upward."

Cendri thumbed the latch, and the cabin of the
shuttle ship was quickly flooded with orange sunlight.
She slitted her lids against the light of the sun, and
looked down at a surface of sea which, from this
distance, looked one even green color. Small islands
were scattered, thick greenish patches, or dark rocky
outcrops; then she made out the shoreline, with brown-
ish edgings which she knew were sandy beaches, and
dark patches of some kind of vegetation. She could see
boats, at this distance only tiny toylike shapes, in the
harbor and out on the waves; there were, further
inland, smooth rolling hills, and strips which might
have been ploughed fields under cultivation, a
blackish-purple color.

As they flew along the coast, Cendri noticed black
shapes, sharp-edged and regular, thrusting upward in a
curious pattern. There seemed a kind of geometry to
their arrangement, although she could not identify it.

She asked, "Those towers—is that the city of Ariadne?"

The pilot made a negative gesture. "No, indeed!"
she said, "Could intelligent women live at such heights?

When the ground shakes, what would happen? Directly below us is the territory known as We-were-guided; in my grandmother's day, or so we are told by the Elders, the ship which brought our foremothers to Isis was guided here to these ancient ruins."

Dal sat up, craning his neck toward the viewport at Cendri's side; Cendri could understand how he felt. She, Cendri, could *see* the mysterious Ruins—were they those of the Builders?—which had brought Dal here; and he, Dal, swaddled in blankets and wedged into a spare seat like unregarded cargo, could not! Her heart ached for him, but there was a part to be played, and already the pilot was frowning disapprovingly at Dal over her shoulder.

"Tell it to lie down and be quiet or it may be hurt," she said, not as if she cared, and Cendri, feeling she would choke on the words, said, "Lie down, Dal. It won't be long now."

As if she were speaking to a troublesome dog. Just like that. And Dal was the Scholar for whom the Matriarchs had sent—but they didn't know it!

Cendri had never felt so much like an imposter as she did at that moment. She tried to catch Dal's eye; but he would not look at her.

All this had seemed like a joke, on University. Now it did not seem funny at all.

chapter two

CENDRI HAD SEEN MANY SPACEPORTS THROUGH THE
Unity; mostly, they were very much alike. Chaotic,
confusing, with hurrying hordes of passengers, uni-
formed personnel everywhere, and all manner of
concessions and services. By contrast, this seemed
hardly a spaceport at all. A low concrete wall surrounded a long expanse of thickly planted vegetation which
felt soft and springy underfoot; paths were worn in the
sand here and there, and there was one big area where
there was no vegetation at all, only a blackened spot
where the shuttleship had landed. There were about
half a dozen other small shuttleships at one side of the
enclosure, inside a long, low, roofed building open at
one side to the weather; beyond the concrete wall was a
view of distant hills, grey in the distance.

There were only two other buildings inside the
enclosure; one looked like an enormous warehouse of
plastic prefab; the other was a good-sized building with
an assortment of vanes, antennas and other instrumentation protruding from a sort of dome on top.

Cendri and Dal were the only passengers anywhere
in sight. There were no slidewalks; the pilot herself
helped Cendri down the steps of the shuttle ship [Dal
was left to scramble down as best he could] and
beckoned to a tall, thin man in a loose, whitish pajama

15

suit, a red baldric tied around his shoulder. He was wheeling a small motorized dolly-platform.

The pilot said, "The personal belongings of the Scholar Dame from University are to be sent to the home of the Pro-Matriarch Vaniya. Will you make certain of that when a conveyance is available?"

He bowed without speaking, and Cendri, staring at the red baldric—she could not think of any world in the Unity where men habitually decorated themselves in this way—happened to intercept a glance between the man wheeling the platform—some kind of porter, apparently—and Dal. The man stared until he was sure he had Dal's attention; then, with one hand, taking care to avoid being seen by the pilot, made a curious gesture. He held his right hand with all four fingers, bunched, touching the thumb; then slowly drew the thumb apart from them, murmuring something too low for Cendri to hear.

The pilot was waiting, and Cendri started and hurried after her. The anthropologist within her was taking notes. Of course; in a society where women dominated, there would be many kinds of male bonds, secret societies and recognition symbols among men. Male bonding in groups appeared to be universal— Cendri was too good a scholar to say that anything, in a Galaxy-wide civilization, was *actually* universal, but male bonding was certainly a widespread phenomenon, and, Cendri had been taught, was the major form of social cohesion. That was one reason why such planets as Isis/Cinderella, with women socially dominant, were extremely rare. She could think of only two, in fact; this world where she now stood, and its own mother colony, Persephone. Except for the ill-fated Labrys experiment, she could remember no others.

Dal would have to help her study the male groups. If she was doing archaeological work for *him*, he would have to make up his mind to doing some of *her* work. She followed the pilot along the path, lifting her thin-sandalled feet fastidiously. She had not expected a world quite so primitive, and had been prepared for slidewalks, at least.

Why had the man with the red baldric greeted Dal? Was it simply a universal greeting between males?

Inside, the building with the instrument domes on top was divided into several separate areas by what looked like low, movable screens of translucent paper or plastic, painted with landscapes and flowers in bright colors. Beyond one such screen she saw an office filled with instrument consoles and television monitors; there was a low buzz of people, machinery, low-voiced conversation. In the larger space, a variety of people were coming and going, and it was here that Cendri finally decided what seemed so strange about the place.

It was not entirely the absence of enormous expanses of concrete and skyscrapers; Cendri had been on other worlds with little travel and no funds for expensive installations. Nor was it the absence of passenger traffic; there were many worlds whose citizens were content to remain at home, for cultural or psychological reasons. No, it was something else which made this world seem completely different. It was the absence of *uniforms*.

Two or three people were dressed like the shuttleship pilot, in brief metallic-cloth bands across breast and hip; but one of them was behind some kind of booth providing a service Cendri was not yet fluent enough in the written language to identify, and the other was emptying a trash container, so that this dress did not signify "shuttle ship pilot" or even "spaceport officer." There were many people coming and going on unidentifiable errands, but so far she had seen so many different costumes that it was dizzying. Many were dressed in a sort of loose pajama suit, shirt and trousers, making it hard to tell at once whether the wearer was male or female. Besides the pajama suits, and the brief functional breast-and-hip bands [she even saw a man wearing one such costume] there were loose, flowing robes, some hooded and some not; a few in

kilts to the knee, leaving breasts bare [no sexual taboo
on this, for both men and women wore them]. She
noted one or two men with elaborately curled and
coiffed hair, but some of the women, too wore this kind
of hair-dress. There seemed to be no specific dress
difference between males and females. Cendri felt
confused. How could you tell anyone's function or
status without some kind of uniform to mark what they
were doing? On the Unity ship which had brought them
here, one could immediately tell ship's officers and
functionaries, from stewards or service personnel. But
everyone here seemed to be dressed chaotically, without regard to function or even to gender. Cendri was
used to this on University—where most people followed the dress of their native world, except actually
within official University areas—and at spaceports
where men and women of various cultures mingled.
But such diversity within citizens of a single culture
group was unusual; Cendri had been on field trips to
many different societies, and she could not think of a
single one where it was not immediately possible to tell
men from women by some immediate cue of dress, hair
style or manner.

How do they tell the men from the women? she
wondered. There must be *some* cultural clue; she
simply wasn't experienced enough in this society, yet,
to guess what it was.

She wanted to ask a million questions; she wished she
were here on a normal research assignment in cross-
cultural anthropology. But she remembered that the
Matriarchate had put themselves on record about that,
a long time ago, in one of their very few communications with the Unity:

"The Matriarchate of Isis is not an experimental
society, and we will not allow ourselves to be studied by
scientists as if we were one of those glass-sided insect
colonies we give to our little daughters for toys!"

Hurrying through a long corridor at one edge of the
building—she noted that it, too, was only semi-divided
from the offices and waiting rooms, by the thin,

translucent screens which looked movable—she thought about that.

Cendri's Mentor, Dr. Lakshmann, had grumbled a lot about this. A most unscientific attitude, he had called it; unworthy of any society; ungrateful, anti-social. Cendri had protested—she had been only a Student then. Surely it was their own society, she had said, and they had the right to keep people out if they wanted to. Lakshmann hadn't been convinced. Paranoid, he had called the Matriarchate. But then a society which had convinced itself that women were mistreated within any society as enlightened as the Unity, would have to be paranoid. Cendri had tended to agree. After all, women were the equal of men, by law, on University, which represented the Unity at its best, its official policy. If there were fewer Scholar Dames than Master Scholars and Scholar Doctors, surely it was only that fewer women were willing to compete for these advanced academic prizes. Psychologically, Cendri had learned, women were less competitive; she had seen it in herself after her marriage to Dal. Cendri herself had had no trouble attaining Scholar rank; she was acknowledged —and by men—to be the superior of most men of that rank. Most women who became Scholars, and Scholar Dames, were superior; there were no mediocre Scholars, the mediocre woman Students dropped out. Didn't that prove that women, in the Unity, were actually regarded as somewhat superior? Cendri knew that she herself would have attained her quals for an advanced degree if she hadn't done what women were too likely to do, and taken time off after her marriage.

Obviously, then, the Matriarchate's attitude was pure paranoia. . . .

They had reached the end of the corridor; the pilot gestured Cendri into a small room, inside the translucent semi-divided screens, and made again the gesture of salute within the Unity, hands clasped before her face. Then, with a smile that made her look, for the first time, like the young girl she actually was, she said,

"It has been my honor and pleasure, Scholar Dame, to escort you and conduct you to the Chamber-of-reception-for-honored-guests. I truly hope I shall see you again while you honor Isis with your presence. The Pro-Matriarch Vaniya has been informed of your arrival; if you will be content to rest here and make yourself comfortable, Scholar Dame, she will soon send someone to welcome you. If you desire refreshment—" she indicated a console against the wall, "the control at the top will dispense hot liquids for your pleasure, and the control at the bottom, cold ones. I myself, unfortunately, must return to my assigned duties. Will the Scholar Dame give me leave to go?"

Cendri said, "Certainly, and thank you very much," and the pilot withdrew.

There was no furniture in the Chamber-of-reception-for-important-guests, but a few thick cushions were scattered about the floor, which was covered with a soft rug in neutral colors. Cendri went to examine the screens; she had thought the landscapes were printed on, but they were actually painted, not very skillfully. Behind her Dal said, "Well, how does it feel to be a VIP, Cendri?"

Immediately she was contrite, apologetic. She had almost forgotten Dal! She said hurriedly, "Oh, darling, I'm so sorry. The reception should have been for *you*—this is awful, isn't it? She was atrociously rude—she treated you like a dog, or something!"

Dal laughed, and Cendri was enormously relieved. They could manage to weather this somehow, if Dal could continue to treat it as a joke. She honestly didn't see how she could endure it otherwise.

"I gather men here *are* treated pretty much like dogs. Even five hundred years ago on Pioneer, we never branded our women, or made them wear property tags!" He chuckled as he fingered the numbered tag around his neck. "But I suppose a world of women would have to go to extremes."

"They certainly do," Cendri agreed indignantly, "I don't think I'm going to like it here, Dal!"

"Well, that's lucky! I had to take a lot of kidding in the Scholar's Room in the College of Archaeology—saying you'd get to like it, that if I had half a brain I'd never let my wife loose here to see what it was like with women on top . . . that sort of thing. I told them I trusted you and you were a sensible girl, but just the same—every one of those bastards thought it was *funny!*" He shook his head, ruefully. "Laughing stock of the whole Department, those last weeks before we left!"

"Oh, Dal, I *am* sorry—you should have told me—"

"Nothing you could do about it, love. Anyhow, I told them I'd have disguised *myself* as a woman with plastic what-do-you-callems for a chance to get at the Builder ruins, and sometimes I almost think I meant it," he said, laughing.

Suddenly she remembered. "Dal—the porter, the man in the red baldric—the one who took our luggage; he made some kind of sign at you; a signal, it looked like a password—"

"Oh; that," Dal said, "Yes, I noticed—"

"What did he say? I couldn't hear him?"

"He said, *We were not born in chains,*" Dal told her, "Must be some kind of religious society. Like the Khorists, on Betelgeuse Nine, who greet everybody with *Infinity is Peace,* remember? Of course, that's more in your line than mine; I don't know much about subcultures and subgroups and things like that." He smiled. "Or, really, give a damn."

"I had thought it might be some kind of male bonding society," she mused, "but it sounds—I wonder if it is some kind of underground, a kind of resistance movement against the government or something like that—"

Dal looked uncomfortable. But he said, "Come off it, Cendri, outfits like that would be secretive; they wouldn't walk up to a perfect stranger and make revolutionary statements at him!"

Cendri frowned; revolutionary statements? Well, she supposed *We were not born in chains* might be regarded as a revolutionary statement on a world where men literally wore tags or brands and were legally the property of their women. She hadn't thought about it that way. But certainly Dal was right; if it *was* intended as a revolutionary statement it would hardly have been a greeting to a perfect stranger, let alone someone from another planet!

"I'll need to find out something about how the men live in this society—" she began, then suddenly felt tired and shaky. This was not the time to argue. She went to the console and said, "Let's have some drinks. Hot or cold, Dal?"

."Cold," he said, "but you look as if you could use something hot, Cendri. Here, let me get it for you." He installed her on one of the cushions and went to the console.

The control at the top dispensed, in a preformed fibrous cup, a hot liquid which reminded Cendri, as she sipped it, of a hot fruit soup; but it was pleasantly tart, and after sipping about half of it she felt sufficiently revived to feel curious about Dal's cold drink and ask to taste it. It was dark brown and tasted like iced cocoa, but after a small sip she felt so stimulated that she began to wonder what it contained. Caffeine? An amphetamine-like alkaloid? Social drugs varied greatly from world to world.

Dal sat beside her, looking at the painted screens. She looked at the small squarish letters in the corner, saying, "You read the language better than I do; what does it say?"

Dal narrowed his eyes. "The name of the artist, I guess. Yes; *Painted by the—students,* I guess—*of the school for the daughters of fisherwomen.* Not much of a painting, but good for schoolgirls, I suppose." He shifted his weight, restlessly. "I wonder how long they're going to keep us waiting? It seems to me this is no treatment for a VIP."

She shrugged. "That depends on what their cultural attitudes are toward time and punctuality. In some societies, we'd already have been kept waiting an inexcusable length of time, and depending on our relative status as VIPs and the status of the one appointed to meet us, our official greeter would abase himself in the dust, or commit suicide with chagrin. On the other extreme, if it's a society with a very loose attitude toward time and punctuality, nobody might get around to remembering us for a couple of days. I suggest we make ourselves comfortable, because we'll have to relax and accept *their* attitude, whatever it is. That's the first rule for fieldwork in anthropology—find out the society's taboos and attitudes toward time, and just accept them."

Dal scowled angrily. "Damnation, Cendri, I made a casual comment, I didn't ask for a lecture on anthropology!"

"I wasn't lecturing—" Cendri began, then sighed. "Sorry, darling. Habit, I guess."

"It's all right," he said generously, "just remember you're not supposed to be an anthropologist at all, and I don't think the Dame di Velo would know a taboo if it walked up and spat on her!"

Cendri looked at him in amazement. "Don't they give instructions like that in your department? How can anyone possibly get along on any strange world without first knowing their taboos and cultural imperatives?"

"We manage to get along," he said, tight-lipped, and she sighed. "Dal, let's not quarrel. Please."

"It seems to me that *you* were doing the quarreling," he said, and Cendri bit her lip and didn't answer. There was no point in making him angry. This trip was going to test his forbearance to the uttermost. It was humiliating enough for him to accept an outwardly subordinate position on this trip, and even now he was wearing the collar-tag, locked on and marked with a number which proclaimed him, on this planet, legally her property. She would have to bend over backwards not to add further weight to his humiliation. She leaned again to look at the paintings on the screens, stood up to examine those on the other screen.

Abruptly, it tilted toward her, fell; startled, thrown

off balance, she clutched at Dal, and they fell together to the floor, the screen collapsing on top of them. There was a rumble like distant thunder; all over the building she heard cries, the sound of collapsing screens and interior walls. Shocked, clinging to Dal, she thought; *it must be an earthquake!* The drink console rocked back and forth, but did not fall; *it must be on rollers!*

The tremor went on for several seconds; subsided. A little greyish powder sifted from the stone wall of the building, behind the screen, but the exterior walls had withstood the seismic shock; and now Cendri understood the purpose of the screens. Rigid interior walls might collapse, and have to be tediously rebuilt; Dal lifted the collapsed screen off them with one hand.

A young woman with a red baldric tied around one shoulder appeared in the gap left by the collapsed screen. She said quickly, without salutation, "Come with me at once; there may be aftershocks, and the building must be emptied!"

Dal helped Cendri to her feet; Cendri met the amazed stare of the woman with the baldric and moved away from him. They followed her quickly through a corridor cluttered with the fallen screens, some of them splintered and torn; out of the building, and on to a long expanse of vegetation. She said, "You are the Scholar from University?" At Cendri's nod she said quickly, "Forgive my ignorance of diplomatic courtesies, but you must stay here. I must go back and make certain that all the pregnant women and visitors are out of the building. If you will wait here, I will send someone to you as soon as possible." She hurried away, looking backward with a troubled glance.

Dal shook his head in astonishment. "Some welcome to this world! Do you suppose they have this kind of thing very often? You noticed the heavy equipment set on rollers?"

"I noticed," she said. "They seem to have everything ready for earthquakes! I seem to remember—" she frowned; before coming here she had read—quickly, scanning for anything of importance—everything she could find about the settlement of Isis/Cinderella. The planet then known as Cinderella had been considered, for some reason, undesirable for colonization or homesteading. If it was notably seismic, that was completely understandable. Yet it had been the only planet available for the Matriarchate. They seemed to have developed sophisticated methods for dealing with earthquakes—light interior construction, heavy equipment on rollers, and she would be willing to make a guess that they also had taboos about untended fires! Even now she could see flames shooting up from one corner of the building, and people were running and shouting and dragging hoses, mounted on small motorized platforms. The firefighting techniques looked efficient and quick.

Dal whistled in surprise. "Cendri—they are women, fighting the fire!"

"Well, Dal, it *is* a Matriarchy—"

"But surely, for heavy manual work, dangerous work—" he protested. "Surely men are physically stronger, wouldn't work like that fall naturally to them?"

"I'd have thought so," she said, "but we don't know, yet. I wouldn't comment on it, if I were you."

He said shortly, "I don't suppose anyone would listen if I did."

The women, in thick short protective coats of woven fiber, cut away the torn screens and dragged them to where they could burn out, unattended. There was black smoke which looked as if some electrical fixtures had caught fire, but it was quickly extinguished. Abruptly it was all over; women with smoke-smudged faces coiled up the hoses and trundled away the platforms, and the people who had been sent out of the buildings began to drift back toward them. A few women were still spraying down the open hangar and the shuttleships, to prevent any stray spark from damaging ships or fuel.

Cendri wondered if their luggage was safe; they had brought a great deal of reference material, books,

tapes, recording equipment. Ought she to go and see?
But when Dal expressed anxiety she hesitated.

"They told us to wait here, they'll send someone for
us. Look, I think that must be someone coming now,
that woman is pointing at us—see?"

The woman she indicated was one of those who had
come last from the burning building; because of their
actions and obvious concern Cendri had tentatively
identified them as having something to do with the
machinery and instrumentation there. She was pointing
Cendri and Dal out to a woman in a pale-blue flowered
pajama suit, very loose, with a broad-brimmed sun hat
and her dark hair in a long braid down her back. The
woman spoke to her informant and then began to hurry
toward Cendri and Dal. As she came, Cendri could see
that the woman was very young—younger than Cendri
herself—and that she was heavily pregnant.

She stopped a little way from Cendri, and waited,
saying hesitantly, "Scholar Dame Malocq?"

Cendri identified herself noncommittally. Until she
knew more about the customs here, she knew it would
be a breach of etiquette to do almost *anything*. It might
also be a breach of manners to do *nothing*, but sins of
omission were usually less serious, in most cultures,
than sins of commission. Dal, she observed—not
having her extensive training in cross-cultural
protocol—had already bowed; but the woman's eyes
did not rest on him even for a moment.

She said, "I am Miranda, third daughter of the
Pro-Matriarch Vaniya; my venerable Mother has asked
me to come and escort you in person to her country
home. As you can see—" she made a nervous gesture
toward the people jostling around the building, from
which a few gouts of smoke were still drifting, "we have
had some troubles, and since the quake was felt in the
City, too, the Pro-Matriarch was not free to come and
greet you herself. She sent me to welcome you, and beg
that you will forgive the apparent discourtesy."

Cendri made a formal bow, hands clasped before her

face in the manner of the Unity. "The Pro-Matriarch does me too much honor, Lady Miranda."

"Rather, it is you who confer an honor upon us, Scholar Dame," Miranda said. "A conveyance and driver await us at the entrance, if the honored guest will follow me."

Cendri followed her, her brows ridged slightly; something was beginning to puzzle her.

Her manners are too formal. They don't fit what else I've seen here; the absence of uniforms, the haphazard way everything else seems to be run. Yet she welcomed me as if she was familiar with Unity protocol.

She wished she could discuss this with Dal; but the way in which the shuttleship pilot and the Lady Miranda had ignored his existence warned her; too much attention to Dal in public could even endanger her own status. She soothed her guilt, reminding herself to have a good long talk with Dal about it as soon as they were left alone.

Will he even care? He's an archaeologist, he couldn't care less about their social structures and customs. . . . She thought, suddenly, that it might be a good thing she had been sent here instead of the Dame di Velo, who might not know how to cope with this unusual and delicately structured society. And yet, if it weren't for sheer accident, she would never have been allowed to come here at all. She told herself she should be grateful to Dal for devising the strategem which had brought her here, but instead, for no reason at all, she found herself nursing a resentment so intense that it shook her to the core.

". . . honorable Scholar Dame?"

"I am sorry," Cendri said, recalling herself with an effort. "I fear my mind was wandering; what did you ask me, my Lady?"

"Your Companion—" she did not look at Dal, "may ride with the driver, if it wishes; I trust it is tractable and obedient?"

"Very," said Cendri, and dared not look at Dal.

"Tell it, please, to get into the front compartment with the luggage—" she watched, with amazement, as Dal climbed in without waiting to be told. "It actually understands our language?"

Cendri said dryly, "My Companion, Lady, is a Scholar on University."

Miranda raised her eyebrows in surprise, but made no answer.

The driver was a woman, stout and greying; she wore rough dark clothes. She indicated with a careless gesture that Dal might curl himself up in the seatless hard space next to the gear levers where the luggage had been stacked. Cendri herself was ceremoniously ushered into a box-like interior, well-carpeted and thickly cushioned with pillows and soft textures. It did not seem to Cendri that it would have crowded them unduly to allow Dal to ride inside, but she did not know what taboos this would have violated. She was beginning to feel an immense curiosity, a curiosity so great that she could barely restrain herself from asking numberless questions which had nothing whatever to do with her ostensible mission.

Instead she said, as the Lady Miranda settled herself awkwardly among the cushions—she was *very* pregnant—"I trust the quake did not cause too much damage."

"Very little," Miranda said. "A woman in charge of a painting crew was bruised when a vehicle rocked against a wall, but she made certain none of her charges was injured; a woman in the Communications Room stayed at her post a little too long, broadcasting warnings down the coastline, and inhaled smoke from the electrical fixtures; but she will recover. Another woman was hurt when a trash container fell over on her—I believe her ankle was broken. And of course there are dozens of screens to be recovered and repainted, but that is work for the children of the city, and actually they are always pleased when new screens must be put up in public places, so our school children will be happy."

"Are there many such quakes here?"

"Unfortunately, a great many." Miranda added, in quick reassurance, "You need not be afraid, Scholar Dame; you will be lodged in the house of the Pro-Matriarch, near the ruins at We-were-guided, and the ground never trembles, for those who built it hold the ground under their protection."

Interesting; if the society which built the ruins, whether or not they were the hypothetical Builders, had the technological know-how to locate their city away from tectonic stress lines! Unlikely, though, that they could be the Builders. The city was far, far older than the Isis/Cinderella colony, which had been here less than seventy standard years, but certainly not old enough to be the mysterious Builders who were supposed to have seeded the Galaxy millennia before any known race. No surviving technology would have enabled a society to predict tectonic stress and seismic activity—or freedom from it—from any site more than a few thousand years in advance.

And from what Miranda had said about the builders of the ruins holding the ground under protection from quakes—they evidently had some quasi-religious veneration of the site. She wanted to know about that. She wanted to know *everything* about this culture!

Builders ruins! Builders! Who could possibly care about a prehistoric race who might not even have been human, when the whole Galaxy, the whole Unity and beyond, were filled with endlessly fascinating cultures which were still *here*, alive, working, to be seen and studied! Again she felt the sense of frustration. Did these women of the Matriarchate want to keep everyone away from their culture until it was dead, and had to be studied like that of the Builders, from almost undiscernible clues left behind by their few imperishable artifacts?

Not, she thought, looking through the clear plastic of the vehicle's window, that the Matriarchate was likely to leave many imperishable artifacts to be studied millions of years later. Her first impression of the city

was of low, regular buildings, made of something like
sun-dried adobe, smoothed and decorated with bright
paintings, which varied so much in quality that Cendri
suspected each house was decorated, not by professional artists or painters, but by its own inhabitants.

The houses were arranged in clusters, irregularly, in
park-like gardens. The car moved leisurely along
narrow streets which seemed reasonably full of men
and women and little children, dressed in the same
confusing variety of clothing Cendri had seen on the
spaceport. There was no uniformity, though in general
those who were working—a man hanging lengths of
brilliantly dyed fabric on a wooden framework, a
woman pushing a barrow piled high with bright green
globes which could have been vegetables or
playthings—wore rather less than those few who were
doing nothing.

The earthquake had not made havoc in the city—
probably due to the specialized construction of the
houses—but everywhere there were piles of rubble
being cleared away, and people hauling out broken,
torn or smoke-damaged wall-screens to be repaired. A
group of men were working in an excavation which had
evidently caved in.

There were children everywhere; those beneath the
age of puberty went naked except for sunhats and
sandals, and looked browned and healthy. The older
ones were working alongside their elders, helping to
clear away earthquake damage. The younger ones were
playing games which looked, to an inexperienced
observer, like aimless running around, although a
group of small girls was squatting in a patch of sand,
playing some kind of game with flat stones, and a mixed
group of preadolescents were turning a jumprope and
jumping through it in precisely-timed patterns.

It was late afternoon, and the sun moved, low and
slanting, over the roof of a low white building, surrounded by ornamental shrubbery. "You have come
here at an unfortunate time, Scholar Dame," said the
Lady Miranda. "This is the Residence of the High

Matriarch of Isis, which is also the Temple of the Goddess. It was she who sent for you—or rather, for the Scholar Dame di Velo; but at this moment our beloved Matriarch lies in a coma, near to death."

Cendri did not know what, if anything, it was proper to say. Depending on the society's attitude toward death, such an occasion might call for condolences—or for congratulations! She murmured non-committally, "I am sorry to have come at an inconvenient time."

"I fear the inconvenience will be mostly to yourself, Scholar Dame," the Lady Miranda said, twisting the end of her long braid. "I fear that if our Mother and Priestess should die without naming a successor, it will be a long time till we know which of the two Pro-Matriarchs will assume her rank, ring and robe; so everything is likely to come entirely to a stop until we have consulted the Inquirers. And, I fear, your work would be halted, too, until such time as we have resolved the differences between the two Pro-Matriarchs—my mother, Vaniya, and her rival and colleague, Mahala. Those differences, so my mother tells me, are very many, and go back to the days when they were little girls squabbling over games on our motherworld of Persephone."

Cendri felt troubled. She had been intensively trained in the ethic which forbade a sociological student, or an anthropologist, to take either side between rival factions on any world; was it proper that she should actually be lodged in the home of one of the rivals? Well, she supposed it had all been arranged long before she came here, and indeed Miranda's next words confirmed this: "I myself know nothing of politics, nor of the many rivalries and differences between them," she said, "I am the loyal daughter of my mother, regardless of what the rights and wrongs of the matter may seem to others. And my mother has told me; on the last day when the High Matriarch could speak coherently, it was of this she spoke; that you should be brought here, and lodged at our house, which is located so near to the ruins at We-were-guided that from the upper rooms, the Ruins can be seen clearly, and from our front gates, it is only a little walk along the shore. It seemed to the High Matriarch that your work could best be done from there. And of course this has made the Pro-Matriarch Mahala very angry; partly because she hates my mother, as I have said, and perhaps, I think, because the Mother Rezali had not confided the honored guests to *her* care. But then, during all her years on Isis, the Pro-Matriarch Mahala has made it a point of honor to disbelieve in the Builders—"

"*You* believe in them, then?" Cendri asked.

"Oh, yes," Miranda said. "I have communicated with them very often. But Mahala, you understand, is one of those women who believes in nothing unless it fits certain rules she has invented for herself, and so she says that our contact with the Builders is all superstition and nonsense. She has not examined the evidence, you understand. She is, I believe, a very stupid woman."

It took Cendri a moment to digest this unbelievable statement. *Communication? With the Builders?* She blinked at Miranda's matter-of-fact tone, forcibly reminding herself that the Builders—if they had ever existed at all, which most reputable scientists doubted—were supposed to have left their ruins no less than two million years ago! Surely, surely, the Lady Miranda's statement must have some symbolic, or religious, interpretation! And she could not even inquire about it until she knew precisely what weight was given to religious matters in this society!

She felt intensely frustrated, but she made her voice noncommittal again. "It will indeed come most conveniently to our work, to be located so near the ruins. That was most thoughtful of the High Matriarch."

"It was a decision demanding courage," Miranda said, "and now it is likely to go for nothing—depending, of course, on who is appointed High Matriarch in her place. Her death at this time may undo all the work she has done—she has believed for many years that we on Isis should have more contact with the Unity, but it has taken this long for the time to be ripe for this opening gesture; inviting the Scholar Dame di Velo here to explore the ruins. There are still those who fear any kind of contact with the worlds dominated by men; they feel they can only bring contamination to our society—" she broke off and said anxiously, her fingers nervously twisting her long braid. "Please—my mother said I must be certain not to offend you, since you are from a world dominated by males—and there are those here who feel you will have nothing to offer us but temptation—I'm not saying this at all well," she said, with her diffident smile.

Cendri said neutrally—the one thing she must *not* do was to question, publicly, the prime postulate of their society—"The worlds of the Unity are not, of course, dominated by males, Lady Miranda. Oh, perhaps a few hundred years ago, on such worlds as Pioneer and Apollo, there were certain—certain inequities. But on my own home world they were never very great, and on University, men and women are quite equal."

Miranda raised her feathery eyebrows in obvious skepticism. She said, "I am not, of course, well enough informed for intelligent comment on this, Scholar Dame. But it does conflict with everything I have ever heard."

Cendri smiled. "And of course I could never convince you, Lady Miranda. The simplest thing would be for your world to send some—" she hesitated, phrasing it carefully, "Some of your finest students there, so that each woman might see for herself that she is welcomed as the equal of any man, and accepted only on the basis of her individual talent and aptitude for scholarship."

The Lady Miranda laughed. She said, "The very fact that men are accepted as scholars points to prejudice and inequity," she said. "It is a biological fact, long proven by any impartial scientist, that the average man's brain is smaller than the brain of a woman, that female children are taller and heavier at puberty, and of course *after* puberty, males are so much at the mercy of their compulsive sex drives that it is impossible to educate them. Male *children*, of course, can be educated, if it is skillfully done. But only in a society where males make the rules could anyone accept the idea of a true scholarship for adult functioning males."

Firmly Cendri reminded herself that she was not there to debate, or to defend the Unity, or the world of University. She said diplomatically, "I am sure in your experience you have found it so, Lady, but I do assure you that on University we have many great male scholars."

Miranda nodded, and after a moment Cendri realized that she was being *humored*; that Miranda was being diplomatic and polite. "Of course they have taught you to think so, Scholar Dame, and you have never had, I am sure, a chance to do research without cultural bias."

Since this was exactly what Cendri would have liked to say to Miranda, she wanted to laugh. "Let us hope for a day, then, Lady, when your scholars from Isis can see for themselves."

Miranda returned the smile, with spontaneous friendliness. "I wish we might! It has been spoken of, you know, in the councils of the High Matriarch—that we should send scholars to University, have more trade into the Unity, share problems with other worlds; we need to know more about water-table technology, and the mathematics of reserve technology and arid-land cultivation; and more about pelagic ecology. The High Matriarch believed, too, that we have a responsibility to the women of the Unity, to show them the example of a sane society in function, and that until they are shown our example, they could never follow it. But so many of the women here are paranoid on the subject! They still believe—or, in the case of some politicians, pretend to believe—that the worlds of the Unity are just lying in wait to seize us again, and put us under male domination, as they did with out first colony on Labrys . . ." she paused, looked at Cendri and asked "You know the story—?"

"I only know that the colony on Labrys was destroyed," she said. "The official story is that an overanxious administration miscalculated the speed with which their Sun was to go Nova, and resettled them on a world with an unstable orbit. There are not many records; most of those which remain call it a colossal bureaucratic blunder, for which the Unity paid a heavy indemnity. But indemnities, of course, cannot wipe out the loss of life, and it would not be at all surprising if some people called it a plot against the Matriarchate."

"It *is* so called," said Miranda, soberly, "and there are those who think me a traitor because I have said that I, myself, would like to go and study on University—"

"I hope someday you may," said Cendri, and Miranda smiled gaily and said, "I would like to see other worlds. I am not afraid of male-dominated worlds! I—" she laughed again, a merry, defiant sound, "I *defy* any male to dominate me!"

She sounded completely confident, and Cendri thought how incongruous it was that this young woman, delicate, pretty, pregnant, should express such defiance. She would have said, if she had been on her own home world, *There are a great many men who would really enjoy trying it, my dear, and you might enjoy it, too, if you would give it a fair chance! In some things, dominance is not so bad!* Miranda was pregnant, surely she must have found *that* out! But of course she could not say this; so she only rejoiced that the Lady Miranda was in a feminine gossiping mood— she supposed this was a typical mode for a world of women—and encouraged it.

"You yourself would like to study on University? Are there many women interested in that, do you think?"

"I am sure there are," said Miranda. "There are many women from the College of Ariadne who have volunteered to assist the Scholar Dame from Unity in her researches, if she will have them. But there are also those who fear that this is sacrilege, that your work there will deprive us of the love and concern of the Builders—"

"The—" Cendri swallowed hard, "the—the love and concern of the—the Builders?" For a moment she felt certain that she must have misunderstood Miranda's speech. Miranda's eyes were glowing.

"Oh, yes! You will feel it, too, you are a woman—"

Cendri blinked again. How could she possibly do any dispassionate work on the Builder ruins when she found them an object of religious worship—a worship which, judging from Miranda's expression, fell just short of idolatry!

Frankly, she didn't care all that much whether the Builder ruins ever got explored or not. That, of course, was Dal's prime concern; as for Cendri herself, the longer the exploration of the ruins was delayed by the deathwatch on the dying High Matriarch, the longer it would give her to explore and make notes on the fascinating and supposedly impossible society of the Matriarchate.

The vehicle was stopping before a building somewhat taller than the ones inside the city walls. The Lady Miranda said, "Here is the Residence of my mother, the Pro-Matriarch Vaniya. Welcome, Scholar Dame. You must not be frightened," she added earnestly, "even though it is built with an upper story, we are so near to We-were-guided that the ground never shakes here, and you are as safe on the second floor as in the arms of the Goddess."

Now I wonder, Cendri thought, *is this an observed seismic phenomenon, or is it an article of faith, because of the supposed love and concern of the hypothetical "Builders"?* She could not ask; she would simply have to take her chances. After all, earthquakes could strike anywhere, on almost any world, and she had never been afraid of living on an upper story; her small apartment on University was on the eighteenth tier of a hugh residence complex, and she had never given even the most fleeting thought to earthquakes before this. She assured Miranda seriously that she was not afraid, and Miranda smiled.

"And I am not afraid of all the threatened dangers from the Unity, Scholar Dame."

Cendri had been on the verge of alighting from the vehicle; she stopped, her hand on the door-latch. She said in amazement, "The dangers of the Unity? What, I must ask, could we possibly have that is dangerous to you?"

"War," said Miranda, and her face was suddenly grave. "It is a historical fact, Scholar Dame, that every society where men were allowed to rule has been destroyed from within by wars, because of the competitive, aggressive nature of the male animal. It is this, I think, that they fear."

Cendri blinked at Miranda and said, "But our society—the Unity—is flourishing undestroyed, after more than five hundred years of peace, Lady Miranda. I cannot understand your logic at all."

The Lady Miranda looked confused.

"I *told* you I didn't understand politics. You must talk to my mother about it. Come," she said, leaning across Cendri and opening the door-latch, "let me welcome you to our home, Scholar Dame."

Cendri, moving her cramped knees carefully, got out of the car, watching Dal, equally stiff and cramped, and scowling as if he had had an unpleasant trip, getting out of the front along with the hauled-out baggage.

I have a lot to tell him. How long will it be before we are alone to talk? I don't dare to speak to him in public here! She smiled at Dal, trying to encourage him, but he avoided her eyes; and Cendri's heart sank.

This was the beginning of the most complex and difficult assignment she had ever had; her first work as an independent professional, not a student. And she wasn't even free to concentrate on it, because all her emotional energy was taken up with worrying about Dal's feelings! It was justified, she could sympathize with Dal completely, but still, she could not help resenting the drain on her energy!

A short flight of steps—the first she had seen on Isis, except at the elaborate Residence and Temple of the High Matriarch—led up to the front door; the room into which Miranda led them was spacious, hung about with thin draperies and divided by the screen-like movable partitions, in pale colors. The floor was matted cleanly with what looked like woven reeds or tatami matting. All around the room were evidences of children's play, toys and cloth dolls, a child's shoe lying abandoned at one edge of the room, but the children themselves had been hastily cleared away; Cendri fancied that she could still hear childish voices, raised in surprise and protest at the interruption of their games.

Yes, what is an Ambassador from another world to them? A Scholar from the Unity, and her mission, means less than nothing. When will I see these people as they really are, and not as they choose to present themselves to me? Will I have any chance at all, to do that? A sociologist can fade into the background, have a chance to observe. But I am here to serve elaborate political aims—aims of the Unity, aims of the Matriarchate—and studying the ruins is only a pretext. What I am is living proof that the Unity will not endanger their way of life. That is my real mission, even though the Unity did not tell me so. I wonder if Dal has guessed it yet?

The Lady Miranda was looking around the untidy, child-littered room distressfully. "Is it true that on the world of the Scholar Dame there are rooms reserved for formal meetings and policy?"

She seemed so disturbed that Cendri paused a moment to frame her reply carefully, to soothe that disquiet. She said at last, "Every world has its own customs, Lady Miranda, and there is no great authority somewhere in Limbo to say with arbitrary words which customs best express the human spirit." She felt sententious as she mouthed this banal cliché—it had been an epigraph in an elementary text of Comparative Anthropology—but it lightened the careworn look on the Lady Miranda's face. She said, "Excuse me for a moment, I must see if my mother is able to receive you—" and hurried past the screens, leaving them alone. Cendri looked quickly at Dal, but he raised his eyebrows noncommittally and said nothing. In the distance—privacy must be difficult or impossible in houses with this kind of open construction—she heard a low-voiced colloquy, then Miranda came hurrying back.

"Will the Scholar Dame forgive my mother? The earthquake has caused much damage in the fisher-woman villages along the shoreline, and the Pro-Matriarch has been urgently summoned to see what damage has been done and what help must be given to the poor women there; many boats were smashed in the harbor. She has left word that she will return at sunset, unless some very great urgency should delay her, at which hour she will be pleased to welcome you and dine in your company. Meanwhile, may I make the Scholar Dame comfortable in the chambers which have been prepared? And if there is any other way in which I may serve the Scholar Dame, she has only to ask."

Cendri replied politely that she was content to await the total convenience of the Pro-Matriarch. She was getting very tired of these elaborately formal speeches, which seemed to rest uncomfortably upon Miranda's lips. She added that it would be very good to rest after the journey.

"If the Scholar Dame will follow me—"

The rooms lay at the top of two flights of stairs, elaborately and carefully balustraded, and one of them closed off with a device which was evidently a kind of nursery gate to keep small children from tumbling

down. On these upper floors she saw the first solid
interior wall construction she had seen anywhere on
Isis/Cinderella, although the walls were masked, in
part, by the light movable screens which seemed the
normal wall-decor for this world. Walls and screens
were painted with murals that looked like children's
work; and, tired as she was, Cendri was still taking the
mental notes of the trained anthropologist. Children
were very much in evidence, not banished to a separate
part of the household or community. Miranda opened a
door which had been gilded, and said, "These rooms
have been prepared for the Scholar Dame and—and
her Companion." For the first time she glanced, briefly
and shyly, at Dal, and Cendri had the odd impression
that she wished to extend him, too, some courtesy, but
did not know what form it ought to take.

She thought in wonder, and some indefinable irritation, haven't these women ever *seen* a man before?
They act, quite literally, as if they had never set eyes on
a man, and that is preposterous, there are men all over
the place! What *is* it?

*I can't expect to understand it, after only an hour or
two. . . .*

The room was hung all round, inside, with curtains;
literally a cyclorama of curtains, surrounding the entire
room. Miranda showed Cendri how they could be
pulled back—"So that you can have darkness and
privacy, or light, at your wish," she said, and adjusted
them, with what seemed an automatic gesture, to admit
indirect light while keeping out the glare from a
window which faced the sun. Behind another fold of
the curtains she indicated a door, saying, "Here you
may refresh yourself as you wish; the Scholar Dame has
no objection to sharing bathing facilities with her
Companion? If it is so, I am instructed to tell you that
there is a male facility at the foot of the stairs—"

"I have no objection," said Cendri quickly.

At the center of the room was a bedstead; quite the
highest and narrowest bed Cendri had even seen. She

wondered how she would possibly sleep in it without falling out. Miranda indicated racks for clothing, shelves—Cendri noted that they were carefully braced on what looked like gimbals and had movable arms which could be extended to hold the books in the shelves, a reasonable precaution for a world prone to continuing seismic tremors—a mirrored enclosure with a padded seat, and at one corner of the room an alcove, cushioned deeply and filled with luxurious pillows, as if the entire alcove had become a thick, comfortable bed. The Lady Miranda said, with a quick glance at the alcove, "When our Mother informed me that the Scholar Dame had brought a Companion, it was this room we set aside for her to inhabit, a room with an Amusement Corner." She glanced, quickly and surreptitiously, at Dal, and suddenly, looking at the piled, luxurious pillows, Cendri understood, and felt almost inclined to giggle, or to blush in embarrassment.

The separation—that high, narrow, obvious bed, and the sybaritic "Amusement Corner"—tells me more about how this society regards sex, than a whole series of erotic films, or any number of lectures about sexual customs! She saw that Dal had understood, too, for his mouth twitched a little at the corners, and Cendri was suddenly afraid he would laugh out loud while Miranda was still in the room. She said, hastily, "You are too kind, Lady; everything seems more than comfortable."

With a few more formal phrases, and assurance that their luggage should be brought soon, the Lady Miranda turned to go, with a final request that if everything was not as the Scholar Dame liked it, she had only to request assistance.

"We are honored and content," Cendri said. It was a risk to include Dal in the pronoun, but by including the "Amusement Corner" in her room—again the hidden mirth bubbled up inside her—they had taken at least a tacit notice of his existence! She said with a formal gesture, "We ask only one thing; if we offend in anything against your customs, we ask that you accept that it is done in ignorance and without intent to offend."

It was the first time she had ever had occasion to use this little memorized speech suggested for contact with any alien society, and in her years of training she had come to think of it, too, as a cliche, so banal and stereotyped as to be virtually meaningless; she was surprised when it drew the first genuine, spontaneous smile from the Lady Miranda.

"You are kind, Scholar Dame. I trust you will be happy here." Again the quick, embarrassed look at Dal; she added in a whisper, as if greatly daring, "Both of you," and, coloring, withdrew.

When the door had closed, Dal drew a long, whistling breath. He dropped into the "Amusement Corner" cushions, saying explosively, "What do you think of all *that*! Sharrioz! What a world!" He chuckled. "If they want to get into the Unity they're sure going to have to change their ways!"

Cendri started to protest—there was no evidence that they wanted to get into the Unity at all—then held her peace. This was just a way of working off the long tension of being treated like a nothing, part of Cendri's baggage, a mere convenience for her amusement or pleasure. *Poor Dal!* she thought, and was eager to make it up to him, but didn't quite know how.

"Let's look and see what kind of bath they've given us. Some studies judge a culture by the quality of their plumbing, you know."

"I know," Dal said, good-humored again. "I told you that, remember. The ruins on Serpens Delta Four had eight separate and distinct classes of latrine and bathing facilities, each for a different class of society, and judging by the ritual objects we found, there were rigid taboos against one caste going near the bathing facilities of any other caste! We might as well explore this one before it gets to be an artifact!"

"We really do the same work, in a way, don't we, Dal?" she said, voicing a thought that had come to her before. "I study cultures while they're still going on, and you study them after they've stopped, but it's the same work, isn't it, darling?"

"I suppose so," Dal said, kindly but without enthusiasm. "Although, of course, there is no way to measure a society objectively while scientists must observe it through subjective judgments, either their own or the judgments of the society in question. No society can ever be judged except in historical perspective," he added, and Cendri, who had heard this before without agreeing with it, and knew she would never agree with it, let it pass without comment. Together they went to explore the luxurious bath assigned to them by the Pro-Matriarch.

"If a culture *could* be judged by plumbing, we'd have to give this one high marks, wouldn't we?" Cendri said at last; it was unbelievably elaborate, containing not only elaborate toilet and bathing facilities, but showers of different sizes and heights, and some fixtures about whose use she was not certain, though she guessed that one very shallow, waist-high tub, with guard-rails and a headrest, and faucets fixed to give only warmish water, with no hot or cold, must be a special fixture for bathing very young babies without danger of dropping, chilling or scalding. Others she could not even make intelligent guesses about; body-care facilities could be judged only by actually observing their use.

Dal looked dubious. He said, "I'm not sure; societies which place too much value on luxurious body-care have usually been decadent, historically speaking. Viable and vigorous societies tend to be more spartan in emphasis; but the overemphasis on physical comfort is what I would expect of a society where females define the major priorities."

Cendri frowned, not sure she understood. "All societies work for physical comfort as they define it, don't they, Dal?"

"You know better than that," Dal chided. "The pursuit of luxury appears, normally, only after a culture has expended its primary energies. Women are usually out of the main stream of culture, since the real work of a society is done by men, and only when the real aims of the society are accomplished do the men have leisure to pamper their women by creating non-essentials such as physical comfort. Historically, when this happens, a culture has begun to die, since the men have nothing better to do than to pursue the goals and aims set by women . . ."

Cendri said tentatively, "But perhaps in a culture where the primary goals were *determined* by women, priorities would be differently ordered—"

"That is precisely what I was saying," Dal said with weary patience. "A culture where women's priorities took precedence would reach decadence at a very early stage. This society is still new, but I notice already the early signs of decadence; a very low level of organization, and an unstructured hierarchy without visible incentive status, which fits very well, with the other signs of decadence; undue emphasis on physical comfort, and a lack of time-values; for instance, the idea that if you are made comfortable while you wait, you will not protest at the wasting of your valuable time as a trained specialist. This indicates, of course, a contempt for the Unity's values, and for the Unity's time—"

They were interrupted by two people who brought their luggage, a man and a woman; when they withdrew, Cendri had lost all interest in the argument—she had heard it in her study of Cultural Institutions—but Dal would not be silenced.

"There are certain priorities which, in a colony as new as they, *must* take priority over anything as unnecessary as physical comfort. First comes conquest—if there are no actual enemies to involve them in war, then the terrain and the climate must be conquered and reduced to submission—then expansion, and the achievement of hierarchy, and directives for structuring social goals. A society which gives priority to things which are important only to women would never achieve any of these stages in a vigorous or viable form." He smiled. "And such a society never lasts long, so study it while you can, Cendri; it's not likely, with these priorities, to achieve anything lasting enough to have any kind of historical value or perspective." He added, indulgently, "Of course, you wouldn't be interested in historical perspective, would you, Cendri? Women aren't—it's excusable, of course, probably necessary for biological reasons, but women always tend to live in the present, and leave historical perspectives for men. And women never seem even to define this as a fault!"

Cendri wondered if he included the Scholar Dame Lurianna di Velo, one of the most notable archaeologists in the Unity, among those women who were unable to see anything in historical perspective, but she had sense enough not to say so.

"Did you hear anything of what the Lady Miranda told me about the situation here?"

As she had feared, this revived Dal's major grievance.

"How could I, bumping along in the luggage compartment beside the old hag who was doing the driving?"

"I'm sure you saw more of the city than I did," she said, but he was not mollified. "I didn't come here to look at scenery!" he grumbled, "No, not a word of it."

"I thought not, or you would not be complaining about their having kept us waiting," she said. Briefly she explained what the Lady Miranda had told her of the deathwatch on the High Matriarch, and the possibility that whoever took her position might have a totally different attitude toward the Unity.

Dal asked sharply, frowning a little, "What is the attitude of the Pro-Matriarch—*this* one, the house where we are staying? What are *her* feelings about the Unity?"

"I don't know, Dal. The time didn't seem quite right to ask. I should imagine, from the way the Lady

Miranda spoke—she herself said she would like to study on University—that she is not completely prejudiced against the Unity: but I don't really know."

"I should think that would have been the first thing you would have wanted to know," said Dal, frowning. "Don't women ever come to grips with essentials?"

Now she was provoked. She said, "I don't know what *women* do, Dal; I only know *I* used my best judgment about what I could and couldn't ask! After all, we are in a strange society here, and have to find out something of their forms of courtesy and social restrictions! I did the best I could!"

"I'm sure you did," Dal muttered, but it was clear he didn't think that was good enough. She said, trying to placate him, "I don't know what Vaniya's political attitudes are, but she was willing to let us use her house as a base for the study of the Builder ruins, because it was located so near; the Lady Miranda said that the upper rooms here actually looked down on the ruins."

She moved to the window, and drew aside the curtain. They were high up above an enclosed garden, hedged with greenish-gray shrubbery, brilliant with flowers and green leaves. Further off lay a long section of shore, with sandy beaches and a long expanse of slow rolling surf, and a small fishing village, houses clustered and crouching under a cliff, and one tall building, a kind of lighthouse or watchtower. It looked quite old, and weathered.

And further away still, down the shoreline, lay low hills, and on the nearest of the hills, something else. A cluster of thick, black, upthrusting shapes, blackened, squarish; higher than any of the houses of Ariadne, and more regular; and at this distance, windowless, blank, featureless; strange, in their unvarying geometry, their curious proportions. They were not like anything else Cendri had ever seen.

"Dal," she said. "Come here, look at this. Are these

the ruins which the Scholar Dame di Velo called Builder ruins?"

Dal came to the window, his muscular hand holding back the pale folds of curtain. He was silent, staring, and Cendri, watching his face, saw the jawline tighten, the eyelids twitch.

At last he said, his voice muffled, "They are—ruins. More than this I could not possibly say. The Dame di Velo had seen what she considered evidence, to convince her that they were what we needed to prove that the Galaxy had actually been seeded by these people. It would not—not be accurately scientific even to hazard a guess. But yes, they are the ruins of Isis—the ruins we came here to see."

Abruptly he turned from the window, letting the curtain swirl down into place. He strode heavily to the "Amusement Corner," blundering into one of the light interior screens as he went and steadying it with an unregarding hand. Why, Cendri wondered, with firm interior walls and curtains, were the screens here at all, when they had no function of separating off interior rooms? Or did the women of Isis feel that a room simply did not look to them like a room, or *feel* to them like a room, without the customary screens? She knew she was focusing on this silly question to hide her anguished awareness of Dal's pain.

He said, his face pressed into the cushions of the "Amusement Corner," "And to think I can't—can't get out there and do anything about them, can't even go out and *look* at them—it's all going to be up to *you*, Cendri, and you don't even really care at all, do you? I should never have come, I should never have come. . . ."

She wanted to weep, to protest; *I do care, Dal, I do.* But she knew the words would be empty on her tongue. Quietly, she turned away from him, knowing he would never forgive her for having seen him break like this. His work meant so much more to him than anything else, anything in his life. Next to his despair, her own work seemed suddenly trivial, meaningless. But the only thing she could give Dal now was a sense of privacy. Very quietly she went to the far end of the apartment—glad, now, of the interior screens which divided it into several sections—and started unpacking their things and stowing them in the spaces provided.

chapter three

HOURS LATER, WHEN THE LIGHT OUTSIDE HAD DIMMED somewhat, Cendri heard on the lower floors of the house a variety of sounds—footsteps, voices, movement and bustle—and knew that the Pro-Matriarch Vaniya had returned. She knew they would soon be summoned to dine formally with her, so she bathed in the luxurious bathroom, did up her long fair hair in an elaborate coiffure, and put on a gown suitable for formal dining on University. Later she would learn, she supposed, what was proper for such occasions here. But it was not, from what she had seen, a society where minute differences in dress conveyed many cues about status. As she smoothed the narrow pleats in her elegant close-fitting dress, she wondered at that. It had seemed to her reasonable that a society structured by women would have paid enormous attention to dress. Wasn't that one of women's special concerns everywhere?

Dal had recovered his spirits and was stowing their

collection of reference works and making sure the cameras and recording devices had suffered no harm in the packing. He seemed busy and self-absorbed; she hated to disturb him, but finally said, "Dal, shouldn't you get ready?"

He shrugged. "What makes you think they'd invite *me*? Or have you forgotten I'm only the dog?"

She couldn't blame him at all for that. "Let's say I have a hunch, Dal. After all, they went out of their way to notice you by giving me a room with an—" she hesitated, then laughed, a forced laugh, but she knew they *must* make a joke of it or it would be unendurable, "an Amusement Corner."

He laughed too, as she had hoped, and came to drop a kiss on the back of her neck. "It's a bit more elaborate than a dog's bed! If you're good, I may let you sleep in it with me!" His hands lingered, and Cendri felt an overflowing relaxation, a lessening of tension. At least he was not blaming *her*!

"I will try to make them realize you are a Scholar in your own right, Dal."

His smile was a little sour. "Why bother? Enjoy it while you can. Women are always saying they don't get enough recognition, there aren't nearly as many Dames as Master Scholars—this might be your only chance at Scholarly eminence!"

That ruffled her a little; she *would* have been a Dame by now, had she not taken off time after her marriage! Then, with humility, Cendri thought; that's what he means, a man, a serious Scholar, wouldn't have done that. Women just *aren't* as serious about Scholarship as men! "Well, Dal, we will simply have to prove it to them."

He laughed, stroking her hair. "We can't upset the whole basis of their society, darling. Do you think I give the weight of a hydrogen atom to what *they* think of my scholarly credentials?"

It felt so good, to have him laughing with her again! And of course Dal was right, there was no way, and no need, to challenge the basic postulate of the Matriarchate; but she supposed any young anthropologist in a society which was wholly irrational, would feel this way! *The daydream; that she, single-handed, could show them the error of their ways, prove a major influence to bring them into the mainstream of the Unity.* . . . She laughed at herself and turned so that Dal could tie the ribbons of her sash.

She looked at herself in the mirror with satisfaction; no woman of the Matriarchate could say she had not taken the trouble to honor her hosts! *Hostesses,* she amended. Dal, too, was resplendent, with the University decorations which proclaimed him Scholar and Master, and the insignia of his homeworld Pioneer; he had dressed as if for a Scholar's Banquet, and she was proud of him.

The Lady Miranda came for them; after bowing to Cendri, she turned to Dal, with a shy gesture. "The Scholar Dame, *and* her Companion, are bidden to dine with the Pro-Matriarch this evening, and I am bidden to say to you that my mother's Companion, Rhu by name, is eager to entertain and find company and friendship with the Scholar Dame's Companion."

Thank God, Cendri said to herself, *someone at last has taken special notice of Dal, and men, at least, can dine with women!* For a time she had wondered if this society had revived ancient interdining taboos; in some societies men and women did not eat together, but it was usually because women were considered unclean, or unfit to join the dominant males; she had been afraid this culture had simply *reversed* all cultural taboos!

Lady Miranda had taken down her braid, and her long hair flowed down her back; she wore a loose, waistless gown of pale blue, nearly translucent, which made her pregnancy very conspicuous. She must be, Cendri thought, very near to term; she looked enormous. Miranda's eyes lingered on Dal for a few minutes, shyly studying his decorations, and Cendri felt annoyed. *Are the men kept out of sight so much that I'm going to have to worry about women admiring Dal?*

Even pregnant, Miranda's pretty enough that if she seriously tries to get Dal's attention, I *ought* to worry!

Downstairs, in an enormous long room, scattered at low tables and sitting on cushions, many women, and some children were gathered. There were two or three pre-adolescent boys, but she saw, at first, no other adult male. Miranda led them through the clustered small tables, heads turning to watch as they passed, into a small alcove at the far end, where a man and woman were sitting.

Cendri's first thought—is this a polygamous society, is he the husband of all these women and father of all these children?—was quickly dismissed; the man was very young, considerably younger than Dal himself. But it was the woman beside him, rising to her feet to greet them, who drew Cendri's eyes.

Vaniya, Pro-Matriarch of Isis/Cinderella, was a woman of middle age, her face lined and slightly stern. She had the head of a magnificent lioness, framed in a heavy cloud of thick, frizzy, amber-colored hair. She was tall and strong-looking, her forehead high, her nose long and arched; her eyes deep-set and flashing brilliant blue. Her thick body was draped with violet silks, falling in elaborate folds which did not suit her; but she looked imposing. She raised her hands and clasped them before her face, in the Unity's greeting.

Her voice was a light soprano, which nevertheless was strong enough to be audible everywhere in the room; the voice of a trained singer or public speaker.

"It is a pleasure to welcome the Scholar Dame Malocq from University. In the name of our High Matriarch Rezali, I make you welcome for yourself, and for the Scholars you represent."

Cendri said, aware that after the trained resonance of Vaniya's voice her own sounded like a child's, "It is a pleasure and an honor, my Lady."

The Pro-Matriarch's face, stern and unsmiling till now, relaxed in a smile. Her face was unsymmetrical, and when she smiled she looked lopsided and untidy, but good-natured. "And now I am sure you have had quite enough of formalities, my dear Scholar Dame. Please sit here beside me." She indicated a large, soft blue cushion. Awkwardly, Cendri lowered herself. There were societies with chairs, and there were societies without chairs, and she was glad of her young and athletic knees. The Pro-Matriarch turned her piercing eyes on Dal, who raised his hands in the Unity gesture of greeting; after a moment the Pro-Matriarch returned the gesture and Cendri relaxed.

"May I know the name of your Companion, Scholar Dame?"

Cendri said firmly "He is the Master Scholar Dallard Malocq."

Vaniya raised her shaggy eyebrows. Her complexion was tawny, roughened somewhat with age. "Dear me, all that? What do you call it, my dear?"

Cendri colored with annoyance and dismay. "Dallard, or Dal."

"Dal." Her smile was charming and hospitable. "Rhu, you must entertain Dal for me while I talk seriously with the Scholar Dame," she said, turning to the young man on the cushion beside her.

Women were moving around the room, setting bowls of fruit and platters of undefinable substances on the tables, taking their own places. There seemed to be no servants, or if there were, they sat at the table with their betters and were not distinguished by dress or manner. Lady Miranda took a seat beside Cendri, saying courteously, "Allow me to serve you, Scholar Dame," and began to fill her plate with food.

"I trust the rooms prepared for you are comfortable, my dear Scholar Dame," Vaniya said.

"Very comfortable indeed; very luxurious."

"I hoped you would find them so," Vaniya said. "They are the rooms which I myself inhabited with my Companion when I was somewhat younger, but such luxuries, of course, are more suitable for younger women, and I felt it proper to allot them to the honored guest of the Matriarchate. And, to her Companion. Your Companion is charming and attractive," she added, "but I find it surprising that you brought no assistant for your work among us, Scholar Dame."

Cendri, feeling Dal's eyes upon her said firmly, "I thought it had been made clear, my Lady, that my Companion is—" she stumbled over the lie, "—is my assistant, and that I shall require his company and assistance as all times in the Ruins."

"A man, for assistant? But how surprising!"

"Dal is a Scholar in his own right," Cendri said. Vaniya's smile was a little uncertain. "One understands, certainly, that there are male Scholars on University, which is why we requested the Scholar Dame di Velo for work here. But it did not occur to us that a woman Scholar would choose a male for assistant at her serious business!" Now Cendri identified her expression; Vaniya was scandalized. "Don't you find it—" she actually blushed, "*distracting*"

Cendri thought, helplessly, *Oh, damn, this is ridiculous*! The one thing she must not do was blush, now, or she admitted her vulnerability to this idiotic cultural and sexual taboo! She bit her lip, hard, and the pain dispelled the blush she felt rising to her cheeks. Her voice was level. "Not at all distracing, my Lady; our work is kept apart from—" she fumbled for a moment; the language of Isis had no word for *marriage*. "From companionship."

Miranda lowered her eyes; Vaniya frowned slightly in puzzlement. "I am not narrow-minded, I hope; I am not one of those who believes that learning makes a male somehow unmanly, and on some subjects I can converse with Rhu—" her eyes dwelt on him, fondly, "almost as with an intelligent woman. But that is not what I meant, not entirely. You come from a society dominated by men, Scholar Dame—at least one where the academic prizes are mostly reserved for men. So it would seem you might well have chosen a fellow woman for the prestigious post of your assistant, rather

than choosing a man who could have won scholastic
honors on his own. I understand how rude it must seem
for me to criticize your choice, and I can well understand that a young woman might well desire for her
Companion to be trained in her own field so that she
might have the pleasure of his attendance on an
assignment far from her home world. But you could
have brought a capable woman for assistant, my dear;
we would willingly have extended hospitality to your
Companion, simply for your convenience and—" she
smiled, indulgently, "the amusement of your leisure."

Miranda was blushing; she said something almost
reproving to her mother in an undertone. Cendri was
debating half a dozen answers, realizing—and the
memory stung—that the Scholar Dame di Velo had
chosen a male for *her* assistant, and that she, Cendri,
had originally intended to accompany Dal in much the
same capacity that Vaniya now indulgently allotted to
her "Companion." But any answer would only satisfy a
selfish desire to defend her own customs against
Vaniya's—an ignoble desire for an anthropologist!

Finally she said, "Within the Unity, Lady, men and
women do not compete for posts of honor. We try to
assign work to the person best qualified to do it,
regardless of male or female, and it would never occur
to me that I should appoint a woman for assistant, any
more than a man would choose a male assistant
because—" she broke off, remembering that the male
pronoun was not used except in a sexual connotation,
"because the male *was* male."

Vaniya said, thoughtfully, "Yet there is a proven
biological difference which simply unfits men for certain tasks. It would seem to be kinder not to force men
to compete in spheres where they are not qualified."
She glanced at Rhu and Dal, saying, "You two must
really not take this personally, but, Scholar Dame,
don't you find it tends to unfit a man for his real
function, when he is allowed to develop his mind too
much?" Cendri noted the deliberate use of *he* and *his*.

"Men are such magnificently physical creatures at their best, and many women feel that allowing them to cultivate womanly talents such as art and music will make them weak and even impotent. Of course, there are exceptions—" she looked dotingly at Rhu. "But are the men of the Unity still—still pleasing to women?"

Cendri saw that Dal looked ready to explode; she looked warningly at him, but he only smiled. "Lady Vaniya," he said, "five hundred years ago on my homeworld of Pioneer, our men shared at least one of your beliefs, that the cultivation of art, music and scholarship would indeed make men womanly and weak. Only in the last hundred years on Pioneer have men been allowed to cultivate serious scholarship, and my own grandfather looked with scorn on the idea that a real man could be a Scholar, far less an artist or musician."

"Then your world—Pioneer—retains some traces of matriarchal rule, Dal?" inquired Vaniya seriously, and Cendri had trouble keeping her face straight. Dal refused to look at Cendri, but his voice was sober. "I am not enough of a Scholar to discover any such traces, Lady."

Oh, damn you, Dal! Cendri thought, trying not to choke on stifled laughter, nobody alive could be enough of a Scholar to discover traces of matriarchal rule on Pioneer, because there weren't any! If ever a culture was patrist and woman-suppressive, it was *that* one! This was *wicked* of Dal! Making fun of the Pro-Matriarch, right to her face!

But thoughtfulness displaced her laughter. It wasn't just reversal of woman-suppressive cultures, then; it was an exaggeration, of trends already present in the Unity, on worlds such as Pioneer, which went to extremes; if all the softer and more scholarly talents were unmanly, and men's sphere restricted to the warlike and competitive, this too could tip the balance of stereotyping for sex-roles. . . .

Again she was angrily conscious of all the questions

she could not ask. Her stay here was going to be a frustrating experience! She applied herself to the food on her plate; it was good, though unfamiliar. In any case, Cendri's training had conditioned her to eat virtually anything edible to humans without distaste or disgust; people had such widely different ideas of the palatable that any cross-cultural student had to be able to join in any kind of meal with apparent, if not actual, enthusiasm. She noted that most of the food seemed to be grains and seeds, with portions of fruit and greens, and wondered if there were taboos on meat eating.

"Scholar Dame—"

"My Lady—?"

"Forgive me; these formalities seem un-natural," Vaniya said, "Our society does not use them; my daughter—" she looked indulgently at Miranda, "studied your forms of courtesy and convinced me that I must use them, at first, to make you welcome; and one can understand that on a world like University where many cultures meet and mingle, a veneer of formalities would smooth social relationships. But I am hoping you will find friends here, as well as interesting work. Have you a personal name, Scholar Dame, and would you find it offensive if we used it to you?"

"My name is Cendri," she said, "and I would not object at all . . ." she felt a flow of elation which had nothing to do with the question. *I was right! I knew these formal manners didn't fit what I had seen of this society—the clothes without social distinctions, the haphazard layout of the city!* As when she had first used memorized textbook clichés for intersocial structuring, and had found they were not lifeless formulas, but actually *worked*, she was excited. It made her work seem real to her—her *real* work, not the lifeless Builder ruins.

"Cendri—it is a pretty sound," Vaniya said, "Has it meaning in your language?"

"It means—a spark, a flash of flame, a live coal," Cendri said, searching for equivalents in Vaniya's language, and Vaniya touched her hand lightly. "As I can see you are in truth, through the formal manners the Unity has put on you. I felt sure you were a woman like ourselves, though my daughters were sure that, coming from the Unity, you would be either weak, submissive, dominated by men—or else harsh and competitive, corrupted by striving against them in daily life."

Cendri knew Vaniya meant a compliment, but to her it did not sound much like one. She felt herself as competitive as any man, and as qualified to compete. But she accepted the words in the spirit in which they were given. "My Lady is kind."

"But if I am to call you Cendri, you must call me Vaniya; or perhaps when we know one another better you will call me Mother, as all the women of my household do, even those who are not the daughters of my womb."

It was a cue for Cendri and she picked it up. "Then all these women are not your daughters, Vaniya?"

"Daughters of my household, but not of my body," Vaniya said, and seemed not ill pleased to expand on this theme. "You have met Miranda, who is the youngest daughter of my body, and who is bearing my heir," she said. "I have three other daughters of the body, although one has gone to live in the household of her life-partner, with her children, and one is away tonight in the city. And this—" she indicated one of the other women at the table with them, "is my eldest daughter Lialla, and her life-partner Zamila."

The two women she indicated smiled shyly at Cendri. Cendri noted that they were seated very close together, and they were taking turns feeding a very small child with a spoon. *Life-partner.* So the women do pair off, then. Where do they get all these children? Artificial insemination? Where in this world are all the men?

If the men are kept away from the women as carefully as this, maybe it is no wonder they are regarded as dangerous animals. . . . but that train of thought em-

barrassed her and she turned her thoughts to analysing
all the names she was told. Most of them were
three-syllabled and euphonious, like all the female
names Cendri had heard there.

"Also within my house are two foster-daughters and
their grown children and life-partners—" she told
Cendri their names, but Cendri was losing track, and
found it hard to assimilate so many names and complex
relationships. ". . . and my foster-sisters, and the
grown daughters of the life-partner of my mother, and
three or four women of our remote kin, who have come
to live with us so that we may share companionship and
work in fields and household, and visit the sea in
company. My youngest male child, Lar, went to the
Men's House nearly fifteen turns of the sun ago, so that
no males now live under this roof except my dear
Companion—" again, the doting smile at Rhu— "and
three grandsons not yet a decade in age. I should also
mention our household Inquirer, Maret—" she indicated a grossly fat, fair-haired person at a nearby table,
who was rocking a small sleepy child in an ample lap.
"Maret is a woman-by-courtesy; it was born *Mar*, my
foster-sister's eldest male child, but many years ago
it was given the privilege of wearing woman's garments—" (Cendri wondered how anyone ever told
the difference, since all garments appeared unisex, but
maybe the differences were too subtle for an outsider to
see) "—and of performing sacrifices at the shrines of
the Goddess, to be called *Maret*, and to live here
among us as a sister."

And now that Cendri looked carefully she could see
that the grossly fat person was breastless and that there
was a faint shadow, carefully shaven, along the jowly
jaws. An effeminate? Or a eunuch? Was the transfor-
mation from male to *woman-by-courtesy* surgical or
merely psychological? And what kind of functionary
was a household Inquirer? She concealed the sense of
revulsion which rose, uncontrollably, in her at the sight
of this gross ugly man who had renounced his gender to

live among woman. Apparently this society rewarded feminine behavior even in men, and she should have expected it.

What's the matter with me? I'm an anthropologist, I'm not supposed to make judgments like this. It must be fatigue. She listened to Vaniya saying, "But enough of me and mine, you will learn as you live among us."

She sought for a neutral topic. "Miranda told me that your High Matriarch lies very ill. Is a stranger allowed by custom to inquire about her health?"

Vaniya sighed. "Our beloved Mother and Priestess has fallen into a coma. She is neither recovered nor dead; it is uncertain whether she will even recover consciousness to designate whether I myself, or my colleague and fellow Pro-Matriarch Mahala will assume her ring and robe. This is a doleful state for one who has served the Goddess for more than eighty years; yet I cannot bring myself to regret it, Cendri, for it has brought us the one thing we must have; *time*"

"I do not understand—"

"Our beloved Mother's last conscious words were to bid me make you welcome to the ruins at We-were-guided, and lodge you with me," Vaniya said, "and even Mahala dares not disobey that command, while our Mother and Priestess still breathes. But when she breathes her last, then—then we cannot know who will assume her ring, and if it is Mahala—if it is Mahala, her plans for We-were-guided do not bear thinking about!" Vaniya frowned, then, with an effort, smiled at Cendri and said, "So you must make haste, my dear Cendri, to explore the ruins and verify that they are, indeed, the ruins of the Builders—which we *know*, but once this is confirmed by an independent outside scientific study—"

Cendri asked, trying to make her voice level and courteous, "Is the Pro-Matriarch Mahala opposed to the study of the Ruins?"

"You must not trouble yourself with our politics," Vaniya said, and though she smiled, the words were a warning; *a keep-off sign,* Cendri thought, despite their cordiality.

She said, "Surely you understand, Vaniya, that such as archaeological exploration is a long piece of work; there is no way we could possibly do this in a few days, or months!" Dal had spoken in terms of years! "Archaeology is the most deliberate of sciences; ruins which have stood for millions of years cannot be evaluated in a little while! And if your High Matriarch is likely to die at any time—how long is she likely to live?"

"Our surgeons will not even hazard a guess, although Lohara said she might linger for a season or more; and of course, it is possible she will recover her consciousness and speak me her successor, in which case—" she smiled, rather grimly. "I have one of my own household stationed near her bedside, so that if she does so, Mahala could not conceal it!"

Rhu said, "And no doubt the Lady Mahala has likewise stationed one of *her* Inquirers for a similar purpose?"

"No doubt, sacrilegious bitch," Vaniya said, then, with an effort, added, "But you must not trouble yourself about politics either, Rhu, this is no proper welcome for our honored guests. Miranda, will you sing for us, my child?"

Obediently, Miranda took a small stringed instrument from a case near the window, sat down with it in her lap, and began to sing. Her voice was very pure and clear, evidently well-trained, though not, Cendri judged, of performing quality for public display. She sang several songs, all short, all mournful, in a strange melancholy minor scale. To Cendri's questions, she explained, in a soft, diffident voice, that they were mostly rhythmic songs of work-women; songs of the looms, of the herdwomen, songs of the sea and the nets, songs for weaving cloth and spinning it. She added, to Vaniya, "Will you not have Rhu sing for our guests?"

Rhu protested to Vaniya in an undertone, but she said briskly, "Don't be shy!"

"I would prefer to listen to the Lady's singing," he said, not looking at Miranda.

"Miranda should not tire herself now."

"My *lyrik* is in my room—"

"Use mine," Miranda said, timidly, and Rhu glanced at Vaniya for permission, then took it, protesting faintly, "If I re-set the strings for my voice, the Lady will have the trouble of re-tuning them afterward for herself—"

"I don't mind," Miranda said, not looking at him, "Please sing, Rhu."

"As the Lady and the honored guests wish." With courteous resignation, Rhu began to tune the instrument he had called a *lyrik*, bending his head close to the strings. Cendri watched him beneath lowered eyelids—she suspected that staring at him was at least a social error and perhaps more. Rhu was, she suspected, four or five years younger than herself and Dal; thin and dark, his hair elaborately curled and waved. He wore a tunic of metallic blue fiber which left his tanned shoulders bare; a tight belt of silver plates circled his narrow waist, and his long slim legs were bare, except for silvered sandals ornamented with pearls. He had a narrow, curly beard and small moustaches, and his thin face looked sad. He asked Vaniya, "What shall I sing?"

"Whatever you like, my dear," she said indulgently, "A hunting song, please, men always like them."

Nodding, he began a long ballad which, as nearly as Cendri could make out, celebrated the pleasures of the chase, of the spear, of carrying the slain beasts home in triumph. Cendri had no interest in the subject, though she tucked away the random knowledge that while these women lived in cities, much of their life still entered upon the agricultural cycles of the year.

In spite of the boring recital of the pleasures of the hunt, she had to delight in the voice, a superbly trained baritone which Cendri judged would have won him fame as a concert singer on virtually any civilized world. Rich, full and golden, it swelled to fill the room without being loud, or died to a whisper which was, nevertheless, audible to the furthest corner; women stopped talking to listen, and when one of the children prattled something, its mother quickly hushed it.

A voice like this, tucked away on Isis?

When the song ended, she spoke a few words of compliment to Rhu, who smiled with shy pleasure. "The Scholar Dame is kind, but I wish she could have heard my voice before it was spoilt by changing; as a child I had truly a fine soprano."

Vaniya said regretfully, "Yes, Rhu has splendid technique, but of course it is wasted on a man's roughened voice."

Dal said directly to the Companion, "If you ever get tired of living on this world, a voice like that would make your fortune anywhere inside the Unity. Believe me."

He blushed like a boy. "The honored guest is kind; how may I thank him?"

"Sing something else," Dal said, and Rhu glanced at Vaniya for permission, then bent his head close to the harp, and sang, in a low voice ;

> I am only a man
> And I have no part in Paradise;
> Twice have I tasted bliss
> And twice have I been driven forth;
> Once when I left my mother's womb
> And again when I was driven forth
> From my mother's house.

The golden baritone dropped to a mournful croon, his hands swept the strings with an anguished cadence;

> When I am done with life
> Will the Goddess take me, perhaps,
> To her loving breasts?

Cendri discovered that she was blinking away tears; not only at the beauty of the voice, but at the agonized sadness of the song. Dal, too, looked visibly shaken.

"Men's songs are so sentimental," said Vaniya lightly, "but that one always comes near to making me cry. Men enjoy self-pity so much, don't they?" As Rhu put the harp in the case and returned it to Miranda, she filled a cup with wine and held it indulgently to Rhu's lips. "Here, my dear. Rhu has given us so much pleasure, I think he deserves a treat."

Suddenly Cendri was filled with an overwhelming revulsion. In spite of Vaniya's kindness, despite the pleasant atmosphere and the excellence of food and wine, she found it hard to conceal her sense of disgust and shock. She had read about this phenomenon in her textbook, one of the manifestations of culture shock; she supposed it was due to fatigue.

Vaniya looked sharply at her.

"You are weary, Cendri. The journey must have been long and fatiguing."

"Yes," Cendri admitted.

"Then you must go and rest—"

"But before we leave you, Vaniya, may we ask if we may begin our work at once in the Ruins—?"

Vaniya sighed regretfully, and said, "Alas, I still have much to do with the disasters which the earthquake left behind; I shall have no leisure for some time to take you there; perhaps in a few days I can arrange to take you, and then, when you have been properly introduced to this—which is a very sacred place to us—you will be free to work there as you choose."

Cendri, listening carefully to the words of the Pro-Matriarch, realized; in spite of their solicitous courtesy, she had just been warned not to try and go there on her own. *Why not*? She told herself that it was natural enough, the ruins which Vaniya called We-were-guided were one of their greatest shrines or sacred places; but the argument did not quite convince her.

Maybe it isn't the Pro-Matriarch Mahala who is opposed to the exploration of the Ruins. Maybe it's Vaniya herself! Twice, now, they've side-stepped a direct answer on that!

She made, resignedly, the only possible answer, that they awaited a time of the Pro-Matriarch's convenience. As they climbed to their room, she was anticipating without enthusiasm Dal's probable comments on that, and on the society as they had seen it tonight; but Dal was silent and thoughtful. Finally he said, when they were safely shut into their room, "Did you ever hear a voice like Rhu's?"

"Not since the Orpheus Musicians visited University; they had a baritone almost as good."

"And Vaniya keeps him for a pet and snubs him—a talent like that! I'd like to kidnap him and smuggle him off to University! Might cause a diplomatic crisis, though. There must be some kind of penalty for alienating the affections of the Pro-Matriarch's Companion. And speaking of Companions—" he put his arm around Cendri's waist.

"If you're *very* nice, I may let you sleep in the Amusement Corner with me."

Cendri laughed, putting her arms up around his neck. "Don't you be arrogant with *me*, love, on this world I could have you put out at night like a puppy dog!" But she let him scoop her up in his arms and carry her to the padded alcove. It was considerably more comfortable than that high, narrow bed!

"This seems to be my only proper function on this world," Dal murmured against her lips, "I might as well take advantage of it!"

"Don't be ridiculous, darling," she whispered, drawing him down to her, "We'll call it a second honeymoon."

Dal had made a joke of it. And yet there was a trace of bitterness behind the words which told Cendri that in Dal's heart it was very far from being a joke.

Late in the night, Cendri rose and went to the

window. She looked down on the ruins of the ancient site which the Pro-Matriarch had called We-were-guided. Dal slept, satiated and, she hoped, a little comforted and pacified. How would she keep him from going mad with frustration here? When she herself would be doing *his* proper work, and he must pose as her assistant and subordinate. . . . she had been foolish ever to accept this deception!

Dal had insisted. He had said it was enough for any Scholar simply to have the privilege of working on the Builder ruins, and in any case he would have the credit for the work when they were back on University. Yet she quailed at the thought of seeing his pride wounded, day after day, in a society like this where he was reduced to the status of a housepet like Rhu, a boy kept for a woman's pleasure! She marvelled at Vaniya—the woman was many times a grandmother, and her Companion young enough to be her grandson!

Well, in the Unity it was not unknown for some rich woman to dote on a handsome and talented youth, and to keep him as a sort of pet. But there it was always done with a little more respect for the young man's pride, and the woman usually felt some shame about it. Cendri told herself that her revulsion was just a cultural prejudice.

She turned her eyes to the moon-flooded landscape, which covered the low slopes behind the city with such brilliance that shapes and outlines were clearly percep-tible. At the center of the ruins of We-were-guided, surrounded by them, and at their very center— *enshrined*, the thought came without volition—lay a familiar outline, dwarfed by distance; one of the old models of starship.

Was this the very ship in which the women of Isis/Cinderella had come to their world?

The original Matriarchate—Cendri remembered— had been founded a few hundred years before, by a group of historians who held a mad theory that the original human stock had come from a world with a primitive matriarchal culture, and that decay in human cultures had set in when the worship of a Mother Goddess, a planetary Earth-mother, had been over-thrown and superseded by climatic changes which convinced the primitive society that the worship of sun and rain gods, regulating the weather, was more important than the Goddess cults.

So the Matriarchate is founded, then, in religious fanaticism and it will never be understood except by understanding its religious beginnings. . . .

The Matriarchate had recruited women from all over the Unity and settled on a planet which they renamed Persephone. For a few generations they had remained part of the Unity, and Cendri had read of a few scientists who had been hired to work there and their research lavishly funded—Persephone had been a rich planet then—to re-discover what the Matriarchate believed, or professed to believe, was the original form of humanity, female in form, and without the y-chromosome creating maleness.

Some interesting research had been done, but the parthenogenetic females created by this research had proved sterile after the second generation, and the Matriarchs had resigned themselves to retaining some males in their society as breeding stock.

About that time they had founded their daughter colony of Labrys; after the bureaucratic blunder which wiped out almost eighty per cent of the Labrys popula-tion, they had become paranoid, and withdrawn from the Unity—that was one version; the other was that the Unity had ejected them for being in violation of the First Principle, that all worlds participating in the Unity should grant equality to all citizens. Persephone had insisted on its right to determine *who* should be defined as a citizen. And after that, there had been almost nothing heard of them. The remnants of the Labrys colony were repatriated, embittered. Then, less than fifty years ago, Persephone, undergoing climatic chang-es, had taken over, on normal Unity homestead laws, an uninhabited pelagic planet, almost without arable land, known as Cinderella. As non-members of the

Unity, they had had to pay an enormous surcharge for the privilege. They had promptly re-named it Isis, and dropped almost out of contact.

During the early stages of the negotiations about the Builder ruins, Cendri had heard the Dame di Velo raging about that. Even then—the Dame di Velo had been a young woman when Cinderella was resettled as *Isis*—she had known about the ancient ruins on Cinderella and had convinced herself they were Builder ruins. The Dame herself had tried to raise a fund to homestead Cinderella by archaeologists instead, and keep it in perpetuity for a mine of information about the supposed Builders. But the colony of Persephone had outbid them.

"A tragedy," the Dame di Velo had called it, "the greatest tragedy of my professional life; that a world which was a mine, a veritable mine of archaeological information, should be turned over to a crackpot culture, for them to spin and weave and fish and ignore the most famous artifact in the known Galaxy!"

But scientific foundations traditionally found it hard to raise money, and the Unity's basic stipulations stated that no viable colony should be denied the right to homestead any arable planet. So the Matriarchate settled on Cinderella/Isis, and closed their doors to the Unity. They traded, Cendri had read, in pearls and nacre from their oceans, in magnesium, arsenic, selenium and gold. Their jewelry was famous to the luxury trade everywhere. They imported platinum and titanium, and certain fluoride compounds—Cendri was not sure whether it was for their plastics industry or for their teeth—and a few organic chemicals. But until the negotiations which culminated in the invitation to the Scholar Dame di Velo to come here, no citizen from the Unity had set foot on Isis.

Cendri had grown cramped and cold, standing by the window, and was about to return to the comfortable nest of cushions where Dal still lay curled up, when she saw a light below.

The city of Ariadne was dark at night. Cendri had

expected that; most of what was usually called "night life" was oriented to solitary males from the spaceport districts, and based mostly on selling them sex and entertainment. Remotely she wondered what the solitary males on this world *did* for entertainment. There seemed to be nothing akin to marriage as it was known on Cendri's world and Dal's. Cendri had become accustomed to extreme differences of sexual customs from world to world. On University, for instance, her best friend had come from a world where group marriage was the norm and the worst perversion imaginable was to make love in groups of fewer than four. And considering the number of children she had seen in the dining room tonight, there must be *some* allowances for sexual contact.

But whatever they did at night on Isis, they did it silently and in the dark, without need of bright lights. She had seen dim lights on the upper stories of the few buildings that had them, but otherwise all was dark; so the row of lights, slow, winding, bobbing quietly along at a steady pace, drew her eyes and her attention. She had thought it the torch of some kind of night watchman—if night watchmen were *men* here—could any world, even a matriarchy, be free of crime? But there were too many of the small lights for that. She drew back the curtain a little and leaned out the window. It was a torchlight procession, winding slowly through the gardens behind the Pro-Matriarch's house and down along the shore.

Well, she had wondered what they did at night in Ariadne to amuse themselves. Now she had seen something, though of course she had no idea what it meant. A moonlight picnic? There were two moons, large and beautiful, in the sky. A skinny-dipping party? A religious festival? They might be going out to hunt, fish, swim, eat, copulate, or pick mushrooms which only flowered by moonlight, as they did on Cendri's own home world at one season. Near the head of the procession she could make out a tall, broad-shouldered figure which might very well have been the Pro-Matriarch herself.

She watched the lights winding along the shore, where the surf tumbled and boomed softly with small breaking whitecaps. They moved further away and became small twinkling fireflies in the distance. Then they reappeared, no more than tiny points of light, winding slowly into the very center of the ruins which Miranda had called We-were-guided.

And their spaceship lay there. Thinking of Miranda's rapt expression when she spoke of contact with the Builders, Cendri wondered; was this, then, the procession of some sort of religious cult which had grown up around the ruins? Had they gone—Cendri found herself shivering—to try and appease the supposed spirits of the Builders for their imminent invasion by outworlders bent on learning their secrets? Perhaps, even, to appease their supposed wrath? Again she shivered—ancestor-worship cults were notoriously bloodthirsty! Were they offering sacrifices at the Builder's shrines? And *what* sacrifices? They seemed a peaceful, enlightened culture, with an adequate technology, but religious cults were by definition outside of a society's rational structure.

Again she sought out the distant twinkling lights, adorning ruins and spaceship. They had formed into a circle. A garland of lights, Cendri thought drowsily, watching it. She yawned, tired and thoroughly chilled—Isis' culture did not evidently run to central heating, though in view of the daytime heat and general subtropical climate that was not surprising; but now it was distinctly chilly. She thought longingly of the warm cushions, and Dal's warm body, even in sleep wonderfully comforting and reassuring.

Yet she stood as if compelled, watching the distant torches that festooned the ruins like Festival lights on the Sacred Tree of the Vhanni on Rigel Four—the light that had begun to glow, like a reflection of the huge pale moons, at the summit of the ruins. She was not conscious of cold now. She stood in amazed fascination, watching the light, the slow, suffusing, comforting glow. It was like a voice in her heart, filling her with kindliness, love, warmth. . . . her heart went out toward the light, and for a moment she felt like the child she had been, running to hide herself in the lap of a nurse. . . . a fragment of Rhu's song lingered for a moment in her mind, *When I am done with life, will the Goddess take me to her loving breasts.* . . .

Cendri started upright, shaking herself. Had she been asleep? The moons had set, but the light lingered, a faint glow around the ruins, the echo of the voice in her mind—had it ever been there, or had she been dreaming? Reason said, *I was dreaming*, but enough of the warmth lingered that she was reluctant to dismiss it as a dream. She was enough of a scientist not to trust her own perceptions when they seemed to deny reason.

She turned and called softly "Dal—"

He came awake slowly, confused, "Cendri? Where are you?" She could see him feeling about in the bed for her beside him. Had she been asleep, standing bolt upright at the window? Was a bizarre dream enough cause to rob him of his rest? But she said softly, "I'm here at the window, Dal. Come here, I want you to see something—"

"*Sharrioz!* At this hour?" He sat up, bewildered, then padded softly, naked, across the room to her side. "Sweetheart, is something wrong?"

"Dal, look—toward the ruins—"

Blinking, he pressed his face to the pane. "Lights—down there in the ruins—"

"I saw them leave the house—hours ago now, I suppose. I have no idea what time it was, but the moons were still in the sky. They went into the ruins—"

"Well," he interrupted, "Why shouldn't they? Vaniya said, at supper, that they were a religious shrine. Maybe they go to say their prayers by moonlight, or something. That's *your* job—to study this culture!"

She reminded herself that his truculent tone was not

an insult; that he had been roused from a sound sleep to see something Cendri herself had not been sure she saw.

"That isn't all," she said, "I saw a light in the ruins—near the tip of that building, do you see, the one with a tip like a broken horn. . . ." The light, to Cendri, was still faintly there, and the sight of it some-how roused again, in her, the memory of that brief, ecstatic glow. . . .

But she was not sure, not now. If she had fantasied it, or if it had been an illusion, born of a glimmer of reflected moonlight on some unknown shining surface . . . she would not suggest it. Not unless he saw it independently, and felt what she had felt, what she seemed to feel faintly even now, would it validate her own perceptions.

"There is a light . . . no, not a light, a kind of glow. Are you sure it wasn't moonlight, Cendri? Or per-haps some kind of luminescent material—we have no idea what kind of materials the old Builders may have had." He broke off, yawning hugely. "Are you sure you didn't dream it?"

Cendri realized she was *not* sure. One moment she had been full of the flooding light, warmth, the suffusing joy she could not identify, happiness for no known cause; the next moment cramped, cold, the moon set.

"I *did* see a glow—" she insisted forlornly.

"I'm sure you did." Dal yawned again. "Maybe that high place is reflecting the glow of the rising sun out on the ocean, dawn can't be very far away." With sudden solicitude he felt her cold hands, bent to touch her chilled feet.

"Darling, you're chilled through! Have you slept at all, or have you stood here half the night watching torchlight processions and things? Here, let me warm you up."

She put her arms around his neck; tenderly, as he had done in their first days, he picked her up and carried her to the cushioned corner, covering her, enfolding her in his own warmth, taking her cold feet into the curve of his body to warm them. Snuggled close, she persisted. "Dal—when you were looking at the lights—did you *feel* anything?"

It was dark, but she could feel him looking at her in amazement. "*Feel* anything? Cendri, you're half asleep," he said tenderly, "Just that I can't wait to get out there! Thanks, by the way, for making it clear to the old girl that I *am* a Scholar and that you'll need me; I was half afraid I'd never be allowed out there at all."

"Oh, Dal! Could you doubt it?"

"I wasn't sure. I mean—you're one of them, a woman, they respect you—I thought you might take this chance to try and prove what you can do on your own. . . ."

She thought, appalled, *does he still not trust me?* And then, troubled by her own thoughts, *does any man ever trust any woman? Completely? Is that why men on some worlds try so hard to dominate women . . . not arrogance but fear?*

"Dal, Dal—I couldn't do anything without you. . . ."

"I wasn't sure," he said, shaking, holding her tight —not now, she sensed, to warm her, but to reassure himself. It shook Cendri's certainties. She had always seen Dal so strong to her weakness, powerful where she was without strength. But now?

"Cendri, don't you think I know how much you've resented this, resented not being a Dame when I was made Master Scholar, I couldn't blame you if you . . . if you took advantage . . .," he murmured, and she clasped him tight, troubled and shocked beyond words at her own thoughts. Was this place corrupting her too, where these women gave her illusions and delusions about her own power? Abruptly, frighteningly, she wished they had never come here.

"Oh, Dal, hold me," she begged, suddenly, "Hold me tight, don't let me go! I'm afraid! Oh, Dal, hold me!"

chapter four

VANIYA'S DUTIES CONTINUED TO OCCUPY HER, TO THE
exclusion of her alien guests, for the next ten days.
Cendri was not altogether displeased; she welcomed
the opportunity to study the strange society into which
she had been admitted. Already she was envisioning,
with pride, a report with her name on it, studying these
women who lived essentially without men; a report
which would surely make secure her borrowed status as
Scholar Dame.

She kept copious notes, scribbling them in the
antique script of her childhood for secrecy's sake; she
still remembered that one recorded statement from the
Matriarchate—*we will not be studied by your scientists
like one of those glass-sided insect colonies we give for
toys to our little daughters.* A voice-scriber might be
found and turned on by accident; but there was no one
on this planet, not even Dal, who could read the
language and written script of Cendri's home world.

Miranda continued to be friendly, and on several
occasions invited Cendri to join the life of the women
of the household, inviting her into sewing-rooms,
weaving-rooms, gardens and nurseries. Yet she knew
that the essential life of the Matriarchate eluded her.
They did not live their lives without men—considering

73

the number of small children in Vaniya's household. And the general level of the society seemed somewhat too unsophisticated for widespread acceptance of artificial insemination. A considerable number of them must have quite active relations with men. But she wondered how they managed it; one never saw a man around this household, except for occasional menial work.

Yet Miranda's growing friendliness encouraged her to think that sooner or later she would be allowed to see beneath the outer surfaces of the society of the Matriarchate. And Miranda seemed endlessly curious about the Unity—almost as curious, Cendri thought, as she herself was curious about the Matriarchate.

One day they were in the garden of the Residence, among the flowers and herbs of the ornamental walks, when Miranda asked abruptly, "How long have you and your Companion been together?"

Cendri, automatically converting from the timescales of University, said, "About a third of your Long Year."

"Did you take him as Companion only for your—your stay here on Isis?"

Cendri smiled gently and said, "No; no, we intend to stay together as long as we both desire it. It is not common for a marriage to endure lifelong—" There was, as far as she knew, no word for *marriage* in the language of Isis, so what she actually said was *life-partnership*. "—but it is not unheard-of either, and at present we have no thought of separating at any time in the foreseeable future."

"Then your Companion is actually your—your life-partner as well?" Miranda said, in astonishment. "How strange it would seem to me—to anyone here, to take a male as life-partner! Strange and far too—too—" she paused, fumbled for words, finally said stiffly, not looking at Cendri, "—too sexually exacting, even exhausting."

Cendri wondered exactly what kind of idea Miranda

had of a man's sexual needs and demands—or, for that matter, of her own. She knew sexual needs were mostly psychological, and largely conditioned by the society anyway, but did she really believe men were sexually insatiable? She remembered that the shuttleship pilot—or was it Miranda herself, on their first day here?—had spoken of the impossibility of educating men because they were so much under the compulsion of their sexual needs. How could any woman have a realistic idea of what men were like when she never knew any of them at close hand? She said, "No, I don't find it so, Miranda," but she was embarrassed anyway.

Miranda said, "But—aren't you lonely, with no other women in your household? It seems so un-natural to me, and odd."

Cendri was used to this; on University, one of the commoner patterns was group marriage, and she was accustomed to the mixture of pity and curiosity from women in such marriages, feeling that Cendri must be lonely with no other women, and bored with only one man. She said tranquilly, "I have many women friends, Miranda, but our pattern of life, Dal's and mine, has its basis in the idea that one man and one woman, and their children, form the basic unit of society, and that the man and woman are closest to one another, best friends and intimates, with everyone else somewhere outside that bond."

"But how can you really have woman friends when you do not share the important things of your life with them?" Miranda asked. "Can a man really—really be close to a woman that way?"

Cendri smiled at the young woman. They were the same age, and Miranda was, by her own world's standards, very well educated; yet she had never been off her homeworld of Isis, and this alone would have made her seem, to Cendri, provincial and somewhat immature. She said, "On University we see many life patterns; in mine it is taken for granted that a man can be a closer friend to any woman than another woman."

"But women are so much alike, they can understand one another so well," said Miranda, and she sounded a little wistful. "I am lonely—I was partnered at school, but I was too young, I suppose, to choose wisely, and we quarreled and separated last season; so I am bearing this child alone. My mother and sisters have been kind to me, but it is not the same." She hesitated and seemed about to say something further, then sighed and asked, "Have you no children, then?"

Cendri told her no—she and Dal had agreed to delay children until they had both gained the credentials they wanted, and had decided on which world they wished to live, or whether they would stay on University indefinitely.

"It would seem strange, to be forced to consult some man's convenience for a decision of that sort," Miranda said, and Cendri laughed and said, "Dal is not 'some man' to me, but my life-partner, as you would say, and I would not make any decision without consulting him, any more than he would without consulting me. It is truly mutual, Miranda, no matter what you have been told about what you call the maleworlds. I am not *forced* to consult his decisions, it is my choice."

"But how very strange," Miranda said. "Among us, most women take a life-partner when they are about my age; but a woman can share decisions with other women because we are so much alike."

"Does not your mother share decisions with her Companion?"

"With a *Companion?*" Miranda said, raising her eyebrows in incredulity. "No, no, of course not. But she is old enough to keep a Companion, her decisions at her age are her own; no woman my age would keep a male." She laughed, nervously. "I suppose you are used to many different life patterns and choices then—"

Cendri nodded. "If you were on University you would see many of them, too. And yet you would, I suppose, choose to remain with the one which gave you the emotional satisfactions you learned to need from childhood. Most people remain lifelong with the sexual patterns they learn before puberty. It's very rare for anyone to change. Some people have tried—a woman from my world joined a group-marriage on University. She was my friend, brought up to the kind of marriage *I* learned, one man and one woman, yet she joined—for a time—in a group-marriage where all the other members had been brought up to think of this as the only endurable or decent marriage." She was silent, remembering. Jerri's brief attempt to cross cultural lines had been a disaster; most such attempts ended in suicide or mental breakdown.

Cendri said after a time, "In the early decades of University, such cross-cultural marriage experiments were hailed as a broad step toward intercultural understanding. There were so many tragedies that now most people think, on the contrary, that they should be forbidden by law. I suppose the real truth—if there *is* any real truth—is somewhere in between."

Miranda nodded, understanding that. She said, "Yes, to me our way seems as right as if the hand of nature itself had written it in our flesh, in our bodies, our wombs, our hearts; and yet I can see that this is because from my earliest days I have been taught to think so, and to someone not so taught it would seem strange and even disgusting. Does our way disgust you, Cendri?"

Cendri said honestly, "I don't know enough about it to know how I really feel about it." She had, in any case, undergone lengthy conditioning, during her training as an anthropologist, to free her of some of these prejudices; but she could hardly say so. She wished she could question Miranda about some of the things that puzzled her; wished there was some way to do so without rousing her suspicion that she was not quite what she seemed. She wondered about their relations with men, wondered if the "life-partnerships" between women involved physical sex—she supposed they did,

close relationships and even sexual partnerships between the same sex were not unknown even on
University—but she did not know how to frame her
questions without violating some as-yet-unknown
taboo.

Miranda stooped to a flowerbed beside the path,
picked a small pale blue flower. She stood turning it this
way and that in her hands as she said, "There are times
when I—I like to wonder what it would be like to live in
some of those other ways which seem so—so unspeak-
able to our women. You say that your Companion is
your life-partner too. But—you are from the Unity,
from the maleworlds, does he not—not own you, then?
Are you bound to him by a bond you could not break at
will?"

Cendri smiled and said, "To dissolve our partner-
ship, I would merely have to go before the Civic
Authority on University, and make with him a joint
declaration that we wished to separate; no more than
that. If one of us was willing and the other unwilling, it
might be a little more complicated—an Arbitrator
would have to hear the case—and if there were children
we would have to make mutually agreeable arrangements for their care and education. But a marriage
cannot persist if either does not desire it; that would be
slavery."

"And you would let him go like that, if he wished to
leave you?"

Cendri countered, "Would any woman wish to keep
a man who no longer wished to remain with her?"

"It would seem to me strange to consult the wishes of
a man, especially of a Companion," Miranda said, and
she was frowning a little. "I had thought perhaps it was
the reverse of the way it is here; that perhaps in your
worlds a man owned a woman and was responsible for
everything she did. . . ."

Cendri shook her head. "No, although I believe
there have been worlds—Pioneer, many generations
ago—where this was true. And in some cultures a man

is required to provide for the support and nurture of any children he may have fathered."

Miranda said, "That *does* seem strange, for a man to be responsible for a child; how can any man possibly know that a child is of *his* fathering, unless he has kept the woman locked away from everyone else?" Again she seemed on the verge of saying something else, and again hesitated, drawing back; Cendri wondered if indeed the time were ripe to ask something about the unknown mating customs of Isis, but instead Miranda frowned a little and said, "It seems so natural that the woman, who bears the child, should take all responsibility. Yet I can see that your way could have its—its attractions," she added, her lips curving for a moment in a faraway smile. Cendri wondered who had fathered Miranda's child; if, for a minute, she had actually forced Miranda to think beyond her own cultural prejudices. Then Miranda said, "But if you had—had a child, and separated from your life-partner, as I from mine, would you not simply do as I have done, return to your mother and sisters so that they could care for you and your baby?"

Cendri laughed. She said, "That is the very last thing it would occur to me to do. I am not even certain where my own mother lives now; she could not wait for me to be old enough to go to my chosen lifework as a Scholar, so that she could return to her own! I have not seen her since my seventeenth year! I suppose some day we will meet again, as friends, but each of us has her life to live; on our world we do not recognize biological ties after a child is old enough to fend for herself."

"That seems to me as cold-blooded as the fish," Miranda said with distaste. "How else are women distinguished from animals, except by the nurture they give their young?" She laughed, then said, "It is good to hear someone challenge the ideas I take for granted! I like talking of such things with you Cendri, I think I shall always like to do so, but I should warn you, not to speak too freely of such matters to the women of this

household. Many of the women here would be shocked
and disgusted by the way we have been talking, they
would think you dirty and perverted for speaking of
such things—and me no less perverted for being willing to hear them spoken! Don't tell them, will you,
Cendri?"

She smiled at the off-worlder and sniffed deeply. "I
thought so; the fish-flavoring herbs are in flower, by the
South wall. Come, let us gather some and take them to
the women in the kitchen; they will want to gather them
while their fragrance is strongest, and dry them to
season the fish when next we visit the sea."

She gathered a bouquet of the strong scented greyish
pink flowers to take to the kitchens, Cendri helping
her. When they came into the kitchens, one of the
women wrinkled her nose in disgust.

"Pheu, you smell like a fish dinner, Miranda, you
smell as if you have been visiting the sea—"

Miranda laughed. "Well, and so I have, you can tell
that by looking at me," she said gaily.

The other woman turned away, abashed. "What a
way to talk, Miranda! And before the distinguished
guest!"

"You first spoke of it," Miranda said, laughing. "We
are all grown women here! And if we want herbs to
season our fish, we must then smell like the sea! And I
like the smell, for it tells me the season for visiting the
sea is near—what is it, Zamila, does the smell make it
too hard for you to wait?" She crushed the strong-
smelling flowers between her palms, bruising them, and
as the aromatic smell spread through the room, the
women began a little nervous giggling which Cendri did
not understand.

Dal, too, when Cendri got back to the upper apartment they shared, wrinkled his nose against the strong
smell which clung to her hands.

"What in a hundred worlds is that stink, Cendri?"

"An herb of some sort, used for seasoning fish; I was
helping Miranda to gather it," Cendri said, abstracted-

ly. Did the talk of "visiting the sea" have something to do with their seasonal religious festivals, then? "I gather the scent is highly prized for flavoring their meals."

Dal sniffed. "I don't remember tasting it myself, and frankly I'm just as well pleased. Don't you get bored spending time with these women? Picking flowers and rubbish like that?"

"Of course not, Dal, it's my work, and I'm getting quite fond of Miranda."

"Don't get too fond of her," Dal said morosely, "I don't trust women who live without men. It doesn't seem normal or healthy, and I'm not sure I like the idea of my wife spending a lot of time with women who pair off like that. Miranda hasn't bothered you, has she? Are you sure you can trust her?"

After an incredulous moment Cendri realized what Dal meant. She said, "That's so ridiculous I won't even dignify it with an answer, Dal," and went to wash the smell of the herb from her fingers.

Miranda's lonely. She said so herself. And she certainly went to some trouble to find out whether I was rigidly prejudiced against their way of life. And her sisters have all chosen women for life-partners—oh, that's ridiculous, Miranda knows I'm not that kind of woman.

Anyway, what makes me think I have any right to be so condescending about what's normal? If men are kept out of the society except for breeding, and the women spend all their time with one another, naturally they develop all their love and affection for each other. How can you love a variety of people who are regarded as dangerous animals who have to be registered as property? And naturally, where there's love, there's probably sex too. You've seen homosexuals before this! Don't be so damned smug and condescending, as if you had a right to approve or disapprove! It's their society! It's all very well for Dal to find fault, he's not a trained anthropologist . . . there's no excuse for you doing it!

Just the same, she felt sorry for the women, not allowed to keep a Companion till they were Vaniya's age, and forced to get their love, even their sex, from one another. No, not forced, they chose . . . did they really choose, without open options in the society?

I guess my own cultural prejudices go a lot deeper than I ever realized . . .

The Pro-Matriarch was not present that night at dinner; but prodded by Dal, Cendri approached Miranda.

"Is there any possibility we could begin our work in the ruins soon, Miranda?"

Miranda avoided her eyes, saying, "I really know nothing about it, Cendri, you must ask the Pro-Matriarch."

"I know you sometimes make decisions in her place—" Cendri persisted, but Miranda said, "No, not about such matters, only those pertaining to the household. I really don't have the authority, Cendri. I know how you feel about your work, but you must await my mother's decision."

Later when they were in their room again, Dal fumed. "How long are they going to put us off? Why did you let her put you off again?"

"Dal, I went as far as I could. I know I made Miranda very uncomfortable—"

"Maybe if you made her uncomfortable enough, she'd start demanding a decision from Vaniya! Cendri, if we don't hear something definite in a day or two, I think we ought to go to the *other* Pro-Matriarch— what's her name, Mahala—and see if *she* can do anything for us. Maybe we can use the rivalry between them to get things moving!"

"Dal, I really don't think we ought to. I don't want to alienate Vaniya—"

"Damn it, Cendri," he exploded, "*You're* doing the work you're interested in, you're studying these people—"

"Dal, lower your voice," she said sharply, "If they

overheard *that*, it would be the end of our welcome here!"

He dropped his voice almost to a whisper. He said, "But what of my work, Cendri, the work we came here to do for the Unity?"

"Vaniya has been occupied with the damage from the quake—"

"Oh, come *on*! If quakes are as common as that here, it wouldn't be up to the Pro-Matriarch to handle it all personally! That's the excuse she's making—just to delay us!" He went to the window and stared down morosely at the distant ruins.

"Have you found out, yet, why they call them We-were-guided?"

"I've had no chance to ask, Dal."

"*Why not? Sharrioz!*" he stormed, "the ruins are what you're mainly supposed to be interested in, here! What *do* you and Miranda talk about?"

Cendri sighed and said, "Nothing in particular, Dal, nothing that would interest you." It was true, and she resented it; all the things she was learning about this world, all the strangenesses, the wonder of the difference, meant nothing to Dal; she had learned that in the first few days. Suddenly she was overcome by a surge of resentment so enormous it was all she could do to keep from throwing something at him.

He expects me to be interested, even enthralled, in his damned ruins. Yet he won't take the slightest interest in my work!

Dal threw himself down in the padded alcove where they slept. "Aren't you coming to bed?"

"Later, Dal," she said, turning her back on him. "I want to write up my notes for today. One of us ought to do some work."

He scrambled up; stood over her in a rage.

"That's not fair! It isn't *my* fault we haven't started the work we came here to do!"

"I didn't mean that," she said, sighing. "I'm sorry, Dal. Tomorrow I'll try to find out if Vaniya will see me, and put it to her that we should really begin our work in the ruins. And if not—well, perhaps you are right, perhaps we should approach the other Pro-Matriarch."

He said, a little placated, "Is the High Matriarch still in her coma, neither living nor dying?"

Cendri nodded. "We may have to wait until she recovers or dies, Dal. That may be what they are waiting for."

He grumbled, "And what if the political party who doesn't want the ruins touched, comes into power then? I think we ought to make some attempt to start work; so that at least the Unity *knows* whether or not they are genuinely ruins of the Builders, or just some ordinary extinct civilization—"

"I couldn't agree more, Dal," Cendri said, sighing and putting away her notes. She could not write them up in peace when Dal was in this mood. It seemed there was only one way to placate his bruised pride. She tried to make allowances for it; this was the only function he was supposed to have here, it was no wonder that he tried to make an impression the only way he could, to leave the stamp of his body on Cendri, to make up for his humiliation otherwise on this world. But she found herself helplessly resenting it, enduring it, without desire, feeling used and exhausted.

But how would I expect him to feel, here? Loyally, trying to stifle her resentment, she allowed him to lead her to the padded alcove. *Amusement corner*, she thought wryly, *whose* amusement?

Hours later she woke, to a sound like a thunderclap. A moment later she heard screens toppling over in the main part of the room, the cries of children wakened roughly out of sleep, and thought; *an earthquake! Again, so soon*?

Dal was sitting up at her side, listening to the sound, everywhere in the house, of collapsing screens, rattling dishes, crying children. There was a soft, urgent rapping on their door. A low voice called, "You are safe, Scholar Dame, the worst is already over, but you must join us outdoors; it is better to remain outside until we are sure there will be no aftershocks!"

Cendri threw on a random garment, hurried down the steps, Dal at her side. She heard crying children, the sound of older children sleepily protesting. A woman she knew only by sight clutched at her arm and asked, "Will your Companion carry my little son? He is too heavy for my arms, and too sleepy to walk!"

Dal hoisted the child good-naturedly, only saying to Cendri in a low voice, "They could have asked *me*!" They went out on the lawn. It was an hour or two before daybreak; the air was cold, and the grass soaking wet with dew, the heavy smell of herbs hanging in the air. The women of the household were gathering on the lawn, in all stages of disarray and partial dress. Vaniya, her hair standing up wildly around her head, but nevertheless as composed and calm as if she were at a diplomatic banquet on University, was moving from group to group, talking in low, encouraging tones. Rhu, at her heels, looked drowsy and unkempt, barefoot, in a long white tunic. Vaniya came quickly, but without visible signs of hurry, toward Cendri, as Dal put the child down beside its mother.

"You are unhurt, Cendri? Good. But truly, there is no danger; there has never been any quake but the mildest, so close to We-were-guided. I hope your Companion was not too frightened? Most men are afraid to sleep above ground level." She turned to one of the women crowding close and said, "Send a messenger to the Men's House, and reassure them there is no need for alarm."

The woman hurried away. Although Vaniya seemed calm, Cendri could see that something was troubling her; her eyes moved restlessly from group to group. Everyone seemed to be out of the house now; no more women or children were coming down the steps. Vaniya said, distressed, "I do not see Miranda—where is she? Where is she? Rhu, do you see her? Cendri?"

Cendri looked around for Miranda, but the tall

woman with the long dark braid and the heavy pregnant body was nowhere to be seen. Vaniya asked a woman nearby, "Where is Miranda? Do you see her anywhere?" and another, "Her room is next to yours, did you not see her come down the steps?"

"No, Mother, I thought her already gone—"

"Goddess protect us!" Vaniya turned, her face drawn with dread, and hurried back toward the steps. "Miranda! Miranda!"

Rhu ran after her; caught up with her at the foot of the steps, remonstrating firmly. "Let *me* go! You must not trust yourself inside again, there may be aftershocks!"

"You, Rhu? *You*? No, indeed, you would not be safe there!" she said in amazement, "She is my daughter, bearing my heir—I must go and find her—"

Vaniya's eldest daughter, Lialla, caught Vaniya by her arms. "Indeed, Mother," she said urgently, "You must not risk yourself, you are needed here! Zamila and I will go; but I think it most likely that Miranda simply slept through the first shocks! I almost did so myself!" She turned to Rhu, and said, "Look after her, don't let her follow us!"

Vaniya remained, twisting her hands nervously, ignoring Rhu, who was trying without success to persuade her to move away from the steps, to sit down and rest. Cendri came slowly toward her, and the Pro-Matriarch said with staccato nervousness, "I am afraid for her. She might have been hurt by something falling in her room, she might have tripped and fallen on the stairs, she might have been overcome by premature labor—I knew I should insist that she have someone to sleep in her room—"

Cendri said comfortingly, "It is most likely that she slept through the whole quake, Vaniya; it was the screens falling which wakened me."

"But Miranda is such a light sleeper," Vaniya fretted. Then, slowly, turning toward the groups of women, "I must go and see whether anyone else is missing—"

"That I *will* do for you," Rhu said firmly, and hurried away. Vaniya sighed and watched him go, letting herself lean heavily on the stone balustrade of the steps to the Residence. She said defensively, "I should go, but Rhu is really very capable and responsible—"

He came back after a time, saying, "Every soul in your household is here and safe, save only Miranda. Has she been found?"

Vaniya's answer was drowned by cries from the women; Cendri felt the stone balustrade beneath their hands tremble, with an obscene rippling and cracking; Dal grabbed Cendri from behind and held her upright as the balustrade broke away; Vaniya stumbled and went down. Inside the front door of the house were feminine screams; Vaniya gasped, "It is Miranda—," and struggled to her feet, thrusting away Rhu's hands. She plunged up the stairs, but Rhu hurried past her, shoving at the door; it stuck, cracked, finally came open, awry on its hinges. Inside, in the gap, Lialla and her partner appeared, leading Miranda between them. She was limping, and Vaniya cried out, stumbling up the steps toward her, clasping her daughter in her arms, crying out in dismay.

"Mother, mother, you must not be frightened," Miranda protested, holding her close. "I twisted an ankle on a fallen screen, no more, and I felt it better not to try the stairs alone, for fear of falling—" She held her mother reassuringly, in a tight hug. "Really, really, I am not hurt—my ankle pains me, that is all—"

Rhu reappeared, thrusting himself through the gap. "The balustrades are cracked and fallen; no more harm is done," he reported. "Is it—is it well with the Lady Miranda?"

"Yes, thanks to your strong arms," Miranda said. "We could not open the door, Mother, it stuck from inside until Rhu added his strength to ours. . . ."

"The Goddess be thanked," Vaniya said with a long sigh of relief, holding Miranda a little away to look gratefully at her, "When I did not see you among the household on the lawn, I thought I would die of terror!

Is the child truly safe, Miranda? Shall I send for our midwives, to be with you until we are sure that the shock will have no ill effects?"

Miranda laughed, holding her hands across her bulging belly. "She is alive and well, and telling me in no uncertain way that she does not like to be hurried on the stairs," she said, gaily, "and I am out of breath, and when we get inside again I will need a length of bandage for my ankle, but I am not in labor, nor likely to be for another change-of-the-moon! I was only frightened when we found the door wedged shut, and if there had been another shock it might have fallen on top of us, the hinges were warped. But all is well, thanks to Rhu—" she gave him a little quick smile; he colored and looked away. "It is my pleasure to serve the Lady," he said in his queer formal way.

Miranda, limping heavily on her right foot, came toward Cendri. "I trust you were not frightened, Scholar Dame, nor your Companion. We are safe here, the ground rarely shakes so close to We-were-guided—" she pointed toward the ruins. "See, they have endured unfallen for more centuries than we can measure, though some day you may indeed measure how much time has gone by that they still bestow their love and concern among us."

Cendri looked up at the ruins, thinking, somewhat bemused; yes, that's true. How is it that the ruins there have never fallen? Did they build in such a way that they can resist earthquake? Or did they choose a place known to be free of quakes? It could, she thought, hardly be *that*; so close to Ariadne, which had twice in the past ten days been ravaged by a light quake. . . .

"Look," said Lialla, "the quake must indeed have been severe; you can see the glow of fires inside the City wall. . . ."

Freed of anxiety about Miranda, the Pro-Matriarch was quickly recalled to her duty. She said to Rhu, "Go quickly, and summon my car, and a driver! Has Maret checked the instrument to find out where the quake was centered?"

"Here, Mother." The huge gross body of the woman-by-courtesy came toward them, a sheet of paper hanging from its pudgy hand. "The recording instrument showed the center of the quake to be very near here; possibly it was worse inside the city, but it was not serious at all, the worst must be over."

"Thank you, dear child," said Vaniya, patting the puffy white fingers. "It must be over then, a quake of that strength rarely has any aftershocks, and, the Goddess be thanked, it was on land so that we need not fear any great waves on the shore! But still I must go and make certain all is well with the High Matriarch, and I must see if there is any serious damage reported to the city Mothers. Also I must be certain all is well with my colleague Mahala." She looked uneasily at Miranda. "I do not like to leave you when you are hurt—"

Miranda smiled. "Mother, don't fuss; it is only a twisted ankle and my sisters can look after me perfectly well. If you don't believe me, ask Maret, she will tell you!"

Vaniya turned uncertainly to the woman-by-courtesy. "Maret, is it well with my daughter and my heir, is it safe to leave her?"

Maret smiled vacantly; the wide blue eyes went blank and the face turned vacant, sagging unpleasantly. After a moment Maret said, in an odd, dazed voice, "Miranda is well and her child has taken no harm. . . ."

Cendri wondered; is Maret a clairvoyant or some kind of soothsayer, or simply a charlatan? Shamans in some cultures renounced their gender. . . . She bent and picked up the long slip of paper which the limp fingers had released when Maret let his—or was it her?—eyes go blank. It appeared to be a perfectly ordinary readout from one of the old style seismographs. Strange, the mixture of science and superstition, that Maret would be in charge of this and simultaneously consulted for clairvoyant advice!

Miranda took an unwary step and grabbed at the nearest thing, which happened to be Dal. Abashed, she took her hand away as if the contact had burned her, and Cendri reached out and steadied her. She clung gratefully to Cendri, saying, "I had better not try to walk until my foot is bandaged—"

Rhu knelt in front of Miranda, a strip of cloth torn from his tunic in his hands, and began to wind it tightly around her injured ankle. She looked shyly away, and Vaniya beckoned to one of the women, who came and briskly brushed Rhu aside, strapping the improvised bandage into place and knotting it tight. Miranda got to her feet, leaning on Cendri, and tested her weight on the ankle. "That's better," she said, "Thank you, Haliya." She did not glance at Rhu even momentarily. "Go and do what you must, Mother, now my ankle is steady under me I can do whatever is necessary. Your car is waiting, and you are needed in the city."

Still reluctant, Vaniya gave Miranda's hands a final squeeze, and climbed into the car. Rhu said, "Shall I come with you, Vaniya?"

"No, my dear, what possible help could you be? Stay here and look after yourself, keep the Scholar Dame's Companion amused and out of the way," she admonished gently, and closed the door.

Rhu turned disconsolately back to them as the car drove away, but Miranda, moving firmly on her bandaged foot, had already begun moving among the groups of women, speaking to one after another. Rhu moved toward Dal; Cendri hoped Dal would not be rude to him; Dal had, indeed, admired Rhu's singing, but he had no respect for the Companion and had, in fact, been scathing, in private, about him.

Cendri listened to Miranda giving orders that if there were no aftershocks quite soon, they should all go inside again and try to sleep, but that no kitchen fires should be lighted until they were all quite sure the danger was past. Admiring Miranda's domestic efficiency—she was arranging for the serving of cold food, and for workwomen to inspect each different area when it was sufficiently light, to discover any possible structural damage to walls and foundations of the

Residence—Cendri looked up toward the ruins, above them on the hill. The sky was paling, out over the ocean, with the coming dawn; the pinkish glow was reflected on the tops of the ruins, and Cendri wondered how long it would be before they were allowed to go there.

Vaniya could use the duties connected with this new quake to delay even further. But what could she do? It was unreasonable to ask the Pro-Matriarch to neglect a city where there had been an earthquake and fires.

Not that Cendri cared; this was the opportunity of a lifetime to study the Matriarchate. But it was hard on Dal. . . . She looked at her husband, who was listening, with a strained patience, to Rhu. Naturally, Rhu assumed that Dal was his own kind; a Companion, a man whose main function was the amusement and company of a woman of high prestige. *I should find out about that. Are only women of high social position allowed to keep a Companion? And what do the rest of the women do?*

Dal had enough good sense not to rebuff Rhu—after all, any insult to the Pro-Matriarch's Companion might very possibly be an insult to the Pro- Matriarch as well. But he tended to avoid him when he could do so without being obvious. . . .

Miranda came back to Cendri. She said, "I think it is all over; that last aftershock was so mild it would hardly have knocked over a screen. But you must be careful on the stairs, the balustrades have fallen. I think we can send everyone back to bed." She stood looking at the seismograph printout which Cendri still held, absently, in her hand, after Maret let it fall, saying, "This was a land-based quake; we can chart them, and even to some extent predict them. And many of them are far away inland, where no women live. We must take some care to warn the males before they go inland hunting, but otherwise there is little danger." Yet she looked troubled. "It is the great volcanic quakes, deep in the sea-bed, which really cause trouble. We have no way to predict them, and no warning for the great tidal waves which devastate our coastland. And sometimes small quakes like this herald the great quakes and waves—"

Cendri said, "In the Unity now, Miranda, there are sophisticated computers which can chart and predict the drift of all the tectonic continental plates, even of undersea seismic activity, and compute the strength of the resulting tsunamis—tidal waves—as well as precisely where they will strike and with what strength."

Miranda nodded. "I had guessed there must be," she said, "even in the days when my mother came to Isis from Persephone, there were some such machines. But they are available only to the richest worlds, and after the Labrys disaster, we had no resources to buy such equipment. All our resources could not make them available for at least another hundred years." She looked, dejectedly, at the seismograph printout in her hand. "Land-based quakes do little trouble, because of the way our houses are designed, and our furniture, and we have very rigid fire-laws. But every year there are tidal waves which sweep away villages, destroy boats, destroy the pearl-harvests. . . . I do not know if Isis can endure another hundred years, until we can somehow acquire such equipment!" She sighed, adding, "And if we cannot hold out here, I do not know what we will do—"

Suddenly, recalling herself, she turned her attention to her guest. "Cendri, it will be quite safe now for you and your Companion to return to your rooms. Sleep again, if you can; we will send breakfast to your room at whatever hour you desire, and later in the afternoon I will send workwomen to repair or take away any broken screens, or replace anything which is damaged."

Cendri said, "I suppose the Pro-Matriarch will be absent most of the day? Is there any possibility that we might be able to begin our work in the ruins soon?"

"Not today, I fear," Miranda said, "Even if the damage in the city is minimal, she must make a visit to a village down the coast which was nearly destroyed by a quake sometime before you landed here. We have had word that their boats and nets have been repaired, and they are ready to begin their yearly pearl-harvest. Since the High Matriarch still lies sick, unable to speak or perform her duties, my mother must go there and give her blessing to the boats and the pearl-divers. Have you seen our pearl-divers?"

Cendri shook her head. "I have heard of the pearls of Isis, of course; they are said to be the finest in the Galaxy."

"They are our major item of trade," Miranda confirmed, "There are some who say that the export of pearls should be stopped—that the pearls are the tears of the Goddess, and that it is not right for them to be sent offworld where She is not held in the highest reverence."

"The whole Galaxy would be the poorer, if the pearls of Isis could not be sent anywhere else," Cendri said.

"Isis would be the poorer, too," said Miranda frankly. "Our world needs many things which we cannot make for ourselves. Our pearls are our greatest asset—indeed, almost our only hope of someday having the equipment I spoke of, which may some day allow us to predict and control the tsunamis which wipe out our coastal villages and kill so many of our sea-farmers. I fear I have not as much faith as those who feel we should trust entirely to the mercy of the Goddess, or even the love and concern of the Builders. But enough of that," she added quickly, "Go and rest, my friend." She put her arm briefly around Cendri's shoulders and hugged her. "If you are not too weary, later in the day, would you like to go with me, and see the blessing of the pearl-divers?"

"I would indeed," Cendri said, "I have not yet visited your seashore."

Miranda blinked, a little, with an uneasy laugh, then recalled herself. She said, "Well, a visit to a pearl-diver's village is perhaps nearly as welcome an expedition. We will leave just after mid-day, unless another quake should happen, which is not at all likely." She turned to look toward Dal and Rhu, saying, "Call your

Companion, he may not know it is safe to go back in the house."

Cendri hesitated—she hated to summon Dal peremptorily, as Vaniya did with Rhu, but it was true he should be told. She beckoned to Dal, and relayed the news.

"We can go inside? Good; this is an unholy hour to get up," Dal said, and put his arm around her waist as they began to climb the stairs; under Miranda's startled look Cendri quickly slipped away from his touch, trying not to feel guilty at Dal's irritable look.

She looked back, briefly, as they went through the warped hinges of the door. No one remained on the lawn now but Miranda and Rhu; Miranda's face, lighted by the sunrise, seemed transformed, quite without her usual aloof shyness; she was talking to Rhu, absorbedly. After a moment Rhu put his hand under her arm and began to assist Miranda toward the steps. Suddenly aware that she was staring, Cendri started and hurried inside.

She told herself not to imagine things. Rhu was Vaniya's Companion; Miranda was the Pro-Matriarch's most cherished daughter and pregnant with her heir. Rhu was deeply devoted to Vaniya, it was no wonder he should exercise the most careful devotion and protectiveness toward Miranda. And yet—something Cendri called instinct made her lift her eyebrows, ask herself: *Rhu and Miranda*?

Nonsense, she told herself. She didn't know enough about the relationship to jump to conclusions like that! She followed Dal up the steps.

In their room, Dal looked with dismay at the books and recordings showered all over the floor. "I should have taken those holders on the shelves more seriously! It never occurred to me there would be another quake so soon!" Disgustedly, he bent to assess the disorder. "I don't suppose that while you were talking to Vaniya, or that precious daughter of hers, you thought to ask if we could get started in the ruins any time in the foreseeable future?"

"As a matter of fact, Dal, I did," she protested, "but Miranda said that this afternoon she was supposed to go and visit a pearl-diver's village, to bless their boats or something—"

"All right, all right," Dal said in disgust. "I get the picture, you let her put us off again!"

"*I* let her?" That left Cendri speechless. "What was I supposed to do, kick and scream and put up a fight about it? Vaniya has duties of her own—I can't insist she neglect them, Dal. Anyway, it will be interesting to see the pearl-divers' villages—"

"For *you*, maybe," Dal said, tight-lipped. "I'm not interested in quaint native customs." He turned away, lifting one of the fallen screens.

"Leave it, Dal, Miranda said she would send workwomen to repair the screens and the other damage—"

"I have to have something to do, don't I?" he asked savagely. "*You* have enough to keep you busy—and do you really think I'd trust those damned women with our reference books and tapes?" He turned his back on Cendri and began gathering up the scattered materials. Cendri sighed, and said nothing. It occurred to her that she was getting a lot of practice in holding her tongue lately. She went and lay down, with no expectation of getting back to sleep; but after a time she fell into an uneasy doze.

She was wakened by a soft, furtive rapping; she looked around, but Dal had vanished into the other room of the suite. She got up and went slowly toward the door, but before she reached it, it was thrust violently open, and a man sidled quickly through the door, shoved it shut behind him.

A man; the first she had seen, other than Rhu, inside the Pro-Matriarch's residence. He was small and bent and hunched, his hair grey, his eyes wide with fear, looking all around himself with quick, furtive, darting glances. His lips were a thin, terrified line; he had been branded, and the brand was like a flaming scar across the wrinkled forehead. Cendri had grown so used, in these days, to seeing only women, that she was frightened. His eyes looked so wild! Maybe here the men really *were* dangerous animals, cultural traits were more important than inborn ones. . . .

"What do you want here?" she said sharply, and at the way he twitched at her voice, she realized he was more afraid of her than she could possibly be of him! His voice was only a shaking whisper.

"I must see the—the Scholar from the Outside Worlds—from the maleworlds—"

"I am the Scholar," Cendri said, baffled, "What do you want with me?"

"Respect, Scholar," he whispered, in his frightened voice, his eyes darting here and there in terror, alert for any movement, with little scared movements of his head. "We had heard—it was rumored—there is a male here from the—the outside worlds—if it is not forbidden—"

"I think he wants to talk to me, Cendri," Dal said in his deep voice, coming up behind her. He shoved her aside—Cendri registered the man's shock at that—and faced the man. "What is your name?"

"Bak, respected Him," the stranger said, in a somewhat stronger whisper. "Truly, you dare speak so, you are here from—"

"There is no time for that," Dal said quickly, and from where she stood, watching, Cendri contrasted Dal's quiet poise with the terrified Bak. "I am the Master Scholar Dallard Malocq. Have you a sign for me?"

Recalling himself, the man made the curious sign Cendri had seen at the space-shuttle port; bunching the fingers together, touching the thumb, slowly drawing them apart. He said, in his shrill whisper, "We were not born in chains—"

"Nor will you die in them," Dal said, "I do not know if those are the words you want, but I think we should talk. Cendri, go and leave us alone . . ."

Slowly, Cendri moved away from the door as Dal drew Bak into the room. He said, "I have been expecting someone. Come and tell me—damnation! What is that commotion? Come in here, quickly—"

He drew him quickly through the door of the bathroom, as pounding feet raced up the stairs. Then, rudely, the door was thrust inward, and two or three sturdy women stepped inside.

Cendri began to protest: "What is—"

"Respect, Scholar," one of the women said, "but we have reason to believe an escaped male has taken refuge here. Our duties require us to search." Cendri began to protest, but they moved quickly around the room, opened the bathroom door, called to her companions; after a moment they reappeared with Bak struggling between them.

"Be quiet, you," said the leader, roughly, jerking him along with one arm. "It's the Punishment House for you this time, Bak, and probably a flogging as well! When they learn you've intruded into the quarters of the Scholar from University—"

Dal stepped toward them; made a menacing gesture. He said, "Let go of him! He is *my* guest, and came to talk to *me*! Take your hands off him, I said!"

Cendri watched, paralyzed in horror, as the woman thrust out her truncheon and gave Dal a vicious blow in the stomach. He yelled and fell, doubled up, to the ground. The woman said angrily, "Restrain your Companion, Scholar Dame, or we will be forced to hurt it!" Unprovoked, she gave the writhing Dal a savage kick, jerked hard on Bak's arm.

Cendri said, struggling for composure, "I don't understand. This man—" she indicated the cowering Bak, "has done nothing; it came and asked, politely, to speak with my—my Companion. I do not understand why a guest of the Unity should be hauled away as a captive."

The woman guard raised her face, her jaw set and contemptuous. "You are not now in the maleworlds, Scholar Dame, and males cannot intrude with impunity into the houses of women. You—" she said to Bak, whose defiance had collapsed, so that he stood shivering between his captors. "Who owns you?"

He stood defiantly silent.

"Speak, you!" shouted the woman guard, striking him across the face. Obstinately he remained silent; she came and jerked at his collar, forcing his head up. She studied the red brand across his forehead a moment, then said in angry disgust, "The Pro-Matriarch Mahala! See, Scholar Dame, it's a plot to discredit you; we've seen you here and we know you'd never have invited *this* here—" she made a sneering gesture, "but there are women all over Ariadne who might believe it! And then there would be no chance for you to do your work here without scandal! Take it away," she ordered. "We'll hold the creature till Mother Vaniya has time to deal with it as it deserves!"

Cendri moved to Dal, knelt beside him.

"Dal—did they hurt you?" she begged. One of the women, who held Bak's limp arm, guffawed; the leader of the women guards turned, with a savage gesture. "Hold your noise!" she commanded, "The Scholar Dame's from off-world, you have no right to make donkey noises about everything you don't understand; just tend to your prisoner there, girl!"

She ushered the women and their prisoner out of the room. Cendri was shaking all over.

Dal swore as he picked himself up. His hands cradled his bruised stomach.

"I never thought I'd want to hit a woman, but *Sharrioz*! I'd like to cram that truncheon down her throat!"

"Dal, what was that all about? They said he came from the Pro-Matriarch Mahala—a plot to discredit *me*?"

"That's nonsense."

"Dal, what was it, then? Do you *know* who he was?" she surveyed him in dread. "You know you must not get involved in their politics—"

He frowned. "Look, Cendri, this is my affair; don't meddle. I know what I am doing." He glanced at the timepiece he wore, and said politely, "The Lady Miranda will be waiting for you. Go along to visit the blessing of the pearl-divers, or whatever it is, and don't worry. I can look after myself, Cendri; I was doing it a long time before I ever met you."

"Dal—" she hesitated, frightened. "Oh, Dal, don't get into any trouble," she begged. But he only repeated, smoothly, "The Lady Miranda is waiting for you."

chapter five

THE VILLAGE OF THE PEARL-DIVERS WAS ONLY A LITTLE way along the shore; it seemed to lie at the very foot of the ruins, and Cendri looked up at them in frustration. How long would Vaniya continue to stall them off? If Dal, she thought, could get into them, start the work he had come to do, he would not be tempted to engage in dangerous and, certainly, illegal intrigues with the men. She thought, between dread and anger, *that could get us sent away from Isis. University makes it very clear that the Scholars who go to study a culture must not entangle themselves in politics . . .*

"Look," Miranda said. "We are in time; there is my mother by the sea-wall—"

Vaniya, draped in impressive folds of crimson and purple, was standing before a little group of slender, naked women, hair cropped close to their heads, formidable knives strapped to their waists. Cendri could not hear what she was saying, but she passed before the women, and one by one, they knelt and she laid her hands on their heads and then on their knives. Then they all knelt, and after a moment Cendri heard a high, chanting lament.

Miranda murmured, "They are singing a memorial for the women killed in the last pearl-diving season. It is a very dangerous trade; in this little village alone, four women were killed last year. Would you like to go nearer?"

"Yes, I think so—"

Slowly, they picked their way across the shore, littered with seaweed, driftwood, rocks and shells. Cendri looked at the flimsy houses, built just above high-tide mark, at the small boats, circular, and built of wood and fiber. "Are they all pearl-divers in this village?" she asked, looking at the women and children clustered on the shore watching the ceremony.

"Nearly all. They have been bred for generations for the diving, and from the time they are very little girls they are taught to remain under water for a longer time every day. I can swim well, but when I was a small girl I had a friend here in this village; she was in my school. Even then she could stay under water for a time that made me dizzy and my ears ring." Miranda said. "Once I nearly drowned because I *would not* come up before she did, and I lost consciousness; if the matron had not fished me out I would have died. It was then I learned that all the differences between women are not due entirely to education and training, but are inborn, part of the self, and competition is useless, a game for men . . . look, my mother is putting a blessing on their knives. That is in order that the Goddess may keep away the creatures of the sea, and they may not be forced to shed blood in Her holy realms . . ."

"Is your Goddess a sea-Goddess, then?"

"She is the Goddess of the whole; the World-mother," Miranda said, "When the First Mothers dwelt on Persephone, they worshipped the Goddess by *that* name; here She is Isis, the spirit that inhabits rocks and soil, air and winds; but we worship her especially in the sea, because it is from the Sea, so our scientists and our wise-women alike tell us, that all life comes on any world."

No wonder they renamed this world, Cendri thought, struggling with a smile, *who could worship a Goddess by the name of Cinderella?* She asked, "Is fishing forbidden, then, if blood cannot be shed . . .?"

"Oh, no," Miranda said, "the Mother sends food from the Sea, and," she added, with a quick shift from religious faith to practical wisdom, "we have not enough arable land to raise all of our food as yet. But blood is shed there only in the last extremity. Most fish are taken with nets; it is less of an offense to the Goddess, or so many of our people still believe, and will not eat spear-caught fish. And when we visit the sea and the men are allowed to go spear-fishing, many women refuse to eat the fish caught by blood spilled in Her waters." She laid her hands over her pregnant belly and said, "I shall not visit the sea this season, I shall have a child at my breast—" she sighed. "Look, they are lowering their boats; let us go up by the sea-wall where we can see them put out. The pearl-beds are offshore, by the rocks—you will see them from there."

They climbed the stairs together. Miranda was heavy now, and stumbled, and Cendri took her arm, steadying her on the last steps, which were slippery with spray and sea-wrack left by the tide. She asked "When will your baby be born?"

"With the next Full Moon, or so the Inquirers have told me," Miranda said. "I will be glad when she is here, I am weary of dragging around like this."

Cendri wanted to know who the father was, but was not yet sure enough of herself to do so; men were never mentioned, and it was all too easy to forget their existence! She noted, however, that Miranda spoke of her coming child as "she"; would she be disappointed if her child were a male? Well, she would certainly find out when it was born, she might even find out something of the customs surrounding birth.

"Look, the boats are away, that is the closing hymn," Miranda said. "When it is over, Mother and Rhu will come down to us. Cendri, why did your Companion not come down with us today?"

"Dal—Dal gets headaches in the sun," Cendri improvised uneasily.

"Still, most men are glad of an opportunity to come to the seashore when they are forbidden otherwise." Miranda said, shading her eyes to watch the small boats sculling toward the distant rocks which marked the pearl-beds. "One of our legends says that pearls are the tears of the Mother at what men have done to her beautiful worlds . . . I *know* that is only a fairytale," she said defensively. "I learned at school how it is that the small sea creatures make pearls and their lovely shells of nacre. But it is a pretty story—" She smiled shyly at Cendri and drew out a narrow chain from the folds of silk at her breast. Delicately encased in a small filigree case of silver wire, a large rose-colored pearl shimmered like some sea creature itself. "This is my loveliest treasure—"

"It is beautiful," Cendri said, thinking she had never seen quite so large and beautiful a pearl.

"Tell me, Cendri, is it true that in the worlds ruled by men, pearls and jewels are given to women by men, to—to reward them for their sexual functions?"

Cendri blinked, startled by the phrasing of the question. At last she said, carefully, "I cannot say that this has never been a practice among men. But I think, most of the time, when men give pearls—or any jewels—to women, they give them because they love them, because they want to see them even more beautiful, because they want to give pleasure to—to the women they love."

Miranda smiled and cradled the pink pearl in her hand, tenderly. "I am—I am very glad to hear it," she said, her fingertips lingering on it as a cherished thing. Cendri thought; *I wonder what man gave it to her? A gift from the father of her child, perhaps?* Again she felt the sense of frustration; in the study of any society, one of the first things an anthropologist had to know was something about their mating customs, and so far, it seemed, children sprang into being by spontaneous generation! And even with Miranda, friendly as the Pro-Matriarch's daughter had been, Cendri did not feel secure enough to break the taboo.

Vaniya, resplendent in her brilliant robes, slowly came along the pier toward them. She said to Cendri, "So my daughter has been guiding you and showing you our rites—do you like our pearl-divers?"

"They are certainly brave," Cendri said with a shiver.

"They are born to this work, and trained from infancy for it," Vaniya said, "and they are well-rewarded; there is no work in our society more highly regarded than to descend into the bosom of Isis and bring up her tears for all women everywhere to admire, and to the ends of your Unity, our pearls are considered the finest. In fact, our divers are so well-rewarded and so admired that it is all we can do to persuade them to take off a year, now and then, to bear daughters to inherit their craft! Some day, perhaps, our scientist will find a way to avoid wasteful bearing of sons in crafts where the blood lines are so important. We *can* create parthenogenetic females for this craft, of course, and that would give us more divers for a short time, but the daughters so born would be sterile. And many of our fisherwomen are ignorant, and feel that such conceptions are an offense against Nature. I can understand why no woman wishes to take a season off from her work, even though we pay them well for their resting time, only to discover she has not borne a daughter to inherit her craft but only a useless male. Some have

even been know to kill their male children. I am forced
to judge such women and punish them, but it goes
hard!"

Miranda said, "In the worlds of the Unity it is
possible to insure the conception of male and female at
will—is this not so, Cendri?"

"Yes, certainly."

"That would have a certain limited social usefulness," Vaniya said, "it might well be encouraged
among such as the pearl-divers. But it could have
dangers too—would *any* woman be content to bear a
male if she could win status and recognition with a
daughter? And then where would we be? You are not
old enough to remember, Miranda, but when the Grey
Plague killed only males, many women were frenzied
with fear they would be doomed to live childless.
Fortunately the Goddess was merciful, and twice as
many males were born in the next three seasons, but we
have had a frightening scare. Men, too, have their place
in the balance of nature, and you must never forget it,
Miranda."

"Oh, Mother," said Miranda impatiently, "You
older women are always so afraid that any new way of
doing things will be an offense to the Goddess! If She
had not intended women to use their minds, she would
have made us all stupid! I think if you had your way, we
would all bear our babies squatting in the reeds like our
foremothers!"

"You might do worse," said Vaniya, smiling serene-
ly. "But I have no wish to live in reed huts, and if I were
the reactionary you think me I would not have brought
Cendri here. And I know it is true that in the Unity
children can be conceived male or female at will. But I
do not know if it is so great a blessing. Is it usually a
matter of choice on your world, Cendri?"

"Not entirely," Cendri said. "It has been prohibited
on some worlds and strictly regulated on others,
because of the desire of men or women for one sex, or
the other, has indeed disturbed the balance of nature.

Now it is used rarely, and by special permission; if a family has had two children of one sex and wish for another. Although on a few worlds it is taken for granted that every woman will bear one son and one daughter."

"I suppose that is fair," Vaniya said, "though it seems dull and regimented to me. And of course men are useful to the world, also," she added, with a carefully polite glance at Rhu, hovering, as usual, in the background. "I myself find as much pleasure in Rhu's company and conversation as that of another woman, but of course Rhu is quite unusual; and I am growing old and can afford to ignore convention a little."

Rhu said, in his slow, hesitating voice, "Have you forgotten that it was Gar, of the household of Gracila, who designed a way to deal with fluoride effluents in the plastics industry, so they would not pollute the waterway of the Goddess?"

"I have just finished saying that there are extraordinary men in the world, my dear," Vaniya said, patting him carelessly on the cheek. "The Goddess knew what she was doing when She created humankind both male and female." She turned her attention to Miranda again. "My child, where did you get that exquisite pearl?" She touched the rose-colored gem with an admiring finger.

Miranda widened her eyes, saying innocently, "Didn't you give it to me, Mother?"

"You know perfectly well I did not, child, I have never seen it before. "

"I think it must have been a gift from one of my kin-mothers," Miranda said, quickly slipping the chain inside the neck of her frock, "but I have forgotten which one, I think I have had it a long time. Are you growing forgetful, Mother?"

"Don't be impudent, child," Vaniya reproved, but she smiled. "If it was a sea-gift you could have said so, Miranda, we are all grown women here! A man, of course, would not have known its value." She slipped her hand through her daughter's arm, as they turned to go. "Hold firmly to my arm, the stairs are slippery here, and I would not like to see my granddaughter endangered by carelessness. You should not have come up here now, dearest."

"I wanted to show Cendri the boats—"

"Yes, it was a kind thought, but still—to endanger yourself so," Vaniya fretted.

Cendri heard a gentle voice at her elbow. "May I offer my arm to the Scholar Dame? It is indeed slippery here; and while it is right and natural that the Pro-Matriarch should offer her support to the one who bears her heir, I am sure that she would be most unwilling to see the distinguished guest suffer a fall."

Cendri took his arm, without hesitation; Rhu, from everything she had seen, was the soul of propriety, and would never make such an offer if it was not suitable. She took his arm, steadying herself against the slipperiness of the seaweed under foot. "The sea-view is beautiful; I am grateful to Miranda for bringing me here, even if it was unwise to risk herself on the steps."

"The Lady Miranda is always most kind," Rhu murmured, and looked away. Suddenly, with sharp perceptions, Cendri remembered the morning, and the sunrise on Miranda's face as she talked to Rhu, and thought; *he loves her.*

And yet, on a world where love is not much regarded as part of the social structure, it must be difficult to love . . . On Cendri's world, and on many of the worlds of the Unity, love between man and woman served a useful social bond, social cohesion, establishing mating bonds and making social arrangements for the care and nurture of children. Serving this purpose, love was respected and admired, and on many worlds indissolubly bound up with sexuality. But here, where social bonds and sexuality seemed not to be allied, could love, as such, exist at all? Even in the Unity, there were some who considered romantic love a myth . . .

"The Scholar Dame is silent," Rhu ventured, "I had hoped your Companion would accompany you; I feel remiss, that I have not sufficiently bestirred myself to entertain him. Perhaps I could arrange a hunt, or some form of expedition to divert him . . ." he broke off, turning his head toward the sea.

"The tide!" He leaned forward, touched Vaniya's shoulder, and said, urgently, "Look at the tide!"

"What's this? What's this?" demanded Vaniya, turning around in irritation at his unaccustomed urgency; then she saw what he had seen, and gasped, "Goddess protect us all!"

The tide had gone far out—far, far out, sinking and sinking as if it were draining into some bottomless pit over the horizon. Stranded fish were gasping and dying, squirming ropy sea-things laid bare, and Cendri could see, at the foot of the rocks near the grounded boats of the pearl-divers, the long, ridgy rows of shelled creatures, thrusting up through an inch or less of sea-water.

After a moment of shock, Vaniya quickly mastered herself.

"Miranda," she ordered, "Get back up the beach—inside We-were-guided, if you must; but go, go quickly!" She turned to Rhu and said, "Get her to safety, at once!"

Miranda pulled away from her mother's hand. She said, "Send your Companion to safety if you must, Mother, but I have a responsibility—these are my people, too!"

Vaniya touched the younger woman's swollen body. She said, "Your responsibility, Miranda, is to *her!*" She added quickly, to Cendri, "Go with them, at once! There is great danger here, it is no place for men or pregnant women! Within We-were-guided you will be on high ground."

Cendri stared, confused. "Danger? In low tide—"

"It is not only low tide," said Vaniya, breathless. "It is the tide-drop; far out at sea the earth shakes, and before long a great wall of water will smash the shore here! Go, quickly! See—" she pointed, "they have seen, they are hurrying to the shore! I must stay here at least until I am sure they are on their way to safety!"

Miranda insisted "Mother, my place is at your side—"

Suddenly Cendri knew what was happening. She had read it somewhere—that the extra-low tide, sucking and draining back and back, was the warning—usually the *only* warning, and it was a matter of minutes—of the dreaded tsunami or tidal wave! She looked uncertainly at Vaniya, understanding Miranda's qualms; despite her strong presence, Vaniya was not young! Making up her mind quickly, she took Vaniya's arm, saying urgently, "Take your child to safety, Miranda! I will stay beside your mother and make sure she gets to high ground before the water strikes!"

Miranda smiled, gratefully; quickly pressed Cendri's hands and hurried away with Rhu. Vaniya spared only seconds to follow them with her eyes; Miranda leaning heavily on Rhu's arm as he guided her across the slippery beach and up toward the hillside at the top of which lay the ruins of We-were-guided. She turned back to Cendri, accepting her presence without question, and Cendri thought, yes, of course; I am a young, able-bodied, unencumbered woman; my place, on this world, is at the center of any danger! She felt frightened, but determined to remain and prove herself worthy of being a woman in this culture.

"What can I do, Vaniya?"

Vaniya pointed to a tower built above the cliffs. "Your legs are younger and faster than mine; run, Cendri, and make sure they have seen—find out why they have not rung the alarm! Then come back and we will make sure that everyone seeks higher ground—we will guide them up into the ruins, no wave has ever come into We-were-guided!"

Cendri ran down toward the tower; her feet slipped on seaweed and her thin sandals were cut to ribbons by the sharp rocks; she ran on, limping and stumbling, and knew her feet were bleeding. On the steps of the tower she hesitated, seeing the door swinging open; was anyone inside at all? She could see the bell inside the tower, but no one seemed near it.

"I wonder what has happened to the watch?" said a worried voice behind her, and Cendri turned to see a young woman with closecut curly red hair, in a dark pajama suit. "If she were there and alive she would have rung the bell already—come, quickly! If she is in no state to ring it, we must somehow manage to do it ourselves . . ."

Together, panting, they hurried up the twisting, worn stairs. *Of course, a watch-tower would be the first thing built in a village given to tidal waves . . . this one must be very old . . .* the woman at her side thrust the door open, drew a harsh breath of consternation.

"Look, it must have been the earthquake this morning, no one thought to come and make sure she was not hurt . . ."

Cendri felt her throat catch as the woman with red hair pointed. On the floor of the small, bare room, a woman lay at the foot of an overturned shelf; her skull was crushed by a heavy pot which had evidently fallen. Cendri saw in one glance that she had been old, and skinny; blood matted her grey hair at the scalp, blood spattered her shabby robe, but she must have died instantly. The red-haired woman went to her side, but Cendri said urgently, "No! We can't do anything for her! Where is the bell?"

The red-haired woman, looking greenish sick, got shakily to her feet. "You are right—but it goes hard—there, up those stairs—"

Trembling, Cendri set her foot on the stairs. They, too, had been damaged by the earthquake; some of the wooden struts were missing, and dreadful gaps showed below, but they climbed, setting their feet carefully against the need for haste, clinging to one another for balance on the rickety structure. They came out into the open bell-tower, and Cendri saw the ropes dangling from above. She grabbed them, yanked. She heard the cry of warning as the red-haired woman grabbed her round the waist from behind, holding her firmly, even so, the recoil of the great bell-rope nearly knocked her off her feet. Above her the great clanging of the brazen sound made her cry out, clap her hands to her ears as the echoes reverberated, clanged, howled at her. They swung the rope again, getting into the rhythm of the swing now, hearing the bell ring wildly along the shore, raising echoes and starting sea-birds, screaming, from the rocks.

The red-haired woman pulled her hand off the rocks. "Now we must go—they have heard," she said, and pointed below; Cendri, stunned and deafened by the bell, could not hear, but she could see women and children running from the houses in the village. She looked, aghast, at the boats marooned on the rocks, the women stumbling hopelessly toward the shore.

"Can't anything be done to save them—?"

"Maybe some of them will get to shore," the woman said. "But we must go! Quickly! The tower is high, but the structure has been damaged by the earthquake, and if the wave strikes it, it may be washed away! Hurry!"

Cendri needed no urging. They hurried down the stairs, slipping on the damaged stairs, emerging with claustrophobic thankfulness into the sunlight. Women and children were hurrying toward higher ground, struggling up the slopes toward the black, angular loom of the ruins. Cendri ran back toward Vaniya.

"Come, you must go, Vaniya—"

"Why had Grania not rung the watch-bell?"

"She could not," said the red-haired woman, hurrying up beside Cendri. "Respect, Mother and Priestess, you must come to safety too, your life is not yours to risk, but belongs to your people! Look, everyone in the village has come out to safety!"

Vaniya let them guide her along, with a sorrowful look at the marooned boats.

"And they had just repaired their nets and boats," she said, sadly. "There will be hunger in the village this winter, and I fear all of Isis will suffer if the pearl-harvest cannot be gathered!" She stood, her head turned to the women making for the shore, and her lips moved as if she were praying; but when Cendri and the red-haired woman urged her on, she went with them, stumbling.

It is too much of a shock for a woman her age . . . Cendri thought, Yet she, too, felt an overwhelming dread; would the pearl-divers, the crews of the boats, make it to shore, or to high ground, before the wave struck the shore, smashing through the houses and buildings and washing everything out to sea?

The path upward toward the ruins was steep, but looked well-traveled, and Cendri remembered the procession she had seen, her first night in the Pro-Martriarch's residence, the torches winding along the shore like a garland of lights; they must have come along this way . . . She was aware of pain in her bleeding feet, and of Vaniya's faltering steps, leaning more and more heavily on her; yet at her concerned question, the Pro-Matriarch said only, "I am very well; I only wish I knew everyone in the village was as well as I, and as able to reach safety . . ."

"Take care on the stones here, the path is broken," the red-haired woman said, guiding Vaniya's steps carefully, then looked across her at Cendri. "Goddess guard us! It is the Scholar Dame from the Unity—how could you let her risk herself in danger, Mother Vaniya?"

"There was danger for everyone," said Vaniya, looking gratefully at Cendri. "And it is as I thought, the women of University are as brave and competent as any of us!" She gave Cendri's arm an affectionate squeeze. "You have saved many lives today with your bravery, child. You said Grania could not ring the alarm—" she added to the woman with red hair. "Why not, pray?"

"Because she was dead," the woman said, "She had evidently been killed by falling pottery in the quake this morning, and no one thought to go and see if she was safe . . ."

Vaniya sighed and said, "Sad, sad; she and I were schoolfellows. But there is no time now even to mourn." She turned back, watching the women and children climbing hastily up the path, and moved away to make room for them to scramble inside the ruined city. Now they could see below them the giant wall of water, towering, looming a hundred feet high, rushing, racing at fearful speed. It smashed across the rocks and the abandoned boats with a crash; swept along across the shore and Cendri saw the tower engulfed in water, saw the houses break like matchwood and dissolve into a foaming spray of spars and boards, saw boats rise and spin away on the water like chips afloat in the surf. The sound was like the end of the world. She saw the tower itself sink and go as if it had melted into the water, and shuddered; if she had resolved to risk staying there, she would not have lived a minute in the furious boiling waves. It crashed down along the path, surging up, lapping halfway up the hillside, a foaming maelstrom of white spray; slowly, the boiling water subsided, smooth and innocent, then began to race back toward the shore. Cendri stood, appalled, seeing as it withdrew that every trace of human structure was gone from the shore; scattered beams and planks remained, but as the surging white water boiled down, there was no single house remaining, not a sign of tower or boats, gardens or sea-wall. The shore lay bare and littered, wet and foaming, with fish washed up dying on the land.

Vaniya covered her face with her hands; but only a moment later, resolutely lowered them and straightened herself, with gallant resolution.

"Well, it is over," she said, "and when the next tide comes in, some, at least, of the boats may be recovered. When the village is rebuilt, it must be re-built on higher ground, and a more effective lookout kept. We can all see the damage to structures we have built; now we must find out if there has been much loss of life." She moved toward the clustered women and children, and Cendri saw a group of men, huddled at one side, waiting.

She said, "Where is the village Elder-Mother?"

"I am here, Vaniya," said a small, stout, grey-haired woman. And Vaniya said, "Take the roll of your village. The Goddess be thanked," her eyes falling on the group of women, naked to the waist, with the strapped-on knives that marked them as pearl-divers. "Some of you, at least, are safe—"

"We saw the tide-drop, and at first thought it a low tide so that we could harvest the pearls without diving," said one of them, "But then Narila said it was no normal tide, and insisted we should leave our boats and run for the shore—I did not want to abandon my boat," she admitted honestly, "it was new-built; but I went with my sisters, and halfway to shore we heard the watchbell ringing—"

Vaniya moved from group to group, counting and assessing the losses. After a time she came back, slowly, to where Cendri waited, and looked in horror at her cut sandals and bleeding feet.

"But you are hurt! And I did not even notice! How could I have been so neglectful, when you had so heroically helped us!"

"It is nothing," Cendri said, though her feet smarted with the sea-salt in the cuts. "My shoes are too thin for walking on the shore, that is all!"

The red-haired woman who had helped Cendri to ring the bell and to guide Vaniya to high ground stooped and pulled off her own sandals, saying, "Take mine, Scholar Dame, No, truly, you must take them, I am from a village like this and I am used to walking barefoot on these stones, my feet are hardened; really, I only wear shoes for the sake of vanity, when I am teaching my classes!" She made Cendri sit down, pulled off the thin torn sandals and strapped her own on Cendri's feet. After her first protest, Cendri was glad to accept them, seeing that the red-haired woman walked without the slightest sign of discomfort on the rough stones.

She knelt on her heels beside Cendri and said, "I have been hoping to see you, Scholar Dame, I was one

of those who volunteered to work with you in the ruins;
Mother Rezali sent word to the Women's College
asking for students there who could help you in your
work. My name is Laurina, and I am a teacher of
history. But we were told you had not yet begun your
work in the ruins."

Cendri blinked, startled. Everything had been happening so fast that she had not even realized that she
was actually on the threshold of the Builder ruins! She
looked up to where, only a few hundred meters behind
her, the great ruins rose; strange, looming, dark,
immeasurably ancient, lost in Time . . . Her first
thought was an almost wild protest; no! I shouldn't be
here, it isn't fair, Dal should have been here *first* . . . it
meant so much more to him. . . .

But there was nothing to be done about that now.

Vaniya said, looking at Laurina, "I have had no
leisure to bring our guest here, what with quakes here
and in the City, and the High Matriarch still at death's
door. And even now—with all these women homeless
—" she looked around the huddled women and children, the little group of men clustered apart from them.
"I regret—" she said, and for a moment, again, Cendri
felt a flash of anger; she thought, we came halfway
across the Galaxy to study these ruins, and they put us
off for one thing after another. . . .

It seemed for a moment that she could almost *hear*
Dal saying, *A world where women established the
priorities would never get very far, or accomplish
much* . . . and then she was ashamed of herself. The
Builder ruins had waited . . . waited a very long time.
At least two million years, if they were truly the ruins of
some ancient race which had seeded the entire Galaxy
with life years ago; but even if they were simply the
ruins of some ancient civilization established on Isis
long ago, they had waited patiently for centuries,
millennia, and they could wait long enought for Vaniya
to see to her homeless fisherwomen. There *were*
priorities higher than scientific research, after all, even
if the outsider from University couldn't see them!

She said, "Of course you must see to your people, Vaniya. But since I am so near to the ruins, may I look around at them for a little?"

She could see, in the blink of an eye, that Vaniya was not pleased; that she was almost helplessly reluctant. But she had no excuse whatever; and furthermore she had just expressed her gratitude to Cendri. "To be sure you may. But stay near the entrance until someone who knows her way around can show you how best to go through the site. It will be dark soon, and you could easily become lost inside."

"I will go with her," Laurina said, and Vaniya nodded; then one of the women from the wrecked village called to Vaniya and she turned to them, reluctantly turning her back on Cendri and Laurina.

"Come," Laurina said, "I have been here more than once, I know how to get inside. Come, there is a door in the wall—"

As she climbed through the opening, Cendri wondered again at the stability of the structures. They might not be ruins of the legendary Builders. But they were old—so old that Cendri's half-experienced eye could not judge how old they were. She had had a quick hypno-learner course in archaeology, and she could see at a glance that they did not belong to any of the known civilizations or cultures; they were not Sarnian Empire or Pre-Voltian, as most extremely ancient ruins had turned out to be on isolated planets in this sector of the Galaxy.

Yet, old as they were, she was struck at once by how *new* they looked. They had not, it seemed, endured millennia of earthquakes and volcanic action on an unstable and seismic planet. They had not been buried under the sea for generations and risen, wave-beaten but recognizably artifacts of intelligent life, like the Windic ruins of Aldebaran Nine. They might have been abandoned less than a hundred years ago. The paving stones in the empty spaces between the buildings were up-ended by the inexorable growth of grass and small underbrush growing up, but the buildings themselves—huge, black-glassy structures, upended, high, untouched by the centuries—were smooth and beautiful. Ruins? Cendri thought. *Ruins?* They are far less ruined than the Residence of the Pro-Matriarch after the last quake!

How have they survived all these years?

She looked around again, trying to make notes in her mind. Dal would be eager to hear every detail, everything she could tell him—*it wasn't fair!*

She said to Laurina, who walked at her side, "You say you have been here before. Is it all like this?"

"No," Laurina said. "There are lesser structures behind the two great towers here. Across this courtyard—"

Slowly they crossed the courtyard, and Cendri said, "You told me there are women in the college who have volunteered to assist me—" She wondered why she had not been told.

"Indeed there are," Laurina said. "We were sure that the Scholar Dame would need some unskilled help, although you must have brought some qualified assistant from the worlds where women are—" She stopped, hesitated and said, "From the worlds of the Unity, where men rule."

Cendri smiled and said, "In our worlds neither men nor women rule, Laurina, but everyone does such work as—she—" she said, stumbling, remembering the male pronoun was thought indecent, "as she is qualified for. My Companion is my assistant. But we will certainly welcome such help as the women from the college of Ariadne can give us."

"I have heard," Laurina said, "that in the Unity, and on University, most of the majority of the—the Extra-scholars are men."

"Well, it is true that there are more men than women," Cendri said, wondering if this was going to be the same argument that she had had with Miranda, about how poorly men were qualified for scholarship. Instead Laurina said, "And still you became a Scholar Dame?" She pronounced the words almost with awe.

"In worlds where women are not considered first for scholastic prizes you still won such prizes?"

Cendri said, "Yes," feeling guilty without knowing why; after all, she would genuinely have been a Scholar Dame by now if she had not taken time off after her marriage.

Laurina gazed at her, almost rapt with admirat on. She said, "This is an inspiration to all of us, honored guest, because it shows us—it shows us that perhaps there is hope for us outside the Matriarchate, that perhaps what the elders fear is not quite so dangerous. See, a woman from outside, and you are not a slave or in subjection to any man, and you have won academic standing on your own! You are an inspiration to every young woman of the college of Ariadne, Respected Scholar Malocq!"

She was so dazed with admiration that she stumbled on a stone and Cendri laughed and helped her up. She said, "I am really very ordinary, there are hundreds of women like me on University, Laurina. And you must call me Cendri."

"Really? May I?" She sounded so awed that Cendri laughed again, trying to put her at her ease. She said, "And I will be glad of the help of the women at the college, far more than of their admiration; but I hope they realize that a scholar's work on an archaeological site is not all observation and inspiration! They should be women who have no objection to hard manual labor, for we may have to do a lot of digging and searching, through layers of the past . . ." But even as she said it, she wondered; this site seemed so perfectly preserved . . .

Laurina said, "I think you will find that our young women are not afraid to get their hands dirty in a good cause! It is only the weaker sex which is overly concerned with what work is suitable to its pride or its image!" She added, "Actually, there has been a considerable amount of competition for the honor of actually working with the Scholar Dame—"

"Cendri," she corrected smiling.

"Cendri—oh!" Laurina broke off, staring, and after a moment Cendri saw what had attracted her stare, even before Laurina's startled "Miranda!" After a moment of shocked staring, she turned her eyes away, in embarrassment. In a small alcove in the courtyard, on the edge of what Cendri recognized as a fountain, though the jets of water had been dry for hundreds or thousands of years, sat Miranda and Rhu, close together, their hands clasped, gazing into one another's eyes in what Cendri instantly recognized as complete mutual absorption.

Even if Cendri had been inclined to think it entirely innocent—and she had had no reason to think otherwise—Laurina's shocked turning away, and the swift, guilty way in which Rhu raised his eyes from Miranda's face, would have told her that this was clandestine—and shocking. Miranda rose to her feet, struggling for self-possession. Cendri wished desparately that she could do or say something to ease that look of guilt and shame on Miranda's face.

I don't know what the sexual taboos are here. But it's certain that Miranda has broken them, whatever they are!

Laurina said calmly, "I think the Pro-Matriarch is waiting for you, Rhu." He raised his eyes, momentarily lambent with the first real defiance Cendri had seen on the face of any male on this world; then, with a glance at Miranda, he dropped his eyes and went, scrambling up the steps and out of the fountain court.

"Laurina—" Miranda said.

"Yes; I was visiting my great-great grandmother in the village and I made Cendri's acquaintance when we went to see to the alarm bell," Laurina said calmly.

Cendri asked Miranda, "Do you know Laurina, then?"

Miranda said, "We were at school together." She was recovering her composure, but her face was still flushed. "I was too short of breath, after coming up into the ruins, to do anything else, and the sight of the water made me feel sick and faint—"

"Really, Miranda," Laurina interrupted, her voice high, not looking at her friend, "You don't owe me any explanations, it is for your mother to say, but is it really fair to Rhu? Oh, I admit he is pretty enough, but you know how easily such men have their heads turned by such attentions! You know he will be blamed if anything happens to you!" She turned and began to go back, and Cendri said, slowly, "I suppose Vaniya will be anxious about you, Miranda. You really should go and let her know you are safe."

"Yes, I suppose so." Miranda pressed her hands across her back as if it hurt her, and began slowly to cross the courtyard. She sighed and walked with her head cast down, after a moment raising her eyes defiantly to Cendri.

"It isn't what you think! Rhu has never touched more than my fingertips! And it was not his choice to become a Companion—!"

"Miranda," said Cendri gently, "I'm not sitting in judgment on you!"

"But Laurina is so sure I have shamed myself and my kin-mothers, and so magnanimous about not revealing the guilt we do not have—" Miranda sputtered. "I am not ashamed!"

"No. Why should you be?" Cendri said, and walked slowly at her side. The sun had set; twilight was falling over the great, dark shapes of the ruins, and she shivered, suddenly, with cold. Miranda stumbled in the near-dark and Cendri put an arm around her, feeling a sudden surge of affection and sympathy. She said, "Miranda, lean on me, you mustn't fall." She noticed that Miranda's hands were clasped protectively over the pink pearl at her throat. She said softly, "Was it Rhu's gift, then?"

"Yes. He came by it honestly," she added at once. "It was given him by the Elder of the Weaver's Guild, who is very rich, for a song he wrote for her daughters—he is not only a singer, he is a maker of songs as well! And he gave it to me—it was not a sea-gift," she added, defensively.

"You love him," Cendri said gently, after a moment.

Miranda nodded. In the darkness, Cendri could not see her expression, but her voice was filled with pain.

"I do not understand it myself; they say this kind of love is for a woman to give her child, her sisters, her kin-mothers. This is why I had hoped you could understand this, you seem to think it is not strange to love a man—"

"No, Miranda," said Cendri gently, "it doesn't seem strange to me."

But on Miranda's world, Cendri thought, romantic love served none of the social functions of family formation and child-nurture which it served elsewhere. Here, the major bonds of social cohesion were family bonds between women, and sexuality had little or no part in them. A woman who found herself irresistibly drawn, emotionally, sexually, personally to a man, might well believe that this was a strange and unlikely perversion; might find herself at a loss to understand, or even express, her own desires and hungers.

She asked softly, "Is Rhu the father of your child?"

Even in the darkness, Cendri could sense Miranda's shock and horror. "What do you think me? What woman could possibly know a thing like that?"

And now Cendri really did not know what to think or say. She turned to Miranda in the darkness. "Come, they will be worrying about you. Let me help you on the steps, they are a little irregular."

Miranda clung to her, trustfully, and Cendri felt a strange flooding emotion; protective, tender; an emotion new to her, and disturbing. She wondered if this was how these women felt about one another. *Or is this how I would feel about a daughter if I had one?* Unwilling to explore the emotion, she turned to thinking of Dal. How troubled he would be when he discovered that she had been into the ruins! He is going to want to know everything, she thought, and I won't have much to tell him, I won't be able to tell him nearly enough!

And suddenly she did not really care. The ruins could wait. They had waited a long time—not, perhaps, the two million years of Builder ruins, but still, they had waited a long, *long* time! They could wait a little longer. She, Cendri, had an opportunity which might never come again to a woman of the Unity, and she intended to make the most of it!

Dal could wait. But he wouldn't wait much longer; circumstances had forced Vaniya's hand, and now there could be no excuse for further delay.

chapter six

JUST INSIDE THE WALL OF THE RUINED CITY, WHERE Vaniya had gathered with the women from the destroyed pearl-divers village, they had lighted torches and fires. Laurina came out of the darkness to join Cendri; and Vaniya beckoned Miranda to her side.

She said, "We must go and speak to Them, give them thanks for the shelter they have given us from the great wave. Later we can all go down—for the time being, the homeless can be housed on the grounds of the Residence. But this comes first. Cendri—" by torchlight her eyes gleamed, "You are here to learn about Them, so you must have a place among us now; and it is fitting, since you have risked yourself for our people." She took Cendri's hand in hers. "Come and join us when we speak to Them.'' With a little *frisson* of excitement, Cendri realized that Vaniya was speaking of the Builders.

Can she really believe this? That a civilization a million years dead can hear? For a moment the scientist in Cendri struggled with scorn—Vaniya, Pro-Matriarch, capable administrator, stateswoman—and she could be so superstitious? Then Cendri admonished herself to wait and see. Religious faith gave life and emotional force to a culture; and Vaniya might well be speaking symbolically of a form of observance, without any superstitious or irrational component at all . . . *except insofar,* Cendri reminded herself, *as any religious observance is irrational.*

She let herself be drawn into a place—*of honor?*—at the head of the procession, between Miranda and Vaniya. Laurina walked close beside Cendri. Rhu, she realized, had withdrawn into the shadows and walked alone, separated from the women—but equally separate from the men of the pearl-divers village, who followed at a distance, barefoot, shabby, rude and uncouth.

I feel sorry for Rhu. No place among the women—but even less among the life of what they call the Men's House. Of course. He has what they consider a privilege, and they envy him—to live among women. But this privilege makes him an outcast among those who would otherwise be his peers. Paint a monkey green, and the others will tear it to bits.

They walked by torchlight into the very center of the ruins, through black shadows and empty echoing spaces, along a path that felt strangely smooth under their feet. It was very quiet; no one spoke, not even a whisper, and to Cendri the silence was strangely full. She told herself not to be superstitious, but she found herself thinking it was easy to understand how primitive emotion had peopled all ancient things with ghosts. It was as if the ancient Builders were watching them, as if the darkness beyond the torchlight were peopled with the ghosts of those ancient people, ringed about with invisible eyes that watched the women winding their way through the city which had once been theirs, wondering and waiting.

At the very center of the ruins lay an open space, vast enough to have been a spaceport. And there, by the shadowed torchlight, Cendri saw what she had seen by moonlight from the upper window of the Residence; gleaming faintly by reflected light, the structure of the antique-fashioned ship. Was this, indeed, the ship which had brought the foremothers of the Isis colony here? If so, it was no wonder they held it in reverence. The pilot of the shuttlecraft had said it; they were *guided* there . . . what folly had prompted the colonists to set their ship down at the very center of a ruined city? Cendri knew almost nothing of the art of piloting ships, small or large, but she *did* know that on a world with no established spaceport, you found the largest uninhabited tract of wild country you could find, and put it down *there*!

She felt Vaniya's hands on her elbow, guiding her forward toward the old ship. The hands forced her gently to her knees. She was half annoyed, half in a curious state of suspended belief . . . *an anthropologist must be ready to join the people of her research at prayers. . . .*

She blinked; it seemed that a dim light had begun to glow and shimmer around the structures of the ancient ship. Natural phosphorescence; reflected moonlight, she told herself firmly.

And with the glow came the warmth, the light, the suffusing tenderness. She felt a flood of love poured out on her, and poured it out lavishly in return. Some fragment of wonder in her cried out, "Oh! Who are you?" and the answer came, a steady pulsing glow; I am; that is enough. Love me, love me as I love you. . . .

It was cold. The torches had died to a glimmer, and Cendri blinked herself awake, shivers of ice running down her spine. What had happened? She was walking

slowly away from the dead city, outside the walls,
moving as if in a dream. Next to her Miranda moved,
her face by moonlight dazed and enraptured. Laurina,
too, looked irradiated. Vaniya turned her eyes to
Cendri, and smiled, with so much tenderness that
Cendri felt a lump in her throat; she wanted to throw
herself into Vaniya's arms, and sob out "Mother;
Mother, I love you—"

"What is the *matter* with me?" Cendri thought,
dazed. *What's happened to us? Whatever it was, it
happened to all of us, not just me! Look at them!*

Some form of hypnotic experience? Some mass
hallucination? Or had anything happened at all? Had
she, suggestible and lonely, isolated from all her normal sources of emotional satisfaction, gone into some
kind of religious daze with these women? Firmly, she
struggled against the need to let go, sink herself into
this hypnotic flood of joyous love.

Nonsense, absurdity. . . .

She forced herself to look around, firmly calculating
what could have happened. Of course it was some kind
of illusion; and equally of course, this was what
Miranda had meant when she spoke of the love and
concern of the Builders. But whatever had happened, if
anything *had* happened, it was certainly not the spirits
of the Builders, from two or three million years ago,
sitting there around the old spaceship and pouring out
floods of hypnotic love and emotion on the women who
came there!

Most of the women shared the dazed look of
excitement and delight which was on Miranda's,
Vaniya's face—Cendri supposed that she looked much
the same. Most of the girl children over eight or nine
had some trace of it; they looked sleepy and joyous.
The smaller children were restless and crying, and their
mothers were leading them along or carrying them. The
men. . . .

It was all too obvious that whatever the experience
had been, none of the men had shared it; one or two of

them looked awed, but most of them, stumbling along in the semi-dark after the women, looked cross, tired and bored with the waiting.

She was almost too tired to think straight. There was no way she could evaluate it now. Was this why the Matriarchy regarded this as a holy place, a sacred precinct? She wished she could discuss it at leisure with Laurina, who was a scientist and historian and might have some sort of objective attitude, but this was neither the time nor the place.

Now that the ecstasy had subsided a little—or the hypnotic illusion—she realized that her feet, torn on the rocks and imperfectly protected by Laurina's too-large sandals, were very sore. She was limping painfully by the time they came into the grounds of the Residence, and her eyes felt sore and ached in the lights streaming from every window. Servants came flocking out with cries of welcome and Vaniya's older daughter, running to welcome them, cried out with relief.

"We were so frightened, Mother—we knew you had gone to the pearl-divers village and afterward, when we saw the wreck the great wave had left, we feared you had been hurt or drowned—"

Vaniya seemed to have returned entirely to herself. She gave orders that tents should be set up on the grounds of the Residence, that the men should be housed in the Men's House, that the sick, the pregnant and the elderly should be taken into guest-rooms within the residence itself. She commanded food to be served for all, and while they were waiting for it, one of the women whose task it was to assist Miranda in the running of the household, came up to Vaniya and said, "Respect, Mother, we have had trouble here; an intruder, a male belonging to the Pro-Matriarch Mahala, broke into the house, and managed to gain entry to the quarters assigned to the Scholar Dame from University, and to her Companion."

Cendri blinked, the last vestiges of her daze vanishing. So much had happened since this morning that

she had forgotten the intruder, the branded man called
Bak, who had come to talk to Dal and given him that
peculiar password. Vaniya looked displeased, but said,
"I might have expected that of my colleague; I am only
curious to know why she did not think of it sooner. Did
you question it?"

"No, we held it for you to deal with, Mother."

Vaniya shrugged. She indicated the refugees clustered on the lawn of the Residence and said, "As you
can see, I am very much occupied with these homeless
people. But I suppose you must bring the intruder to
me."

The woman summoned the fierce-looking guards
who had burst into Cendri's rooms and taken Bak away
over Dal's protest; but they came back quickly.

"Respect, Mother—the prisoner has escaped!"

"So?" Vaniya said, almost without interest. "I
suppose it has run home to the bitch who loosed it upon
us in the first place, but there will never by any way to
prove it. But how did it escape? Was the cage damaged
by the quake? Who saw to the fastenings?"

"I did, Mother," said the main guard, "Respect, but
I saw to the hasps myself and they were all in good
order. Some human hands let it out of that cage, and
that's a fact." She glared at Cendri, her face grim. "The
Scholar Dame's Companion tried to interfere when we
took it away. I'd like to know where that one was when
the prisoner got loose!"

Vaniya said, "Go and fetch the Companion."

Cendri said, "Vaniya—"

"Hush, my dear, if your Companion is innocent it
won't be hurt. I might have suspected Rhu, but it was
with me all day." She sighed, told her oldest daughter
to continue arranging for the housing of the refugees
from the pearl-divers' village, and went into the house,
with Cendri and Miranda.

Dal, brought before Vaniya, firmly denied any
knowledge of the prisoner.

"I have been working in the room allotted to us, all

day," he said. "I have not seen anyone since the guards took the prisoner away." And to all of Vaniya's questions he repeated the same thing.

One of the Guards said, "I have the means to make it talk." She flicked the rope at her waist suggestively.

Vaniya frowned a little. She said, "I am not fond of such business, but I suppose I really have no choice." She glanced at Cendri and said, "As a matter of form, since it legally belongs to you—I suppose you have no objection to having it interrogated by force?"

Cendri looked, appalled, at the barbed whip in the woman-guard's hand. She said, "Indeed I *do* have an objection!"

One of the guards snickered. There was a little nervous giggling. Vaniya said gently, "Come, come, my dear, you must not be squeamish. It is the only way to get the truth from one of them. I am sure Mallida will not hurt it any more than strictly necessary!"

Cendri said sharply, "What you do not realize is that my Companion is not property, but a citizen of the Unity, and a Scholar on University. His word is as good as my own; he is covered by diplomatic immunity!" She realized too late; male pronouns were indecent. Just now she did not care.

Vaniya looked at her, frowning a little. She said, after a moment, rather sadly, "I had hoped you were enough one of us, my dear, not to stand on technicalities of that sort. But it is true that you live by different laws. Can you truly trust your Companion's word?"

Cendri set her chin and said, "Yes."

"Ask him before us if he had any part in the freeing of the prisoner, then."

Her heart pounding—*my system must be flooded with adrenalin*—Cendri said, "Dal, did you have any part in the freeing of the prisoner?"

"I did not," he said, but Cendri noticed he did not look her in the eye. *Oh, God!* she thought, *he's lying.* This put her in a terrible position. If she backed up Dal's word, and he was later proven a liar, she had destroyed the credibility of University citizens—not to mention making it impossible to accept her statement that a man's word could be trusted! Yet if she proclaimed Dal a liar, what was the alternative to having the truth beaten out of him by the fierce Mallida's barbed whip? Ferociously she thought; *I don't give a damn what happened to that poor bastard, I'm not going to have Dal hurt!*

She said, "I accept my Companion's word." *But,* she thought, *I'll have to talk to Dal about it later!*

Vaniya shrugged. She said, "It doesn't matter much, since the prisoner accomplished nothing of what he had come to accomplish. Set it free, Mallida."

Cendri found her hands were still shaking as Vaniya beckoned them to her side, saying, "And now let us forget all this unpleasantness and have our dinner." And, though the meal was good as usual, she found she could not eat.

"I feel to blame," said Rhu in his gentle voice, speaking to Cendri in an undertone, "I have been remiss in my duties as the host of the Scholar Dame's Companion. After all—" he spoke directly to Dal, "I am your only possible peer and friend here, since, like myself, you are excluded from the Men's House. I should have made more efforts to entertain you, Dal; perhaps set up a hunt to divert you."

Dal said awkwardly, "That's all right, I didn't expect it—"

"But Vaniya charged me with your entertainment," Rhu said, "and idleness breeds trouble in males . . . I am sorry for any trouble you have had. And now that the Scholar Dame has been inside the ruins—"

Dal started, glanced sharply at Cendri, and she felt a clutch of dread. She had been going to tell Dal herself, when the time was ripe! She had known he would be distressed, that she would visit the ruins without sending for him, but she had hoped she could make him understand the unplanned, almost accidental character of her visit there! Now his face was lambent with wrath;

she could tell the signs, even though he managed to keep his voice calm when he spoke to Rhu.

"I did not know; Cendri had not seen fit to tell me."

"Oh, I am sorry," Rhu said apologetically, "I meant only—now, I suppose, the Scholar Dame will have need of your services there, since I understand you have been trained to function as her assistant. I envy you," he added, sighing. "Since there will be women from the College of Ariadne to assist the Scholar Dame, may I volunteer my services to entertain the Scholar Dame's Companion? I would like to come—"

Vaniya said indulgently, "The Scholar Dame will have enough to do in looking after her own Companion, my dear, without being burdened with your care as well."

For a moment Cendri thought Dal would explode; she grabbed his wrist, out of sight between the cushions, and squeezed his hand warningly. He was silent, and Vaniya said, with a glance at Cendri, "May I indulge my dear Companion in this whim, then? If it is careful to keep well out of your way—"

Cendri could feel Dal's obvious distaste, and at the same time, she did not feel inclined to go against Vaniya's wishes. She hesitated, caught in the middle, but finally found it most politic to say, "Rhu will be welcome, of course."

"I thought so." Vaniya said, smiling, "since you will have Laurina and perhaps other women from the college of Ariadne to assist you with the real work."

Cendri knew this was making it worse, but what could she say? She knew it would make trouble with Dal, and she was tired and exhausted, and her cut feet ached miserably in Laurina's sandals. She wanted to get away and fall into bed, and she knew there would be a scene with Dal. Dal tended to take out on her all the frustrations of the days, when he must keep silent and pretend to be nothing but a frivolous attachment for Cendri's leisure time. Tonight when they were alone, it was more than sullenness, it was rage.

"Confound it, Cendri, I tried to make it clear I didn't want Rhu along, and now, our first chance to visit the ruins, you've spoiled everything by saddling us with that damned little parasite! Now Vaniya will expect me to spend my whole day entertaining him and keeping him out from under foot, and I won't get a damned thing done!"

"Dal, I'm sorry," she pleaded, trying to conciliate him, "I truly am, but all the work we do here is dependent on Vaniya, and I didn't feel I could refuse her this small courtesy."

"Small courtesy! My first chance to do some of the work I came here to do—"

"Dal, Vaniya accepted my word that you had nothing to do with the prisoner's escape. Diplomatic immunity is broken on the suspicion you had anything to do with their politics—you *know* that! She could have insisted that you be questioned by force, and there wouldn't have been a damned thing I could do about it! I felt I owed her something!"

"Diplomatic immunity be—" he swore, grimly, a gutter obscenity from Pioneer. She caught his arm, pleading.

"Dal; Dal, tell me—*did* you set that man free?"

He set his mouth. "It's better if you can say honestly that you don't know, Cendri. Keep out of this, I told you!"

"Oh, Dal, you *know* you mustn't meddle in their politics—" She felt frightened, apprehensive, but Dal only shrugged. "I know what I am doing. And in all the confusion this afternoon, when they heard about the tidal wave—well, as I said, the less you know, the less they can blame you." He turned away to ready himself for bed; stopped, shaken, at the sight of her bleeding feet.

"Cendri! Darling, what happened?"

"I cut my feet on the rocks," she said, and found herself telling him about the tidal wave. He listened, tightening his mouth when she told about going up into the rickety bell-tower with Laurina to ring the alarm.

"Sharrioz!" he swore. "I was standing here at the window and saw the wave hit and the tower go! And you were *in* that thing?" He held her hard enough to hurt. "Cendri, Cendri! Damn a world like this—sending a woman into such danger!"

She leaned on him, the exhaustion and pain of the day suddenly coming down on her. It was a temptation, to let him comfort and coddle her, forget his own humiliation in solicitude for her. Yet, even while she let him lead her into the bath, while he washed and bandaged her cut and torn feet, she rebelled against the female deviousness of that.

"Dal, women here are expected to take risks as a matter of course. I didn't want them to despise me, or think the women of the Unity are an inferior species! They already think women in the Unity are subservient and owned by men!"

He seized her shoulders and held them. "Are you more concerned in proving points about the Unity, and women Scholars, or about the work we came here to do? Cendri, when I saw that wave hit, when I knew you'd gone there with Miranda—you'll never know how I felt! Cendri, you're my wife! I can't let you risk yourself that way!"

Suddenly she was angry, flamingly angry. "Dal, I have a right to take my own risks! It's *my* decision, isn't it? Or do you *really* think you own me, as they seem to think men own women in the Unity?"

"I have a right to be concerned about you," he retorted, "Or would you want me *not* to care?"

She sighed, inwardly shaking, but not willing to keep the argument alive. She said, "It doesn't matter, love; I'm safe. And now everything's all right; tomorrow we are going into the ruins, and it was all for the best, because now Vaniya can't delay any more. And you can get started on what you came here to do."

"I suppose that's true," he said, reverting to his earlier grievance. "But you've arranged it so I'll have to spend the time looking after Rhu—"

"Dal, I thought—"

"I know what you thought," he stormed, "you thought you'd get rid of me, not have me hanging around to show up how little qualified you are for this work, so you could botch it up any way you wanted to without having me around to critcize—"

"Oh, Dal, no—" she protested, flushing. Actually she had been a little afraid that she would have to turn to him so often for help and advice that their carefully concocted story would not hold water; what would they think if the Scholar Dame from University continually consulted her supposed assistant at every possible moment and before making even the simplest decisions?

"This place is corrupting you," Dal accused, "they've told you so much garbage about how self-reliant and independent women ought to be that you're beginning to believe you can get along without my help! I ought to walk out and let you show yourself up for the fake you are! Are you so damned cocksure you think you can do it all yourself?"

"Dal, that isn't fair," Cendri said, feeling tears welling up behind her eyes.

"Fair—" he shouted, "how fair have you been to me?" All his frustration came out in a rush. "You've tried to make me into a simpering effeminate like Rhu, trailing you around and picking up any crumbs you're willing to throw my way! I'm not like that, Cendri, I'm a man of Pioneer and you're my wife, and the first thing we're going to have understood—"

"Dal, lower your voice," she begged, in sudden deadly fear; interior walls were flimsy here, and although they were speaking in their own language, the Scholar's speech of University, Dal's tone spoke—literally—louder than words. On Isis men did *not* raise their voices like that to women!

"And *don't* you tell me to lower my voice! Do you think you can order me around the way Vaniya does with Rhu?"

Cendri put out her hands to conciliate him, then

suddenly something inside her snapped. She was weary of these nightly scenes where she tried to placate his hurt pride and then endured his angry lovemaking as if every night he should stamp on her body the imprint of his own strength, leaving her bruised, humiliated, without desire.

She flung her head back.

"All right, damn you, Dal! Do anything you please. Raise your voice. Yell. Rave. Storm. Carry on like one of your great-grandfathers on Pioneer threatening to beat his woman and show her that her proper place is in his bed! See what it gets you! Once already today I put my credibility on the line and risked everything I've accomplished here, to keep them from beating you to rags! We're not on Pioneer. We're not even on University! We're in the Matriarchate on Isis, and do you realize that if *I* raise *my* voice, I can have you put outside in the male kennels to sleep there? If you lay a hand on me, Dal, I will call for help, and you have already had a taste today of how they treat a male who misbehaves!" She was shaking. "I am tired of this, Dal! I'm doing my best for both of us, and every night, every night I have to face this, and I'm sick of it, Dal, sick of it!"

Dal lowered his hands. His face was dead white.

"You've just been waiting for a chance to do this to me, haven't you, Cendri?"

She shook her head. "I've been bending over backward *not* to do it, Dal. But I've reached my limit! I can't take any more!" She bit her lip hard, trying not to cry. "It's not my fault things are the way they are on Isis! But you're blaming me for it! You wanted me to come here, you forced me into this position, into this *impossible* position, and now you are making it impossible for me—" her voice broke and she sobbed.

White-faced, Dal reached for her; she flinched, and his jaw dropped in consternation. He whispered, "You're really *afraid* of me, Cendri? Love, what's happening to us?"

She fell against his shoulder, weeping. "You begged me to come here, you begged me, you promised me it wouldn't make any difference who got the credit for it, you said it would be the two of us sharing our work, and now you're treating me as if I were your enemy—" She couldn't go on.

He held her gently, trying to soothe her. "It's this damnable place," he said, "You're beginning to act like these accursed women here. I can't understand you any more, Cendri! Would you really have turned me over to them?"

She shook her head, her eyes blurring with tears. But when he would have carried her to the padded corner, she began to cry again. Not this, not that he should soothe his hurt pride again with lovemaking. . . . He tried to coax her, calm her, but she continued to shake her head, sobbing, and at last, angrily, he let her go and went wrathfully off to his corner.

"So now you're going to use sex to discipline the wild animal?" he flung at her in a rage. She did not trouble to reply, though she knew that was not how it was at all; rather, *he* had been using his sex as a weapon to impose his will on her, and when she refused to be manipulated that way, turned the accusation back on her. Silently, she went and climbed into her high solitary bed. It was just as narrow, just as cold and uncomfortable, as it looked. She thought longingly of the warmth of Dal's body, but she knew she could not give in now. In the end she cried herself to sleep.

chapter seven

HE WOKE STILL SULLEN, AND DID NOT SPEAK TO CENDRI as he moved around the luxurious bath. But when she came back after a long hot bath he was standing at the window, looking down at the ruins, shrouded in thin morning fog. He could not keep back a smile as he turned to her:

"Today's the day, Cendri! Somehow I never thought we'd actually get inside them, I thought they'd keep stalling and stalling us—"

"I'm glad, Dal," she said, and he came to her, contritely pulling her into his arms. "Cendri. I'm sorry I bullied you last night. I won't do it again. It just got to be too much for me, that's all."

"I'm sorry too, Dal." She leaned her head against the warmth of him. "I just—exploded, that was all. The waiting makes me nervous, too."

"And then when you wouldn't sleep with me afterward—it was just the breaking point, that's all. But it's over. Let's try never to get out of synch with each other again, shall we?"

"I'll try, I promise."

"I still think we could have made it up, if you'd been willing—"

Softened and warmed by his touch, Cendri still found a small core of anger remaining. Did he really think that things could have been settled by coming together sexually, when nothing of the basic conflict had been dealt with? Was that really a universal male failing? Gently, she freed herself from Dal's arms. "We mustn't get off to a late start, Dal. It's going to be a long day. Have you the recording equipment ready?"

Instantly diverted by the memory of his long-awaited work, he went off to assemble it, while Cendri thought, surprised and shocked at herself, *How devious I am! That's a female way of handling it, and I despise it!* She had always despised such elusive female maneuverings. Yet how quickly the technique had come to her hand when she wished to make use of it!

She had known all along that this place was damaging Dal. Now, uneasily, she explored the possibility that it might be having an effect on her too—or was it simply making her see, with her surface consciousness, things she had done unconsciously all her life? Damning the whole Matriarchate under her breath, and Dal along with them, she started gathering together the materials they would need.

They made a considerable assembly stacked on the floor of their suite, and Dal surveyed them with a frown. "We'll never be able to carry all this. Do you suppose Vaniya will lend us a couple of people, or servomechs if they have them? I'd prefer servos, it goes against the grain to have other people carry things for me. If Rhu's bound and determined to come, maybe I can talk him into carrying some of this stuff!"

"That might be useful. Anyway, some of the woman students from the College of Ariadne were supposed to be showing up to assist us."

"To assist *you*, you mean," he grumbled, then deliberately made himself grin. "Well, at least it will be only young *women* flocking around to share your prestige and admire you! I often thought that if the Scholar Dame di Velo had had a jealous husband she could never have had the kind of career she had! Funny thing," he mused. "She's not good-looking, she seems as old as the Windic Ruins, and as for sex appeal, my grandfather might have thought her a fine-looking woman, but certainly no younger man ever did! And yet, when she started talking, nobody ever noticed any younger woman, no matter how beautiful she might have been. I was often surprised that you weren't jealous of her, Cendri."

She slipped her hand within his arm and murmured, "I was, a little. Didn't you know?" And privately she thought; Vaniya has something of that quality. It's the quality of power, of force of personality, which has nothing at all to do with personal attraction.

"Poor woman," Dal said, "I wonder how the Scholar Dame is getting on? I can't forget that I got my chance through her misfortune! "

"She'd want you to do your best by it, and enjoy it," Cendri comforted him, and he sighed, "I know," as they went down toward the huge dining-hall and its morning component of frisky children and Vaniya's assembled family and hangers-on, trying for a word with the Pro-Matriarch before her duties took her away for the day. As they went to the places now reserved for them by custom, Dal muttered, "Actually, I wish we could eat a bit informally in our rooms and be on our way without all this fuss, but I suppose Vaniya would be mortally offended!"

"Yes, I'm afraid so."

"Why can't they just give us what help we ask for, and leave us to get on with the job? After all, it's what they brought us here to do!"

"Dal, you're thinking in terms of the Unity and of University again," she chided, trying not to sound as if she were lecturing him. "That special idea—that time is a limited commodity and wasting it is somehow morally wrong—belongs only to a very few cultures in the Unity."

"Well, they're the cultures that get things *done*," he argued. "They *sent* for an expert from the Unity, why don't they just let you do what they sent for you to do?"

She shrugged. There was no way to convince Dal; he *was* in essence the male from Pioneer who valued attention to business and strict efficiency and a regulated approach to time, and she had long since accepted it. Her own world was time-oriented—although perhaps not so compulsively as Dal's—but at least she now regarded it as a preference, not a moral absolute!

Vaniya, at the low table where she sat, with Miranda and Rhu and one or two other favored members of her household, such as the guests from the Unity, was listening to petitions, as she did every morning at breakfast. Cendri listened as she let Miranda fill her plate with small, crisply-fried shellfish. The petitioner just now was a man, in a brief tunic outfit, and Vaniya listened, frowning, as he presented a petition from the Men's House of—Cendri did not know what the area represented, or whether it was a single household, a district, a village or a whole city—to organize a hunt.

"Are your rations really so inadequate?" Vaniya asked. "I do not like to think of anyone suffering from hunger. At the same time, I am most reluctant to grant this permission just now. Our reports from the seismic equipment warn of continuing quakes in that district, and it is unwise to expose yourselves to danger until the conditions are a little more settled. During one of the last quake seasons, almost a hundred men were killed in the inland Land Reclamation district, which is why the project has been cancelled. If we cannot allow any of our subjects to go inland for anything as vital as Land Reclamation—although I have asked for some woman volunteers next season—certainly we cannot allow it for the frivolous purpose of a hunt!"

"Respect, Mother," said the man, stammering, "but our hunt is not—not frivolous. The Inland area produces nothing and cannot even be reclaimed. The meat that grows there of its free will is a valuable addition to the protein reserve."

Vaniya made a wry face. "A most uneconomical use of land reserves," she said, "and I am personally not inclined to substitute use of slaughtered creatures for the crops the land might grow if it were reclaimed. Even when one understands the additional need for

protein in the male's food system, it seems to me
irrational. It is not particularly reasonable, to rationalize your love of hunting by such arguments. I am sorry
to deny your people a pleasure, but I am afraid I must
refuse, for the present. I will give orders to supplement
your protein rations by one-fifth, which should suffice
in such a season as this, with extra allowance for
athletes and manual laborers and growing youths. Will
that content you?"

"Respect, Mother Pro-Matriarch, but I have here a
letter from our Supervisor stating that the crops this
season will not support an increase in the protein
allowance." He bowed and handed it to her, and
Vaniya frowned over it, letting the food on her plate
turn cold. Finally she said "I am sorry; I am so
accustomed to men who rationalize the desire for
hunting with specious arguments, that I had not been
prepared to see a genuine need." For her, Cendri
knew, that was a gracious apology. "Well, I suppose
you must organize your hunt, then, but be sure to
consult the City Mothers before your route is fully
planned, and make certain to avoid known eruption
areas."

The man bowed. He said, "In gratitude, may we
invite the Pro-Matriarch's Companion to be our honored guest on this hunt?"

Vaniya glanced at Rhu, and said, "No, I think not,
he is not really strong enough for the journey. He
would burden you. You didn't really want to go, did
you, Rhu?"

Rhu lowered his eyes to his plate and murmured, "I
am at your command, Vaniya."

"Then I think not," said Vaniya, "But we have an
honored guest of the City of Ariadne at our table.
Perhaps, Scholar Dame, your Companion would enjoy
the diversion of a hunt after being cooped up in the city
like this since his arrival?"

Dal's glance at Cendri said plainly, a command, "*Get
me out of this!*" The first day in the Ruins—and some
point of protocol might send him off on a Hunt? She

could see that in his face as clearly as if she were reading his mind.

She said coolly, not looking at the man, "I am sorry to refuse, but I thought it had been made clear that my Companion is my trained assistant. I cannot by any means dispense with its presence as we are beginning our work."

Dal looked grim. Well he might, Cendri thought, when it was taken so completely for granted that Cendri had the right to give him orders like this. She tried to catch his eye, give him a reassuring smile—after all, when all was said and done they *had* to make a joke of it—but his eyes were resolutely averted.

Misunderstanding—fortunately—the frown on his face, Vaniya said cheerfully to Cendri, "I hate saying no to men, don't you? They *sulk* so. Perhaps another time a hunt can be organized especially for your Companion, when the land is safer."

The man bowed and withdrew. Cendri saw him gesture surreptitiously, unobserved by Vaniya, who was applying herself heartily to her breakfast. After a moment she saw Rhu return the gesture, below the rim of the table. His lips moved; Cendri could not hear what he said—in fact, she thought, he had probably not spoken aloud—but she was perfectly sure that what he said was, "We were not born in chains."

The light was growing, and the sun clear of the horizon. Vaniya firmly stamped one or two more papers and handed them to her private secretary, a childlike young woman, fair-haired, and well advanced in pregnancy. "We have heard nothing of the promised students from the Women's College. At what hour did they commit themselves to be here, Calissa?"

Calissa said, "Laurina, who teaches history at the college, is already here. I believe she brought a message—"

Laurina came into the dining-room. She was wearing a wide sunhat and, Cendri was glad to see, stout shoes. She bowed to the Pro-Matriarch and said clearly, "I am ashamed for my colleagues. And for *your* colleague, Vaniya."

Vaniya said, looking as if she were bracing herself against bad news, "What has Mahala done now, child?"

Laurina was squirming. She was very fair-skinned and somewhat freckled under the short curly red hair, and her pale skin was pink between the freckles. "As you know, Vaniya, Mahala is one of the Trustees of the College, and she has sent word—" she lowered her eyes and twisted her hands, in agonized embarrassment, "that none of the woman students shall work with the Scholar Dame until Mahala has had a chance to speak with her, and make certain that—that—"her voice gave out and she glanced pleadingly at Cendri. "Scholar Dame, I am ashamed!"

Cendri was angry—for Dal's sake; they needed some kind of help in the ruins. She was also angry at the insult. She said, "Does the Pro-Matriarch Mahala think I am likely to harm the students, Laurina?"

"That woman!" Vaniya grated, "shameless, insolent, discourteous to our honored guests, dishonoring the will of the High Matriarch—what excuse does she give? What reason can she possibly have?"

Laurina said uncomfortably, "That until she has seen and—and spoken with the Scholar Dame she does not consider it wise to expose her students to the hazards of male scholarship."

"In the name of the Goddess," Vaniya exploded, "How can scholarship be male or female? That is like speaking of the feminine nature of the atomic table of the elements, or the maleness of a volcano! Laurina, truthfully, has my fellow Pro-Matriarch gone mad?"

"I am not qualified to judge, Vaniya. But I am ashamed of my students for hiding themselves like shellfish at low tide!" She looked at Cendri, hesitantly. "Will you have me as their unworthy representative, then?"

Cendri smiled at her, realizing how much bravery it

must take to defy the Pro-Matriarch Mahala. In a society like this, where law seemed to be at a minimum and everything handled by personal relationships with superiors and mothers and older kin, it must have seemed a shocking thing to Laurina to go against such a ban. "I hope you will not get in trouble for coming without the others, Laurina."

Laurina's smile glowed at her. She said, "I don't care if I do or not," and Cendri sighed a little, even while Laurina's gesture moved her. Evidently the young woman had developed a full-fledged case of hero worship. She would have thought Laurina, who was about her own age, was too old for such a school-girlish attitude, but perhaps on a world where one's immediate social superiors were *all* women, this kind of thing lasted longer.

Laurina added earnestly, "It was not absolutely forbidden. But the Pro-Matriarch spoke, and of course everyone was afraid to make her angry, so the matrons at the college suggested it would be wiser and more courteous not to go. But I am my own woman, and I do not see how merely listening to what the Scholar Dame has to say can damage me. I do not suppose she will force her opinions upon me, if I cannot accept them in conscience!"

Cendri wanted to laugh at the young defiance of that. She discovered instead that she was moved. "I am happy to have your help, my dear, and perhaps when the other students see that I have not damaged you in any way, they will decide that their consciences and their duty will permit them to come."

"But this is sheer politics!" Vaniya fumed, "How dare that woman set the whole city at odds this way? Is she hoping that if Rezali dies without naming a successor, some grand outcry from the people will place her upon the High Matriarch's seat? What will it profit her to do this?"

Cendri thought it prudent to ignore that. She could not, after all, make any legitimate comment about local politics. She told Vaniya that, since the promised students had not appeared, they would need some help in carrying their gear and that it was ready to transport; bringing Laurina with her to their room, she gave her charge of the graphic recording equipment. She hated to feed the young woman's crush on her by singling her out for special attention this way, but Laurina, as a student, was better fitted to deal with such a responsibility than Vaniya's unskilled servants and poor relations who had been assigned to the task.

Surreptitiously she saw Laurina examining the equipment. Dal was organizing the materials, putting them in order for use. Somehow everything got organized— even Rhu volunteered to help—and they started through the garden toward the shoreline and the path which led upward toward the ruins at We-were-guided. Vaniya stood and watched them go. Cendri thought she seemed distressed; but whether it was at the action of her fellow Pro-Matriarch, or something else, she could not be sure.

Of course this is not what she wants. We-were-guided is a holy place to her. How can I make her understand that we will not desecrate it? Or will our very presence do that?

She knew Dal would never understand this. He was trained in all the traditional disciplines of archaeology, but he was oriented only to measurable things; micrometric measurements of the skulls of tomb inhabitants, computer analysis of tools to judge the size and physiology of the hands, limbs or appendages that had used them, measurements, judgments based on arbitrary standards.

But could he really understand, from these things, the true essence of the past? Could computer analysis of a tool and the hand which held it ever provide the complex reasons why a society assumed its form? She had applauded louder than any other student in her section when a famous anthropologist, returning from a study of the customs of the Delta Kamellins, a curious crew of aboriginal humanoids in the Orion system, said he wasn't interested in the statistical analysis of the comparative length of their sexual appendages, or of how frequently they used their anterior, as contrasted to their posterior appendages; his interest was in the complex social and emotional factors which caused them to choose one appendage over the other, and those things were not subject to such analysis.

So with Cendri. She was interested in the complex and living culture of the Matriarchate. She could have been equally interested in a past culture like that of the hypothetical Builders. But Dal was not, she felt, interested in the *life* of the Builders at all. He did not care what kind of beings they had been, or what motives lay behind their ruins or the daily rituals they had once performed in those ruins. He wanted to know what they had done, and when, and even to a certain limited degree *how*. But the *why* would forever escape him; and the tragedy of this was that he would not miss it.

And she knew it was useless to argue with Dal about all this. She could only—if she were fortunate—follow his study and analysis of the ruins, and come to her own conclusions about the things *she* wanted to know about the Builders. And even that was a poor substitute, she thought with a bitterness so deeply submerged that she was not fully aware it was there, for spending her own precious and irrecoverable time on Isis doing *his* work instead of her own research into the live, growing, *real* culture of the Matriarchate which was all around them. How could Dal be content to waste his time on beings which had been dead for years, centuries, millennia?

As they began to climb the hill toward the ruins, she turned and got a glimpse of Dal's face. This, she reminded herself, firmly, was his moment. She had been doing her own work since she landed, her notes were full and precise, and even though there were tremendous gaps in her knowledge of the Matriarchate—their mating customs, for instance, still lay in utter darkness—she had still more than tripled all extant knowledge of the daily life of the Matriarchate. Until this very morning Dal had not had the slightest chance even to begin his work. And even now, he must pretend to take a subordinate position to Cendri.

She herself had spent an enormous amount of time on the ship outbound, on tapes and hypno-learners, and she felt she could give a passable imitation of a professional archaeologist. But she new within herself that she was just that, an *imitation* of one.

She saw that Laurina, close beside her, was apparently bubbling over with a thousand unspoken questions, politely repressed in honor—or awe?—of the Scholar Dame from the Unity. *If she were* a real Scholar Dame, she thought, at least part of her commitment would be to teaching, and not merely to her own research, and she realized that this, too, was an important part of her mission to Isis. They were going to judge the quality of the Unity's scholarship by *her*. Cendri Owain. The Scholar Dame Cendri Malocq.

Laurina, encouraged by her smile, asked shyly, "May I ask the Scholar Dame—" she had evidently been well briefed, and reminded herself overnight, of the forms of courtesy in use on University, "what instruments she carries for use in her research?"

The formal terms of courtesy should have made Cendri feel at home, as she would have felt with a teaching assistant from her own college on University. Instead, for some reason, it made her feel lonely, excluded, apart from the easy companionship of the women to which she had been briefly admitted, here on Isis. She said, "You were to call me *Cendri*, Laurina. And yes, of course, you may ask me anything you like. The instrument in your care—" she indicated the graphic-recording console, "is to record, as permanently or temporarily as I wish, whatever I see or hear today. It is like photographic camera equipment—do you not have that on Isis?"

"Yes, of course, our little girls use them for toys, and

also they are used in nurseries or hospitals, when patients or infants must be continually observed without disturbing them," Laurina said. "But where are your supplies—"

"That is the way in which they differ; no perishable supplies or sensitized material for storage of the record is needed," Cendri told her. "Once it is activated, we need only activate a certain sequence to replay, projected on any desired space, a complete holographic record of what we have seen and heard. We can even—not here, but on a world with the adequate compensating machinery and equipment—reproduce, to a small and limited degree, replicas of certain artifacts, so that the cultural treasures of one world need not be removed so that other worlds can enjoy their semblance. And if, a hundred or a thousand years from now, some new research lightyears away should cast additional light on what we find here, scholars on University could, to some extent, find out what we have discovered here, even if these ruins should have been since obliterated by tidal wave, earthquake or time."

"That is not likely," Laurina said, "Already we know that within We-were-guided, the ground never quakes, and no tidal wave can reach so far."

Cendri thought, *I wish I could be sure of that.* But she knew already that this was an article of faith with the women of Isis, and in fact, the ruins themsleves could not have stood so long unless located in a spot singularly immune to the general seismic properties of the rest of the continent of Isis.

They were approaching the ruins now, crossing the area directly in front of the enormous black-glass gates. She dropped back beside Dal, and said, in a low voice, and in their own language, to avoid overhearing, "You should go in first, Dal, if we can manage it. I owe you that."

He smiled briefly at her, and said, "That isn't important now. But before we go in I want to get graphics of the exterior—*look* at those gates!"

"I'd say, whatever they were, they were larger than human, wouldn't you?" she asked, looking at the vast, towering arches far above their heads. He made a negative gesture.

"Can't tell anything at all by ceremonial doors and gates; to find that out, we'll need to find the doors they used all the time, every day." But it was not a reproof, just an impersonal comment, and Cendri thought, with a sigh of relief, *he's himself again. This was what he needed.* There had been a time when they had shared their studies like this; before their marriage, before she had—though temporarily—abandoned her own.

She saw Rhu and Laurina, and Vaniya's servants, burdened with their equipment, watching them, wondering what the alien scholars from University would do now. Suddenly she wished she could get rid of all of them, get rid of the pretense that *she* was the Scholar Dame from University, and he her unregarded assistant, so that they could be free to interact in their own normal pattern, without pretense or sham. But when she said so to Dal, almost yearningly, he shook his head.

"Out of the question. Let's not get involved in side issues now, Cendri, there's a job to be done."

He was right; there was no point questioning the postulates on which they were free to explore the ruins of Isis. After all, wherever they might have gone, there would have been *some* kind of adverse working conditions. She said, "You want graphics of the exterior. Shall I teach Laurina to use the recorder so that I can be free to make written or voice-scriber notes?"

He frowned. "That might be a good idea," he said, "but I hate to trust it to a stranger, and a woman at that."

"Dal, *any* qualified assistant we get here is going to be a woman," she reminded him, and he chuckled. "Right you are. And you did tell me she was a professor of history at the college here, so she must have a considerable amount of intelligence." He turned around, glancing at Laurina, and beckoned her close. "Show her how to work the thing, will you, Cendri?"

Laurina looked shocked. She whispered, "Do you allow it to talk to you in that tone?"

Cendri felt a moment of despair. The brief moment of naturalness between herself and Dal had suddenly evaporated again, into the pretense that was their life on Isis! She said, with a trifle more sharpness than she intended, "My assistant is a scholar in his own right on University, Laurina, and as such he is fully qualified. We do not make distinctions of this kind on University. There is work to be done, and we have no time to waste in preserving such artificial distinctions. The important thing is that together we are qualified to make these explorations, and which of us gives the orders is a matter we do not really stop to consider." She thought: maybe I can actually make a point about scholarship on University!

Laurina looked crushed. She said, almost in a whisper, "I did not mean to offend the Scholar—I mean, I did not mean to offend *you*, Cendri. Forgive me—"

"That's all right." In a sense, Cendri knew, she was *using* Laurina's hero-worship for her to enforce a point of view which went against all Laurina's cultural and ethical preconceptions. Was she justified in doing this? Could the end ever justify the means? There was no time to explore complex cultural and ethical questions now. She said, with a pleasant smile, "I presume you would *like* to know how to use the graphics-recorder?"

"I would indeed," Laurina said, and she looked awed, "if you will trust me with it."

"Very well, then." Cendri moved to her side, and began demonstrating the complex controls. She found Laurina a quick pupil, and after a few minutes had no hesitation in turning it over to the woman for the recordings.

"From now you record everything that we see and explore," she instructed. "First of all, get the gates from all angles. . . ."

Slowly, working together, they recorded the giant gates, the two huge black-glass towers just inside the gates, and the courtyards inside *them*. Then, slowly, they began to explore the streets of the ancient city—although "streets"was hardly the word for the huge, regular, but strangely ordered spaces between buildings. After a very brief survey, Dal beckoned Cendri to his side. She went, ignoring Rhu's shocked stare.

"I want to check out a preliminary impression," he said, low-voiced. "First of all, what strikes you first about these ruins?"

She knew immediately what he meant.

"Their newness," she said, "they don't look as if they had been here more than a couple of thousand years at most. I'd amost say a couple of *hundred*, but that's impossible; they were here when Cinderella was discovered and mapped."

He nodded, biting his lip. He said, "Right. And on a planet as seismic as this, how in the *hell* did they manage to escape the quakes?"

She hazarded, "Some form of building that can resist almost infinite earthquake stresses?"

"Impossible," Dal said, "Technology can do a lot, but not that kind of resistance. It's like the question of the irresistible force and the immovable object—*how* immovable would they have to be, to resist a Force 9 or Force 10 quake? The very *definition* of such a quake is—total destruction of all man-made structures and virtual destruction of the land configurations. I'm going to have to get a look at the seismic patterns—you told me they had basic seismographs—but statistically speaking, a planet like this should have at least one Force 9 quake every two or three thousand years, and for this particular area we could make a statistically defensible prediction that nothing, and I mean *nothing*, could survive from one civilization to another, giving each civilization Rakmall's Limit of twelve thousand years."

"Would Rakmall's Limit apply to a nonhuman technology, Dal?"

He scowled and nodded, evidently thinking deeply. "To a nonhuman *civilization*, perhaps not. But I can't think of a technology which could survive Rakmall's. I'll have to explore all these structures—I hesitate even to call them *buildings*, now. Maybe we can get a clue to the level of the technology which built them. I do think we can confidently say they were not human or even humanoid. Look—" he swept his arms in an all-encompassing gesture, "The size, the arrangement of the structures—it makes no sense for any culture I have seen. I can say confidently one thing; they are no known civilization or technology." He sighed deeply. "*Sharrioz!* How I wish I had a fully accredited team with me! An expedition, say, of ninety to a hundred men, equipped in all specialties—"

Abruptly he dismissed all that. He said, "Let's get on. Let's go straight through, making a graphic record of the exterior of every structure, and we can code them at our leisure."

Again they started through the ruins, pace by pace. The sun climbed, began slowly to decline. Dal finally yielded when Cendri demanded a brief stop for rest and refreshment, seeing that Rhu was exhausted and sweating in the subtropical heat, and even Laurina, fascinated by what they were doing, and bent on proving she could handle the graphics recorder, looked wilted.

Vaniya's servants had provided ample and pleasing food, and Cendri would have liked to sit down by Dal and talk over the morning's work; but as Rhu approached them, reluctantly, she recalled the social prohibitions of the Matriarchate. She and Dal could perhaps be dispensed from these prohibitions for the duration of their work. He was also their Companion, and had a right to share her meals, she assumed, but she remembered Vaniya's scandalized question about whether or not she would find it *distracting*. If she sought Dal's company out of working time, she gave weight to that belief. She turned to Laurina, and they sat together on some oddly-proportioned steps (did the original inhabitants of this place have legs fourteen feet long, or did they fly?) spreading out their lunches, while Dal, trying to conceal his annoyance, resigned himself to Rhu's company. She noticed that Vaniya's servants, mostly women, separated themselves, drawing near to Cendri and Laurina—though not near enough to listen to what they were saying—while the few men among them kept strictly separate.

Dal after a period of time, checked his timepiece and the angle of the sun. "If we are going to finish the preliminary survey today, we have no more time to lose. Laurina, you make a graphic of the steps from all four directions before we leave here."

"How dare you," Laurina flared. "I do not take orders from any male! We are not now in the male-worlds!"

Shocked, dismayed—this was what she had been most afraid of—Cendri sprang to her feet. She had an irrational impulse to throw herself between them—to *protect* Dal? Laurina had scrambled upright, and was facing Dal in angry indignation.

"Laurina," Cendri said sharply, and suddenly knew what she must say:

"If you wish to work with us, you must to some extent respect and accept our customs! I explained to you that on University, we do not make these distinctions. Furthermore, my—my assistant—" she almost choked on the words, but this at least was necessary, "did not give you an *order*, but made a courteous request of a fellow worker. If you are not prepared to grant the same courtesy to my assistant as to myself, we can dispense at once with your assistance!"

For a moment Laurina remained motionless, staring at Dal in angry defiance, and Cendri had a moment, her heart pounding, of dread. Vaniya's servants, she thought, looked ready to tear Dal limb from limb, and Rhu had turned as white as the bleached limestone of the courtyard under their feet, and was bracing himself against a column as if his bones and muscles no longer had the strength to hold him upright.

Then Laurina dropped her eyes. She said, hesitantly, "I am sorry, Cendri—I forgot. I am—I am not accustomed—"

Relief washed like a spring-tide through Cendri's body and mind. She said gently, "I know; custom of a lifetime is very hard to break. Dal, too, was heedless; among these surroundings, a request should have been relayed through *me*." She gave Dal a hard look—did he *know* what he had almost precipitated? But at least they had proved a point . . . or she hoped they had. If this point had to be made again and again, it might indeed be better to dispense with Laurina's assistance—or the assistance of any native of Isis/Cinderella!

She was glad she had left her voice-scriber running. It was sound-activated and would provide a complete record of the episode for her mentors on University. She wondered what it would provide in the way of semantic analysis. She watched, a little fearfully, as Laurina went toward Dal, not sure which of them she now wanted to protect, for Dal was glowering; but Laurina said, with shy formality, "If the Scholar Dame's assistant will inform me which angles of the steps should be recorded, I will endeavor to supply it with the adequate graphics."

Dal looked a little taken aback, but he was willing to meet Laurina halfway; was, Cendri realized, aware of the enormous emotional step the woman of Isis had taken. He answered with perfectly correct formality, "We should have a recording from each direction, and one from the top of each flight of steps, in order. If the respected teacher will avoid facing the instrument directly sunward, the quality of the recordings will be greatly improved."

Rhu, Cendri realized, was watching the episode with a surprise which reminded her of—for a minute she could not remember what it reminded her of. Then she knew. The male, Bak, who had penetrated into their quarters with a message for Dal, and had been captured. *He* had looked like that at Dal, when Dal brushed Cendri aside and took over questioning him.

Poor little devil! Maybe Rhu will learn something from this, too, about life on University.

Is that fair, to expose him to that kind of hope, when his world is so narrowly circumscribed? Life for him, at least, will never change!

But for the present the recording proceeded smoothly, and they worked their way, court by court, open space by open space, through the ruined city, with Dal—she knew—describing his impressions on a voice-scriber set to a throat-mike so that he could subvocalize and make his personal notes; Cendri making the record by voice in the language of Isis for the use of such help as they might later have from the students and assistants there, and Laurina handling the graphics recorder which would provide visual holograph commentary on everything they had seen that day.

The sun had begun to decline downward, substantially altering the quality of the light, when they came to the enormous open space at the very center of the ruins, where the antique spaceship lay. Cendri approached it hesitantly, against her will feeling something of the wonder and awe she had felt there last night. Or had it all been hallucination, illusion, delusion, a kind of mass hallucination? Tentatively, she glanced at the spaceship, at the faint light she had seen in the ruins, but, though deep canyons of shadow lay across the city, darkening the area around the spaceship, there was no sign nor glimmer of reflected light.

Had it all been illusion, then? She glanced at Laurina, and saw, in shock, that a faint trace of the ecstasy and awe were outlined on her companion's face. Laurina said in a whisper, "I wish I could be sure that They did not feel our presence was irreverent, Cendri."

Cendri felt like saying a fervent, "Me, too!" But she knew this was completely irrational. She glanced at Dal—had he too been touched by the wonder of the site, by any trace of that contact?

Evidently not; Dal, was murmuring into his voice-scriber, transcribing his personal notes on each successive feature of the ruins. He looked happy and completely preoccupied with what he was doing; but as Cendri approached him, he broke into a grin.

He said in their own language, "Cendri, is that what it seems to be?"

"The spaceship? Yes, of course."

"*That* doesn't belong to the ruins. It's not more than three hundred years old, and it looks in worse preservation than *they* do!"

She had noticed that herself. She said, "As a matter of fact, it has been here sixty-nine years, sidereal Unity time. It is the ship which carried the Isis/Cinderella colony here."

"Hell of a place to land a starship," Dal commented, voicing the thought Cendri had had, "What do you suppose made them pick out a spot like this?"

She could not comment on that without going into the belief of the Pro-Matriarch that they had been *guided* there, and that would inevitably have led to some kind of discussion of her own experience there. And unless Dal himself sensed something in the area, she could not bring it up. He would call her imaginative, superstitious . . . she couldn't face that, not now.

And if he *does* feel it, how will he be able to make his exploration of the ruins? she wondered. She herself could hardly force her dragging feet to cross the great expanse of—was it stone? Concrete?—around the starship.

Dal furrowed his brow and murmured, "What is it they call this place?"

"We-were-guided," she said, and he raised his brows and said, "Extraordinary. I wonder what made them think of *that*? That would be *your* province, of course, alien psychology. . . ." and went a little closer to the starship. "What a *very* strange place to land. I wonder why?"

Laurina was moving around, slowly recording the ruins and the ship from all angles. Cendri made a note of the time and angles, but her mind was busy elsewhere. Faintly, dimly, like an illusion, a dream within a dream, she remembered the night before, when a flooding warmth and joy had gone all through her. . . .

Laurina said, "I wonder, sometimes, if They are angry that after They had brought us here, we did not do as They probably wished, and come to live with Them here. . . ."

Cendri blinked at the question. She started to say, that was ridiculous, then realized that Laurina's answer to that particular question could tell her as much about the society of Isis as Dal could learn about the ruins. She said carefully, "Why didn't you do so then? Live here inside the ruins, that is?"

"I don't know, Cendri; it was, of course, before I was born," Laurina said. "Perhaps only the High Matriarch could tell you, for it was her predecessor, I believe, who made the decision. I can only guess, as a historian, that perhaps the buildings seemed, to them, unsuitable for human occupation. Or it may be that They did not wish to be disturbed except at their own time and in the proper way. It is obvious that They are much older and wiser than our people."

Cendri decided not to think much about that answer now. A time would come when she could sit down with one of her mentors on University and subject it to intense semantic analysis.

But it also occurred to her to think; Vaniya must have been alive when the decision was made. Perhaps she would know. . . .

Dal came toward them, as they moved through the abandoned area of the spaceship's landing, and went toward the remainder of the structures. He spoke directly to Laurina.

"Have you been inside any of the structures?"

Laurina shook her head. She said, "I have been told that it is impossible to enter any structure in We-were-guided."

Dal frowned and considered. Then he turned resolutely to one high, towering structure, and laboriously dragged himself up the high steps. Cendri crawled up after him, and after a minute, Laurina, bracing the graphic-recorder console on her arm by its strap, struggled up behind them. They crowded together on the small platform at the top.

"No doors," Dal said, glancing up into the dark expanse above them. "I ought to find out what's inside."

But when he pressed forward, he frowned, flattened himself, then said, "Come feel this, Cendri."

She touched it with gingerly fingers. "What is it, Dal? It feels like glass, but I can't see anything."

"Unusually clear glass, maybe," he said, "or some invisible material which bends light around it—it's not transparent, though—" he pressed his face against the unyielding barrier. "It just looks as if there's nothing there. Extraordinary."

Cendri nodded. "What is it, then? Force-field?"

"How should I know? I hate to try and use a laser on it; but somehow, sooner or later, I've got to get inside one of these structures. . . ."

"We have some force-field disruptors in the equipment," Cendri said, "They'll break almost any known kind of stasis field, if that's what it is."

He nodded, signalled to one of Vaniya's servants who was carrying assorted equipment, and took out a small graduated series of force-field breakers. He ordered Cendri and Laurina down off the platform, and aimed the disruptor field at the barrier. There was a growing light and a painful subsonic whine, but no result. Dal tried one after another of the field-breakers, but with equal lack of results.

"No luck," he said at last. "Whoever put that thing up there, they meant it to stay. Maybe when we get a little further along, I'll pick one of the smaller buildings and try to cut into it with a laser."

Laurina said, hesitantly, "But suppose They do not want us inside?"

Dal turned on her, and he looked about to explode;

but fortunately he remembered in time where they were. He said, with careful patience, "If They don't want me inside, I'm afraid They will have to tell me so Themselves."

"But They do not speak to men," Laurina said, looking shocked, and Dal grinned. He said, "Then They will have to tell Cendri, and *she* can tell me—all right, Laurina? Meanwhile, it's going to be dark fairly soon. I knew all along it would take more than one day just to make preliminary explorations. Shall we go back to the gates before it gets dark? I have lights with the stuff, but it's been a long day and there's no sense in overdoing it."

No one moved, however, and Cendri realized that none of them were conditioned to seeing a man make such a decision for an entire expedition. She said, "Let's get going, then. Laurina, you know the way back, would you like to lead the way?" And they started back toward the gates.

There was still some light left outside the gates, and the sun was not wholly down. On the shore below them, the women of the wrecked pearl-divers' village were moving along the shore, gathering up what the tide had brought in from the wreckage of their village and their world.

"They are fortunate," Laurina said. "A great deal of timber has been brought back by the waves—look, they are hauling it up above tide-mark—and now not so many men will need to risk their lives inland, cutting more timber and beams. We have had great waves before, though never such an enormous one. Within a few days, some preliminary shelters will be built, and by the next season, the houses will be ready to live in, and the life of the village will go on. Although I suppose the High Matriarch will order that the next watch-tower be built up higher, perhaps almost as high as We-were-guided."

Cendri said in dismay, "You mean they'll go down and live there again?"

Laurina looked grave. She said, "Yes, Cendri, they

have no choice. We cannot abandon the pearl-beds which were planted there, which have been there for a generation now. Without our pearls, Isis has nothing. A little gold from sea-water, a little magnesium, a few biologicals—but it is our pearls on which we depend, and these and the other villages down the coast are our lifeblood."

This is no planet for colonization, Cendri thought. The Scholar Dame di Velo had been right. This planet should have been turned over to a scientific foundation, for study of the Builder ruins—if they *are* Builder ruins—and never turned over to a colony at all. It's never going to be a viable settlement.

She doubted very much if they could even manage to hold out long enough to get the tsunami-prediction equipment which, Miranda had thought, would make such a difference to their world and their people.

She said something of this to Dal, low-voiced. He said, "If they really *were* Builder ruins—well, that might make a difference. We have nothing else which can be authenticated as being directly of Builder origin. If they had been Builder ruins, I am sure the Unity would have offered to resettle the Isis Colony elsewhere, at its own expense, on a planet more suitable to their agriculture and their way of life, in exchange for unlimited opportunity to study the Builder artifacts—"

"Do you really think they would accept such an offer from the Unity after what happened on Labrys? They have reason to distrust the Unity—" Abruptly she heard, as if by delayed action, something else he had said.

"You say *if they had been Builder ruins* . . . Dal, do you *know* that they're not? And if they're not, what are they? Do you know?"

"No, to both questions," Dal said, "But whatever they are—Cendri, don't be naive! They are too new to be Builder ruins! Unless—" and he wet his lips, hesitating. "I hardly dare to believe—to hope—"

"Dal, what is it?"

"Only one thing could have preserved them like

that," he said, "It is only a theoretical construct, no known civilization was able to use it—"

"What, Dal? What are you talking about?"

"Time stasis," he said.

"Time—" she broke off. "Oh, Dal!" she said, chiding, "I thought it had been conclusively proved that was impossible by all the laws of physics—"

"Impossible by the *known* laws," he said, "but they used to say that about trans-light speeds and antigravity and antimatter black holes—"

She said, "Goodness, Dal, isn't it enough to challenge all the accepted scientific theories about the Builders? You've seen what that did to the Dame di Velo! If you're going to start talking about wild theories like Time stasis—"

"No, no, no," he interrupted, almost pleading, and she thought, *I never realized how much this meant to him!* "Don't you see what it might *mean*, Cendri? It would mean that the Builders left all their records and artifacts for us, when we could get around to a technology that would understand them! We'd have to break into it, but they've left a key for us, we just have to learn to use it! All the Builder technology—think of it, Cendri! But it will mean none of our force-field breakers will be any good, no laser ever made will cut inside—we'd need theoretical physicists of the highest order here, but if we get in, the whole Builder culture is waiting there for us! Think of it, Cendri!" He was pale and sweating with excitement.

She felt almost angry. Wasn't it enough, she wondered, that she was prepared to tolerate his attachment to *one* crackpot theory, the existence of the hypothetical Builders who had seeded the Galaxy with intelligent life, without being required to be patient and tolerant with *another* one? Time stasis indeed!

Although, come to think of it, it might possibly explain why the ruins were so *very* well-preserved!

But it was getting dark, and all of Vaniya's people were standing there, waiting. She said, "Do we need to do anything more today, Dal?"

"No, you can send all the people who are just fetching and carrying, back home," he said, "but I think we'll need Laurina to arrange about tomorrow."

Cendri dismissed Vaniya's people. Rhu, though reluctantly, begged leave to go with them; Vaniya, he said, might require his presence when she returned from the city. Dal, Cendri and Laurina sat on the steps in the courtyard with the dry, forgotten fountains where she had seen Rhu and Miranda—was it only yesterday?

"We have hardly made a beginning," Dal said, "though we have graphics of all the exteriors, I think. Tomorrow—I think we need a plan and a schedule." He pulled out writing instruments and a storage-note copier. "Let me see; tomorrow I want to take soil scrapings, and try to get access to a computer to analyze them. I have to bring up a laser, and see if we can cut into one of the smaller buildings. Maybe X-ray equipment first, to see if we can get a line on what's inside; we don't want to risk damaging the contents of any building. I want to try and adapt the force-breakers, too, to work with a couple of little-known frequencies; we tested only the most common ones today. That will take two days. Meanwhile we will have to send to University for everything known of the other suspected Builder ruins, though I have copies of the Dame di Velo's notes, and I'll have to recheck them. Or can I put you on that, Cendri? You, Laurina," he added, "You are a historian?"

She whispered, in shock, "Yes—"

"I want you to take tomorrow off and check your— do you keep your information in libraries or computer terminals or what? I want to know everything that's happened at this site since the Isis colony landed here, and eveything you were told about the place *before* you landed here. Is that fairly clear to you?"

She nodded, and Dal went on, rapidly outlining a clear, comprehensive schedule for studying the ruins, bit by bit, *before* actually getting inside any given structure. Cendri, who knew that the sound of his voice would activate her voice-scriber, listened, admiring the brilliance and clarity with which Dal, after only a single day of observation, could mount a comprehensive plan of attack against the secrets of the ruins of We-were-guided.

He finished winding up the plan, and stretched, yawning. "We'd better get back, then. Supper is going to look awfully good, now we've actually gotten something done," he said, "Ready, Cendri?"

She nodded, and they got to their feet. But as Laurina got up, she reeled against Cendri, and Cendri saw that the red-headed woman had gone pale, her freckles standing out like blotches in the lowering sunset.

"Laurina, what's wrong? Have we tired you too much, this first day?"

"It isn't that," she said faintly, looking after Dal as he started down the hill. "Cendri—Cendri, I am—I am frightened. I had never believed that a male could—could make a clear and comprehensive plan like this, full of logic and good sense. An adult, functioning male."

Cendri said with a sigh of weary patience, "I told you, my—my Companion is a Master Scholar on University."

"I can understand—on worlds where males make the rules, their kind of scholarship is accepted as best, it *must* be," she said, shaking, "but this—this is *real*. It is, perhaps, a little too linear, a little too left-brained, but it is real scholarship, real intelligence. It frightens me, Cendri, because I could not have done as well myself. And if a male— an adult male, subject to the compulsive sex drives which keep them from learning—can do this well, then where is the virtue or benefit in being a woman? I'm frightened, Cendri. Do you really want to destroy all the scholars on Isis this way, letting them know that a man can so easily equal or almost surpass their best accomplishments?"

"I do not see how any scholar worth the name could be destroyed by having her assumptions challenged,"

Cendri said, but then she *did* understand. Laurina's whole way of life was based on the assumption that women were a superior kind of being, that no man could possibly be capable of her kind of rational thought.

Dal had said something like this about Pioneer; that when it was brought home to them that there were women actually as strong and capable as men, some of the men of Pioneer felt their masculinity challenged. Was this the kind of culture shock Laurina was facing?

Cendri could see that Laurina's self-confidence, her very self-concept, had been shaken to the roots. Could she survive that, undamaged? Could the culture of Isis survive being told such things?

Was a way of life, good in itself and workable, expendable just in order to make a point the Unity wanted made?

She put her arm around Laurina, feeling the young woman lean on her. Protectively, she started down the hill, saying, "Laurina, it's not that serious—" but she knew Laurina could not take it in, not yet. Laurina's open hero-worship gave her, Cendri, a responsibility. How could she let Laurina be damaged this way? She wondered if Laurina would be there tomorrow to work with them—or if she, Cendri, shouldn't dismiss the girl for her own good. But wouldn't that be true of any worker they got from Isis? Sooner or later they would have to know the truth.

Had they really been sent here by the Unity to destroy the culture of Isis.

Was a culture which lived by a lie really worth preserving, then?

The first law by which an anthropologist lived was—*do nothing to damage the culture you are sent to study.*

But if they live by laws which cannot survive against other cultures—what then? The history of culture was full of cultures which had been destroyed—vandalized—by forcing them into contact with irreconcilables. The history of the Galaxy was the worse for that destruction. Distressed beyond words at what she seemed to have done without meaning any harm, she said nothing except, "I think you are over-tired, Laurina. Maybe it will all look better to you tomorrow."

She had *not* been sent here to show the Matriarchate of Isis the error of their ways! They had a right to their own truths and their own culture! It was not up to her to destroy it!

She would speak to Dal, and warn him about what he had done. Meanwhile—she stumbled, realizing that she herself was wearied almost to exhaustion. There was no way she could make rational judgments about comparative truths and ethics now. She said, "I'm tired, aren't you, Laurina? I'll be awfully glad to get into a hot bath and some fresh clothes, and have one of Vaniya's good dinners."

chapter eight

BUT THEY DID NOT GO TO THE RUINS AT WE-WERE-guided the next day.

Dal was in high spirits that night as they washed off the grime and dust of the ruins. He sang, and teased Cendri good-naturedly about her "admirer." And at Vaniya's table that night he spent some time, of his own free will, talking with Rhu—which, Cendri thought, would ease somewhat the friction of having it known that her Companion did not like Vaniya's. Later, before they slept, he said thoughtfully. "I think I may start teaching Rhu to operate some of our equipment. Maybe all the kid needs is self-confidence. He's not so dumb, he's just been taught never to open his mouth, that's all." And Cendri was greatly relieved.

But the next morning, as they were making their preparations for the day, and Vaniya was receiving petitioners, a messenger entered the hall who made Vaniya frown and Miranda look deeply troubled. But Vaniya, as always, was calm.

"Well, Clarita, I know you for my worthy colleague Mahala's messenger; how can I serve you?"

"Respect, Pro-Matriarch, my message is not for you, but for the honored guest of the Matriarchate," said the woman. "I bring a message and an invitation for the Scholar Dame from University."

Vaniya frowned and said, with obvious reluctance, "The Scholar Dame has begun her work and is engaged."

The woman Clarita said smoothly, "Is this the message I am to bear to the Pro-Matriarch Mahala, then, that you would not allow me to deliver the message to the honored guest of the Matriarchate?"

Vaniya chewed her lip and said, with ill grace, "No, of course not. Cendri—" she turned toward them, "the Pro-Matriarch Mahala, my colleague, has sent you a messenger."

Clarita turned toward Cendri and made the Unity's formal gesture, hands clasped before the face. Cendri had grown so accustomed to the informality of the Matriarchate and Vaniya's household that it startled her, seemed completely inappropriate. Clarita said, "The worthy Pro-Matriarch Mahala regrets that she has seen nothing of the Scholar Dame from University, while her colleague Vaniya has had the privilege of entertaining the honored guest and showing her the hospitality of her household. It is now the pleasure and the privilege of the Pro-Matriarch Mahala to state that she has arranged a formal entertainment for the Scholar Dame this afternoon, and to invite her and her Companion to attend as guests. We have arranged an athletic competition in her honour, and her Companion is respectfully invited and urged to compete in any event of its particular interest and skill."

Cendri blinked. An—an *athletic competition?* And Dal invited to compete? She looked uncertainly at Vaniya. Dal was wearing his *Get-me-out-of-this!* look. Cendri felt completely at a loss. She said in an undertone to Miranda, who was—as usual—sitting close beside her, a mark of honor, "Now that our work has begun, I hate to break if off like this. Is there any way I can refuse without making trouble?"

Miranda shook her head. She said, in a troubled voice, "No, I'm afraid not. This is the highest mark of honor that can be given to an individual, to arrange such an entertainment for her particular, special benefit. In a sense it is an attempt to reproach my mother that she has not done so—as if my mother had been neglectful, not paying enough honor to our honored guests. To refuse would indicate that you have allied yourself entirely with my mother's political adherents. I don't understand politics, but I know that this is something you cannot do, coming from the Unity."

This was the second time that Miranda had specifically disclaimed any knowledge of politics, but Cendri thought that she had nevertheless a very good grasp of them. She liked Vaniya; the Pro-Matriarch had showed her kindness, it seemed, far beyond ordinary courtesy to an official guest. So had Miranda. And yet the official policy of the Unity absolutely forbade aligning herself with any specific political faction. She raised her eyes to Mahala's messenger and said with resignation, "Tell the Pro-Matriarch Mahala that we shall be honored."

Dal looked glum; but he had heard Miranda's words,

and was resigned to the loss of a day. The messenger Clarita said, "I shall bring word of your acceptance to the Mother Mahala. She bade me say further that you are requested most cordially to lunch with the Pro-Matriarch in private before the Games—"

Damnation, thought Cendri. She knew Dal was counting on at least a half day to consider and consolidate the previous day's work. She was tempted to plead the press of work; but Clarita added, pointedly, "Thus you will confer upon the Pro-Matriarch Mahala an honor which has already been given to the Mother Vaniya," and Cendri resignedly told the Messenger that it would be a pleasure.

"Would your Companion care to compete in any of the events? Does it swim, box, wrestle or race? Some excellent prizes have been offered by the Council of Elders, and it is welcome to compete for any or all of them."

Nonplussed, Cendri glanced at Dal, who was frowning in amazement. She floundered for a sufficiently diplomatic answer. "My Companion is not sufficiently familiar with the rules of contests of such sort on this world, and requests politely that it may be excused."

Clarita bowed. She said, "The Pro-Matriarch will await you at the noon hour, then, and you will be her guests in the Official Box." She added to Vaniya, "The Pro-Matriarch Mahala cordially requests that you, Mother, your Companion, and such of your daughters as wish to see the entertainment shall be invited to join them in the Official Box as well."

Vaniya said, "Tell my colleague I am obliged to her and I shall be present if my duties allow." When Clarita had gone she sat frowning, letting her food get cold, not speaking. Finally she said to Cendri, "I suppose this, or something like it, was inevitable. My colleague has been jealous of me since we were little girls on the mother-world of Persephone. I had thought—actually, I had *hoped*—that when she prevented the students from the college from coming to assist you, Cendri, that she had simply decided to wash her hands of the entire project, and take her chances that the High Matriarch will recover long enough to name *her* as successor." She frowned. "I must go at once to inquire about our Mother, see if Rezali's condition has changed. This new maneuver by Mahala means that she is not quite as secure as she might be. She wants to make certain that she will have some connection with the Scholar from University—" Cendri realized that by now, Vaniya was simply thinking aloud. With an effort, the older woman smiled at her guest. She said, "In any case, my dear, you and your Companion are certain to enjoy the games."

She excused herself, and Cendri, resigned to the loss of a day, consulted Miranda about the proper dress for such an event, and went to make ready.

To her surprise, Dal was less irritable than she had feared. "We can't spend all our time working," he said, "and I know you wanted to see something of what the men do here. It will take us a day or two to evaluate yesterday's data, anyhow."

Cendri nodded, deliberately trying to look on the bright side. This might even remove some obstacles from her way; she remembered the message Laurina had relayed; *until she had seen and spoken with the Scholar Dame,* Mahala was unwilling to trust to the scholarship of a male-centered world. This might serve to reassure the other Pro-Matriarch that Cendri was not a threat to the Matriarchate. While she robed herself in the light cool robe which Miranda had suggested for such an event, she had to dismiss a recurrent thought that she was being disloyal to Vaniya.

Fiercely she berated herself. She was an anthropologist, a scientist of University. She wasn't supposed to form any alliances here that would jeopardize that; allying herself with any faction whatsoever would obviously be unethical. Theoretically she should have the same kind of regard for the unknown Mahala as for Vaniya, for Miranda.

Restlessly she went to the window and looked down at the distant ruins of We-were-guided, lying bland and unrevealing in the sun.

It is a bond between us. We have stood together before their shrine, felt—felt something. It was real, it wasn't an illusion.

And yet I am not supposed to form such bonds. . . .

"Athletic competition," said Dal, coming up behind her. "Why, of all things, an athletic competition? You're supposed to be the anthropologist, Cendri, why should their entertainment take that form?"

"I don't know, Dal."

"I could understand it, if it were the *women* of the society competing—demonstrating their strength and aggression. But why do they have *men* competing?"

Cendri could only hazard a guess. "Possibly it's the one form of aggression they permit men in this society, a socially allowable form of outlet? I'll have to see it first, Dal, I can't make guesses."

Since none of the cars would hold all of the Pro-Matriarch's party, Vaniya elected to go in one vehicle with Miranda, leaving Dal and Cendri, with Rhu to escort them, in the other.

They had not been in the city of Ariadne since their first day there, the day of the earthquake. Much of the rubble had been cleared away, but the amount of construction being done startled Cendri, and she asked, "Is this all the aftermath of the quake the day we came here, or the small one the other night, Rhu?"

"Oh, no; there was a great quake here, almost one of our Long Years ago. Had Vaniya not received a warning from the Inquirers and from We-were-guided, the city would have been destroyed. As it was, many, many lives were lost. Now I see they have the recycling plant in operation again, to process gold and magnesium from seawater for export." His face gave a cynical twist. "But our balance of payments is nothing to me. I am much more interested in the rebuilding of the Symphony Hall. Vaniya has promised that if I continue to please her—" Cendri thought she had never heard anything as bitter as Rhu's voice, "she will arrange to have my first two symphonies performed, as well as the cantata I am now finishing."

"Do you compose too, Rhu?" Dal asked, and the Companion sighed and said, "I turned to composing after my voice was destroyed by growth. There was really nothing else for me."

Dal said impulsively, "I wish you would not say that your voice was *destroyed*. It has only matured and is more beautiful than ever."

Rhu stared bleakly out the window. "A man would say so."

Cendri said quickly, "Rhu, you have the most beautiful voice I have ever heard. On any world in the Unity it would make your fortune; thousands would be at your feet in admiration."

Rhu looked at her, his face twisting. "I cannot believe there is any civilized world in the Galaxy where a rough voice like mine is preferred to the beautiful soprano I once possessed."

Cendri said, feeling the sadness in his words clutch at her heart, "I wish you could sing on University; you would soon believe the truth of what I say."

"The Scholar Dame is kind," Rhu said, shaking his head sorrowfully, "but it is too late for me, even if somehow I could have that experience; I do not think *I* could ever believe it, now."

Dal laid a hand on his shoulder. He said, with a warmth that astonished Cendri, "Rhu, my friend—look at me." Cendri could not see his hands; he kept them out of sight; but she guessed quickly at the gesture as he said softly, "You were not born in chains—"

Rhu looked, in terror, at Cendri. He said, "No, no—not here—"

Dal was motionless for a moment. He said, "Cendri is not—" then sighed. "Very well. When we arrive at the Residence, if you wish."

Shocked and hurt by this mark of distrust, Cendri

realized she should have known it all along. Dal had a mission here which had nothing to do with the Ruins.

I knew it, that day when the fugitive Bak was caught. . . .

This is against the laws of the Unity! she thought, then berated herself as naive. Who but the Unity could have sent Dal on such a mission, primed with the passwords he would need? So much, she thought wrathfully, for the University code of ethics, of noninterference in the basic codes of a society!

Are they going to interfere in the Matriarchate, try to twist it their way? She wondered how Dal could stoop to this—to entangle himself in Unity politics. Dal was a scientist! The ethics of a Scholar of University should certainly supersede the political struggles of the Unity! Isis had a right to structure their society in their own way! How could the Unity dare to send agents dedicated to destroying it, altering it, arbitrarily, to fit Unity standards?

She turned away, afraid that Dal could see the anger in her face, relieved as the car drew to a halt and Rhu said, "This is the Residence of the Pro-Matriarch Mahala."

It was, in its own way, as imposing a dwelling as Vaniya's home, although longer, lower, all on one floor. There were wide lawns and flower and herb gardens, shrubbery and playgrounds were a group of half-naked children were playing. The walls were decorated with murals, as usual on Isis, but the quality of the painting was so much better that Cendri surmised—rightly, as she later discoverd—that Mahala had gone against custom and had her walls decorated by a professional painter rather than by members of the household.

There were no steps here. Cendri remembered that most houses in Ariadne were built without stairs or upper rooms because of the constant danger of earthquake. In the large front hall, a young woman greeted them formally and ushered them inside, saying, "The honored guests from University, Mother Mahala." Rhu was ignored as if he had been one of the small children on the lawns.

The Pro-Matriarch Mahala rose easily from a large cushion where she had been sitting, examining some papers, and came toward them. She was a small, wiry, dark-haired woman, in a brief kilt that left her withered breasts bare; but, perhaps in deference to Unity custom, she had thrown a scarf about her upper body. Her voice was light, low and quick.

"It is a pleasure; you honor me, Scholar Dame, and you, Master Scholar of the Unity." Cendri blinked; it was the first time in their stay on Isis that Dal's position had been spontaneously recognized.

And yet this was the woman who had sent a message forbidding the women of the college of Ariadne to associate with male scholarship? Cendri felt completely confused.

"I had hoped to meet you before," Mahala said, in her quick light voice. "I do not know how much my colleague Vaniya—how she hates me!—has told you about the political situation, but I presume it is not much."

"She has told us that your High Matriarch lies at the point of death and that she has not named either of you as her successor," Cendri said.

"That is true. Unfortunately, before lapsing into unconsciousness, Mother Rezali insisted you must be lodged with Vaniya, because her Residence is so near to the Ruins of We-were-guided. I have tried to encourage you to visit me, but I do not suppose my messages reached you; finally I was forced to arrange things in a way even Vaniya could not ignore. I apologize for placing you in this position, Scholar Dame." She smiled, then looked at Dal and said, with a sudden grin, "And I suppose I should also apologize on behalf of my people for the position in which you have been placed all along, Master Scholar, but the customs of the Matriarchy are what they are; and I could not abate them for the sake of a single guest, no matter how worthy. I trust it has not been too much of an inconvenience, Scholar Malocq."

Dal said, politely, "No more than any Scholar would accept for the privilege of exploring the ruins of the ancient people who built the site, Mother Mahala." Cendri noted that he used the title spontaneously and with ease, as he had never seemed able to do with Vaniya. Cendri, too, was not immune to Mahala's charm. If Vaniya was, as Cendri had occasionally thought her, a magnificent golden lioness, Mahala was like a small friendly kitten; but Cendri warned herself not to underrate this woman's intelligence or shrewdness.

Mahala waved them both to seats on the cushions at her side. She said, "Now we will talk a little before this entertainment. I am sorry that you chose not to compete, Scholar Malocq—" her eyes dwelt for a moment, appreciatively, on Dal. "You are handsome enough to give us all a treat on the field of competition; but I suppose you felt you could not join in the unfamiliar contest. A pity. Another time, perhaps, you will give us that pleasure." As food was brought in by women of her household, she served them herself, and said, "I had thought that my message denying you the assistance of the women of the college would have brought you to me at once, Scholar Dame."

"It did not occur to me," Cendri confessed. "I am not very skilled in politics; I thought it simply an expression of hostility."

Mahala laughed. "I was too subtle, then; I was hoping to create a situation which would bring you to me, to confront me—even in anger— so that I could see you away from Vaniya's influence. I am quite aware that she holds the ruins of We-were-guided in a completely superstitious awe, and I feared she might attempt to delay exploration indefinitely." She gestured. "Do eat while we talk, we do not have a great deal of time. I don't suppose you know why I am anxious to see the ruins explored?"

It was Dal who said, "Surely you don't have any scientific curiosity about the Builders, Lady?"

"Not a smidgin of it," Mahala said frankly, "but if they are genuinely the ruins of a race which seeded the entire Galaxy, then Isis will become the center of scientific interest all over the Unity. We are a poor planet, Scholar Dame—" Cendri noted that in spite of her defiant decision to treat Dal as an equal, and her attempt to include him in the conversation, she found herself automatically addressing Cendri; even to the enlightened Mahala, it did not come easy to speak directly to a man. "We are a poor planet. We have few exports. And you have experienced our earthquakes, though we can deal with them and even predict them a little. And, worse, our terrible tidal waves."

Cendri said, "Yes; I saw a village wiped out by one, it was terrible indeed!"

"I heard about that," Mahala said. "So you know that our pearl harvest for this year is reduced by at least a third, until the pearl-divers can rebuild their boats and their nets. We need the kind of predictive seismic equipment the Unity can give us. Yet we are caught—caught between the quake and the great wave! We need, we desperately need, what the Unity can give us. We cannot afford to buy it—you have seen that, I think!"

It was Dal who said, "Lady, the Unity has grants for member worlds, to allow them to rebuild their worlds and bring a homestead world up to the necessary level of efficiency. Surely the predictive equipment would so much improve your agriculture and your industry, freeing you from the continual destruction of quakes and tsunami, that it would pay for itself within a very few of your Long Years."

"This may be true," Mahala said, "but we are not a member world of the Unity, Master Scholar, nor likely to become one, for reasons I am sure you are intelligent enough to understand have no personal insult. We are what we are. We cannot accept the conditions under which the Unity would grant us membership."

Cendri said quietly, "Respect, Pro-Matriarch, but I do not quite understand. What is it that you cannot accept about the Unity conditions?"

"They would demand that we re-structure our society to admit males to a completely equal franchise. We cannot accept that the Unity has a right to decide whom we shall admit to citizenship. Our history tells us that every society where men are admitted to equality soon comes under their domination. Males—again, please understand, this is no offense to you personally, Master Scholar—are not content with equality; they cannot endure a society where they do not dominate. And every society dominated by men has soon come to accept male values of aggression, competition, and, eventually, war. And this has destroyed every culture known in the Galaxy, one after another—you are a scientist, Scholar Dame, you are familiar with Rakmall's Limit?"

The question was put to Cendri, but it was Dal who answered, "I know what Rakmall's Limit is; it is the extreme outside margin of the time during which a culture can resist entropy. But—with respect, Mother Mahala—I do not believe Rakmall's Limit is determined by the position of men in a culture."

"The scientific research done on Persephone has determined otherwise," Mahala said. "A culture rises from the animal into matriarchy; as the matriarchy decays, men take over, entropy begins under the name of progress, technostructures and entities multiply needlessly, social experiments begin, and from there the political, historical and evolutionary process appears to be predetermined. It was upon this research that the Matriarchate began the Persephone experiment, an attempt to build a culture which could resist decay, progress, and entropy, by indefinitely delaying or eliminating the stage at which males seized power from the primitive mother-right. Patrilineal cultures always signal the beginning of entropy and decay, and the death of a culture by aggression and war."

Cendri listened with fascination. In a few minutes,

Mahala had told her more of the basic assumptions behind the culture of Isis than she had learned from Vaniya's household and her own observation in many days. But she found herself quite unable to agree with Mahala's analysis.

Damn, she thought, *I wish I were here as an anthropologist, openly. I could talk to Mahala and she would understand.* She felt a pang of disloyalty to Vaniya.

She said, hesitating, "I am—I am something of a historian, Pro-Matriarch. In primitive pre-space cultures, the matriarchal societies, too, underwent degeneration, when they in turn began to oppress men. . . ."

Mahala smiled. "But we do not oppress our men," she said, "Our men are completely content and happy, because they know they live under a rational culture which will never destroy itself, and that we are here to protect them from their baser impulses, and free them for what they are best suited to do." She gestured to a hovering servant, and added kindly, "Let me help you to a little more of this delicious melon, my dear Scholar Dame."

Dal said, "Are you aware, Mother Mahala, that the Unity has been instrumental in reversing some of the very abuses of which you accuse it? On my world of Pioneer, which joined the Unity approximately four hundred years ago, the Unity demanded the enfranchisement of women as a condition of admission for Pioneer, and the men of Pioneer agreed; not cheerfully, but we agreed, and women on Pioneer are now free to be the equals of men. Are you saying that cultural customs are so sacred that Pioneer should have refused to enfranchise our women, to preserve our customs of long standing?"

Mahala narrowed her eyes. She said, "I know only a little of Pioneer. However, I cannot believe that what the Unity did made so much difference, after all. It is hardly equality for women, if they are simply freed to live as equals in the kind of culture designed by men for men; a woman, to be equal in such a culture, can only be equal by doing the same things men do; and equality in a corrupt male-dominated culture is probably not worth having. Women can fulfill themselves only in a culture designed by women; the difference is that in a culture designed by women, both men and women can know true fulfillment." She added, with a charming smile, "But there is no need to argue politics now. I do not expect you to agree with me, Master Scholar." She turned to Cendri and said, "However, Scholar Dame, I am sure you can see my point. If the ruins at We-were-guided are of sufficient scientific interest, then the Unity will, perhaps, give us trade allowances, including the earthquake-predictive equipment we need, in return for concessions for scientific study, without demanding that we violate the basic principles of our social structure."

Dal said frankly, "It is quite possible, if the ruins prove indeed to be those of the Builders. I—" he broke off, with a glance at Cendri, and she said, "I am not yet ready to form any conclusion about the actual age or origin of the ruins at We-were-guided. It seems most likely, from their state of preservation, that they are of much more recent origin than the Builders; old, indeed, and perhaps unique in the known worlds of the Unity, but probably not ancient enough to be those of the Builders—if, indeed, the culture called the Builders ever existed, which is rather doubtful and remains to be proved."

She was proud of herself; for once, she thought, she had managed to sound precisely like a professional archaeologist. She caught Dal's eye; he was smiling, a faintly superior, tolerant grin, and she felt stung. What had he expected her to do?

"In any case," said Mahala, "I shall hope that they prove of sufficient interest to draw the scientific community to us, and give us the equipment we need without concessions which would ruin our culture and doom it to follow the rest of the Unity to the death decreed by Rakmall's Limits. At least, my dear Scholar Dame, you are *studying* the ruins left by the

Builders—or whomever the makers of the ruins may have been—and not offering incense and flowers at their shrine! And now, I see that my worthy colleague has arrived, so allow me to escort you to the games in your honor, and I wish you a most enjoyable and entertaining afternoon."

As they were driven to the amphitheater allotted for the day's games, Cendri was thoughtful. Mahala's charm had made an impression on her—enough of an impression that she felt seriously disloyal to Vaniya, for whom she had come to feel genuine affection. But Dal, she knew, was in a deeper predicament. Mahala had, in a sense, offered him—by way of an offer to the Unity —his uttermost desire; a free hand for Unity scientists to come here openly and study the Builder ruins; to bring a fully equipped team here and give them systematic study over a period of years. Yet she had tied this concession—one Cendri knew Vaniya would never have made—to a condition Dal, with his fairly obvious undercover mission to the men of Isis, could never accept: a pledge, on the part of the Unity scientists, not to meddle with the social structure of Isis and the enslavement and disenfranchisement of their men.

In the Official Box above the amphitheater, where they had an excellent view of the huge oval playing field, she and Dal were seated in a position of honor. Vaniya was at her side, with Miranda, too, joining them in the box. The stands were packed with women of all ages, from young girls to old ladies, shouting and applauding enthusiastically as a large number of athletes—all male, and all naked except for colored ribbons tied around their heads—paraded in the amphitheater. Cendri blinked with surprise; this was the last form of entertainment she had expected here. But on reflection it made sense; as much sense as some of the spaceport-area sex displays of female beauty. It was, perhaps, even a little more tasteful, since they had come together, at least ostensibly, for athletic competition, and nudity in athletics had come and gone, as a fashion, since pre-space days. Flower sellers vended their colorful wares through the amphitheater; Miranda bought a basket of blossoms and offered it to Cendri, displaying their use by tossing down flowers to particularly handsome specimens parading, readying themselves for the early contests; pretty adolescent boys running races and displaying agility at leaping and vaulting.

Dal whispered under his breath to Cendri, "Damn it, this is embarrassing!"

"I don't see why it should be any more embarrassing to you than it was supposed to be embarrassing to me when you took me into a show once in the port district and were admiring the pretty girls there," Cendri whispered back, and Dal's face took on a dull color. He muttered, "I never thought you minded that, you didn't tell me."

Some of the women discussed the fine points of the athletes with considerable technical understanding; they played a leaping game with rackets—Cendri had seen something like it on University, hitting a ball back and forth over the net—and prizes were awarded by Mahala herself, varying from the trivial, garlands of flowers and shells for the boys' contests, to silver and gilt badges and medals, huge boxes of confections and baskets of fruit, and elaborate sports equipment for the contests among the older men. The women shouted and cheered, threw down flowers and colored ribbons, and urged on their favorites in loud voices. The men strutted and preened, displaying their prowess and good looks without any undue modesty. Cendri found the display embarrassing, and was embarrassed, too, at the frankness with which the women admired the men.

"What a pity your Companion does not choose to compete, my dear," Vaniya said, eyeing the men in the arena with a look Cendri could only describe to herself, privately, as lecherous, and looking regretfully at Dal. "He is so *very* handsome. Dear Rhu, alas, is quite hopeless at athletics, but then," she added, sighing, "one cannot have everything."

Cendri looked at Rhu's downcast eyes and flinched at

Vaniya's tactlessness. She caught Miranda's eye as Miranda murmured something under her breath to Rhu. It was a disturbing thought. Did Rhu, with his intelligence and his musical talent—yes, and his good looks, too—really feel inferior because he could not compete in the parade of athletic and sexual display down there in that arena?

The afternoon was to culminate with displays of boxing and wrestling, and Cendri gathered that these were the major events for which everything else was only preliminary, and the prizes for these were really valuable. A sort of intermission was going on now; the women bought iced sweets, chattered enthusiastically about their favorites, flung flowers at athletes waiting in the amphitheater, and watched displays of dancing and parades by—Cendri gathered—the Men's Houses of various households in the city. Dal rose, and murmuring an excuse, slipped out of the box—Cendri supposed he had gone to look for a rest room somewhere. Rhu called after him, then rose and with a word to Vaniya—who nodded indulgent permission—went after him. Cendri, watching Vaniya leaning over the rail and watching the handsome men in the arena, thought Vaniya was kind really, despite her tactlessness. She was unfailingly kind to Rhu, it would probably never have occurred to her that she was showing contempt for him. Indeed, Vaniya was kind to everyone of her household, she was a conscientious leader of the women of the city.

Is she the superstitious fool Mahala thinks her? I simply can't believe it!

Miranda stirred uneasily, and Cendri thought; her baby might be born at any time; she must find this a long afternoon, sitting on these hard benches—for even in the Official Box, where the benches were cushioned, they were hard, not particularly comfortable for a pregnant woman. She slipped out of the box, and Cendri went after her; she was anxious to see what she could of behind the scenes.

The rest room facilities were luxurious, as every-

where on Isis, with large mirrors at which many of the
women were preening themselves and lavishly re-
applying cosmetics; this was, Cendri realized, one of
the few social events where she had seen cosmetics
worn at all, and clothing was more elaborate than she
had yet seen. Miranda was delicately outlining her large
blue eyes with a shadowy variety of colored pigments,
an effect which Cendri found bizarre but pretty; female
adornment varied so much from world to world that it
was hard to tell just what kind of social or sexual cues
any given adornment was supposed to convey. Laurina,
the young teacher from the college of Ariadne, was
there too; she greeted Cendri with her usual blend of
wide-eyed awe and puppyish friendliness, and Cendri
was glad to see her. She glanced uneasily in the mirror
at her own face—her society did not wear cosmetics
except to repair an obvious defect, to cover a freckle or
birthmark too small to bother about removing, or color
streaked hair to a uniform hue; at Miranda's suggestion
she had worn a little pink cosmetic on her cheeks, and a
little gilt glitter on her eyelids, but even this modest
paintwork seemed blatant and overdone. Laurina,
however, commented on how pretty she looked.
Women were crowding around the mirrors, and Cendri
realized, from the narcissistic chatter and attention—
quite unlike the usual haphazard attitude to clothing—
that this was an event intended for display on both
sides. She filed away everything she saw for later
analysis. It was the first event she had seen at which
men and women frankly displayed their attractiveness
to one another.

And yet—she saw too, not only in the secluded rest
room but on the stairs, as she went back with
Miranda—the women were excited and some of them
over-wrought, but in spite of their awareness of the
men, they made no overt move toward them. In a nook
of the stairs, however, she saw two or three couples—
pairs of women—seeking partial privacy for intense and
passionate kissing and fondling. Cendri, who had never
seen public lovemaking between women before, was

embarrassed, turning her eyes away from the couples. She had seen so many different sexual patterns on so many worlds that nothing in the gamut of human sexual behavior could really surprise her, but this seemed stranger than anything she had seen yet. She would have thought that the presence of the men would have turned the women toward *them,* caused them to fix their attention on the handsome males in the arena. At her side Miranda sighed:

"At times like this I am lonely," she said in an undertone, "I even miss my old partner—" And then, in a low voice, "Or I regret that—that there is no way Rhu and I can be together like this! What is the matter with me, Cendri, that I am so unlike my own people? I find that I envy you and your Companion more than I can say!"

Cendri said nothing—what could she say? At last, hesitating, she said, "Every society has its own rules, Miranda, but they are made by the people in the society, there is nothing necessarily ordained by divine authority about any of them; and in every culture I have ever seen, there are some who do not fit into the patterns of its society. I don't know what you can do about it, in this world you live in, but you shouldn't feel bad about yourself because you are different."

Miranda blinked fiercely, clinging to Cendri's arm. She said, "I wish—I wish—I don't know what I wish. Maybe I wish we were part of the Unity, so that Rhu and I could go away together somewhere, to a world where it wouldn't be shameful for us to want to be together all the time—I feel so disloyal to my mother, when I say this!" She struggled for self-control, standing between Cendri and the balustrade of the stairs. Women returning to their seats edged past them, maneuvering—Miranda was so pregnant that it was not easy to pass her on the narrow stairs—and giving them indulgent looks, winks and smiles. Cendri realized that they accepted that she and Miranda were one of the couples she had seen. But she had no time to worry about that, though it was embarrassing; she was concerned with Miranda, who was crying noiselessly, tears streaming down her face. Helplessly, Cendri dried Miranda's eyes with her own scarf, urging, "Come along, come back to your seat, Miranda. Don't cry like this here, don't—"

Miranda gulped and struggled with her tears. She said, sniffling, trying to smile at Cendri, clinging to her, "How do you know so much about people, Cendri, when I thought you would only know about dead civilizations, and people who have been dead for millions of years—"

It was like ice-water; could Miranda possibly guess that she was more a student of cultures than of archaeology? She urged gently, "Come back to the seats, Miranda—I have lived on University, that is all, and we have so many different kinds of people and societies there." She urged Miranda up the rapidly emptying stairs and corridors. At one crossroad she stopped, looked down; it led—evidently—directly down toward the quarters where the athletes readied themselves for the arena, the dressing rooms—*or, since they performed naked, the undressing rooms?*—and saw Dal. He was at the center of a group of men, clustered tight around him, and for a moment she felt brief unease. Rhu had made it clear that despite his preferred status as a Companion—or perhaps because of it—he was not welcome or even safe in an ordinary group of men from a Men's House.

But it was also immediately obvious that Dal was in no danger. They flocked around him; athletes, naked, sweaty, or wrapped in loose towels or capes, still wearing the ribbons and garlands of the arena; other ordinary men of Isis in their drab clothing. But one and all were wide-eyed, clustering around him with something like reverence. Was he lecturing them, conspiring with them, making incendiary statements? Or was it simply a kind of hero worship—they were simply eager to see, touch, listen to a man from the worlds where men were not woman's property? In all the time she had been on Isis she had seen no such male assembly.

Was it even *permitted*? Would Dal get into trouble over this? Or did anyone on Isis even know or care what men did among themselves?

Was Dal an inspiration to them, then . . . ?

He turned, made his way slowly through them; they reached out to touch him, reluctant to let him go, but made way deferentially, did not hinder him. Cendri realized that they must get back at once to their seats, the important part of the show was beginning. Also she was reluctant for Dal to know she had been watching him. At Miranda's side she went quickly along the area behind the seats and back into the Official Box. Miranda hung back, saying in a whisper, "I don't want my mother to see that I have been crying—" and pushed Cendri forward to sit next to the Pro-Matriarchs. Dal and Rhu slipped into the Box, taking seats at the back, and Cendri noticed out of the corner of her eye that Rhu slid into a seat close to Miranda.

She leaned back and whispered to Dal, "Where have you been? I saw you with the men—"

Dal's eyes were hard. "Keep out of this Cendri. I mean that."

The final contests began. Cendri, seated in the prominent Official Box, could see the women around the arena, watching the struggling men, wrestling, struggling, locked together, were leaning forward in fascination and excitement. Cendri could see all the signs of frankly sexual arousal—flushed faces, moist lips, dilated eyes. She had never seen women react this way; the nearest thing she had ever seen to it was when she had watched men at some of the sex-display entertainments in the spaceport night-life areas. The women here applauded, made loud appreciative comments, whistled and shrieked, threw down flowers and garlands in excitement. Cendri, comparing the reactions of the women to the reactions of the men in the cruder sex-display areas in the Unity, realized they were virtually identical. She had always believed— naively, she now realized—that women were immune to visual sex stimulation of this kind.

Well, what had she expected? This had been the only contact she had seen between men and women. They didn't associate in any normal way with men. Somehow or other they must have sex with them—and it's physical sex, they didn't react very favorably when Miranda mentioned artificial conceptions in the Unity—but I still don't know under what conditions it takes place. Judging from this, the taboos are very strong and definite! She thought of this and recognized that she was behaving, almost automatically, like the trained anthropologist and cultural expert she was, but on a deeper level, she realized, there was something more personal.

Poor women, they haven't any idea of what men are like as people. . . .

The winner of the final wrestling match, a huge muscular fellow with great bulging biceps and pectorals, and a gleaming golden mop of curls, obviously dyed, was being garlanded with flowers and serenaded with a song by the men of the city. He looked around the stands, winking, leering, mugging in a way she had seen no man on Isis do, soaking in the appreciative squeals of the women in the stands. He came directly below the Official Box, and Mahala rose and spoke a few gracious words, handing the prize down to him—it was a complete and fairly expensive hunting outfit, warm clothing, boots, bow and arrows, sleeping bags, tent, and a number of other items whose uses Cendri could not even guess. She noted, from Vaniya's quiet explanation, that the items of clothing had been provided in duplicate for each of the major entrants so that each could take home his prizes for immediate use. A lottery was being held to give away the unclaimed prizes, and the men in the arena were laughing and strutting and jostling one another good-naturedly, but the women in the stands, the events over, were rising and crowding toward the exits.

"Let us wait a few minutes," Vaniya said. "Miranda, you do not want to be jostled in the crowds now."

"When is your baby due?" Mahala asked, coming to Miranda and taking her hand in a gracious gesture.

"Not very long now," Miranda replied. Her tears were dried now and she looked calm, though weary. "I had thought it might have come already by now, but they come when they will."

Mahala turned to Vaniya and said, "So you will have an heir at last, if it is a daughter. How proud of her you must be!"

"I am indeed, cousin," said Vaniya. Cendri knew that in the language of Isis this did not denote relationship but was a term of courtesy between equals. "And our Inquirer, Maret, tells us the child will be a girl, so it is indeed my heir who awaits birth." She stood at the rail of the box, looking down at the handsome naked men good-naturedly pushing one another out of the way as the remaining prizes were distributed and every competitor received boxes of confectionery and bright ribbons and garlands. With everyone standing near the exits it was crowded in the box, and Cendri was shoved against the other women. She felt a body pressed tight against hers, knew it was the ample form of Vaniya; the Pro-Matriarch put an arm around her waist, and Cendri let herself lean on the older woman. Vaniya's cheek pressed hers, and Cendri, responding for a moment to what seemed a spontaneous gesture of affection, let her head rest a moment on Vaniya's shoulder. Then she realized, startled and more than a little shocked, that the heavy body was pressing hard and purposefully against hers, that Vaniya's hands had strayed to her breasts and were fondling them gently, but insistently. She tensed in embarrassment, her first, startled response to pull sharply away, in outrage and dismay. Then she remained very still, thinking faster than she had ever thought in her life.

In a sense it was a compliment, a mark of total acceptance, that Vaniya should treat her this way. Such an event seemed to be a legitimate occasion, among the women of Isis, for near-public displays of sexual arousal; and Vaniya, forgetting or ignoring her alien origin, was treating her as one of their own.

At the same time, she thought ruefully, textbooks on anthropology gave no hint as to how one should react in such a case. She knew she ought to feel revulsion, rage, disgust; instead, what she felt was a kind of helpless tenderness. She stood very quietly in the circle of Vaniya's arms, neither responding to nor rejecting the caress, and after a moment Vaniya, aware of her reaction—or lack of it—took her hands away and smiled, almost in apology. She said softly, slipping her hand through Cendri's arm, "Forgive me, my child, I had really forgotten, for a moment, that you were not one of us."

Cendri gave the plump arm a gentle, momentary squeeze, and they moved out of the box on to the stairs, as Vaniya said in an undertone "I am an indiscreet old fool. Are you very angry with me, little Cendri?"

"Angry? No, Vaniya, I'm not angry," Cendri said gently, and Vaniya, squeezing her arm again, moved away from her to Miranda's side.

"Cousin," said Mahala, "You have waited so long for an heir, and you are so beset now with cares, your guests from University, that you cannot enjoy this fortunate time; if it is your will, I will gladly have the honored guests from the Unity to lodge with me, so that you can give all your attention to Miranda and her coming child, and to making ready for the birth-festival. Would that release you from care, cousin? I will willingly relieve you of this duty."

"I am sure of it," Vaniya returned with a dulcet smile, "but it was our Mother's will that I should have them where they can be convenient to their work, and personal cares and conflicts must come second to my duty to our High Matriarch. I am sure there are many other duties and responsibilities to your hand, cousin."

Cendri thought; *they really hate each other, don't they*? She watched the rival Pro-Matriarchs descending the stairway, and again the image touched her mind;

Vaniya as a great tawny lioness, Mahala—she had seen Mahala, in private, as a small friendly kitten; here she saw her as a sleek, prowling black panther!

They moved to the stairs and she found Dal at her elbow. His face was tense, storm-clouded. He said, in an angry whisper, "I saw that wretched old dame trying to paw you, and you didn't seem to mind at all, you were letting her put her hands all over you, and grinning at her—I knew the women here were filthy and corrupt, but damn it, Cendri, when you join in that kind of thing—"

"That's enough, Dal," she said, in a sharp undertone. "For them it's normal. Vaniya wasn't crude about it, and from her it was a compliment. If I wasn't offended, how dare you make an issue of it?"

"Compliment!" Dal said in outrage. "It's their world, they can do anything they damn please, but when you stand there letting her maul you, and stand there smiling up at her, looking *pleased*—and say you weren't offended—"

"Lower your voice," she ordered sharply. "Have you forgotten where we are?"

"How in the hell can I forget?" But he did drop his voice to a whisper again. "Lousy, corrupt—and you're my *wife*! How could you—"

"Dal, for mercy's sake, what was I supposed to do? Yell, slap her, make a scene, precipitate a diplomatic incident? When she saw I wasn't reacting, she let me go and apologized for forgetting I wasn't one of them. Can't you see that's a compliment, Dal?"

"Some compliment," he grumbled, unappeased, and held her back so that they were some distance between the two Pro-Matriarchs, who had reached the bottom of the stairs and were exchanging—Cendri supposed from their looks—formal courtesies prior to entering the waiting official cars. Dal said, "Listen, Cendri, I think we ought to think seriously about leaving Vaniya's house—I'll be damn glad to get out of the place—and moving to stay with the other one, Mahala.

She's a reasonable woman, in spite of her fears of the Unity. We can relate to her in a way we never could to Vaniya, with all her superstitious nonsense about the Builders and their sacred site."

"Dal, I really don't think—"

"Look, after all, it's a way of demonstrating that we aren't really allied to Vaniya's political faction. And today something happened which made me realize—"

Cendri never heard what happened or what he realized. At that moment loud cries of dismay and lamentation rose, spread through the crowd. She heard Vaniya cry out in grief and felt fear clutch at her heart—what had happened? Had something happened to Miranda? No; Miranda was standing next to her mother, crying out, adding her own voice to the rising chorus of lament. She hurried down the stairs toward them.

Mahala raised her eyes to Cendri and said, her voice low and tense, "Catastrophe, my dear Scholar Dame. Our Mother and Priestess, the revered and beloved High Matriarch Rezali, has left us and ascended to join the Goddess. We have just had word; she died but a few moments ago, without ever recovering consciousness."

"And so," Vaniya said, her face pale, "We are without a High Matriarch. And there is no way of knowing, cousin, which of us would have succeeded to her ring and her robe."

Cendri looked at the two rivals, in shock. She had not known the dead woman, the late Mother Rezali was nothing to her. But what would this mean to her work? What would this mean to Vaniya and her household?

Mahala said blandly, "I must go home at once. I am certain that the Mother Rezali will attempt to communicate with me from the great barrier, and I must be ready to receive her word. I pray—" She turned to Cendri and bowed, "Excuse me, Scholar Dame, that I leave you without ceremony. Vaniya, I confide to you, as Mother Rezali wished, the care of our honored

guests, since I am sure you will have no other duties at
the moment."

Cendri saw Vaniya's large broad face flush pink with
wrath; but she merely bowed to her rival and said
nothing. When Mahala had stepped into her official
vehicle and driven away, Vaniya took Cendri's arm in a
tight clasp. Miranda came close to her mother, flushed
with anger.

"That woman! How dared she? You must go home at
once, Mother, I am sure that the Mother Rezali will
communicate with you—Maret must be told at once to
await the word—" Quickly, she gestured to the waiting
car, motioned Dal and Cendri into it, ushered her
mother inside. Rhu clambered in last, taking his place
close to Vaniya and saying soothingly, "Do not disturb
yourself, Vaniya, you must remain calm to await
word."

"Yes, yes," Vaniya said distractedly, "I cannot
believe that Rezali will appoint *that* woman High
Matriarch in her place—yet there is always the
chance—"

She saw Cendri's puzzled face and said, "Forgive me,
my dear, but I fear that until the Mother Rezali has
made her will known, your work must come to a halt."

"Make her will known?" Cendri said, "I thought—
the word you received—I thought the High Matriarch
was dead!"

"Why, so she is," Vaniya said, "but when a woman
of our people is appointed to the post of High
Matriarch, she secretes a duplicate of her ring of office,
and her robe of power, in a place known only to her.
And then, should death take her before she has
designated her successor, her spirit will appear to her
chosen successor, and tell her, or an Inquirer in her
household, where the ring and robe have been hidden.
So that whichever of us first discovers her ring of office,
and her robe, where they have been hidden, becomes
High Matriarch in her place. And I must go and await
some communication from the other side of the great
barrier, telling me that our beloved Mother Rezali

wishes me to carry on her work among our people, and whispering to my spirit where I may find her ring of office to show the City Mothers."

She fell silent, deep in thought, her eyes going blank, and Cendri, blinking, thought; what a development! Now all their work depended on a kind of mediumistic treasure-hunt!

Dal whispered in her ear, "What a *hell* of a way to run a government!"

And for once she did not feel even a little like arguing with him.

chapter nine

THE NEXT FEW DAYS DAL AND CENDRI SPENT IN THE ruins, measuring, taking soil-scrapings, making computer analyses of the buildings and structures. Dal adapted a force-field breaker to attempt again to enter the structures without damage, trying frequency after frequency, but decided to delay any attempt to cut into them until he had X-ray pictures of the interior. To devise these in a way that would penetrate the unknown force-field, he said, might be a long task and demand conferral by long-distance relays with sources on University.

"We could do more damage trying to get into them than we realized," he told her, "if we could break the

force-field and just walk in, that's one thing. But if
they're in time stasis, nothing we could do will break
into them because, essentially, they're not in this
dimension at all."

That sounded like nonsense to Cendri and she said
so. "If they're not *here*, how can we touch them, lean
on them, press against them—"

"Cendri, I don't have time to give you a complete
course in temporal mechanics. Just take my word for it,
unless living on Isis has made you unwilling to trust
male scholarship." But he laughed, and Cendri knew it
had become a joke between them again. She was
profoundly relieved.

"I wish we could get a good temporal mechanic
here," Dal continued. "The trouble is, the only ones I
know on University are men, and I don't suppose any
of them would be willing to wear some woman's
property tag, although to get a chance at a site which
might actually be *in* time stasis, I know some mathema-
ticians who would do more than *that*. I don't know any
temporal mechanic who is a woman—" he continued,
as they came out of the site late in the evening, and
turned to Laurina. "Are there any specialists in mathematics on your world—the mathematics of temporal
conditions and stress?"

Laurina looked bewildered. She could talk to Dal
now without too much self-consciousness, but as always
when she was confused or felt insecure, it was to Cendri
she turned before answering. "Truly, I don't know; I
know so little of mathematics. My own specialty is
history. I can inquire at the college if you like, though."

"Do that," Dal directed. "The help of anyone who
had a grounding in temporal mathematics would be a
help in determining if this place really *is* in time stasis."

"It cannot be that," Laurina argued, "or how could
the inhabitants communicate with us?"

Dal made a wry face and did not answer. He did not
argue with Laurina's beliefs; but he would not dignify
them by comment, either. He simply said, "I'd take it

as a great favor if you could put me—us—in touch with the most highly regarded mathematician at your college. He—I mean she—would certainly have tried to investigate something of the math of temporal stress, I understand it's the most exciting field in mathematics in the last two or three hundred years."

Laurina said, with the queer stiff formality she still sometimes used with Dal, "I am certain that any scientist would consider it an honor to work with the respected Scholar Dame from University and her Companion."

As the great pale sun of Isis drew lower in the sky, they came out of the site and saw a procession passing along the shoreline road toward the city of Ariadne. As they drew near, Cendri saw that it was mostly men afoot, although there were a few cars and surface vehicles of the kind used on Isis. Most of them were young, and wearing the brief kiltlike garments worn by manual laborers of either sex. The few men among Vaniya's servants went down to speak with them and after a moment Dal followed. To Cendri's surprise, the men called out greetings to the women, and Vaniya's servants answered; after a moment, shyly, so did Laurina. Cendri's face must have shown her curiosity, for Laurina explained, unasked.

"They are men from the great dam project, about a hundred kilometers south of the city, coming here for the festival. They will camp along the shoreline, it is the only time of the year when they are allowed spearfishing in the coastline waters. And in four days now—has no one told you?—is the highest of our holidays, when we visit the sea and invoke the Goddess as bringer of life. But certainly—" she hesitated, diffident. "You are the friend of the Lady Miranda, surely she has invited you to join with us in this festival?"

Miranda had mentioned it, once or twice, in such a way that Cendri knew it was somehow connected with the unknown mating customs of the Matriarchate, concealed by the society. Cendri felt a flicker of excitement. Was she, then, enough accepted by them that she would be allowed to witness this festival?

Laurina said, "But no, the lady Miranda is so near to the birth-time that she will not join, this year, in the festival. I had thought her child would have been born long before this." She went on, "It is our Longest Day, and this year it coincides with the double Full Moon, when both our moons show their smiling face; which happens only once in every nine or eleven years, alternately. So this year the festival is particularly sacred; I hope that by then we will have a new High Matriarch to perform the rites. We visit the sea three times in a year, but this, the Longest Day, is the holiest and most blessed of our festivals. Cendri—" she hesitated, then smiled, "you are here alone, without sisters or kinswomen, and it is for us to offer you hospitality and companionship. Since Miranda has not thought to do so, let me be the one to invite you to join us at this highest of festivals."

Cendri felt the flicker of excitement again. Actually to be allowed to witness their highest festival! Nevertheless she felt compelled to ask, "Is it permitted for an outsider, Laurina?"

"I feel that the Goddess could hardly smile on a woman who did not join us in her worship on this day," Laurina said seriously. "All women are of one blood, and since you are here on this world she has blessed with her presence, it seems to me unthinkable that you would choose *not* to join us."

So not only was she *invited* to join them; it might even be taken as an affront to their Goddess if she did *not*! She thought, if I had come openly as an anthropologist, to study them, they might have taken pains to conceal some of their rites from me! Perhaps it is as well I did not . . .

As she returned to Vaniya's house, she was pondering this. The sexual customs of Isis were evidently some form of visitational marriage, then, preceded, and formalized, evidently by the rite called "visiting the sea." She said to Laurina, "So many men! I had not known there were so many! Do they all live outside the city, then? Are they colonists, living in separate villages?"

"Men, colonize anything?" Laurina said with a blank look, halfway between amusement and incredulity. "No, but some Men's Houses have been taken there under their overseers, or leased by their owners, to work on the great dam. They are building dykes and when they have finished, it will provide flood control all along the delta of the great river which we call Anahit, and energy as well. Some of our best engineers are working there, but of course they need immense crews of male labor. Men are reasonably good at manual labor, provided they are carefully supervised by trained women. Of course their attention span is short, and they must be lavishly provided with amusements and rewards, but mostly the men like to work on such projects; it gives them a chance to use their muscles, which is what they do best; they have a natural instinct for manual work, as you can see by their gift for athletics. They are not as graceful as women, but their strength makes up for that. And they enjoy the extra rations of sweets, and the extra opportunity, outside the city, for hunting. So everyone is happy; the men because of the fun of building the dam, and the women because we will have power and flood control."

Cendri wondered briefly how the men would have reacted to this analysis, but they had arrived at Vaniya's house. But before she had finished washing off the grime of the day's work in the ruins, Miranda knocked at their door and came in.

She looked troubled and distracted. "Cendri, will you come? My mother is very distressed, she wants all of the women in her household with her now—"

"What is it, Miranda?"

"Mahala has sent word that she has found the High Matriarch's ring and robe. We must all go to the Council to verify them—I cannot travel now." And indeed Miranda was ungainly now, dragging heavily around. "Lialla and her partner will be with her, but still—she is fond of you, Cendri, will you go in my place? And it may interest you, to see the solemn formality of investing a High Matriarch—"

"I will go," Cendri promised, and Miranda went away. Dal frowned at her and said, "Damn it, Cendri, do you really want to align yourself so much with the losing Pro-Matriarch's faction?"

Cendri said quietly, "Miranda said it; she is fond of me. And have you forgotten, Dal, why I am really here? If I have any opportunity to see the workings of this society, then I must do so."

"I suppose so. But I'm worrying. If you make an enemy of Mahala—"

"I'm not planning to make an enemy of Mahala, Dal. I am going with Vaniya in the place of an ailing daughter," Cendri said with careful patience, and Dal frowned again, angrily.

"I don't like that, damn it! She's getting entirely too fond of you to suit me! I haven't forgotten how she treated you at the athletic contest—I suppose it's to be expected, that women who live apart from men should develop morbid homosexual tendencies, but you're my wife and you can't expect me to approve of letting you run around with a woman like that!"

"Dal, for goodness sake! A woman like that—what in the world, *any* world, do you mean? Do you honestly believe the Pro-Matriarch of Isis is going to attack an honored guest sexually?"

"Well, I suppose not, but—I saw the way she acted the other day—"

Cendri sighed, knowing she could never make Dal understand. She understood the impulse of affection and excitement that had prompted Vaniya to embrace her, an intimacy which would have been taken for granted in Vaniya's own world; an overture, not an attack, and when Cendri had not responded, Vaniya had behaved unexceptionably! She said, "I'm not going to argue with you about it, Dal, it's customary in their world, and you have no right to make invidious remarks about it. When the men are considered unsuitable for companionship, naturally they find their closest emotional ties among one another. I could cite half a dozen parallels among men, if I wanted to—the warrior caste of Kahornia, for instance, who aren't allowed to approach women except for one season in every four—"

"I know," said Dal, grimacing, "I don't approve of them either; I haven't cultivated the virtue of scientific detachment, and I hope sincerely that I never do, if it means tolerating that kind of thing!" Then he shrugged and laughed. "All right, love, there's no sense quarreling." He came and put his arms around her, kissing her hard. "I'm really not worried; I know you too well for that. But don't develop too much scientific detachment or tolerance, darling."

Cendri was relieved, even though she knew perfectly well that Dal did not understand. He was, after all, not trained in cross-cultural comparisons. She supposed this grudging tolerance was all she could expect, and she was glad he was not making an issue of it. She robed herself in her most elaborately formal garments, suitable for a Dame's Investiture on University, and went down to join Vaniya.

Vaniya indeed looked solemn and distracted, but she held out her hands to Cendri with a warm smile. She said, "It is good of you to come in a daughter's place, my child; it was Rhu who suggested it might entertain you to see this solemnity, and he has pledged himself to entertain your Companion in your absence."

Now I wonder, Cendri thought, as she joined Vaniya's other daughters in Vaniya's car, does Rhu intend to spend the time with Dal, learning more about the position of men in the Unity—or is he taking this opportunity to be with Miranda?

On the ride to the city they passed still more of the groups of men, inbound from all over the continent, and Vaniya, waving graciously as the men bowed to her passing car, said distractedly, "It will be a scandal if we do not have a High Matriarch and Priestess for the ceremonies this year—"

Cendri asked hesitantly, "Is there any doubt of this? Miranda told me that—that the Pro-Matriarch had found the ring and robe of—of her predecessor—"

"So my worthy colleague says, indeed." Vaniya curled her lip. "Yet it would not be the first time that a Pro-Matriarch had presented a forgery. Some women will stop at nothing. As for me—" her broad leonine face was stern, "I have not heard the word of our Mother and Priestess, although I have awaited the word with solemn fasting and prayer." Indeed she looked worn, by sleeplessness and hunger. "But I would yield my place at once, rather than win it unworthily, or without the word of my predecessor. If Mahala has truly the ring and robe of Rezali, then I shall be the first to do homage and swear loyalty to her."

Cendri had seen the Residence of the High Matriarch from outside; but until now, when she came as a member of Vaniya's entourage, she had not yet entered the building. She walked with Vaniya up the long marble steps, between the columns, noting that like many other imposing structures on Isis, they were mounted in what looked like gimbals. She had to admit that it made sense, on a planet as earthquake-prone as Isis, but also it took away something—at least in Cendri's eyes—from the elegant formality of the structure.

Perhaps, she thought, this is why so much of their society, so much of their formal structure, seems to my eyes ill-designed and catch-as-catch-can. On a planet like this, nothing is permanent. Except, perhaps, the ruins at We-were-guided. No wonder this is a sacred place to them.

A small crowd of children—not naked in sunhats and sandals, now, but dressed in their best and looking, as

dressed-up children always do, vaguely uncomfortable
—had gathered to watch outside the Residence, watching wide-eyed and solemn. A great many of them,
Cendri noted, had come into the great hall of the
Residence and were standing there to see what was
going on, and it was typical of Isis that nobody thought
to shoo them out of the center of the great hall. Down
the very center of the hall was a long row of statues in
glass cases. Statues? No; they were elegant wax effigies, elaborately robed, each glass case and effigy set
into a pit protected by sand so that it would fall over
and survive undamaged and unbroken. They were
surrounded by the usual screens and their bases were
also decorated with the usual casual art, each one
(Cendri could read the written language now well
enough to tell) decorated by a different children's
school.

Vaniya said, in a low voice, "Some of these effigies
have come with us all the way from our mother planets
of Persephone and Labrys. Here is our first High
Matriarch, our beloved foremother Alicia." She pointed to a woman whose hair, arranged in an elaborate
triangular coiffure, was silvery white, wearing an
archaic robe. "She was born on the Unity world of
Pioneer, I believe, in the worst of the old days." Slowly
they passed through the hall of effigies, and Vaniya
named, one by one, the High Matriarchs of Isis,
standing here for all time as they had appeared to their
daughters in life. Each wore an elaborately embroidered robe, of the same archaic pattern as the foremother Alicia's, although the details of the embroidery
of each robe, so Vaniya told Cendri, were unique, and
chosen by each High Matriarch to be individual to
herself; after a High Matriarch assumed her office, the
duplicate of her robe and ring were destroyed and she
had one made for her own personal use, bearing an
individual *motif*.

"And here stands our mother Rezali, as she appeared in life," said Vaniya, pausing and bowing briefly

before the final statue. Cendri beheld a withered, little, elderly woman, dark-skinned and shrunken, her scant hair all white. "She bore her ring for eighty years; in the time since we left Persephone she has been our Mother and Priestess, the longest reign of any High Matriarch in the history of the Matriarchate."

Passing the statue—a macabre custom, Cendri thought—they came face to face with Mahala and her entourage. A quick look told Cendri at once that the other Pro-Matriarch, unlike Vaniya, had not awaited her call with sleepless prayer and fasting; she looked calm, rested, refreshed. She went toward Vaniya and embraced her in the formal way she had done before.

"You seem weary and worn, my sister," she said sweetly. "This will be over soon, and you shall go and rest, and be free of the cares you have borne since our beloved Mother Rezali fell too ill to make her wishes known."

How she hates Vaniya, Cendri thought. She has virtually told Vaniya that as soon as she is verified High Matriarch, she will be relieved of all official duties. I suppose politics is the same everywhere.

Vaniya said gruffly, "I hope you have not put your household to the trouble and expense of readying for a move from the Residence of the Pro-Matriarch yet, my sister. No doubt you will soon be moving, but there is still some doubt as to the destination." Her face was set and grim; and Mahala frowned. Without answering, she turned on her heel and led the way into an inner chamber, where a group of women, most of them middle-aged or beyond, sat in a circle on low cushions. Vaniya turned to Cendri, and to Lialla and her partner, motioning them to seats outside the circle, and went forward, with Mahala, to take the two vacant cushions to either side.

One of the women seated on the cushions said solemnly, "The Pro-Matriarch Mahala has claimed that our late Mother, Rezali of blessed memory, has communicated with her from beyond the great barrier

of death and designated her successor by revealing to
Mahala the location of her ring and her robe. Produce
them, Mother."

Mahala gestured to a member of her entourage, and
Cendri saw, in surprise, that it was a fat, blobby, sexless
person, neither male nor female . . . an Inquirer, a
neutered man?

Mahala said, "My Inquirer, Karay, holds them for
your judgment."

One by one, the women examined the objects.
Cendri could see only that they were a heavy ring,
deeply engraved, and a robe of stiff material, heavily
embroiderd with metallic threads.

At last they came to Vaniya. She bent over them,
solemnly, giving them her full attention. At last she
raised her head, and her eyes were lambent with anger.

"These are forgeries," she said, "and clumsy forgeries at that! The ring is a good forgery; but a forgery
none the less. The ring of our revered Matriarch, as you
may see from the effigy in the Hall of Matriarchs, bore
a snake with three eyes; this serpent has two. The
embroidery is done with copper-colored threads; the
embroidered robe of our Matriarch, again I call the
Hall of Matriarchs to witness, is done with a twisted
thread of two strands, one copper and one burnt orange
color. I do not even speak of the patterns, which any
little child could see for clumsy imitations of the real
thing, no doubt hurriedly done by Mahala's own sewing
women, or if she does not trust them that much, by her
daughters and foster-daughters. Councilwomen of Ariadne, I ask that these be rejected for the clumsy
imitations they are! Mahala—" she turned her eyes on
her rival, "how dare you bring this stupid imposture
here!"

Mahala said calmly, "I will await the judgment of the
Council, my sister and rival."

One woman said, "They are obvious forgeries! How
can Mahala insult our intelligence this way?"

"Oh, come," another one interrupted, "is it not

possible that the Mother Rezali might have passed these imitations because of her own failing eyesight and memory? I suggest we accept Mahala's word that these are what they claim to be, and hail her as our new Pro-Matriarch!"

Will it depend, Cendri thought, only on the will of the Council, and not on the objective fact? It is certain that Vaniya believes; she has prayed and fasted and awaited word. Is Mahala more realistic, or simply more cynical?

Vaniya said, with an obvious effort to steady her voice and speak calmly through her tremendous wrath, "The will of the Council makes no difference. The law clearly states that every member of the Council must be satisfied that what the candidate presents is the authentic ring and robe of the former Pro-Matriarch."

"Then," said Mahala, turning directly to the Council, "I beg each of you to be satisfied, Mothers. The high festival is upon us, already the men have come into the city to visit the sea; if there is no government, no High Matriarch, and the city is in a state of anarchy, we may have a rebellion on our hands."

One of the Council mothers said, "This is sacrilege you speak, Mahala!"

"Sacrilege? Nonsense," Mahala said contemptuously. "We are making fools of ourselves before the Scholar Dame from the civilized worlds. Is there really any woman here who truly believes that the spirit of the dead will speak to an Inquirer, or to anyone else? In an age when starships can come and go between the Galaxies, will any woman stand up here and tell me she truly believes this superstitious rubbish? It is for the Council to accept me, or reject, and I beg of you not to ask for further ghost-stories!"

Vaniya stood up, her eyes blazing at Mahala. She said, "I will not sit and listen to this! You, the council of Elders of Ariadne, have been twice insulted by this woman, first by imposture and then by blasphemy! I call upon you, my sisters, to name me your true High

Matriarch, on the grounds that Mahala has proven, by coming before us with a forged ring and robe, that she knows the Mother Rezala will *not* speak to her spirit!"

"I notice," Mahala said calmly, "that even you, Vaniya, have not had the hardihood to claim that she has spoken to yours. You are not a madwoman either—not yet, although if you go on awaiting a ghostly voice to appoint you High Matriarch, you will be so soon."

"Peace, both of you," said one of the Elders, sternly, "the High Matriarch has been chosen like this since we founded the High Matriarchate!"

"I remind you," Mahala said, the honey in her voice now a little sour, "that Rezali's reign has been so long that no woman in this room had yet grown her breasts when Rezali was chosen to rule over us; we were still on the mother-world of Persephone then. We know only that this is how the Council *said* a High Matriarch was chosen. It is quite possible that it has always been what I say it is now, a pious fraud to baffle outsiders!"

"This is heresy," said one of the women, and another simply stared in shock, her mouth falling open.

Another said slowly, "Perhaps there is some truth in what Mahala says. In living memory, no woman has been appointed by any such method—"

The debate dissolved in general clamor. Vaniya finally made herself heard.

"I have been summoned here upon a false pretense," she said, "and there are affairs which demand my presence elsewhere. I hold myself in readiness to meet when I am justly summoned; meanwhile, I bid you farewell." She gestured to the women in her party; Cendri rose along with them and followed Vaniya out of the Council Hall. The children gathered in the Hall of Matriarchs stood in small staring groups, watching wide-eyed. As they got into Vaniya's car, they saw Mahala and her party leaving by another door, and Vaniya audibly sighed with relief.

"A calculated risk," she said to Cendri. "She is

persuasive, she might after all have persuaded the Council to see matters her way. But if she had done so I could have gained nothing by staying there." Again the weary sigh. "I must think what to do." She leaned her head against the cushions and closed her eyes, and no one spoke on the ride back to the Residence.

As they alighted from the vehicle, Lialla put her arm around her mother.

"Vaniya, dearest Mother," she entreated, "will you not eat something and take some rest? We are all in your hands now; you must preserve your strength for the difficult days which will come."

Vaniya stroked her daughter's cheek indulgently, but she shook her head.

"No, my dear, there are more serious things on my mind than food and sleep. I must consult with those who are wiser than I. All of you, I beg you, go to bed." But she stretched her hand to Cendri and said, "Stay with me for a little while, Scholar Dame."

She rarely used Cendri's title; that she had done so now indicated to Cendri—and, Cendri thought, to the other women—that she was not rejecting her daughters, on a personal level, for a stranger, but that she wished to speak with Cendri as representative of the Unity, of University. Cendri followed her into the great, deserted dining-hall. Vaniya lowered herself on to a cushion, sat with her head leaning against another. After a time she said to Cendri, "Believe me, Cendri, I am not ambitious. My sister and rival is a good administrator and a worthy and honest woman; I say this in spite of her clumsy attempt to befool us all today. She truly believes—and I feel this is tragic, it bespeaks so much of the poverty of her mind and heart—that there is nothing beyond what she can see and feel. I would willingly turn the mundane adminis-tration of the government over to her. She is younger than I, and, I think, stronger and more fit to rule in the secular duties assigned to a High Matriarch. If it were only this, I would step down today and spend my declining years surrounded by my granddaughters and fosterlings. But I cannot sit by and say nothing while she robs our spiritual life of its meaning. Fit she may be for Matriarch; as Priestess she has proven herself unfit, not only by her actions of today, but by her attitude over all the years. She seems not fully aware that without vision and awareness of the things which are beyond material well-being, the soul and spirit of humanity dies." A long silence, and for a moment Cendri thought the woman, exhausted, had fallen into sleep. Then she said, "It is this, I think, which has made so many of the worlds ruled by men intolerable to our society; that they rested on material well-being, and gave no thought to the spirit and soul of their people. The Goddess knows, I am eager for their physical well-being; I know there have been priesthoods where a pretended concern for spiritual wealth has been used to defraud mankind—and I say mankind deliberately, for no woman will allow such a spiritual death—to defraud mankind of material comforts and allow riches to fall into the hands of the powerful. And so one of the major precepts of the Matriarchate is that the spiritual and the material well-being of our women go hand in hand, always, and this is why the High Matriarch has also been High Priestess; to remind the woman who holds this dual office that material comforts without spiritual riches are barren of benefit, and that spiritual worth without due attention to the bodies of our sisters is a lie and a sham. I fear that Mahala wishes to separate them, to destroy the whole ethical basis of the Matriarchate, and I am afraid; but she will not do it while I live, Cendri."

Cendri said, "And you cannot produce the true ring and robe?"

This time Vaniya's sigh seemed ripped from the very depths of her being.

"I cannot. Even Maret's far-seeing is silent on this. May the Goddess forgive me, I too have had doubts like Mahala's. Perhaps indeed once Rezali had put off her suffering flesh she has no further thought for her daughters left motherless in this world—or," she added with a ghost of her old grin, "it *is* superstitious nonsense to believe the dead concern themselves with the fate of the living. Perhaps the ancient foremothers in their wisdom felt that the woman who could seek out and engage the finest clairvoyants was best fitted to rule over us."

Cendri had never believed in survival after death, but had seen extra-sensory perception and clairvoyance proven again and again; *that* issue was no longer in doubt, and so Vaniya's conjecture seemed a very likely idea.

Vaniya rose, abruptly. "Will you come with me, Cendri, while I seek the council of those who are wiser than I?"

Cendri looked at her in blank astonishment. "I, Vaniya?"

"Mahala has accused me of ignorance and superstition, says that I am making our world ridiculous before the scholars from University. I want you, who are one of those, to see for yourself that it is no mere superstition which sends me to seek the aid of those at We-were-guided; will you come with me, my alien daughter?" She held out her hands to Cendri, and the younger woman, astonished, yet touched by this appeal, clasped them.

"Of course, Vaniya."

Silently, Vaniya went around the big room, taking up a warm cloak against the chill of the damp night; gave one to Cendri. She took a torch in her hand, and they went out through the damp garden.

A thick sea-fog had drifted in, and the garden was thick with white mist. Cendri could not see more than a few feet beyond her face, but Vaniya moved unerringly along the familiar paths, toward the shore. As they followed the path, now familiar to Cendri, and began slowly to ascend the long hill that led to the ruins, Cendri recalled the first night in Vaniya's house, when she had stood at her upper window, watching the procession winding into the ruins.

Vaniya seemed to know every step of the way. As they climbed, they came up above the mist, and Cendri, looking down, saw it lying, like a thick white blanket, along the shore, flowing and drifting in the moonlight. Above them, clear in the light of the growing moons, lay the ruins; dark, massive, strange, and as she moved silently along the canyons of the dead city, Cendri shivered.

Vaniya looked at the moons, their pale gibbous faces floating silently above the dark spires of the immeasurably old buildings. She said in a low voice, "The highest of our festivals is upon us; it frightens me, sometimes, to think that there might be no priestess to bless our rites." She turned to Cendri in the dark, reaching for the younger woman's hand. She said, and her plump fingers felt cold, "I am not an ignorant woman, Cendri; my mind knows as well as yours that the rites are holy because the minds and hearts of our women, and our men, make them so, and it would be no word of mine, nor of Mahala's, which makes them sacred. Children would be conceived and born, the crops would grow, all things would go on in order, no matter who performs the rites, or even if they are not performed at all. I am not the superstitious ninny Mahala thinks me—Cendri, my child, it was I who piloted the ship which bore us from Persephone to this world! I was a young woman then, I had no thought that I would ever hold any office, far less this highest of offices. It was Mahala who always sought for the power of leadership, and I was content that she should have it, so long as she bore in mind what our people needed. But—Cendri—even though the world would go on without the blessing of the rites, our people *need* them. We need all things done decently and in order, and a people react as they have been taught. Every year since we came from Persephone, our lives have been structured according to the world we found. As on our mother world we were structured to the turn of the seasons, planting and reaping and sowing, here we are structured to the turn of the tides, the rise and fall of the sea. The priestesses do not make this happen. I do not believe that even when the mass of folk were ignorant anyone believed that it was the word of the priestesses which made all this happen, but it is their word which gives license or restraint. I know what happens to a people which believes it is responsible to no one except themselves, and their own whim and will. Yes, if we wished, we could change our society to one based not on the will of the Goddess and the cycles of nature, but on our own will, strongly enforced by laws which the women have made for themselves. Such laws are tyranny, always; we live more content under the gentle hand of nature, by the name of the Goddess, than under laws which we have devised by ourselves and must enforce by fear and threat of punishments. I think Mahala feels this would suffice, but I have seen how the laws made by man at last reach a point where crime is not regarded except whether or not the appropriate punishment is enforced."

Cendri nodded, slowly. A government ruled by custom and tradition, without crime and without rebellion, and without need of law or enforcement. She did not know if she would care for such a world, but the problem of crime and enforcement was an enormous one on every world in the Unity. The women of the Matriarchate had solved it in their own way, which was, by and large, quite successful. They had, at least, a right to complete their experiment without interference from the Unity.

Vaniya spread her cloak on the top of the flight of steps which led into the open square leading down into the ruins of the spaceship which had brought them there. She sat down, inviting Cendri to sit beside her. She said, "I piloted the ship that brought us here to Isis, Cendri. I was a young woman then, I had no children. I had been chosen for education by the Mother Rezali, and had learned a good deal about the workings of the Universe. And so I, and half a dozen others, were entrusted with the ship, while the others were drugged to insensibility—you are too young to remember that in those days the drives were less endurable by a person in waking state, and all except the most necessary personnel were kept under sedation."

The technical language sounded strange on Vaniya's lips. She went on, her voice quiet and thoughtful in the moonlit darkness, her face a pale large blob rather like the pale moons in the sky.

"I was alone during much of all that long trip; I had a great deal of time to think, about the world we had left, the world to which we would go. And at last our ship—there it lies below us," she gestured, "was floating in orbit around this world, and I looked down on the strange planet below, wrapped in its clouds, its oceans moved by unknown storms and quakes and tidal waves, and I was afraid. I was afraid, Cendri, for all I knew of the mechanics of the Universe, and for all the education I had received, and for all my belief in the society we had built on Persephone, against the general trend of the Unity. I was filled with terror and with doubt. Would it not be better for us to return and submit ourselves to the laws which the people of the Unity had made for mankind? I even wondered, and doubted the Matriarchate. Were men and women truly so different, that the laws made by men could not be enforced for women too, and give women freedom enough to do as we would? Should we not return, and work for more of a place for women *within* the Unity, rather than removing ourselves so completely from its entire structure? So I pondered, while I looked down at our new planet below us, and I prayed, though I was not a religious woman then. I knew that we would need all the help we could get, whether from ourselves, or from some force greater than we were. And then, Cendri, I was answered."

"Answered, Vaniya?"

"Answered, my child. By those who dwell here, whom you call Builders. They spoke to me, as they still speak to any woman who will come and kneel before them and seek their counsel. They reassured me, and quieted my doubts. They guided the ship here, and they proved to me—" her voice was shaking with intensity, "that our way of life, the Matriarchate, was what we believed, ordained of old before men had seized power from the women."

Cendri felt a curious cold prickle running up and down her spine. She whispered, "Proved to you, Vaniya? How did they prove such a thing to you?"

Vaniya's voice, too, was not more than a whisper. She said, "They spoke to me, as I know they have spoken to you; I saw your face when we came to the ruins, the day of the great wave, when the village was destroyed, and you proved yourself one of us by risking your life to ring the alarm. But in all the years we have dwelt on Isis, Cendri, in all the years we have come here to worship, they have spoken to no male. No male has ever heard their voice. And thus we *know*, Cendri, we know beyond any possible shadow of a doubt, that the Builders of our race ordained women to rule, and that the Unity was wrong, wrong, wrong! Tell me—" she turned her face, pale in the moonlight, to the younger woman, "during all your time in the ruins, has your Companion ever heard their voice?"

Cold and shaking with chill, Cendri whispered, "No. Never."

"And you have heard it. I know you have heard it, child, I have seen it in your face—"

Cendri whispered, reluctantly, her spine prickling, "I have—I have heard."

Vaniya nodded, slowly, drew Cendri to her feet, her arm around the younger woman. She held Cendri close to her, within the heavy cloak she wore. Together, arms enlaced, holding each other against falling in the darkness, they went down the steps toward the site of the old spaceship.

"Come, child. Come. I know now that they will help me, that they will speak to me; they, who know all, will surely help me to find the tokens of the Mother, so that I may continue to guide my daughters. They will reaffirm my leadership, let me remain Mother to my people. Come, Cendri. Come and see."

chapter ten

CLOUDS DRIFTED ACROSS THE FACE OF THE NEARER MOON; the further, shining valiantly, gave a light substantially dimmed as the women, clinging together, moved toward the dark loom of the old spaceship. Cendri wondered why—and how?—the ship itself had become a focus of the presence, whatever it was. Or had the mysterious Builders simply drawn the ship down to themselves? *We-were-guided,* the Matriarchs called the ruins, thus commemorating the contact with the alien presences.

Builders. Dal was right, then, and these ancient ruins *were* the site of those who had seeded the known Galaxy with their offspring. Her skin prickled, and she felt cold creep along her veins. Had this alien race actually cast their seal on the Matriarchate as their preferred people?

The torch in Vaniya's hand flickered and went out, but Vaniya, her steps unerring in the darkness, guided them on. As they neared Cendri began to feel again the sense of an overwhelming, welcoming warmth that lapped about her, crept up into her whole body, so that she no longer felt the cold or the dampness of the dawn wind off the ocean. She no longer needed to see; her feet were drawn forward by some volition outside of herself. She struggled for a moment to cling to herself, to her own perceptions, not this alien thing that seemed about to overcome her, to suffocate her own personality.

I don't believe in Gods . . . religions are an element of social control—even Vaniya, who is their priestess, said so tonight . . . And yet *something* drew her on, something outside herself, a glow within, a warmth, a sense of being lapped in deep, loving tenderness. Vaniya had fallen to her knees; Cendri was not conscious of any act of will as she fell beside the other woman, kneeling there rapt in the warmth.

I love you . . . you are loved, you belong to me, you are mine . . . Cendri struggled to keep an atom of awareness back from the intensity of this, the sensation of being swallowed up in it . . . no use. She drifted in rapture. She never knew how long she knelt there, suffused, overcome, in the presence which wiped out her critical judgment or her disbelief . . . how could she disbelieve? It was *there,* it was real, it was . . . transcendence. . . .

The sunrise blurred her eyes, and she felt them fill with hot tears. It was gone; she was alone, kneeling beside Vaniya on the chill surface of the ruins, and the towering mass above them was only an old hulk of a spaceship, long past its usefulness. She felt cold and alone, the last traces of the warmth and the presence slowly withdrawing in little ripples from her mind and her senses.

At her side Vaniya sighed, struggling to her feet with a faint groan of pain from stiffened joints. Cendri turned quickly and helped the old woman regain her feet.

Vaniya pressed her hand affectionately. She said in a whisper, her face still blank with the last traces of the rapture, "How strange—and how rational. Mother Rezali indeed confirmed my leadership, knowing how Mahala hates and fears the serpents of the shore." Her eyes blinked, focused on Cendri. "In the sea-caves, so They have told me, I will find the ring and the robe, the true ones and no forgery."

"Must we go, then, and find them?"

Vaniya shook her head. "I will send Maret, and my daughters whom I can trust; you have done enough, little Cendri." Her hand on Cendri's shoulder, Cendri supporting Vaniya's steps, they came slowly up out of the ruins, into the reddening fog along the shore. The sun was rising; it was damp, and as they retraced their steps along the shore, the incoming tide lapped at their shoes and soaked the edges of their long cloaks. In the garden, every blade of the greyish grass and every leaf was soaking, and the opening blooms of the fish-flavoring herbs gave a sharp, penetrating fragrance to the shrubbery. Vaniya breathed it in and laughed softly. "From the smell of the garden I can tell the seasons—you will join us in the festival, little daughter? Truly you are one of us now, since the Old Ones have spoken to you." She gave Cendri an affectionate hug, and Cendri smiled up at her, and said, "Laurina has asked me to join you—"

Looking into Vaniya's face, she was suddenly aware of how old Vaniya must be. She looked strong and vigorous, indeed; but long fasting and sleepless nights, had told on the iron strength of the Pro-Matriarch. "Mother," Cendri said, using the older woman's formal title for the first time, "I beg you, go and sleep, and have something to eat! You are so tired!"

Vaniya sighed, and said, "As soon as I have sent the women of my household to reclaim Rezali's ring and robe . . . my daughters will need my strength in the days to come." And with a faint shiver Cendri realized that Vaniya did not mean Miranda and Lialla and her

children and grandchildren, but all of the women of
Isis, who, if she were High Matriarch, would be her
daughters.

. . . and I too, I am her daughter . . . Cendri thought
with an atavistic prickle, tension gripping her whole
body. As they came up into the house, the women of
the household came flocking into the main hall; but at
the look on Vaniya's face they drew back, and Cendri
knew that they still saw, in Vaniya's eyes, the ecstasy of
contact, the Presence still clinging to her.

*This is the true religious experience, the only thing
which keeps a religion from being mere imposture . . .
the actual touch of something beyond the world we
know . . . and it is real . . . real. . . .*

Vaniya said briskly, "Call Maret, at once; go with
her to the sea-caves along the shore, ten and a half
kilometers beyond the pearl-divers' village. In the third
cave southward, exactly twenty meters from the entrance, the three-eyed snake is painted on the wall. Dig
down two meters and you will find a chest in which
Rezali's ring and robe are concealed."

Lialla whispered, "The Mother Rezali has spoken to
you, then, Mother?"

Vaniya shook her head. "No. But She who is wiser
than the Mother Rezali in life or death sent the vision
to my mind as I knelt to seek guidance in We-were-
guided. Go at once, my children. Lialla, Zamila, bring
me food; I must eat and recover my strength." She
swayed, and her daughters supported her. Vaniya said,
"Send at once for Miranda, she too must be told the
news . . . Cendri, my child, go and rest!"

Cendri left the old woman to the attendance of her
daughters and grandchildren, the flocking women of
her household, and slowly climbed the stairs to her own
room. She felt deathly cold and exhausted, completely
unable to assimilate the experience. She was completely free of doubt; she *knew* that Vaniya's women would
find the ring and robe as Vaniya had said, buried in a
chest two meters below the surface beneath a painted

three-eyed serpent twenty meters inside the third cave ten and a half kilometers south of the pearl-divers' village.

Clairvoyance, yes. I have always been willing to believe in that. But this . . . this presence. . . .

Dal stood up slowly from his place in the padded corner where he slept. His face was stormy.

"Cendri, where have you been? I was worried about you, and when I saw you coming back from the ruins with Vaniya, across the garden—"

She shook her head. "Dal, Vaniya has found the ring and robe of the High Matriarch. She took me with her into the ruins to consult the—the presences there—"

He shook his head in confusion. "Cendri, what *is* it with you and that woman?"

If it had not been so deadly serious she would have laughed. She said, "Dal, do you really believe that Vaniya and I are having a flaming love affair? Do you realize she is old enough to be our grandmother?"

"That hasn't stopped her from keeping Rhu for a lover, has it?"

"Rhu is her Companion; I don't really know what their sex life is like and I honestly don't give a damn. Anyway, that isn't the point. You can't have it both ways, Dal; if you think she's keeping Rhu for a lover, it hardly makes sense to think *I* am involved with her, does it?"

"You are certainly loyal to her!"

Cendri said seriously, "It's true; I love her. But not the way you evidently think, Dal, and that's too ridiculous for words!" She would have laughed, again, but she sensed his jealousy, the deep sense of uncertainty Dal felt, was very real to him. She went to him and put her arms up around his neck. "Dal, darling! That isn't important now! I told you; Vaniya has found the ring and robe of Rezali!"

Morosely, Dal swore. "I hoped the other woman would get it, we might make some headway with her!"

"I'm not so sure," Cendri said slowly.

"A society which picks its leaders on the word of a

clairvoyant is a pretty silly society, all things considered."

"It isn't for you to judge them," Cendri said sharply.

"No, damn it," Dal said angrily. "But Mahala is a sensible woman—"

Translation, Cendri supplied to herself not speaking aloud, *Mahala recognizes Dal's superior position and takes it into account, flattering him.* But she did not say so.

"Dal, I was in the ruins, and the Builders *spoke* to Vaniya! They told her where to find the ring and the robe—"

But even as she spoke she saw the skepticism creeping over his face, and sighed. He frowned.

"The Builders *spoke* to her? Oh, come, Cendri!"

"They *did,*" she insisted stubbornly, "I was *there—*"

"So what did they *say* to you?" he demanded, and she sighed, abandoning the effort. How could she communicate to Dal, in words, an experience that was far beyond them, a feeling, an emotion. . . .

"Look, Cendri," he said reasonably, "your pal Vaniya is a consummate hokum artist. She was trying to impress you. Maybe she has some clairvoyance—a lot of people do. But I've been in those ruins, too, day after day. Nobody and nothing ever spoke to *me.*"

She started to say, the Builders never speak to men, and stopped herself, Dal would never believe that. He shook his head in amused contempt.

"Come and sleep, Cendri, you're asleep on your feet . . . wandering all night long in the ruins with Vaniya! If she's found Rezali's ring and robe, you've got to hand it to her, I suppose. I won't deny I'm sorry; Mahala is the kind of person I can get along with, and I was planning, if *she* became High Matriarch, to start laying the groundwork for a fully equipped scientific expedition to come here to work on the ruins. These ruins are older than any civilization I've ever seen or read about; there's a possibility they *are* Builder ruins, if they have actually been preserved by Time stasis or some such thing. A civilization two million years old,

Cendri! And you expect me to pussyfoot around because these stupid women here have made it into a Temple for their idiotic religion?" He shook his head in disbelief. "But Vaniya's a True Believer, and I hate the idea of having to work with *her!*" Abruptly, he stopped his growing excitement and said in a kind tone, "Sweetheart, you're asleep on your feet, come and rest. We'll talk about it later sometime, if you want to."

Later that day, Cendri, who had slept till mid-day, saw the group of Vaniya's household servants and her daughters, returning, carrying with them a great chest which looked, in fact, as if it had been buried for a long time inside a cave, or somewhere equally damp, for the metal fittings were rusted and the outside was covered with a layer of mud. But Miranda told her, exultantly, that it had indeed proved to contain Rezali's genuine ring and her embroidered robe, and that Vaniya had already sent to summon the women of the Council.

"I hope this will be settled before the festival," Miranda said. They were standing on the steps, and Cendri could see, on the road that led past the Pro-Matriarch's residence, more and more men flocking into the city. Cendri felt a sudden inner dread.

Dal was evidently working for the Unity, fomenting rebellion among the men! If he were to encourage rebellion at the time of the festival, when the city was filled with men from the delta and the great dam-building project, he would virtually have an army at his command! Her disquiet increased that night as they sat at their evening meal, and saw Dal and Rhu talking in quiet tones, apart from the women. Rhu had some connection with the underground movement, which she identified only by the password she had heard once or twice: "We were not born in chains."

But—Rhu? The gentle Companion, the musician, the man wholly without violence? He did not take part in athletic contests; he seemed to lack the physical strength which was the most valued sign of maleness here. Could he truly be working for a movement which would have to succeed, if it succeeded at all, only by violence and a bloody *coup d'état?* And would Dal—Master Scholar of University, committed to their ethic of self-determination for all worlds—would Dal ever lend himself to any such thing?

In this world, Dal is legally my property. I am bound to obey the local laws, I will be held responsible for whatever he does. Isn't it my duty to find out? Yet she shrank from the scene she knew Dal would make if she were to question him.

I am a fool, to be frightened of Dal, to be so submissive. I always thought myself any man's equal. Why can I not act that way? Why does the very thought of his anger destroy me this way?

Toward sunset, a messenger came from the Council of Elders; on the morrow, they would meet with Vaniya and her entourage to determine whether the true ring and robe of the High Matriarch had indeed been found. Grimly, Vaniya ordered her strongest women to stand guard over the chest.

"I would not be surprised at all if Mahala sent envoys to steal it," she said, her mouth tight, and glanced at Miranda. "I wish you were past the birthing time; while you are here like this, we are vulnerable—"

Miranda's blue eyes were wide. "You do not believe Mahala would resort to violence, surely?"

"I do not believe she is incapable of it," Vaniya said, troubled.

But the night passed peacefully, and in the morning, Vaniya, accompanied by her older daughters—again, Miranda felt she should not leave the house, since the birth seemed daily imminent—set forth. Cendri, again, was invited to accompany them.

She had a curious sense of repetition, as if she were replaying a tape on her graphics-recorder equipment, as they entered the Hall of Matriarchs, to face the women seated on cushions, while Vaniya solemnly proffered the ring and robe for examination.

Cendri watched Mahala while the Pro-Matriarch took the robe on her lap and unfolded it. She had noted before that there was something feline about the younger Pro-Matriarch; now Cendri had a curious inner picture of a cat with claws extended and every hair on its back rising, as Mahala, her face taut, examined the embroideries.

At last, her eyes narrowed to slits in her triangular face, she said, "It seems, indeed, to be the true copy of Rezali's ring and robe; although you, Vaniya, having seen them on our late High Matriarch's effigy, could have duplicated them—"

Vaniya said dryly, "If after five minutes of examining them through the glass case, I could go home and duplicate them in less than a single day, then I should be superhuman enough that I might indeed make a better High Matriarch than any rival claimant. But I make no claims of more than human power. As you can see from the chest, it has been buried a long time; and this is the authentic ring and robe. I call upon every woman here to acknowledge that I am duly designated by the spirit of our late Mother Rezali, and to acknowledge me as the true and only High Matriarch of the city of Ariadne and the government of Isis."

Mahala leaped to her feet, her eyes flaming in anger.

"This is superstitious flummery," she cried, "I protest! I call for this matter to be settled by the Council, who must acknowledge that I am at least no madwoman! And surely if Vaniya believes that the ghost of a dead woman has whispered to her spirit where she shall find these things—is she fit to rule over us with all the authority of the High Matriarch?"

Vaniya said quietly, "If you will listen to me, my sister, you will see that I made no such claim. I have no notion whether the spirit of Mother Rezali survives anywhere in this world or any other. I simply state that I hold in my hand the authentic ring and robe of the Mother Rezali, and by the custom and tradition of the Matriarchate which we are all here to uphold, the power of the High Matriarch descends to me. I do not really see that there is any further room for debate."

Mahala said, her narrow face flushing, "How came Vaniya by these tokens?"

Vaniya said, "I am not required by custom or tradition to explain this, only to satisfy the Council that they are authentic."

"No," said Mahala angrily, "I question this whole matter. Why should possession of the tokens of the High Matriarch prove that Vaniya would make a better High Matriarch than I? I submit that the Council should settle this matter without reference to this trash!" Angrily she flung the ring across the room, tried to throw the robe after it; it came unfolded and flopped awkwardly into the center of the room, where it lay in a crumpled heap.

Vaniya said quietly, "We have chosen our High Matriarch in this manner for a long time, Mahala, and I for one do not propose to change it. If you had found the true tokens I would willingly have accepted your rule."

"That," said Mahala, harshly, "is because you are a superstitious fool. Why do you think I tried to counterfeit the ridiculous trash? Because it would have saved trouble and given you all—"She flashed a quick look all round the circle of elders, "a chance to accept me because you believed me superior. I demand now that the Council choose which one of us is best fitted to rule over Isis in the place of Mother Rezali, and let us hear no more of spirits and clairvoyants and ghostly counsel!"

Vaniya smiled, a faint contemptuous smile, "But who gave the Council, alone, the right to settle a matter which, if it must be settled this way, should be settled by agreement of every woman on Isis? For that matter, why only the women of Isis? The men are our sons, too, and we are responsible for their material and moral well-being, to say nothing of their spiritual health. If every woman on Isis, and every man, chose Mahala by acclaim, probably I would not object, although I am not sure that the women in the villages know enough about the problems facing us to know which of us is better fitted to handle them—"

"The Council should settle it," Mahala insisted. "They represent the women of their villages—"

"Do they indeed? Nowhere in the founding of the Council has it been agreed that the women of the villages have entrusted it to the women of the Council to choose a High Matriarch to rule over them; and if they did it would still be a mockery." She looked around the Council, and said, "I am not inflexible, nor am I powermaddened, though I am not sure you can say the same about my sister and rival. But if every woman on the Council here agrees that I am not fit, and chooses Mahala for rule, I will withdraw."

"No, indeed," said one of the women, and Mahala said angrily, "I call for majority choice!"

Vaniya sighed and shook her head. "This is a tyranny devised by the maleworlds, Mahala, that a larger force shall enforce their will on a smaller or weaker one. If you can persuade more people to accept your view, does that mean that it is therefore the *right* view, or only that you can make us pretend to accept it lest we be ill-used by the majority? Do you wish to undermine the whole ethical basis of the Matriarchate, my sister?"

Mahala said inflexibly, "I do not feel it is right that our High Matriarch should be chosen by a superstitious ritual which no sane woman on Isis continues to accept."

Vaniya smiled. "I think I am a sane woman. Will you come to We-were-guided with me, and test the evidence of your senses?"

"In such a matter," Mahala said, "I do not trust my senses."

Vaniya asked, "What do you trust?" The question was mild, interested; it was not a challenge, but it put Mahala on the defensive. "I trust the will of the women of Isis," she said angrily, and Vaniya said thoughtfully, "Even those who have not been trained to think of such things, because they have been taught that we are willing to take on ourselves this heavy burden? Had they all been trained from girlhood to assume for themselves the burden of our world's fate, then perhaps—but they have not. I will not lay it down until I am assured that they are able and willing to take it upon themselves."

One of the women of the Council said quietly, "We could continue to argue this point for the rest of the season, and no other work would be done. How shall we resolve this? Our decisions have always been made by custom and tradition; by this method, we have no choice but to choose Vaniya as High Matriarch." She raised her hand as Mahala opened her mouth to protest, and said, "No—wait. Mahala too has justice on her side; if too many of the educated women of Isis have come to distrust our traditions, they are no longer a sound guide for judgment. A custom is no longer a custom when only a few of the old women accept it. And yet the festival is upon us, the city is filled with men, and the women are preparing to visit the sea; and this debate leaves our people motherless while we sit and debate how we shall choose a foster mother for our women, and for our men too. We cannot accept Vaniya's rule if Mahala refuses to swear loyalty, even if these tokens—" reverently, she went and picked them up, folding the robe and laying it back in the chest, "no longer serve as basis for the choice. Nor can we accept Mahala's rule, unless Vaniya can cede her claim and swear loyalty."

Heavily, Vaniya shook her head. It seemed to Cendri that she spoke with regret. "I cannot obey a decision which violates my conscience and the ethical basis of the Matriarchate. I cannot agree until we have reached a decision which satisfies the conscience of every woman in this chamber—" she looked slowly from face to face, "and does not impose a violation of conscience, undesired, on anyone outside it."

Mahala flickered a catlike smile. She said, "And while we await the struggle with a hundred thousand consciences, we enter the festival motherless, and the business of Isis, trade with the Unity, the disposition of a hundred small matters in the city and the country, must all await these hundreds upon thousands of individual consciences?"

Cendri thought, it was the old argument between majority rule, anarchy or tyranny, the age-old struggle between efficiency and personal liberty. Most societies sacrificed something on both sides and accepted a form of participatory democracy; the tyrants sacrificed personal freedom, the anarchists sacrificed efficiency. Every form of government had its price.

But governments changed. And this one, after a long period of changelessness, seemed to be changing, to be demanding more efficiency—or was it only Mahala and a fractional small few who were changing?

Vaniya said, quietly, "I do not think the problems of trade and industry must all be settled overnight. The Unity has been there for centuries and will be there in another season, or another Long Year. There is no reason to make a hasty settlement which will demand to be settled again when all emotional reactions have stabilized. I suggest that for the moment my sister and I continue as Pro-Matriarchs, as we have done during all these moons of Rezali's illness."

But the festival! Are the men to be motherless at our highest festival?" demanded one of the women. And Vaniya said, "Since Mahala has spoken of our faith as superstition, perhaps it would not trouble her too greatly if I were to assume the burdens of officiating at the festival this year?"

Mahala shrugged. She said, "That part of a High Matriarch's duties, indeed, I am more than willing to cede to any who believes in it. Indeed, if I am chosen High Matriarch, my first act will be to appoint a High Priestess to deal with these matters, so that I may spend my time upon important matters of state. My fellow Pro-Matriarch may indeed take upon herself these duties for the moment."

Vaniya said with equal calm, "This attitude—that you will separate such duties—is the main reason why I cannot accept you as High Matriarch, my sister. But since I firmly believe that in the end the women of Isis will confirm my right to the High Matriarch's powers, I feel it my duty to take this part of them upon myself. Is this agreeable to all of you?"

One after another, the women nodded in agreement, until one woman said, "It must be perfectly clear that the matter is not yet settled! There are many who will believe that Vaniya's appearance as priestess at the festival will prejudice Mahala's eventual right to make such a claim for herself!"

Vaniya frowned slightly, but she said, "So be it; I shall officiate only as Pro-Matriarch, and not as High Matriarch. Is this sufficient?"

Mahala laughed. She said, "Do you really think anyone here, or any of the women of the households in the city, or any of the men who are coming in their hundreds into the city to visit the sea—do you really think any of them cares about the ceremonies in the Temples, or anything else? You know as well as I do, what they care about, Vaniya, and I hope to live to a day when all of these ceremonies are stripped of the ceremony and religious custom we have woven around them, and reduced to their essential social usefulness."

Vaniya asked gently, "As they have done in the maleworlds, Mahala?"

Mahala's laugh was like breaking glass. She said, "I do not believe—as you apparently do, Vaniya—that the maleworlds of the Unity have a monopoly on common sense, or that the women of Isis cannot show ourselves as practical as they are."

Vaniya rose to leave the hall. She walked gently over to Mahala and laid her hands on the other woman's shoulders. She said in a soft, kindly voice, "And when we have done so, Mahala, when we have stripped our society of everything which does not contribute to our material and social well-being, when we have the ultimate in a practical and common-sense culture— then, my dear sister, my dear colleague, how will what

we have differ from the worlds we find where men rule?
What then, Mahala, my sister? What then?"

Mahala blinked, without answering; but Vaniya
dropped her hands and walked away, leaving the other
Pro-Matriarch staring after her.

chapter eleven

ALL THE LONG DAY OF ISIS THE CEREMONIES HAD BEEN
going on. Cendri had gone to see the ceremonies in the
great hall of the High Matriarch's Residence, where
women draped the statues of the past Matriarchs with
flowers in the Hall of Matriarchs, and joined the crowds
where, for the first time since she had been in the city of
Ariadne, men mingled with women in the crowds in the
streets. All that day a suffused excitement had been
growing.

Greatly daring, Cendri had strung her voice-scriber
around her neck, wishing that she could record the
ceremonies with a graphics recorder, to play them back
at her leisure and try to decide for herself what they
meant. Again and again in the streets she saw the men
exchange the greeting, "We were not born in chains,"
but she was aware that she was probably the only
woman who had noticed. On Isis, it seemed, men were
so unimportant that no woman *noticed* what a man did
unless he was directly speaking to her, or otherwise
concerned with her.

It was late in the afternoon when they returned to the Pro-Matriarch's Residence. Miranda made a few minutes to speak to Cendri.

"You are to join in the festival? I thought you would. Think of me while the men are spear-fishing . . . I feel guilty that I am keeping our house midwife from the festival. She says I may give birth tonight, but she has said that every night for the last moon, and I still drag around like this," Miranda said, sighing. "I long for it to be over, I was sure that by now I would have my child at my breast."

"Will you be alone here, then, Miranda, with only the midwife? I will stay and keep you company, if you really want me to—"

"No, no, my friend," Miranda said, laughing. "There will be a good dinner, a festival meal, served here tonight for little children, girls and boys too young for festival, for women-by-courtesy like Maret, and for Companions . . . and for women like myself, too pregnant to spend the night on the shore! We will simply join in the children's festival and make the night a merry one for them while the other women are away." She smiled, hesitated and said, "Rhu has promised he will stay near me, so I will not be lonely—Cendri, I could not say that to anyone else, I am so glad there is someone who does not think it a kind of madness. . . ."

Cendri pressed her friend's hand without speaking. Miranda's predicament seemed perfectly normal to her; but in Miranda's own society, it was indeed considered a kind of insanity; that she might prefer the company of a man to the company of women. But tonight, then, she would see what were the normal relationships between the sexes, which began with the curious ritual they called "visiting the sea." She had heard this morning something like a sermon, which reminded the women, flocked into the square before the Residence, that all life came from the sea and that they must return there to pay homage to the source.

All of the women of the household, in readiness for the festival, had put on long robes, embroidered with patterns of fish and flowers. Miranda had lent Cendri one of her festival dresses, and as she put it on, Cendri speculated about what she would see. She wondered if the men accompanied the women home at sunrise; this might explain why Companions were not expected to join in the festival, while all other men, and women, visited the sea at this time. It would have seemed more rational, if it was a form of visitational marriage—there were any number of such societies—for *all* the men to join in this form of blessing their mating rituals—but then, the society of Isis was not rational.

She said aloud to Dal, "I wish I could dare to take along a graphics recorder. If Laurina didn't know what it was, I just might, but she does."

Dal came and hugged her. He said, "I know this means a lot to you, Cendri, to be invited to go along and watch their top-level festival. I don't know anything much about anthropology and I don't really care that much, but I hope you find out all you want to know."

She hugged him hard in return. It was so rare now that they could communicate like this, without jangling or quarreling. This world, she thought, is having a bad effect on us. Is it just culture shock, or is it the strain on him of living where he's a woman's property? She said, "I'm sorry the festival kept you away from your work, Dal!"

He smiled and patted her. He said, "Oh, I have days and days of work just correlating what I have done already, don't worry about it. When things settle down after the festival, we'll get back out in the ruins. Did you notice how the men today came up to stare? Some of them looked at me the way Laurina looks at you—hero worship! I suppose it's because I'm that legendary thing, a free male. I've been talking to Rhu a lot. He feels inferior, poor kid, just because he's not the athletic type. With his talents, damn it, he feels guilty because he couldn't join in that damned athletic contest and win Vaniya a prize and let her cheer for him!"

"He looks strong enough," Cendri commented. "Obviously he wouldn't make a wrestler, or a boxer, but I'd think he'd make a good runner or hurdler!"

Dal shook his head. "He tells me he was ill as a child and has been a weakling ever since; that is why he was allowed to cultivate his musical talents. Sounds like a form of rheumatic fever to me, a weakened heart. Shocking, not to repair that sort of thing, but I gather it's not part of their social ethic. Pioneer used to be like that, lots of emphasis on survival of the fittest; and my own grandfather never could adapt to the fact that I wanted to be a scholar; if I'd taken up music or painting he never would have survived the shock! Our family were all space engineers, that was his idea of a man's job. I can understand it on Pioneer, but it's funny to find it here."

Cendri said, "The first High Matriarch was a woman of Pioneer, hundreds of years ago."

"Is that a fact?" He smiled, his eyebrows raised. "I've read about the position of women on Pioneer in those days; I'm not surprised that the revolt of the women started there, or that their society embodies the feeling that if men once get the upper hand, women wind up in trouble. But they don't realize that men's societies have changed, too." He glanced at the window. "Love, there are a lot of women gathering on the lawn, you'd better go and enjoy your festival."

She hesitated a minute, holding him, reluctant to interrupt this rare moment of togetherness and content. "You really don't mind being alone?"

He laughed. "Not at all, when you're in a group of women like that! Laurina may have a lot of hero worship for you, but she's probably too much in awe of you to make any—any proposals, and I doubt if you have any yen for little girls like that! Run along and enjoy yourself, sweetheart. I gather the kids in the house have a festival of their own, and maybe Rhu, or Miranda, will sing for us. Or," he grinned, "maybe they'll be holding their own festival somewhere!"

Miranda's secret was not hers to share. She said,

"Maybe," and stood on tiptoe to kiss him. "Good night, Dal. I may be very late."

On the lawns before the Residence she found the women gathering, all wearing the festival costumes embroidered with fish, flowers, queer sea-creatures. Laurina rushed up to her and caught her hand.

"Your festival gown is lovely—oh, it is Miranda's? Come, the sun is dropping close to the horizon, we must be there before moonrise, and I want to watch the spear-fishing."

The sun touched the horizon. As they went down to the shoreline, below them they could see great fires built all along the beach, and dark figures clustered at the edge of the sea, where a full high tide lapped high up along the tidewater-mark. As Cendri came closer she saw that they were all men, bare arms and bare legs glinting in the moonlight, wet with the surf; a few wore breechclouts or loincloths, but most were completely naked, except for heavy plastic sandals that protected their feet from the sharp rocks. As she watched, one of the men—she was almost sure she had seen him a few days ago in the arena, strutting and preening himself after the wrestling—picked up a long spear. The light from the fires gleamed along the point of a barbed metal tip. He pulled a mask down over his face, ran out splashing into the waves, and when they were breast-high, plunged face-down into the water. Others ran after him, until the water was filled with the splashing naked forms and their spears.

Laurina guided her to the fire where the women sat in a group, silent, watching the men. Cendri recalled Miranda in the pearl-divers' village, talking of the spear-fishing—*blood must not be shed in Her holy waters* . . . but for this season evidently taboos were broken. Were *required* to be broken.

A long time the dark forms plunged and waded and splashed in and out of the surf, flung silvery fish on the shore where their scales gleamed brilliantly silver-blue and slowly dulled. A group of women were cleaning and scraping the fish, wrapping them in scented leaves, burying them in the coals as the fire died down. After a long time the smell of cooking fish and the strong fragrance of the fish-flavoring herbs began to mingle with the scent of the smoke. The larger moon floated, huge and golden, high above the water, making a bright pathway across the waves. The tide went out and the wet sands lay glistening; high at the zenith the smaller moon floated, a gilt dish with soft shadows across its face.

The women watched the men coming up from the water, moonlight striking sparks on the metal tips of their spears. The women struck up a song; it sounded to Cendri like a hymn, but it was full of archaic words in a dialect she did not understand completely and she could only make out the refrain.

"Wounding is the nature of love. . . ."

Someone put a plate of fish into Cendri's hands. She ate, like the others, with her fingers. The men did not join them at the fire. A moonlight picnic . . . strange, for a ritual of mating, or fertility ritual. Or perhaps not so strange; the fires, the lapping waves, the dark solemn faces of the men gleaming and wet by the moonlight. The fires died down, and the women drew closer together around the coals. Cendri felt sleepy, but even so she could sense the hush of expectancy around the circle of women. What now? The moons were high in the sky, drawing closer and closer.

Then she saw them coming, a long solemn line, up from the shore. Cendri heard some woman—a very young one by the sound—giggling nervously, and someone near her reproved her in a whisper. At her side Cendri felt Laurina's fingers clutch at her arm, with a deep, convulsive gasp. And suddenly Cendri understood.

So *this* is how men and women come together. Solemnly, by moonlight, in ritual: "visiting the sea." She should have known. Miranda's jokes about fish dinners. And now she was here, a part of it. Something in Cendri panicked, cried out to her wildly to get away, she had no part in this, she could not . . . yet some

other part of her was excited and exhilarated, wanting
to see it through, knowing that anyway there was no
way she could remove herself now from the women of
Isis, clustered here and awaiting their seasonal ritual of
mating. An errant thought touched her mind, *I am an
anthropologist, I wanted to study their customs,* and
then, with secret hilarity, *it's called participant observation.*

Suddenly the male forms were looming over them.
Cendri braced herself, telling herself firmly not to
panic, she could endure the experience; an anthropologist studying planetary cultures got into stranger things
than this, her own Mentor had studied among the
Koridorni and had found himself joining in their ritual
cannibalism. . . .

A man was kneeling on the sand before her, his face
indistinct in the moonlight. His voice was husky and
tentative, and Cendri somehow judged that he was very
young.

"In the name of the Goddess who has bidden us to
visit the sea. . . ."

Cendri thought there was probably a ritual answer,
but she didn't know it. It didn't seem to matter. He put
his arms around her, drawing her down on the cool
sand.

She had expected, feared, something cold and impersonal, a ritual brutality like rape, had braced herself to
endure that. Her preconceptions melted away before
the gentleness of the man whose face she never saw.
His hands on her were clumsy, yet tender; his body on
hers warm and inviting. Her dread melted away; she
welcomed him into herself, giving herself over to the
night and to the soft sounds all around her. Laurina was
close, so close that she could have touched the other
woman, she could hear the sounds and almost feel the
movements of the other's lovemaking. It didn't seem to
matter.

In one small part of her mind she was amazed and
shamed. She had had a lover or two, before Dal, but
they both came from monogamous societies and since

her marriage she had been faithful, neither desiring nor seriously paying attention to any other man. She thought almost regretfully of Dal, but on a deeper level something in Cendri desired just this, accepted it.

At last he moved a little apart from her, but still holding her in the curve of his arm, lightly touching her hair, her breasts. He murmured, "My name is Yan; may I know yours, to treasure it in memory when I have returned to the Men's House?"

Cendri started to speak her name; remembered that all the female names here were three-syllabeled, amended it slightly: "Cendriya."

He repeated it in a whisper. "Lovely, and strange. I shall cherish the memory." He laid something in her hand; it was a chain of carven leather. A belt, a headband? "My gift to you," he whispered, and was gone.

A *sea-gift*. And this was how Miranda had passed off Rhu's fine pearl. Cendri lay back on the sand, weighing the strange experience. Then she was aware of another dark form, kneeling, whispering:

"In the name of the Goddess who has bidden us to visit the sea. . . ."

After the fourth time, during that long night, she stopped trying to count the men who came silently out of the dark, whispering their ritual greeting. Afterward there was always the whispered exchange of names, and each of them left her a gift; a necklace of shells, a small jewel—she could not see it in the dark—on a fine chain; a polished carving of glinting nacre; one, who seemed hardly out of childhood, left her a garland of ribbon which, he told her, he had won in the arena in the boy's foot-race. Some of them left her quickly after the ritual exchange of names; others lingered for a few moments, to lie close to her in tenderness, holding her close and murmuring; one or two talked a little. One man told her that he was working on the delta dam project, south of Ariadne, and that he was the leader of a group of a dozen men there; he talked, troubled and almost compulsively, of a comrade of his who had had his foot crushed in a rockslide and been unable to come to the festival. "We promised each other we would go together," he told her, almost weeping, and Cendri did not know what to say to comfort him. She found herself wondering, briefly, and troubled, if the men paired off as the women did, in long-term partnerships. On the whole she thought probably not; nest-building was a female instinct. But they evidently formed deep and lasting ties.

Another, the very young man who would later give her his athlete's prize, wept for a few moments against her breast, saying that she reminded him of his mother, that he had been in the Men's House only a few moons. Cendri thought it was a strange compliment, until she remembered Rhu's song:

> Twice have I been driven from paradise;
> Once when I left my Mother's womb,
> And again when I was driven
> From my Mother's house. . . .

Here, perhaps, the image of the mother was deep-rooted, ineradicable; every contact with women restimulated the memory of the lost paradise of living in a world of women, every woman would become a search for the Mother. And indeed, in a society where no one could possibly know who had fathered any child—now she understood Miranda's bewilderment at the question—no tie existed save that of the Mother. And there was, in fact, nothing to prevent a grown son from meeting his mother in this way . . . no incest taboo. She cradled the sobbing boy against her breast, and strangely thought that some day she would like to have a child there . . . he calmed, at last, and began kissing her breasts in a most unfilial way.

At last the first glimmer of dawn showed in the sky; Cendri could clearly see the face of the last man who came to her; he was the only one who did not delay to ask her name, simply pressed a beautiful shell into her hand, kissed her long and tenderly, and went quickly away. The men gathered silently on the shore, took up their masks and spears and melted into the rising sun.

Cendri lay on the sand, listening to the tide slowly lapping toward the full again. The women drew together around the cold ashes of the fire, in a close group. Cendri felt Laurina's arms tighten around her, her face against Cendri's, and for some strange reason, wanted to cry. Around her the women were clustered, hugging one another, snuggling together in each other's arms, and Cendri understood; this too was a part of ritual, a ceremonial reaffirming that after the bonds of mating, the deepest and truest ties of the women of Isis were with one another.

Laurina, her face against Cendri's whispered, "I hope I have a baby this time . . . I came away empty last season, I thought my heart would break . . . my daughter is already in her tenth year, I long for a little one. . . ."

Cendri held her tight, murmuring, "I hope you do, if that is what you want." Oddly, and only for a moment, she found herself wishing that she could be pregnant. It could not happen, of course. When she and Dal had agreed to delay childbearing, they had each taken medical treatments to abolish their fertility for a time. Since they were monogamous, Dal had offered to have himself temporarily sterilized and save her the physical side-effects of the treatment. But she had chosen to share the treatment, and though Dal had not been happy about her choice—men of Pioneer took it for granted that they would be the custodian of their wives' fertility—he knew it was not the custom on Cendri's world.

And if he had not conceded her right to take responsibility for her own fertility, she would have been vulnerable now to pregnancy. So that by giving her the choice, he had saved himself possible humiliation; their marriage had included an agreement that she would not bear any child not of his fathering. Would she ever be able to tell Dal about any of this?

She did not protest when she felt herself drawn into a

close embrace, felt Laurina's kiss like a lover's on her mouth. She had been too shaken, too surprised by the strangeness of this ritual mating on the sand, to find the sort of pleasure she normally took in sex; surprised, shocked at herself, she discovered that the woman's touch was bringing her to the release which tension and uncertainty had denied her before. In a surge of tenderness she found herself reciprocating, felt a curious shaken delight as the other woman trembled and cried out under her caresses.

Dal, she thought with last-minute compunction, would probably think this was worse than the fact that I had sex with eleven, or was it thirteen, men tonight. But she no longer cared. Her last waking thought was, *Why should I care what any man thinks?* and even then there was a faint flicker of surprise at it. Then she slept a little, beside Laurina, cradled close in each other's arms.

chapter twelve

THE SUN WAS HIGH WHEN SHE WOKE. ALL AROUND HER women were slowly coming awake, gathering up the small piles of gifts, and concealing them within the folds of their robes as they made their way back to their homes. Cendri woke and sat watching for a moment, then shook her head in amazement, hardly able to realize that she had been a part of it. At her side, Laurina said softly, "I must go back to the city, and see how my daughter fares; she is still a year or two too young for the festival. Will you need my aid at We-were-guided today, Scholar Dame?"

Cendri knew why Laurina had spoken formally, and smiled, touching her hand in kindly reassurance. She said, "Not today, I think, I want to sleep. Tomorrow, Laurina."

All around her the women of Vaniya's household were making their way up from the shore. Cendri joined them, realizing that her festival gown was soiled and bedraggled, and that she was covered with sand. She wanted a bath and a long sleep. It was still very early; no one was about in the downstairs hallway but a few small children, and Miranda, cross-legged on the floor, dabbing listlessly at a screen with watercolor paints adorning it with small delicately-drawn fish and flowers.

Cendri said, "I had hoped your child would be born last night, Miranda!"

Miranda sighed and said, "For a time I thought so, but it was only another false alarm, I did the same with my first child, false labor every day for twenty or thirty days." Cendri had not even known that Miranda had another child, so much had been made of her present child being Vaniya's heir; she said so, and Miranda shrugged listlessly.

"It was only a male; Lialla looks after it much of the time, as she seems to be barren, and Zamila has no daughters either. But Maret has predicted that this will be a daughter." She sighed again. "So the midwife is provoked at me because she missed the festival for nothing, and did not even drink much lest she should have to work later; and Rhu is sulking—there is a proverb, as sullen as a Companion on festival-morning—go and sleep, Cendri, I am not fit company for any woman on this morning!" She laughed a little at herself, but she looked wretched and weary.

"That is a pretty screen you are painting," Cendri said, and Miranda frowned almost angrily. "Such children's work serves to pass the time, and now I am

not supposed to do anything more strenuous than this!"
A small child ran up to her, tangled in a wet breech-
clout, and Miranda snapped at it as she dragged herself
upright and hauled it, in no pleasant mood, off to be
changed and dried.

Cendri went up to her room, feeling exhausted and
let down, all the exhilaration of the night evaporating.
Dal still slept in his corner; Cendri put away the little
pile of sea-gifts in her personal luggage-case without
examining them. Some day, she knew, she would want
to take them out again, look them over, study them,
examine as a scientist, examine their psychological
meaning to the men of Isis and to the women who
received them, but for the moment she was too
emotionally involved with the memory to be detached,
and she was sure she would not want to look at them for
a long, long time.

She was tempted simply to fling herself down beside
Dal and sleep again, but her festival gown was so
bedraggled that she wanted to take it off, and that once
done, she felt so gritty and soiled with sand and
seaweed that she wanted to bathe. Before she had
finished Dal came in and stood beside the running
shower.

"How was the festival, Cendri? Interesting?"

She pretended not to hear him over the noise of the
shower as she carefully soaped the sand and grime from
her hair, enjoying the luxurious bathing facilities of the
suite. When she stepped out, wrapping herself in a
robe, he repeated the question and she discovered that
she was reluctant to say anything at all. She merely
shrugged.

"It was interesting enough. I know you aren't
interested in the anthropological aspects, Dal, so I
won't bore you with them. There was a moonlight
dinner on the shore, and spearfishing, which is only
allowed at festivals. We cooked the fish and ate it."

He scowled. "Something Rhu let drop—I understand
it's a kind of fertility ritual! You didn't take part, did
you?"

She found herself remembering Miranda's phrase, *sullen as a Companion on festival morning*. She thought, suddenly, that she would like to tell Dal all about it, share it—but he was a man of Pioneer; he would never understand how she had felt about it, he would never see anything except that she had been unfaithful to him. She knew he could have tolerated a deeply emotional episode, as he would have expected her to tolerate a genuine love affair on his part; but he could never have understood this kind of simple, undiscriminating sexuality.

He noticed that she had not answered and his frown deepened.

"Cendri, tell me about it!" he demanded, "Fertility rituals on undeveloped planets are all indecent! If you're not ashamed of it, why don't you want to tell me about it?"

Suddenly she was angry. "Because I know perfectly well you wouldn't understand," she flared at him, "You've made it very clear that you regard all these things as senseless native customs and superstition; I'm not going to hold it up for you to ridicule!"

"Cendri, we agreed to share our work—"

"Share be damned!" She was really angry now. "What you mean by sharing is that you tell me what to do and we do it! If you feel like it, that is! You won't say a word about what you're doing with the men, and every time I ask, you tell me to mind my own business, keep out of it! You have refused to let me know anything of what you are doing among the men; how dare you question my work among the women?"

"Cendri," he said quietly, very sober, "if I do not confide in you about my work among the men, it is only to protect you. I think you can guess that it would be dangerous."

"So much for your talk of sharing," she flung at him, surprised at herself for what was surfacing in her now. "If I were truly your equal, Dal, and not just your—your pawn, your figurehead—you would be willing to share risks as well as triumphs! The real reason you will

not share it with me is because you know that what you
are doing is not lawful! Are you trying to start a civil
war on this world?"

"That only shows me that you would never understand."

"Where is your integrity as a Scholar of University?
One of the reasons why the Scholars of University are
so highly regarded as scientists is because they are
above the petty politics within the Unity—"

"We are outside the Unity, Cendri. And how can
you—you of all people—reprove me for taking part in
politics, when you have allied yourself so firmly with
Vaniya and *her* party? If the ruins at We-were-guided
are truly Builder ruins—I don't think you understand
even now what that means, Cendri! Do you realize that
they are the most important artifacts ever discovered in
the known universe, then? Isis *must* be made part of the
Unity, by any means possible! This is the scientific
discovery of the aeon—don't you even *realize* that?
What do the politics of the Matriarchy mean, stacked
up in the scale against *that?*"

She cried, shaken, "And you'd destroy the whole
culture of Isis for your damned Ruins, just to be the
man who opened them to the Unity, just for your own
personal ambition?"

"And you call yourself a scientist!" he stared at her
in scorn and the beginnings of contempt. "I don't
believe you even *care* about the Ruins, Cendri!"

She didn't know what she was going to say until she
heard herself saying it.

"Not in the way you do, no—I don't give a damn!
You don't know half as much as I do about the ruins at
We-were-guided, because you never believe in anything you can't weigh and measure! They mean more to
me than they can ever mean to you! You just see them
as a dead culture, you would let in every Scholar and
scientist and gaping tourist in the Unity, to break into
them, trample all over them, just for your own personal
ambition. I don't give a damn about the ruins, Dal, I

am interested in something more important than that! And I'm not going along with some stupid man's idea of what ought to be done with them! Now get out of here! I want to sleep!"

"Cendri—" be begged, troubled.

"No! Damn it, Dal, get out of here and let me alone!" She wrapped herself in the toweling robe, and threw herself down to sleep. Dal said her name again, kneeling beside her, but she did not raise her head, closing her eyes resolutely. It had felt good, for once to speak her mind to him, to give voice to all the hostility she had been suppressing ever since she came here, his contempt for her own work, the way in which he made her pay for every slight and humiliation the society of Isis put in him. She felt purged and honest. A trace of contrition stirred briefly in her—had she been too hard on him? No, he had deserved every harsh word she had spoken, and she would not undo it all and capitulate again. *As sullen as a Companion on festival morning.* It was just offended male pride. He'd get over it, and then she would speak more moderately, too. Firmly ignoring him, she drifted off to sleep.

She slept for hours, until she was jolted awake by a screen, falling over near her bed. Earthquake, again? She heard small children crying out, and flung on a garment to run downstairs; but evidently the fallen screens were the only damage, and Cendri went back up to dress. It was near evening. Dal was nowhere in the suite. Feeling faintly guilty at the memory of her harsh words, she resolved to hunt him up, tell him as much as he wanted to know about the festival, compound their differences somehow. But he was nowhere in the house, either.

It was too late, in any case, to do anything in the Ruins that day; everyone in Vaniya's household was engaged in clearing up after the festival. It had been silly of her not to share everything with him. He was a scientist, not a man of the Pioneer of five generations ago! He might be distressed that she had gotten herself into the situation without fully understanding it, but he would certainly understand why she could not have withdrawn, once committed.

Anyway, if he was angry, he was angry; what was done could not be changed, and she didn't have to fear his anger. Then she began to worry. Just before she had silenced him, sent him away in anger, he had been trying to communicate with her, to tell her something. Her own nervous guilt, based on his questions about the festival had not recognized until now that he had left that topic and had been trying to tell her something else. But what? Had she really begun thinking like these women of Isis, that whatever a man had to say, it could not be important to her? In any case, anger or no, misunderstanding or no, they must talk seriously about what he was doing among the men. It might be personally dangerous, and she had a duty to share whatever risks were involved.

If she had listened, encouraged Dal to tell her more, from the beginning . . . Cendri grew more and more troubled as Dal did not return. He was nowhere in the house; he was not on the shore with the men servants who were clearing away the wood ashes from the dead fires, he was not in the Ruins, for one of Vaniya's women told her that no one had entered We-were-guided that day. He was not at dinner either, and Vaniya smiled when she inquired if anyone had seen him.

"No doubt it has run away to sulk, my dear; but did you not give it permission to leave the grounds? Our Punishment House is at your disposal if you wish to discipline it," Vaniya remarked. But where Vaniya saw only a question of discipline, Cendri was deeply troubled for Dal's safety. Had he been detected in his plotting? Was he somewhere encouraging revolt or riot among the men, and what would they do to him if it was discovered?

Or—worse—had he run away to confer with Mahala, to join her party? Were she and Dal actually to line up on opposing sides of the political situation on Isis? The thought sent a shudder of horror through her. As a scientist of University she—and Dal—were supposed to be above local politics. Dal had already violated that regulation. Must she do it too? Or—Cendri had been trained into rigid intellectual honesty—had she already violated it, or seemed to do so, out of her deep personal affection for Vaniya and Miranda? Had Dal mistaken this for a kind of political commitment? She must make it clear that it was personal. . . .

Miranda was not at dinner, either. Lialla told her that Miranda was in bed, with the midwife nearby. . . . "But I think it is only another false alarm." Lialla said, resigned. "Her first child was many, many days past the proper time; almost all of those who became pregnant from last winter-festival have already borne their babes, but Miranda is always slow. Some women simply do this."

It was a silent and, generally, a glum meal, the women mostly tired and suffering from lack of sleep. Vaniya, irritable at the silences, asked Rhu to sing, and he said sullenly that his throat was sore and his *lyrik* out of tune. "However," he said, making an effort to be pleasant, "I shall apply myself to composing a song as birth-gift for the Lady Miranda, since she takes pleasure in my poor songs."

Cendri, watching him, thought, why, he really *cares* about Miranda, he's worried about her, as worried as if he *were* the father of her child. Or is it just that *anything* to do with Miranda involves him, emotionally, and he knows he must conceal it? If romantic love is a perversion for women in this world, how much more for men! Pitying Rhu, she knew she pitied herself.

Dal did not return all that night. Cendri slept poorly, rousing again and again, thinking she heard his step in the suite, every small sound anywhere in the house of women, a restless child crying, anyone moving about on the lower floors, disturbing her light sleep. Where was Dal? What had become of him? Was he somewhere in a Punishment House, having broken all unknowing one of the many rules for men on this world?

Long before dawn, sleep deserted her entirely; she sat by the window, looking down into the ruins of We-were-guided, deeply troubled. Her growing insensitivity to Dal's needs had driven him away from her, and now where was he?

Had she really, as Dal had accused, been corrupted by the society of the women of Isis? No, she realized; not really. The Matriarchate had only given a form and expression to a hostility which had—she now knew—begun long before they came here. A resentment, that she had given up her own ambitions to be Scholar Dame, fearing Dal's jealousy; that she had taken time off, after her marriage. But Dal had never asked it of her. It had been her own idea. If Dal had wanted a submissive woman, all the women of Pioneer, trained to it for centuries, and not yet taking full advantage of their freedom, had been at his disposal. He had chosen *her* instead.

And when he forgot, when he fell into old habits from Pioneer, it was for me to protest; not to submit, stifling resentment, until the inevitable explosion. I was not honest with him. Have we lost each other now, forever?

When the sun rose, red and dripping with sea-fog, peering through the cloudbank over the shore like a weeping eye, Cendri was exhausted and frightened. Laurina came early, ready to accompany Cendri to the ruins; but by then Cendri knew what she must do.

She told Laurina of Dal's disappearance. "I am afraid that he, unused to the laws of Isis, has somehow gotten into trouble," she told the younger woman, "and that he is somewhere in a Punishment House. You have been around Mahala's faction. . . . she has some connection with your college, does she not?" Laurina nodded, and Cendri said, "Can you find out what has become of him?"

"I would do more than that for you, Cendri, but why

is it so important to you?" Laurina actually seemed a little jealous, "I am here to give you what help you need."

For a moment Cendri desperately wanted to pour out the truth. She was so tired of this imposture, so weary of the pretense that she was the Scholar Dame archaeologist who knew all, and Dal her unregarded assistant—but tardy caution prevailed; the words, once spoken, could not be recalled. Would these women of Isis despise her if she was only some man's assistant? She said slowly, "Dal's aid is indispensable to me; his special training on University makes it impossible for me to work efficiently without—it—at my side."

Laurina grimaced slightly and said, "It must be hard for the women of University, but after all it is one of the maleworlds. Well, Cendri, I will go and inquire in Mahala's faction. But what makes you think it might have gone to them?"

"One of Mahala's men—anyhow, marked with her tattoo of ownership—came to speak with Dal, secretly," Cendri confessed. "I warned Dal about conspiring with men, but he may not have understood how serious this was." Half-truths; she knew Laurina did not understand, but the woman was content with the explanation and set off for the city.

Cendri was too distraught to work; she even absented herself from Vaniya's dinner-table that night, sending the excuse that she was not feeling well. She spent the evening looking through her notes from the ruins, and writing, in the undecipherable-to-outsiders script of her homeworld, all that she could remember of the ceremony of visiting the sea, knowing she must do so before the memory blurred in her mind. She found it was an exercise in self-control and discipline, but she did not spare herself, even writing down the shaming memory of how she had reacted sexually to Laurina's embraces when the ceremony was ended, firmly forcing herself to make a note of the fact that she had felt ashamed. She realized that her intellectual awareness, that sexual moralities were purely a cultural imprint, did nothing to minimize them for her personally. Afterward she noted, with wry amusement, that the attempt to force herself into clinical detachment from the reaction had given her a very real headache, and in the end she took a sleeping pill, for the first time since she had come to Isis, willing to face the danger of sleeping through an earthquake, or being hard to wake if there was news of Dal, rather than lie awake for hours juggling guilt and fear and the attempt at a scientist's discipline.

The next morning Miranda was still abed, and Laurina came to tell Cendri that as far as she could discover, none of Mahala's people had seen Dal there. "It is not in their Punishment House, nor hidden in their Men's House," she said, "A schoolmate of mine is in charge of their Men's House and I asked her to make an excuse to call a search of the Men's House for concealed contraband, things men are not allowed to keep. So it is not concealed there."

But then where *was* Dal? Cendri was beginning to be seriously frightened. Late that morning, knowing that it was a minor breach of Matriarchal etiquette but by now too troubled to care, she went up to Rhu's quarters. She found the Companion, barefoot and wearing an old and rumpled kilt, his face for once unpainted, bending over his *lyrik*, searching for chords. Was he working on Miranda's song? His face was sullen, but he bowed to her with respect.

"How may I serve the Scholar Dame?"

She said straightforwardly, "My Companion has disappeared. I do not believe he has gone willingly; I am afraid he may have broken some law unwittingly and is being held somewhere, in trouble. Can you help me?"

Rhu's face was closed and unrevealing. He said, "This much I will tell you; he went willingly. Beyond that, you cannot expect me to betray a fellow male. I know that our customs are strange to you, Scholar

Dame, and I am not offended that you ask, but I cannot answer further."

She stared at him in shock and dismay. Somehow, knowing his secret and Miranda's, she had not expected he would draw this barrier down between them. She said, in distress, "Rhu—can't I talk to you simply as a fellow human being, as an equal? Can't you understand that my concern is for Dal, and he is your friend?"

Rhu's mouth tightened, bitterly. He said, "No master can talk as an equal to a slave. I know you are concerned to protect him, you want him back mostly for your own concerns; to be the kind of man I am. If he has escaped into freedom, even though I cannot, I will rejoice for him and never betray him."

Shocked, Cendri said, "He was free on University; he is free here; he will be free again—"

Rhu made a wry face, "Would you really have taken him back there, Scholar Dame, knowing now the pleasure of having him a thing and a toy for your sport? At first I thought there was a different kind of relationship between you. Now—" his narrow shoulders lifted in a shrug. He said, "I am only a man; I know nothing more. Will you have me tortured, to tell what little I might know more than this? It would be useless. Perhaps he has told you; my heart is weak, I would die under the lash. Will you have my life, Scholar Dame?"

Cendri, shocked, put out her hand in an appeasing gesture, and Rhu recoiled, an instinctive movement that shocked her more than anything Rhu had said, *It was exactly as if he feared I would strike him. . . .*

She said, swallowing hard, "No, Rhu. Forgive me. I am afraid some such fate may have befallen Dal—if you decide I might help save him from such fate, I beg you, come to me—" but his face was closed, and she went away, feeling tears rise and choke her.

What could she do? What could she do?

Later in the morning, Vaniya's older daughter, Lialla, sought her out. She said, "Scholar Dame—" she had never come to the informal terms Miranda and Vaniya used with the stranger—"my sister is abed and ill; she has asked you to pay her a visit."

Cendri was still so distressed over Dal's continuing absence that she felt she would be no fit company for the sick; but she knew Lialla would never consider worry over a mere male anything to interfere with the friendly duties between women, so she dismissed her annoyance at the interruption—*in any case, it isn't helping Dal any for me to sit and stew about it*—and went to Miranda's room.

Miranda was lying down, her pregnant body looking enormously humped between blankets. She greeted Cendri warmly, gesturing with amusement to a pallet on the floor.

"Vaniya has insisted that I sleep with the midwife in my room, so I have not even privacy any more, at night. I have missed you, Cendri, but I really feel too heavy and tired to get about. They keep telling me it would be better for me to take lots of exercise and jolt my lazy baby loose from her snug nest, but I am too heavy of foot to think of it without at least a dozen shudders. Listen, Cendri—we are alone, I sent the woman to make me a hot drink—has your Companion been found?"

Cendri said, "No," and wondered whether Rhu had told Miranda what he refused to tell *her*.

"You know I have not been at the family dinner table for days, I have been taking my meals here in my bed—last night Lialla came and kept me company while I ate, taking her dinner at my bedside so I would not fret—so she said, but I think it was for fear I should go into labor if left alone for a few minutes. When Zamila came up to her from the dinner table she began to gossip with her about what was happening, and—you were not at dinner either, Cendri?"

"No, I had a headache—"

"I hope you have recovered," Miranda said, with kind anxiety, "but they seemed to feel it concerned you in some way; a man, a messenger, came to Vaniya. She would have sent it away, saying this was not the hour for receiving petitions, but it insisted amost with rudeness, and spoke with her for a long time, insisting that the women of the household go out of earshot. My mother even sent Rhu away—but when the man was done speaking, she called out in great anger for her guards, and sent the man to the Punishment House. And after, she told Lialla to say nothing of this to the Scholar Dame, since she did not want you worried by trifles. Cendri—I had a strange feeling it might have been something to do with Dal's disappearance. My mother does not know—" she laid her hand over Cendri's, "that your Companion is your life-partner as well, and such a thought would never enter her mind. But *I* know a little, I think, of what your—your Companion means to you, and I think you have a right to know, if this man truly brought a message concerning him."

This seemed to confirm Cendri's worst fears. She said, shakily, "I must speak with the messenger, Miranda. Where is he?"

"In the Punishment House, Cendri, and I fear it was beaten. No," she added quickly, "you cannot go to the Punishment House alone, no woman may except Vaniya's appointed guards, and I do not think they would give you, alone, access to the prisoner; but I will go with you."

Cendri was grateful, but still felt some compunction. "Oh. Miranda, you are ill, suppose you go into labor—"

"Believe me," Miranda said, with heartfelt sincerity, "nothing on this world could please me more! If it has that effect, I shall bless the effort I make!" The midwife returned with Miranda's drink; she motioned her away.

"I will walk a little with my friend, the Scholar Dame from University—" she silenced the woman's protest, saying gaily, "You have been telling me for three days that I should bestir myself and take exercise, and now when I am willing, you would prevent me! Cendri will make certain I do not fall on the stairs, will you not, my friend?"

Cendri supported Miranda carefully on the long flight of steps, feeling intensely protective. *Isis has changed me in one way,* she realized; *my relationships with women will never again be quite the same.* The awareness that she could actually relate to another woman as to a lover, she knew, was going to make some permanent difference in her self-image, but she was not yet sure what form it would take. At the moment, she realized, she felt as close to Miranda as if the woman were her own sister.

It seemed for a moment that Miranda was reading her thoughts when she said, "So now you have visited the sea with us—tell me, Cendri, what do you think of our festival?"

Cendri said honestly, "I don't know yet what I think; I was surprised and—and a little confused. And I suppose, then, there will be an enormous number of births two hundred and eighty days or so from now?"

Miranda shook her head. "No, not really; that will be an unpleasant time to bear a child, in the worst of the summer heat. Most women who want children arrange it, as I did, to try and become pregnant at winter-festival, so that the children will be born at *this* season of the Long Year, and some others, women who work on farms, try to conceive at the harvest so that their children will be born before sowing-time. Although there are always some women so eager for children that they do not care *when* they conceive—my sister Lialla, who seems barren, though she has gone unprotected to every festival for years now. Cendri!" She looked at her in dismay. "Do your women in the maleworlds have no way to avoid conception except to keep apart from men? One of us should have warned you, told you— did you expose yourself, unprotected, to the sea-coming? It can still be remedied, but the process is—is unpleasant—"

Her concern was so sincere, so contrite, that Cendri quickly hugged her as she reassured, "No, no, we have such ways, I am in no danger of pregnancy, whatever I should do, but I was not sure your people did—"

Miranda laughed. "Believe me, it was the first thing to which the Matriarchate gave priority in research! Not many women wish for more than two or three children, if so many, and there are some who wish for none at all, although I must say that seems strange to me—if I could not bear children, I think I would almost as soon have been born male! But then there are also some women who wish for children eagerly, and no sooner wean one child from their breasts than they are eager for another, and of course we are all grateful to them. But did it seem to you that our festival had no meaning but that, Cendri, for the giving of children?" She looked up anxiously at Cendri, and Cendri said, "I have not been among you long enough to know what meaning it might have."

Miranda said slowly, "One of our priestesses could explain it to you better than I. These festivals—Three times in our Long Year we visit the sea; it is our way of remembering, of commemorating that both men and women are the children of the Goddess, whom once we named Persephone and here we call Isis, that all of life including our own comes from the sea; that men, too, have their needs and goals and desires, and that we must join to give them what they need, too, and keep them happy and contented." And now Cendri was more confused than ever, but Miranda did not explain further.

"Here is the Punishment House; I, as Vaniya's heir, have authority to admit you here."

She spoke briefly with the hefty, sun-tanned woman at the doorway, and the woman went away, letting Cendri and Miranda inside.

In the course of her studies Cendri had visited many places of confinement on many different worlds; the Punishment House of the Residence of the Pro-

Matriarch contained four identical small barred rooms, cells, weathertight and immaculately clean. The inhabitants—there were two at present—looked clean and well-fed, warmly clad against the chill and provided with blankets; nevertheless Cendri shrank in distaste from the display, on the wall where every inhabitant of the Punishment House could see them, of a variety of increasingly unpleasant instruments of restraint or punishment, including a variety of long, brutal whips. She also remembered what she had been told upon first landing on Isis; the penalty for any male who attacked a citizen was immediate death, meaning that males being punished could not even resist without incurring immediate destruction like any wild or dangerous animal. She shuddered in horror, thinking of Dal in such a place as this.

Miranda pressed her hand. She whispered, "I know, I feel that way too. It is horrible. And yet most males cannot be controlled any other way; you cannot judge them all by the kind of men whom we know; they are exceptional, you know."

Cendri thought of the boy who had wept in her arms at the seaside, of the gentleness of every man there, of the genuineness of the communication. Not for sex alone, but for some kind of togetherness, some way of re-uniting the sundered halves of the society—she found herself wanting to cry, because even Miranda did not understand.

Miranda said, gesturing, "This is the messenger. He was interrogated by the lash; but Lialla told me he said nothing and at last they were convinced he knew nothing worth telling, more than was in his message. But you should ask him about it, since the message— the message Vaniya did not give him leave to deliver— was for you. Yal," she said, to the man who lay huddled on the bare floor, shivering under his blankets, "I have brought the Scholar Dame from University to you. If your message concerns her, you are now free to give it."

The man Yal slowly, dragged himself upright. Cendri saw with horror that the back of his thick coarse shirt was flecked with blood, and that he moved as if every motion cost him excruciating pain.

He said, "You are indeed the Scholar Dame from University? The Mother Vaniya said that you would have no interest in the message I bear—she said, what is a male to the Scholar Dame?"

Cendri said quietly, "Vaniya was mistaken, Yal. If you bear a message from my beloved Companion, let me hear it."

"Respect, Scholar Dame, the message is not *from* your Companion, but concerning him," Yal said. "I was to say that your Companion, the Master Scholar Dallard Malocq, is being held in the work-settlement of the men at the great dam, and that there he will remain until men of the Unity are sent here, to learn of the conditions under which men of Isis must live and suffer all their lives without freedom. We demand that the Unity shall require the women of Isis to grant us the rights of free citizens, and until the Unity has answered us we shall hold the worthy Scholar Male among us."

Cendri gasped. So this was the end of Dal's work among the men of Isis—to be held as their prisoner, to force action from Vaniya!

It might have worked, with Mahala . . . she wants Isis a part of the Unity, but on their own terms. But Vaniya! Cendri's blood ran cold. Dearly as she had come to love the Pro-Matriarch, she knew that the woman would never compromise with the men.

Miranda said sharply, "That is not the way things are done on Isis, Yal. I can assure you, as daughter of the Pro-Matriarch, that if you return the Scholar Dame's Companion to us, and return to your duties, my mother Vaniya will be ready and more than ready to listen to any reasonable request."

Yal said, "We have done with reasonable requests, Lady; all reason has done for us is to keep every male on Isis in chains."

Cendri begged, "Where is my—where is the Master Scholar from the Unity being held?"

Yal's bruised face moved in a smile. His lips were swollen and darkened with dried blood. He said, "Ah, Respected Dame, that would be telling, now, wouldn't it? And you can see they asked me, and they knew how to persuade me; if I'd known—" he shuddered, "I'd surely have told, wouldn't I? I told them before they sent me, don't tell me anything. What I don't know, they can't make me tell, see, not even if they kill me."

Cendri shuddered; he spoke so matter-of-factly of torture and death. Was this what Dal would suffer for the fate of their messenger? This brave, and stupid, volunteer would die for his cause; but would it do him any good?

Miranda said sharply, "Is it worth it to you to be beaten and tortured for this folly, man?"

Yal smiled again. His smile, in his tortured face, was very terrible. He said, "But there are not enough women on Isis to beat us all to death one by one, woman." He used, not the term of respect, but the simple female noun. "I came here knowing I would be questioned as all men are questioned, by the whip, and then put in chains, as all men on Isis live chained by the will of women. But—" he held out his right hand; made the slow unloosing gesture Cendri had seen before, "we were not born in chains! And we will not die in them!"

He turned his back on the women, deliberately wrapped himself in the coarse prison blanket, and lowered himself painfully to the bare floor of the cell. He did not speak again.

When Cendri had escorted Miranda gently to her room, and left her there in the care of the midwife, she went to her own room, thinking in dread of Dal's fate in the hands of the men.

If they had sought some specific concession from Vaniya, they might have fared better. Vaniya was a reasonable woman, as she had proved when she gave a previous messenger leave to organize a hunt, because of their hunger. But the men had asked the one thing which Vaniya, secure in the rightness of her position, backed up by the will of the Builders—or Whoever and Whatever had spoken to her at We-were-guided—would never grant.

In all the years while we have dwelt on Isis, the Builders have spoken to no male. . . .

Did that mean, then, that the society on Isis was one specially chosen, *right*, the way all humanity should live?

Cendri shivered; then, remembering how the man Yal in his cell had done the same, forced herself to be quiet. No; if she accepted the word of—of whatever had spoken at We-were-guided—that would be to acknowledge it as a God, a supreme Being. And that, despite the almost-automatic reverence she had felt while she knelt there, Cendri could not do. Vaniya believed that whatever spoke there was the voice of a God—or more probably, Vaniya being who and what she was, a Goddess. But Cendri had been raised in the firm agnosticism of the Unity, and she did not believe in Gods—or Goddesses either—except as psychological forces in the minds of those who worshipped them. Far less could she accept that such Supreme Beings, if they existed—which, away from the seductive experience of We-were-guided, she did not believe—would lower themselves to interfere in the political institutions of humanity or to set up women above men, or for that matter, men above women. If Cendri believed in God at all it was in a force of ultimate fairness, which inspired but did not lead its worshippers, and left it to them to work out the details of their societies.

Something had spoken to her in the Ruins. *That* she knew, as she knew her name was Cendri Owain. But the nature of that Something she did not know, and could not guess.

But the fact of the matter was that Vaniya believed, and it was ultimately in Vaniya's hands to put her faith into action. Cendri never doubted that she would do it.

So that Dal might remain in the hands of the men of Isis until he died—or until the Unity sent to ask word of what had happened to its Master Scholar, sent to investigate the ruins of Isis.

And *that* was what the men wanted. That the Unity should come to investigate, to see the conditions of the Matriarchate, should declare them unfit for a world which traded with the Unity. Should enforce freedom for the men of Isis as a condition, not of membership in the Unity, but of trade with it. Cendri shuddered. The Unity could, and would, do it. In the name of Humanity, they would do it. Slavery was repugnant to the Unity, and in the harsh laws of the Matriarchate, where every man was legally some woman's property, they would see slavery, and nothing more.

And Mahala had said it, and Miranda. They were a poor world. They needed, they *desperately* needed, trade with the Unity, a market for their pearls and other exports, they needed terms for the earthquake-predictive equipment which would free them of the quakes and tidal waves, they needed land-reclamation machinery and equipment, they needed scientific training for their scientists and scholars on University. If the Unity enforced sanctions on them, as it did on all worlds which dealt in slaves, Isis could not survive, and their experiment would die with them.

So that the men, holding Dal, had the one instrument which could kill the power of the Matriarchate. Vaniya might trust in the love and concern of the Builders; but they could not save her, or Isis, now.

By the time Cendri had readied herself to dine at Vaniya's table, she was exhausted with her attempts to find some way out of this dilemma. Did Vaniya even understand the plight she would be in, if the Unity should come to investigate Dal's disappearance? If she did not, then she, Cendri, must enlighten her, and she shrank from the thought. Vaniya had not even told her of the existence of the messenger Yal, or of his demand; she had left Cendri to suffer in uncertainty.

Braced with the anger this thought raised in her, she went down to dinner.

Yet her deep affection for Vaniya bade her give Vaniya a chance to tell the truth. After all, she reminded herself, she had absented herself from Vaniya's dinner-table the night before, Vaniya might well have hesitated to trouble Cendri in her supposed illness with such news.

But the meal was much as usual. Vaniya welcomed Cendri back to them with tender concern, inquired about her health, and did not speak a word of the absent Dal. And throughout the meal, Cendri's anger grew, until by the time the dishes were cleared away, she could restrain it no longer.

She said, "Vaniya, I would like to speak with you alone, if I may," and waited until the Pro-Matriarch had dismissed her household. Even then, seeing the lines of fatigue and worry in the older woman's face, Cendri almost relented.

But my duty now is to Dal. I, too, am a citizen and a Scholar of University.

She said quietly, "Vaniya, I have heard that you had news of Dal, and that you did not tell me. I had thought you regarded me as a guest and a friend. In our world this would not be thought the kindly action of a friend."

"Friend? More than that, my child," said Vaniya, gently taking her hand. Cendri drew it away and her eyes blazed.

"Miranda, perhaps, is my friend, Vaniya, but not you; or why was I not told that a messenger had been sent, telling me that Dal was a prisoner of the men's rebellion?"

"Oh, dear!" Vaniya said, and her face was troubled. "My dear child, I did not want you troubled with such trifles. If these foolish men think they can force our will that way, that has nothing to do with you. I am sure you are concerned for your Companion, but after all, it is only a male, and you can all too easily find another. You shall have the choice of my own Men's House, I

will not withhold even Rhu from you if you value him
so highly."

Cendri heard her in amazement and dismay. Had
she, then, never even begun to understand Vaniya, or
her world? No, for she now knew she should have
expected this. The fault had been in Cendri, when she
first agreed to the terms made by the women of Isis.
Dal's fault, too; he was a Scholar and such an imposture was not intellectually honest, either. They should
have demanded—University should have demanded—
to send their chosen Scholar on his own terms, pledging
his obedience to the laws of Isis, and under diplomatic
immunity if necessary; but the imposture, she now
knew, had been a great mistake, and now she, and Dal,
must pay for it. But she would not continue the lie.

She said quietly, "Vaniya, that will not do, and I
think you know it. For all that we have tried never to
offend against your customs, Dal is not a Companion as
you of Isis use the term. He is my life-partner, a citizen
of the Unity, a Master Scholar of University, and the
Unity will not allow him to be disregarded and given up
to imprisonment. I think you know what the Unity can
do if they choose to exercise sanctions against Isis; it
has been done before."

Vaniya's face was pale. She said, "I cannot believe
they would do this for an assistant, even the valued
assistant of a Scholar Dame."

Cendri felt the blood drain from her own cheeks, but
now she was committed to the truth. "Dal is not my
assistant, Vaniya. It is he who is—who has always been
—the Extra-Scholar Malocq," she used the neutral
word in the language of Isis. "It is he, not I, who was
the trained assistant of the Scholar Dame di Velo."

Vaniya's fists clenched. Her mouth was tight, but her
eyes glowed in anger; she looked more than ever like a
great golden lioness, but now the lioness was free and
stalking in fury. She paced the floor, rounding on
Cendri to demand, "And who are *you*, then? Are you
not the Scholar Dame Malocq?"

"I am a Scholar," Cendri said, "I am the life-partner of the Extra-Scholar Malocq, and as the custom is on his home world of Pioneer, I had taken his name for my own. And so it was possible—" her voice failed her there.

Vaniya demanded, in a fury, "Why did you come, then? Only to be a—a sexual playting, a she-Companion, for your Extra-Scholar, then?" Cendri felt she would wither into a small scorched coal under the blazing contempt in Vaniya's voice. She gathered her self-respect, and said firmly, "No, Vaniya. I came for the sake of my own work; I too am a Scholar, and some day to be Extra-Scholar as well, the equal of Dal!" She flung the phrase at Vaniya defiantly.

Vaniya just stood and stared at her. "That I should live to hear a woman and a Scholar say such words— that some day she might rise to be the equal of a male! Have you learned no shame among us, Cendri?"

Cendri set her chin so that she would not cry. She said, "Vaniya, in all save Scholar's credentials we are equals; and I have not completed mine."

"Credentials—" Vaniya said. "Let us have this clear, then. Are you an assistant archaeologist, and your— your Companion—the true Extra-Scholar in that field?"

With all her heart Cendri wished she could leave it at that. Ringing in her mind were the words recorded for a former High Matriarch of Isis—she wondered which of the statues she had seen in the Hall of Matriarchs had said these words;

We will not be studied by your scientists as if we were one of those glass-sided insect colonies we give our little daughters for playthings. Yet she had committed herself now to complete honest with Vaniya.

Standing before Vaniya, looking up into the woman's face as if she were a Student before her Mentor in the first class on University, she said steadily, "No, Vaniya. I am a cross-cultural sociologist and an anthropologist; I came here because so little is known about the

Matriarchate in the worlds of the Unity, and I wanted them to know the truth about you, not garbled lies. I can tell the worlds of the Unity what you really are," she added, hopefully, but Vaniya's face was carved in stone.

"An anthropologist. To study us," she repeated slowly, her mouth twisting a little as if the words dirtied them. She physically drew away from Cendri.

"But we loved you," she said, slowly, in amazement. "We trusted you. We loved you. And you betrayed us!"

chapter thirteen

THE SILENCE LENGTHENED. CENDRI FELT HER EYES FILL with tears, felt them spill over and run hot down her cheeks, but she said nothing. There were a dozen things she wanted to cry out.

And I loved you, Vaniya. I trusted you, enough to risk Dal's life at your hands.

You ask if I have learned no shame among you. I have learned to be ashamed that women can so abuse their power. Tyranny is tyranny, be it the tyranny of the man over the woman, or of the woman over the man.

But she said none of these or the other thoughts surging in her mind. She stood with her head held firmly erect before Vaniya—she had done nothing wrong, she was a Scholar of University, not a spanked child—but she could not keep the tears from scalding her cheeks.

It wasn't a lie. It wasn't betrayal. I loved you, all of you, I lived with you. I visited the sea with you. . . .

She had finally opened her mouth to speak when there was an outcry in the hallway. Vaniya thrust Cendri aside, saying roughly, "What is this commotion in my house?"

There were the sounds of women crying out in surprise and dismay; the doorway was flung open and the Pro-Matriarch Mahala, accompanied by the women of her household, stormed into the hall.

Vaniya quickly mastered herself and said, "Tell me, my sister, how is it that you honor my house? Is this an official visit from Pro-Matriarch to Pro-Matriarch, or a friendly evening call?"

"It is official," Mahala said harshly, "I now demand, my sister and colleague, that you immediately relinquish to me such secular authority as I need to deal with rebellion—or do you, wallowing in your religious observances, even know that we have a rebellion on our hands?"

Cendri, standing forgotten, watched in dismay. Vaniya said, summoning her uttermost dignity, "I have been occupied with the aftermath of the festival, Mahala, and I am awaiting the birth of my daughter's daughter. The peace of the city of Ariadne has been left in your hands, as during all these months of our late Mother's illness. Have you then been unable to maintain it, my sister?"

"It is no time for birth-festivals and merrymaking," said Mahala angrily. "Do you not know that the men have refused to return to the delta and the dam, refused to return to the Inland Land Reclamation Project, refused to return to their duties on farms and factories and along the shore, refused even to go quietly to the Men's Houses when offered a holiday to recover from the fatigues of the festival?"

Vaniya blinked and said, "But, no, I had heard nothing of this, my sister. Where, then, are the men of Isis?"

Mahala gestured, and suddenly, for all her forceful and angry speech, she looked helpless and forlorn.

"They are on the streets of Ariadne, doing nothing," she said. "They are standing about where the cars and drivers cannot pass, they are sitting about on the curbs so that women cannot walk in the streets, they are doing nothing. *They are doing nothing,*" she repeated.

Vaniya shrugged. She said, "When they are hungry, they will go back to work."

Mahala said, "So I too thought at first, but they have been there now all night and all day, and another night is beginning, and they have not moved. Some of them are on the shore, spearfishing; when we sent to warn them away, saying it was out of season, one of their leaders told my officer that the Goddess had given fish to the hungry, and it was theirs for the taking, and refused to desist."

"Beat a few of the leaders," Vaniya suggested, "and they will scatter."

"I have done so, " Mahala said, almost in a whisper, "but we have not enough women in all Ariadne to beat them all, and already the Punishment Houses are full and overflowing!"

Cendri swallowed, thinking of Yal's defiant words: *There are not enough women on Isis to beat us all to death.*

"Finally," Mahala said, "a delegation came to me. They said that since you had not listened to their messenger the first time, but had simply beaten and tortured him, without the courtesy of replying, they would force you to take notice. They say that you care nothing for the Companion of the Scholar Dame from the Unity; so they have sent him with a message for you." She motioned toward the door. "A message, they say, which you dare not ignore."

Between two of Mahala's strongest women guards, Dal came into the room.

He looked tired and sleepless, but he seemed otherwise uninjured. Cendri rushed to him; he touched her hands briefly, smiling a quick, reassuring smile; then put her gently away from him. He said, "I bear a letter for Vaniya from the leader of the United Men of Isis."

Vaniya frowned and said, "I do not recognize any such group or affiliation. Men are not allowed to organize into any societies but the crafts of their trades, or the secret religious societies of the Men's Houses."

Dal said, "They are aware of that refusal, Pro-Matriarch. Nevertheless, they have sent me with a message."

"And you dare to bear it to me? Impudence!" Vaniya snorted. Dal's voice was calm.

"I am here as a representative of the Unity, Vaniya, and I bear diplomatic credentials. You need not respect them, but if you do not, the Unity will exercise sanctions against Isis. May I present the message with which the men of Isis have entrusted me?"

Vaniya said grimly, "Give me the message."

Mahala snorted. "*This* is what comes of your kind of liberalism, Vaniya—allowing some men to learn to read and write!"

Vaniya ignored her, tearing open the letter. She read aloud, slowly.

"'Respect, worthy Pro-Matriarch Vaniya, from the men of—'" she frowned. "It is wretchedly ill-spelled. They list some dozen athletic guilds, and as many more Men's Houses . . . 'since you have seen fit to ignore our messenger Yal and not to deliver the message to its appointed destination, we have seized for ourselves a hostage you cannot ignore. No harm must come to the scholar from the Unity until he carries our message to the worlds where men are free. You will recognize this token of the hostage we hold.'" She tore at the wrappings enclosing something inside the letter, her face pale and taut; unwrapped a large pink pearl on a fine chain.

Her face drained to deathly white.

"Miranda's," she whispered. "But—she was in her room, with a midwife in attendance—" she whirled quickly on the assembled women.

"Lialla, Zamila—Maret—all of you—go quickly, see if all is well with Miranda—"

The women rushed from the room. Cendri heard their feet on the stairs. Mahala pointed to Cendri and said with anger, "It was an evil day, an accurst day when you came to Isis, Scholar Dame!"

"No," said Vaniya, looking sadly at Cendri, "it was an evil day when *that* one came to Isis." She pointed at Dal. He leaned close to Cendri and whispered, "Since we came on the same day, they're both right. As usual. That's the hell of it, they're both right!"

It was all Cendri could do to keep back an outburst of idiot laughter, bubbling up from somewhere deep inside her. But Dal was right. This was the real tragedy of Isis; that these two women, locked in their deadly rivalry, still wanted the same thing; they wanted what was best for Isis, as they saw it.

Suddenly, from the upper floors of the house, loud cries of consternation broke out, and the sounds of running feet on the stairs.

The women burst back into the room in a clustered group, huddling together like frightened small birds.

"Miranda," Zamila wailed. "Miranda is gone! She is nowhere in the house!"

Lialla cried, "The midwife lies unconscious on the stairs; she has been struck and we cannot revive her!"

Vaniya stared at them, blanched, her mouth trembling. Then, slowly, she turned to Cendri and Dal. She said, slowly, holding Miranda's pearl on its chain, clasped against her heavy bosom, "If any harm comes to Miranda, you will pay for this, whatever the Unity may do to me for it."

Cendri began to cry softly. Miranda, her first friend here, loved like a sister—what would become of her, pregnant and ill, in the hands of the men, at the mercy of men with the memory of generations of abuse, slavery, torture! Would they ill-treat her for Vaniya's sake, or to revenge themselves for the treatment of their messenger?

Then, and for a moment the memory seemed incongruous, she remembered the night when she had lain with the other women at the edge of the sea; remembered the adolescent boy who had given her his athlete's garland, weeping against her breast and saying that she reminded him of his mother. Suddenly she was sure they would not harm a pregnant woman, a mother. A Mother. She wished she could share this sudden certainty with Vaniya, but the older woman had not looked at her since that first angry, contemptuous rejection.

"Vaniya—" Mahala said gently, and the older woman turned dazed, suffering eyes on her. Vaniya said, in a stifled whisper, "Miranda! Goddess guard and protect her, my poor child—"

Mahala's voice was gentler than Cendri had ever heard it. She said, "Truly, truly, I grieve for you, sister, I have daughters and grand-daughters of my own. But we have a rebellion on our hands, and although I sympathize with your personal sorrow, the time leaves us no leisure for grieving. We must somehow manage to remove these men from the streets and send them back to their work and their Men's Houses. Will you delegate me the secular authority to deal with it then, sister, if you do not feel qualified to deal with it yourself?"

"I suppose you are right," Vaniya said wearily. "Miranda is my daughter, and she is brave; she must endure whatever comes to her, as every woman on our world must endure the days to come, and I cannot compromise my duty for the safety of one woman, however dear to me."

"Spoken like a true Pro-Matriarch," said Mahala. "There are weapons in the armories; they were used against predators when we cleared the land. I think we must authorize their use, now. They may resist whips and persuasion, but if we fire a few shells into their midst—"

Vaniya stared at her in horror. She said, "My sister, this would be war!"

Mahala's voice was angry. "You who are lost in your religious sentiment, my sister, do you not yet recognize that the men have forced this war upon us?"

Vaniya twisted her big hands together. She said tensely, "My dear sister, of what worth is the Matriarchate if we violate its ethical principles the first time they are put to a test? With these ears I heard you say, when you protested the coming of the Scholar from Unity: the maleworlds perish and are destroyed because every society made by men turns to violence, to war, to entropy and decay. If we must fight and kill to enforce our will on the men, my beloved sister, then we might as well turn over the rule of this world to the men at once, for already we are living as the maleworlds do!"

Mahala's mouth fell open. She stared at her fellow Pro-Matriarch in dismay as the truth of Vaniya's words penetrated to her. "You are right," she acknowledged in a whisper. "It seems that the rule of the maleworlds is already upon us, then, whatever we do or refrain from doing! My sister, what shall we do? What shall we do?" It was a cry of utter despair.

Vaniya held out her arms, and the two Pro-Matriarchs clung together. It seemed to Cendri that Mahala's shoulders heaved as if with silent weeping; over her head, even while she embraced and soothed her colleague, Vaniya stared grimly into the distance.

At last she said, in the gentlest of voices, "Mahala, there is only one answer now. We must seek out aid from those who are wiser than we. Will you come with me to We-were-guided, Mahala, and put the question to those who in the first days of our arrival here, welcomed and counseled us?"

Mahala raised her head. Her eyes were tearless and red. She said, "It goes against reason, Vaniya, but I admit that reason has helped me little in this crisis. There seems no other source for help. Yet I have little hope that we will find counsel there, in the dead city."

Vaniya said quietly, "If you find no counsel there to your liking, sister, then when we leave We-were-guided I shall at once relinquish to you all control of the secular forces of Ariadne. I give you my word, which I have never broken, that I ask only that you come with me, as you have never been willing to do, and hear the words of the wise ones there who helped me to find Rezali's ring and robe. All things are known to them, and they will know what to do in this crisis, too."

Mahala bowed her head. She said, "In this crisis I am willing to turn anywhere, even to a ghost."

The preparations took only a few moments. When the procession left the Pro-Matriarch's residence, it was growing dark, and Cendri and Dal followed in the train of the two Pro-Matriarchs as, each accompanied by her household, they climbed the steep path toward the dark loom of the dead city of We-were-guided. Cendri walked head down, lost in misery, remembering how she had come here before with Vaniya, how Something had spoken to her from the site of the ancient starship. She was hardly conscious of Dal at her side until he stumbled and cursed in an undertone; then she said, reaching for his hand, "Dal, I was so frightened—did they hurt you?"

"*Hurt* me? Cendri, I had to stop them from trying to *worship* me," he said softly. "They did not believe that there were really worlds where men were free. You would not believe how they crave learning . . . I think they want it even more than freedom; because with learning, they say, they could prove they were equal and prove worthy of their freedom! And when they found I was a Master Scholar—Cendri, I was treated with reverence! Reverence!" he repeated. "They wouldn't have hurt a shadow of my clothing, or a hair of my head!" He laughed softly, but it was not a mirthful sound. "Poor devils, poor devils! Some of them feared the idea of learning as much as they desired it! One of them, when he heard I had spent all my life in study, asked if it had not made me impotent! And I thought Rhu was badly off! *Sharrioz!*"

"Dal, did you foment this rebellion?"

He sighed and shook his head. "God help me, no, I was selfish enough to protest. I never thought about anything but my own work of exploring the ruins. I was only the catalyst, coming at the precise time when the men were ready for some such thing."

The night was hot and dark; the moons, waning from full, hovered at the edge of the sky, Cendri moved along, wearily, following the glimmer of Vaniya's torch, trailing in the train of the two Pro-Matriarchs.

She said at last, "How is it that you are coming here, Dal? I thought you were against the idea that the ruins could be a center of religious worship."

In the dark she could not see his face but his voice sounded faintly amused. He said, "I suppose I want to see anything that could make Mahala give way like that. Or maybe, like her, I feel the situation's just fouled up enough that we ought to try anything. Maybe I just have to keep track of what the government of Isis, such as it is"—he gestured at the dim forms of the two women ahead of them—"are going to do now, and how it affects the Unity." He shook his head. "I didn't think anything would make Mahala draw in her horns. She reminds me a lot—in a way, they're not at all alike—of the Scholar Dame di Velo. Come to think, so does Vaniya."

Cendri knew what he meant. It was the aura of personal power, the force of personality, the elusive thing called charisma. She said, "I know what you mean," and in the darkness, Dal reached out and clasped her hand.

He whispered, "You have it too, sometimes, Cendri. When you're mad enough." And his arm went round her waist, so that under cover of the darkness they walked enlaced.

By torchlight, picking their way carefully over the stones, the women found their way inside the gates of the dead city known as We-were-guided, wound slowly through the canyons between the giant unknown structures, where nothing stirred except the dim night-wind, and night birds rustled along the shore. Far below the waves broke and sighed.

Dal whispered, "What happens here?"

"I can't tell you, Dal. You'll just have to—to see." She was remembering, painfully, what Vaniya had said.

In all of the years we have come here, those at We-were-guided have spoken to no male.

But maybe the males never listened. . . .

They came slowly across the great open space, at the far end of which loomed the spaceship. Cendri began to feel the first overlapping waves of the welcoming warmth.

I am here, you are loved . . . I welcome you. . . .

But for the first time she resisted, fighting against the irresistible tide of rapture creeping upward into her brain.

No. No. Not this time! It is too important for that! Do you know who we are? Do you know why we have come here? Who are you?

The licking warmth seemed to hesitate, to flood back, to withdraw and advance and retreat in waves, and then Cendri sensed something else. It was the *same* as the warmth. It had the same mental *feel*. It was not precisely in words; she knew it was her own brain translating the contact *into* words because it was the only way to make the experience of contact comprehensible.

Yes. We—know. A curious positiveness about it, and then a quick crawling sensation as if—Cendri described it later—*as if some enormous force had picked me up, turned me inside-out, looked at every idea or thought I'd ever had since the day I was born, ruffled through my mind turning over all the ideas it found there, patted me on the head like a puppy and put me down again. And all through that trememdous, tender, loving warmth. . . .*

She heard Dal say—and knew he was not speaking aloud, "Did you build this City, then?"

And the voice, answering, still radiating these same waves of loving warmth . . . she glanced at Dal, saw his face glowing with the same joyousness. . . .*No. We did not build the City. We came here from space, when these women came. We had need of them, as they had need of us.*

Now she heard . . . or sensed; how did you translate into words an experience that was not in words at all, a touch that said clearly in her mind, *Vaniya,* and a wordless, *You see, Mahala?"*

I see. But they speak to the man!

And Vaniya's thoughts, flowing with surprise and indignation. *Never before, never, have you spoken to men . . . why now?*

And the alien thoughts, wrapped in warmth; and yet with a touch of chill that made Cendri tremble with sudden terror. *Your mind lied to us. We saw your men only through your thoughts. Now we know that you have lied to us.*

We spoke truth, Vaniya's mind flamed with indignation, *men are not fit. . . .*

As fit as your first Foremother Alicia, when she rebelled against men's dominance on Pioneer. . . .

And Mahala, angry and terrified at once: *What do you know of our first Foremother?*

Whatever your mind knows is known to me, beloved . . . and the surging, compelling ripples of tenderness.

Dal was almost gasping with excitement.

He whispered half aloud to Cendri, "An alien race. Not the Builders, but a disembodied race . . . cosmic clouds? Atoms? Gaseous entities? Needing to live in symbiosis with another race because of their endless loneliness, desiring love. Pretending to be Gods to get it!"

Yes, you are right, my alien son, we have allowed our need for the love of our daughters to blind us to the needs of others who cry out for our comfort . . . and these have lied to us . . . Cendri could feel in her own breast the surge of alien anger. *Vaniya! You have lied to us, we will speak to you no more. . . .*

And sudden, shocking, dead, cold emptiness.

Cendri came awake as if icy surf had splashed over her. The faint light still glowed from the ruins of the ancient spaceship and all around them the faint luminosity of the city shone with its own interior gleam. But there was no warmth, no voice, no lapping ripples of tenderness. The voice was silent. The moonlight had risen high over the city now, and Cendri could see the faces of the women, shocked and quiet, weeping. Vaniya covered her face with her hands, shaking, bereft. Cendri felt shock and pity at the naked anguish of deprivation on the woman's face.

They have been with her so long, so long. Since first she came here as a young woman, coming with her from space to this world, settling here, supporting her, helping her, till she grew dependent on their love and concern. And she led other women to them, so that they fed on this devotion and in turn gave pleasure to those who came to communicate with them.

And by coming here, by asking a simple question, Dal has destroyed these long years of blind, mindless devotion. But what will Vaniya do now? What will she do? Vaniya was looking at Dal with naked hate.

I don't blame her. He has robbed her of her Goddess . . . and yet he did nothing wrong. Why do the innocent have to suffer?

Slowly, with drooping steps, Vaniya turned away from the ancient ship. Her head was bent and she stumbled as she walked. Cendri, impulsively, stepped forward and laid her arm around the old woman, supporting her steps. For a moment she feared Vaniya would rebuff her with a rebirth of anger, but Vaniya was too sunk in her own anguish to care. She leaned on Cendri as they came out of the dead city and started down the hill; then Lialla, behind them, cried out in dismay and fear.

"Look! Look!"

From the gates of Ariadne, a great multitude were surging out of the city, running, plunging upward along the shore, up the hill in a great human wave. Cendri

thought of the tidal wave which had engulfed the
pearl-divers' village on the shore; only this was a
human tide, flowing along the shore, rising slow and
inexorable on the slopes toward the gates of We-were-
guided. And in the moonlight Cendri could see that all
the forms were those of men, moving like a great
groundswell. And one and all, their faces bore the same
dazed rapture that Cendri had seen on the faces of the
women, that day. . . .

Vaniya moaned, moving aside from the surge of
men, stumbling. Cendri held her so that she would not
fall, and heard her weeping aloud. "Profanation," she
moaned, "profanation!"

The men surged into the city, stood before the old
ship. The lights began to glow. Cendri felt the faint
echo of the lapping warmth, but it did not speak to her;
she felt cold and alone, and she could feel Vaniya
shaking, and held the woman tight in her arms, with an
almost anguished desire to comfort her, as the woman,
desolate, deprived of the contact and the love which
was life to her, stood and watched others drinking in
the communion from which she had been exiled.
Others, despised. Men. Not even people.

How long it lasted, Cendri never knew. She held
Vaniya in her arms, trying to quiet her sobbing, until
she was stiff and cramped and aching. And then,
suddenly, it was over.

One of the men, a tall man with long hair flecked
with grey, wearing a coarse pajama suit, came hesitantly toward Vaniya.

"Respect, Mother Vaniya . . ." he said hesitatingly,
and Vaniya wearily tried to pull herself together. She
stood erect, moving out of the support of Cendri's
arms.

"Can it be that you come to me with respect, *here?*"
she asked, and her voice was a whiplash of scorn.
"When you have trampled your mothers in your
profanation?"

"Mother—" the man entreated, "those who speak to

us have given a message which you must know! Men cannot handle this alone!"

Vaniya drew a long breath. She said, "Speak, my son."

The man gestured toward the ocean. "*They* have told us," he said, "that far out in the ocean, many, many, many leagues in the place of fish too deep for diving, the bed of sea shakes, and will shake again and again. And as these quakes move ever closer, the great waves will build up and up, until at last, before nightfall tomorrow, a wall of water higher than this will smash the shore down near the great dam, and if it should strike full on the dam, not a single stone will be left piled upon another. Therefore, Mother—" the man entreated, "you Mothers, and your daughters, who control the cars and the messages and the transportation, we beseech you to help us bring all of our people out of the encampments there, and all of our stores and possessions, lest they be lost forever. The storehouses of grain and building materials could all be swept away, and all our foods and reserves."

Vaniya swallowed hard, "How do you know this, my son?"

"*They* told us," the man said, gesturing formlessly toward the old ship.

"And how do you know it is true?" Vaniya demanded, "that they were not deceiving you as they deceived me? Why should they now begin to give warnings about quakes and tidal waves, when all these years they have not done so?"

The man made a low bow. He said, "Respect, Mother, one of us asked that. This was their answer; that you had never asked them for such help and they did not know they could give it until one of us asked to make our needs known, and they found they could answer."

Vaniya still looked shaken. But she said, "They do not lie. They found the ring and robe of Mother Rezali. Nothing is hidden from them that they wish to know.

Come, Mahala," she said quickly to her fellow Pro-
Matriarch. "You are a quicker organizer than I, and we
have no time to waste now with protocol or rivalry! We
have just time enough—if we hurry—to get every man,
woman and child, and all their stores and possessions,
out of the area of the great dam, if we lose no time.
There will be no time to reinforce the dam; if it is swept
away it must be swept away, but if we are fortunate,
there will be no loss of life. Come, Mahala! let us hurry
to the city, and make all ready!"

She leaned heavily on Cendri as she hurried down
the hill, already moving people of her household
around her to give quick, cryptic orders.

"Lialla, go to the spaceport, find flycraft of any kind
available and muster them for airlifting. Zamila, go
with this man and help him line up all able-bodied men
between fifteen and fifty, and arrange for transport at
once! Thanks to the Goddess, Mahala, most of the men
had not returned to the site of the dam; no one must go
back there unless they are needed to help in the
evacuation!"

Dal and Cendri stood watching as together the
Pro-Matriarchs began organizing their plan. Dal murmured, "I had thought the men would try to stand on
their own feet. But the first thing they did was to yell
for help from the women. . . ."

Cendri felt something very like anger at Dal's failure
to understand. "Dal, don't you see? Something where
men and women have to work together, because
women control all the transport, all the organizational
facilities, all the technical know-how! Do you really
think a society is going to turn itself right around all
night?" She seized his arm, saying earnestly, "Dal, it
wouldn't make a bit of sense to overturn the tyranny of
the women and set up a new tyranny of the men! The
only thing that will save this society is co-operation—
lots of it! Being able to do things together that neither
men or women could do on their own. . . ."

He nodded, but she could see that his thoughts were

elsewhere. After a moment he said, as he watched Vaniya's household quietly organizing transport, "Cendri, do you realize that we have not one but *two* alien civilizations to deal with here? We still don't know who built the ruins—the city. It was probably the Builders, but it will take centuries to *know,* and we'll have to break the Time stasis first. And then—there's the aliens who spoke to—to us, and then to the Men. Cendri, Isis is going to be the new scientific focus of the entire Galaxy! Maybe Mahala's going to get what she wanted after all!"

Cendri could see that, but what was troubling her now was more immediate, more personal.

Where was Miranda? Was she being held at the site of the dam, with the tidal wave racing inexorably toward the shore?

chapter fourteen

THE SUN WAS RISING OVER ISIS; CENDRI LOOKED DOWN on the river below, the spreading delta mouth where the river alternately roared and meandered through flats covered with reed and salt-marsh, where the land had been torn away repeatedly by flood. All night she had watched trucks and cars coming and going, emptying storehouses, taking away the heavy machinery, men and women working side by side. And all night, while the Pro-Matriarchs worked side by side, co-ordinating the efforts of the work parties, Vaniya had repeatedly raised her head to every man who came before her, asking him—steadily enough, but in a voice that trembled— "Do you know where my daughter is being held? If you know who holds her hostage, will you send him to me that I may bargain for her freedom?"

But every man had professed ignorance—Cendri, watching from a distance, had begun to believe that they *were* truly ignorant, that only a few of the ringleaders had been allowed to know the inside of the plot. The words of Yal rang in her mind, *What I don't know, they can't make me tell.* And oh, but Vaniya was reaping the harvest of her harsh rule!

Yet she would not leave her post. Mahala, moved by her anguish, had said at midnight, "Vaniya, my sister, go back to the city, seek your daughter there. I will continue here."

But Vaniya, pale and agonized, shook her head.

"My duty lies here, sister. Miranda is my daughter, and she understands the meaning of responsibility. If we all live through this night, I will seek her out, even if I must kneel before every male on Isis and beg for its help; and I will make such terms as I may honorably make for her release, and if I cannot make honorable terms, I pray the Goddess will give us both strength to endure her fate. But for now my duty lies here; I cannot leave men and women to die while I think only of my daughter and her child."

And Mahala, lowering her head, answered, "I know, old friend. Forgive me for thinking otherwise."

Cendri had been put to run small errands needing no other skill; after a time she was put to work in a hurriedly organized field-kitchen to feed the workers on the site. She watched them slowly, under the supervision of the two Pro-Matriarchs, slowly cross-sectioning the site, performing, she realized, a form of methodical decision akin to triage; what must be removed at any cost (mostly food supplies and heavy machinery), what must be left to take its chances in the path of the wave (mostly structures), and what must be knowingly abandoned. Every decision, Cendri knew, had to be made by the Pro-Matriarchs.

She worked with other women and a few young boys, brewing tea and drinks for the workers, cooking grains and fish for them. She worked here through the night, and as the sun was rising, she came face to face with Rhu, carrying plates of food to a work-party resting for a few minutes on the grass.

"What are you doing here, Rhu?"

"The same as you," he said, with a weary smile. "I have no skills to work among the women, and no strength to work among the men, so I do what I can." His face was pale in the rising light, and Cendri remembered what Dal had told her; that he had a heart weakened by childhood illness.

He said, "I saw Dal on the slope by the site; every man on Isis wants to see him, to look up to him as inspiration. Whatever comes this night, Scholar Dame, life on Isis may be more endurable for men hereafter."

Slowly, Cendri nodded. The basic misconception of the society here—that the inferiority of men was backed by divine command because the Builders would not speak to them—had been toppled at one blow. Men must still compensate for their disabilities of education, struggle for equality as the women had done on Pioneer, and it would not come quickly. Indeed, men on Isis would probably continue to live separate from women, since both women and men were content to have it that way; but since the lower status of men was no longer buttressed by a kind of divine ordinance, it could not survive. Nothing would change overnight. Some things would never change at all. But now there was a kind of hope that had never been here before.

One of the women called to Rhu.

"Take some food to the Mother Vaniya, Rhu; she must eat and keep up her strength, and she may take it at your hands more easily."

Cendri went with Rhu. The field-kitchen was actually over-supplied with workers—every woman who had no duties elsewhere was there—and she was not needed. Vaniya, weary and worn, looked up at them.

"Vaniya," Rhu pleaded, "you must eat something. Here, I have brought you food and wine."

"I am not hungry," Vaniya said, but she sighed, laid down a map of the site, and glanced at a man waiting for her orders. She said, pointing to a segment of the map, "Leave those three warehouses along the edge of the site. They contain only lumber and building cement, and they are not worth the time and machinery it would take to clear them. The water may not ever reach so high, but if it does, then the contents can be replaced with less than the loss of diverting heavy machinery there now."

The man nodded, saying, "Where shall we move the machinery, then?"

"Here." Vaniya pointed again. "Take three of the engineers from the college, and go to strengthen the dikes there; the water might be diverted where it comes in, to flow harmlessly across the lower delta. We will have flooding, but, the engineer from the college tells me, the strength of the wave will not smash there." She raised her hands to her forehead, wearily, as the man and the engineer bent over the map. She said, "We had a copying machine set up in the outer office there, have copies made for each of you, and bring it back to me. . . ." And as they hurried away with it, she raised her head to take the tray of food.

"Rhu, Cendri—" she smiled tiredly as she put a fork to her mouth. "Well, Cendri, you came here to study the Matriarchate in crisis, and now you can see rebellion, anarchy, all those things which try a society—what report will you take back to the Unity, little Cendri?"

Cendri said gently, "I do not know, Vaniya. This—" she gestured, indicating the field office that had been set up around them, "looks not to me like anarchy."

Vaniya yawned, putting her hand to her mouth. She said, "No, perhaps not. In this crisis we do what we must, all our sons and daughters work together for salvation. I wonder, now, that I never thought to ask those at We-were-guided for help in such things. . . ." she yawned again, closing her eyes for a moment. Then, she raised her eyes to Rhu. "Have you any news of Miranda? Of where she is being held among the men?"

Rhu's pale face looked drawn and miserable. He burst out, "No, Vaniya! On my life, no! They betrayed us both!"

Vaniya's broad face looked stunned, disbelieving. "What is this talk of betrayal, Rhu? What could *you* have had to do with it?" And even in this crisis Rhu flushed at the contempt in her voice.

He said steadily, "I came to confess to you; Miranda left the house at my request, she came willingly with me as hostage. She and I—" his voice faltered and Cendri recalled that what he was confessing was something unthinkable in their society. "She and I—we have been much together; she said that she—she loved me—"

"You!" Vaniya stared at him in disbelief. "She has always been kind to you. But to *love* a man—and not even a man, but a Companion—"

"Whatever I am, whatever you think of me, I love Miranda," Rhu said steadily, "and she shared my concern for the plight of men who were nothing in your sight. I was your Companion, but only a—a toy for your leisure hours, while to Miranda I was—I was myself, a human being like herself. We hoped—we hoped *together*—for a world where man and woman could sometimes meet, if they chose, not only at the edge of the sea, in darkness, as animals rut in season—"

"Silence," Vaniya burst out. "How dare you speak of such things now to me—"

"We hoped for a world where man and woman could sometimes meet in the light, wanting one another's welfare and well-being and knowing one another as fellow beings, loving one another," Rhu went on steadily, ignoring her. "And so Miranda, when you would not hear the messenger, resolved to give herself up as hostage, thinking you would do nothing to endanger *her*. You cared nothing for the man from Unity, but you would hear a messenger if Miranda's safety was at stake. She left the house with me, and came to where the men were gathered, believing as I believed, that we were not born in chains—"

Vaniya's face contorted in wrath. "You, my Companion—have you approached my daughter as no man may do? I will have you killed, as the penalty is for any male who attacks a citizen—"

Rhu shook his head. He said quietly, "I have touched her hand, I have kissed her lips and embraced her as a child his mother, and no more; *that* is not what we sought from one another. It was love, Vaniya, not the sea-coming; and if it had been more, even so, she was heavy with child. You misunderstand, as you have always misunderstood."

"So where did you take her, you wretch?" Vaniya interrupted, and Rhu shook his head. "They would not tell me, lest I should reveal all to you. They betrayed us both! And they did not trust me, any more than you trust me. As always, Vaniya, I am exiled from the world of men and from the world of women—"

He covered his face with his hands, and after a moment Cendri realized that he was weeping.

"I would have died before bringing her to harm, Vaniya, she was more than life to me. . . ."

Vaniya looked at him, her face drawn with emotion. "Rhu, Rhu, how could you have done this to me? Have I been unkind to you, or cruel?"

Rhu said, very low, "No, Vaniya. You have been kind, but to you I was nothing. You did not love me. Not as I love Miranda. Not as the Scholar Dame and her Companion love one another. No, Vaniya, you did not love me."

"But who could have expected it?" Vaniya burst out. "How can any woman love a man? The relations between man and woman are ordained by the seasons and the tides, they meet as is ordained, but—but love?"

Rhu shook his head, silent, and said no more. Cendri thought, aching for both of them, that they were both victims of their world. Every society had its misfits. She, Cendri, was luckier than most, for she lived in a society where, if she did not find its ordinances to her liking, she could move outside it, into the open worlds like University, where a dozen cultures met. And as she watched Rhu standing helplessly before Vaniya, she understood something about herself and Dal.

I married a man from Pioneer, knowing he would make demands for a kind of submissiveness I was not trained to. I have a greater need for dependency than the women of my world. And yet I have blamed Dal for being what he is. I now know that when we finish our work here, I must either accept Dal as he is . . . what he truly is, not what my insufficiencies need him to be . . . or leave him. But I cannot try to change him. Isis did not change us. It only showed us, unsparingly, what we already were.

Rhu dashed the tears from his eyes, stood before Vaniya with his head resolutely erect. He said, "When this is over, go to the Builders at We-were-guided. They know all things. They will know where Miranda has been taken."

Vaniya grimaced and after a moment Cendri realized it was meant for a smile. She said, heartbrokenly, "Did you not know, Rhu? The Builders have forsaken me. They now speak only to men."

Rhu said steadily, "Then *I* shall go to We-were-guided and ask them in your name for guidance to rescue Miranda."

Vaniya's face lighted with a momentary hope. She said, "But if she is *here*—"

"Then it is all in the hands of whatever power lies behind man and Builders alike," Rhu said quietly, "but if she is in this encampment, the work parties who are exploring the site will surely find her somewhere. Have I your leave to go, then?"

"Yes. Take my car," Vankya said, "but I cannot spare a driver—"

"I can drive your car, Vaniya."

"I never knew that," Vaniya said, in surprise. And Rhu said, his lips moving faintly in a smile, "You never asked me, my dear."

Cendri followed him out, caught at his hand. "Wait, Rhu," she said quickly, "I must go with you, and Dal—there is no time now to explain it—"

She ran to the hillside where Dal was standing above the site, looking down at the busy scene below. Every few minutes some man, coming up from below with something to be taken to high ground—the more important stores were being moved by machinery, but there was more manpower than machinery—would stop before Dal, bow to the ground before him, say a few words.

Cendri hesitated to interrupt them, but he saw her and came toward her. She caught his hand, forgetful of the watching eyes and the customs of the Matriarchate.

"Dal, come with me to We-were-guided—"

"At *this* hour?"

"Yes—I have something to say to the Builders—"

He said, "They did not build the city, Cendri—"

Impatiently she shook her head. "That doesn't matter now! I said *Builders* because that's what the people here call them, you know perfectly well what—*who*—I mean!"

"Something to *say* to them?"

"Yes! Dal, come with me, in case they don't speak to women now—"

He said, "I don't mind telling you I'll be glad to get away for a while! I'm not really any help here . . ." he moved, uncomfortably, as another man with a heavy load of lumber on his head came past and made a clumsy bow. "I know they mean well, and I know I encourage them being here, and God knows the poor devils need all the encouragement they can get. But still I'll be glad to get away, it's—it's *spooky!"*

Rhu drove Vaniya's car fast and skillfully along the deserted road to Ariadne. It was a drive of more than half an hour, and none of them talked much. Cendri was remembering how she had been driven here to the Residence the first day, Miranda at her side, Dal shoved unregarded into the luggage compartment by the driver.

The Residence looked deserted; it was not yet dawn, and Rhu stopped the car and got out, turning along the shore toward the ruins. A couple of small children, nine or ten years old, a girl and a boy, came down the steps and called to Rhu.

He turned back to speak to them, asking, "Is there any news here of the Lady Miranda?"

The little boy shook his head solemnly. The girl asked "Rhu, is it true that the—the Builders now speak only to men?"

Rhu said, "They spoke to men last night, little one. What they will do in future I know no more than you."

The boy said, "Rhu, does this mean I need not be driven away from my mother's house some day?"

Rhu put his arm for a moment around the boy's shoulder. He said, "I don't know, Kal. But it does mean that your life there may be very different than those of older men. It is too soon to tell."

The small boy looked up at Dal from the shelter of Rhu's arm. He said, "Are *you* truly a Scholar?"

Dal nodded, and the boy said, "Can you win at archery or wrestling?"

Dal shook his head. "I have never tried any of those things. I have had other things to learn which seemed more important to me on my world."

The child said scornfully to Dal, "You do not really look strong enough to be a man! Maybe I would rather live in a Men's House after all," and pulled at the little girl at his side. The children ran away. Dal looked after them, shaking his head. As the three walked along the shore toward We-were-guided, Cendri thought, *there is*

*really no way to tell what this society will be. There is
only one thing certain; it will be different. . . .*

Inside the gates they walked slowly through the
still-shadowed canyons of the dead city. Around them
the enormous structures lay, eternally silent, frozen,
and Cendri could see where she and Dal had been
working, their supplies and recording equipment piled
under weatherproof shielding, the tiniest scratch on the
hugeness of the ruins. Had they really been built here
by a race which seeded all life throughout the Galaxy
millions of years ago? Or simply by some society long
predating mankind? And the mysterious voices at
We-were-Guided—had they any relationship to the
ruins at all? Or had they merely come here, separately,
to live in the alien city, tied to the old starship with their
emotional tie to the women here?

A disembodied race of aliens, existing in a sphere of
pure mind. Cendri knew that there were supposed to be
such races; she had never studied one. There were so
many races; so many that even University with its
enormous explosion of knowledge had only begun to
guess at how many there were! If Cendri had speculated about a race disembodied, she would have thought
that they would be detached, emotionless, that they
would have no emotions. *I always thought emotions
were something generated by hormone reactions and
physical conditioning. . . .*

No, came the answer from all round her, and she
realized that they were standing near the spaceship site
and that the warmth and presence of the aliens was all
around them. *We exist in our thoughts, our feelings.
This is why we became so close to your people. We
hungered for their feelings, their emotions.*

Cendri knew that all of their thoughts lay open, now,
in the Ruins. Telepathy, of course. How else would a
disembodied race communicate? How could thought
exist with no brain to house it? How could emotions
exist with no bodily response to generate them?

I can understand that, came an answer, and she knew
that this time it was Rhu's thought, Rhu's emotion

which stood naked before them all, and Cendri found herself remembering—as, she knew, Rhu remembered—the day she had found them in one another's arms here. *My love for Miranda has nothing to do with the body. I had been taught as a boy that what comes between man and woman is generated of the hormones of mating and has no other existence, yet I came to know otherwise.*

Then, came the bodiless voices whose feel Cendri could not identify as the aliens, *you understand us indeed. We can only exist when we are loved, cared for, welcomed . . . worshipped. . . .*

And Cendri felt Dal's thoughts, directed straight at the alien presences, with anger and something like scorn: *Aren't you ashamed of yourselves for pretending to be Gods to these poor gullible women?*

Stranger, we pretended nothing. We are what we are, and receiving love, we gave it in our turn. If their thoughts saw us as Gods, whatever Gods may be, if the nature of a God is to give and receive love, then perhaps that is what we are, but I can see that in your mind the concept of a God is one who wields power . . . it is not so with these women. Is that, stranger, because you are from what these women call the maleworlds?

Cendri wondered if this was the most fundamental difference between men's societies and women's, after all; that in societies founded by men, the concept of a supreme being was one of Power, and that in women's societies, it was one of Love. . . .

Dal said, and Cendri felt his focused thoughts angry in the sunrise, *You have made them dependent on you!*

We need their love to survive, or we become empty air and die, as we slept in long terrible loneliness before they came. Why, then, since they meet all our needs, should we deny them help in the meeting of theirs?

That, Cendri thought, was an uncommonly good question.

Stranger, only last night did we discover how much they needed help which is simple for us to give; knowledge beforetime of where the ground will tremble, or a great wave strike the shore. If we give them this help they need not impoverish their world to buy machinery which can do this.

Dal's answer was quick and wrathful: *Thus you will encourage them to cut themselves off further from the civilized worlds of the Unity, and persist in their tyranny against men. . . .*

No! Now that we know their men are not what they believed them, dangerously weak creatures . . . we knew their males only through the women's minds, the aliens explained, *but now we know that the women and the men are very much alike, we shall speak to both . . . and as for cutting themselves off from the civilized worlds, we do not want that! We are lonely—and curious! We want people to come here from everywhere . . . and learn to know us. . . .*

Standing close together before the silent, glowing ship, Dal put his arm around Cendri's waist. She *felt* his thoughts, open to her as never before. He was envisioning a team of scientists here; maybe a hundred to start; here to explore the Ruins in depth, men and women working together as equals, to demonstrate to the women, and to the men, of Isis, that there was no tyranny in the maleworlds . . . Cendri was surprised to hear him using the contemptuous term of the women of Isis . . . no tyranny from Unity or University, but that the Unity, and the scientists of University, truly regarded women and men as equals, partners, the inseparable half of a single completed whole, the human race, mankind. This would do more, Dal thought, to *demonstrate* to Isis that they need not fear male equality, than a thousand years of lectures and teaching and propaganda.

When they come to know us, they will understand.

And then she felt his thoughts turn to her, embrace her with a tenderness and warmth she had never guessed. Knowing that here, in the presence of the Builders, her thoughts lay open to him as his to her, Cendri was for a moment ashamed, then, willingly, turned to Dal and embraced him. This it was, then, that

Dal felt for her; an acceptance, a respect, a tenderness, which had nothing, or very little, to do with sex; it came from caring, from shared work, from their long time of learning about one another. And as she held him, feeling her own love, so long forgotten in the irritations of daily life, flood back through her, she thought; *we have found each other again. Dal, Dal, let's never lose each other again* . . . and she knew she was crying in his arms.

Rhu's thoughts blended into theirs, hesitant. *I know now what it is that I have been seeking all my life. Our society does not recognize this, derides it, says it does not exist, yet when I came to love Miranda, I knew it must exist somewhere, and now I know that the dream Miranda and I dreamed was real, even if we cannot share it in this world.* Cendri felt him lay his soft hand on her arm, on Dal's. Then he let them go, and went to the very foot of the ship. He said, and as he spoke the words Cendri felt them resonating in her mind, with the strength of the thoughts opened here:

You know what I am. You know what I feel. I want nothing for myself. But in my blindness, mistaken, I betrayed Miranda into the hands of those less idealistic than I. Help me to restore her to the arms of her mother and the women of her household, and then Vaniya may do with me as she will.

A long silence, and Cendri was aware of the warmth, the tenderness surrounding them, aware of the strength of Rhu's love. And at last, when the glow died, she heard Rhu whisper, "Thank you, oh, thank you!"

The cold dawn wind was around them, and the ruins filled with sunlight, glaring on the towers. The three of them were alone in the ruins; the presences had withdrawn. Rhu said, "Miranda—Miranda—" and suddenly staggered. Dal reached out and caught him, holding him upright. He said, concerned, "Are you all right, Rhu?"

He wasn't, Cendri thought. He was a ghastly color, his face greyed, his breath coming in gasps; but he leaned on Dal only a moment and pulled himself upright. He said, "Miranda—she is in the center warehouse where lumber and building cement are stored! We must get there at once—" he glanced at Dal and Cendri, gasping, his long slender hands clutching his chest. "You heard—you heard Mother Vaniya say—those warehouses, not even to search them, that they were used only for storing lumber and cement, they will be left to break the force of the waves before they strike on the strengthened dikes elsewhere— Goddess!" he gasped, "if she is alone there—"

Dal and Cendri tried to reassure him as they hurried out of the ruins and toward the car. Surely Miranda would hear the search, the heavy machinery moving elsewhere in the construction site, would know that something was afoot. Surely even her captors would not abandon her in the direct path of a tidal wave!

But Rhu was white with terror. He said, "I do not know—I am afraid—so many of the men here—it is ignorance, not evil intent, but they may panic and never think to save her, or they may be so full of anger and resentment, she may suffer for their hatred of Vaniya—"

"Look," Dal said, "from what we heard that wave isn't due till sometime late in the day, and it's not more than an hour or two after sunrise now. We've got plenty of time to get back to the construction site and start hunting for her. She'll be out of there hours before the wave hits. Come on—" he supported Rhu's staggering steps, helped him into the car. "You'd better let me or Cendri drive, you're in no shape to do anything! Rhu, you've done enough! Cendri, can you drive this thing?"

"Oh, certainly, I've watch Miranda, it's simple enough," Cendri said, then, looking at Rhu's collapsed face, thought: *he's used to seeing women take over all the time,* and in a gesture of pure love, said, "You drive, Dal, You're a better driver than I am." He wasn't; but it would do Rhu a lot of good to think so. And, she thought, here on Isis it won't do Dal any harm either!

Dal climbed behind the wheel, swung the car around,

headed down the gravelled road toward the dam site, the surface car eating up Standard Kilometers at a considerable clip. The car rocked and jounced; it had not been designed for rough country roads, but for the streets of Ariadne. It was intended for the sedate rounds of the Pro-Matriarch on her official duties. What they needed was some kind of heavy-duty all-terrain vehicle, but these had all been commandeered for use at the site.

Cendri sat wedged in beside Rhu, all three of them crowded in the driver's compartment. Suddenly the car shot over an enormous bump—a bump? A section of the road had somehow heaved itself up in front of them; Dal jammed on the brake and they rocked and swayed to the edge of the road.

"*That,*" said Dal, with tight control, "was absolutely all we needed. Another earthquake!"

Rhu said, "I cannot see how we needed . . ." and broke off at the sight of Dal's stormy face. Dal climbed out, examining the road ahead and the wheel of the car.

"No harm done to the car," he said, "at least none that I can see. The road is something else." He stood looking at the crevasse, not much more than a foot wide, which had shoved up a hump of earth before the wheel. "Just have to push the thing around it, I guess. Lucky the people of Isis go for *small* surface transit, the enormous people-movers we use on Pioneer couldn't be budged by fewer than ten or twelve men!"

Between them, they shoved and hoisted the car around the obstacle. Cendri put her shoulder to the wheel with the men; seeing Rhu's drawn face, remembering his bad heart, she tried to discourage him, but he said angrily, "I am a Companion, Scholar Dame, but I can do my part when I must," and Cendri gave in, muttering under her breath, damning the male fetish of strength and pride in their muscles on Pioneer and Isis and every other damned planet under the sun! *Any* sun!

The sun was high and they were all dripping with sweat by the time the car was steady on its wheels in the road, and Dal had to lash up a door-handle which twice burst open, with Rhu's belt-thongs before it was safe to drive. But finally they were on their way again, although the car wobbled ominously and Dal said that some arrangement of springs or shock-absorbers meant to steady it underneath had come loose, so that they had to go at a slow pace or it threatened to vibrate itself to pieces. The sun was blinding hot, and Cendri worried at the passing hours; she had not been told precisely at what hour the tidal wave would strike, she had no chronometer in any case, but she knew the margin of safety could not be all that great.

When they finally came within sight of the construction area the car was stopped in the road by a series of wooden barriers. A woman wearing a badge of office advised them that the site was closed, that it had been evacuated, and that no one was allowed inside, except those working with the final removal of heavy machinery from the endangered area.

"Where is the Pro-Matriarch Vaniya?" Rhu demanded.

"She's still inside the site," the woman said, laughing scornfully, "but I'm sure she can get along without her Companion for the afternoon, little fellow. Just go back where you won't get hurt, why don't you? She'll come looking for you when the danger's over."

For a moment Cendri thought Rhu would strike the woman. Frightened, she grabbed as his arm—*any male who attacks a citizen can be summarily destroyed* . . . But Rhu's conditioning held. He drew back and said, "Respect, but I insist, I have an important message—"

"*Do* get out of our way and stop annoying us," said the woman impatiently, and Cendri realized what she must do. She got out of the car and came around to the official . . . although it was hard, she thought, with a fraction of her awareness still focusing on Unity standards, to think of this woman as an official when she was wearing a pink flowered pajama suit! But by the badge pinned to the suit she knew the woman was in charge. Cendri said severely, "I am the Scholar Dame Cendri Malocq, and Vaniya sent us on an important mission concerning her daughter and heir; let us through at once!"

The woman pursed her lips. "Right; I did hear her daughter was missing," she said. "Go right ahead, Scholar Dame, but you'd better leave the men here. There are a few rough laborers working on the site still, but Companions and children are supposed to be kept out."

Cendri said coldy, "I will be responsible for their safety," and the woman, though she still looked hesitant, said, "Well, you know best, Scholar Dame, though I'd advise against it." As Cendri passed the barrier, the woman reached out and touched her on the arm. "The Pro-Matriarch Vaniya is near the edge of the dam's inner wall, supervising the last of the machinery being removed. The quake a little while ago cracked the outer sea-wall, and they gave up trying to strengthen it to survive the waves. The whole line of machinery —they pulled it back to try and strengthen the inner dike, so there will not be so much to rebuild. But it's a risk. Within the hour—" she consulted a timepiece pinned on her belt, "we have to have every last human being, man or woman, out of there, and every piece of machinery we have to be sure we're saving!"

Suddenly Cendri recognized the woman. Two days ago, as the sun rose over the shore, this woman had lain next to her and Laurina on the shore, they had embraced as sisters. She saw that the recognition was mutual; the woman quickly put an arm around her shoulders. She said, "I'll go with you, they'll let you through without any more trouble if I'm there. Come on, hurry—do we really need the men with us?"

Cendri nodded, not explaining, and they hurried down the barricaded road, moving to the edges as heavy machinery lumbered through. With one piece she saw the Pro-Matriarch Mahala, who called, "Everything from the North level is out, Larida!"

Cendri's companion nodded, hurrying her along. She said, "There's not much to go now. Is it true they've found a new way to predict quakes and tidal waves,

then, to give us advance warning?" Cendri nodded and
she said, "Wonderful, we can start to fight that way.
Come along, this way—" she looked back at Rhu with
concern. "I don't think it ought to come. Nobody's
going to have time or energy to carry it if it faints."

"Rhu," Cendri said, concerned by the pallor of
Rhu's face, "Why not stay here? We can take the
message to Vaniya!"

Stubbornly the man shook his head.

They saw the inner sea-wall now, dikes piled high
with sandbags and heavy reinforcements, and withdrawing from them with the last of the machinery, the
tall heavy form of Vaniya. Cendri ran toward her.

"Vaniya! Vaniya," she called. "We know where
Miranda is held! She is here—have you found her?"

Vaniya stopped, looking at Cendri in disbelief and
dismay.

Here? Cendri, she cannot be, every building has been
searched!"

"The three warehouses of lumber and cement, the
ones you said not to go near—" Cendri gasped, "she is
being held in the center one—quickly, quickly—"

Vaniya turned without another word and hurried
toward the outer sea-wall. Cendri, looking down the
slope, saw that everything possible to remove had been
removed, and only the skeleton of buildings remained.
Vaniya flung over her shoulder "How did you find this
out?"

"It was Rhu—" she turned and sought with her eyes
for him. "Where is he? Has he fainted?" she cried out,
quite forgetting that the male pronoun was not proper.
But there was a commotion on the slope, women
shouting.

"You can't go down there—hi! Come back! It's too
late, everything's out of there—" and as Vaniya hurried
toward them, Cendri at her heels, the women guarding
the slope said angrily, "Some damned man ran down
there, some curled-hair pet forgot its ribbons, I
suppose—"

Vaniya said tightly, "My daughter—she is down there, in the warehouse—"

"Oh, no, Mother Pro-Matriarch," said one of the women soothingly, "there's nobody at all down there, trust me. Everybody's out, you know, we searched every building except those old empty warehouses, and there's nothing there but cement and lumber, who would bother going in there? Anyhow, she'd have come out a long time ago."

Vaniya said shakily, "She might be in labor and unable to walk—"

"She'd have had enough warning, surely—" the woman broke off, shading her eyes against the sun. She said, "Goddess! There *is* someone coming out of that warehouse—*two* people!" She checked her timepiece, and said, "We may have *just* time—" and hastily, signalling toward the figures below, began to run down the slope.

Vaniya began to run after them; Cendri caught her, held her back by force. "No, no," she urged. "They will get her out if it is humanly possible—please, Vaniya—come back behind the inner wall—Dal, help me—" she begged, supporting the old woman's weight, "Look, Vaniya, they have them both—Rhu was carrying Miranda, carrying her in his arms, now they have taken Miranda from him, they are carrying her—"

"They're carrying Rhu, too," Dal broke in, "I knew he shouldn't have gone in—oh, my God!" He stiffened, staring out at the horizon, and Cendri knew, in horror, what he had seen. A siren went off somewhere, and the few people left between the sea and the inner dike dropped everything and began to run. Cendri thrust Vaniya along, twisting her head to see the four strong women, carrying Rhu and Miranda, hurrying toward the inner dike. Cendri and Dal between them boosted the Pro-Matriarch's heavy body over the wall, but she struggled away from them, hurrying to where the women were laying Miranda on the grass. One of them, looking at Miranda sharply, said, "I will see if there is a midwife in the crowd up there," and ran up toward the barriers.

Miranda was deathly white. She said, "I am all right, I tell you, I need the midwife more than I need anyone else's help. Cendri, is it you? What is this all about? Rhu would explain nothing, he simply grabbed me up in his arms and ran, what is happening?"

But before anyone could answer—Cendri realized in a flash that Miranda, confined in an empty warehouse, knew nothing of the tidal wave or the warning from We-were-guided—there was a great, crashing roar like the end of the world, and Cendri saw a great wall of water which looked miles high racing toward the shore with the speed of a gigantic jet. Miranda heard the roar and cried out in terror, and Rhu, lying collapsed on the grass, his face drawn in pain, whispered in agony, "Miranda—"

"She is safe, Rhu," Dal said, leaning over him. "You're both going to be all right; just lie back and relax."

"Miranda—" he whispered again, and she turned over, slowly, painfully, reaching for his hand. She whispered, "Rhu—Rhu—"

The agony contorted his face again; he struggled for breath. Miranda held his hand tightly; leaned over and kissed him on the lips, but when she drew away his face was slack and still. Alarmed, Dal felt for a pulse; shook his head.

"He's gone," he said. "Poor, poor heroic little devil!"

Miranda began to sob helplessly. Vaniya bent over Rhu, gently closed his eyes. And then, with a great roar, the tsunami struck below them. Cendri saw the warehouses go, with one great explosion of flying lumber, heard the roar as the outer sea-wall burst and sagged inward like a child's sand-castle, and the water came racing, flying inward with such a sound of thunder that Cendri was deafened, and, watching the great wall of water, felt certain it would roar inward, sweep them

away where they stood, with the wreckage of the
dikes. . . .

But although the flying spray drenched them with
salt, stinging their eyes and splashing high against the
dike above them, it held, and, miraculously, began to
recede. Cendri sank down, gasping, Vaniya looked at
Rhu's body with deep regret.

"How heroic—for a man," she said, in wonder.
"What could he have cared for Miranda! But even a
dog can be heroic—"

And suddenly Cendri was angry, with a blazing fury.
She stood up, towering over Vaniya in uncontrollable
rage.

"Do you know what he did?" she demanded. "Do
you *know* that it was Rhu who saved her, who killed
himself for her? If he had waited until your officials
here got through arguing, she would be down there in
that smashed matchwood that used to be a warehouse!
She and her unborn child both! If he hadn't acted on his
own initiative, without waiting for some woman's
permission, your daughter and your heir would be lying
dead down there, and you would never even have
known it! Even a *dog* heroic? He loved her, Vaniya! He
loved her!" she repeated, collapsed into Dal's arms and
began to cry.

Vaniya looked shaken. She said slowly, "How do
you know this?" and, wiping her eyes, Cendri explained how she and Dal and Rhu had gone together to
We-were-guided.

"Then you had a part in it too, Cendri, and you—
Scholar," Vaniya said awkwardly, and after a moment
Cendri realized she had spoken to Dal. He said, still
kneeling by Rhu's lifeless body, "I only wish I could
have done more, Pro-Matriarch; not only to save
Rhu—he was my friend—but to show you, perhaps,
that men can show all the good qualities which you of
Isis reserve for women."

Vaniya bowed her head. She said, "Some day,
perhaps, I shall know how best to thank you."

Miranda was sobbing, holding Rhu's cold hand in hers. She whispered to Cendri, "For this to happen—for this to happen *now*—when we might have seen our dream—"

Cendri held Miranda close, but she said nothing. Let Miranda keep the dream that some day, if Rhu had lived, they might have had one another in the way Dal and Cendri had each other. It could never have been. They were both children of the Matriarchate, and that bold a change would not come in Miranda's lifetime, or, perhaps, that of her unborn daughter. Cendri and Dal had begun as equals, had found one another through shared work and shared interests and mutual respect. Rhu and Miranda might have tasted the outer fringes of this kind of love. But it could only have turned, for them, to bitterness and disappointment. Now Miranda would keep, forever, a romantic memory of what might have been, and the knowledge that the man she loved had given his life for her. And Rhu—with her heart torn, Cendri remembered his plaintive song;

> When I am dead
> Will the Goddess take me, perhaps
> To her loving breasts?

Miranda cried out suddenly, holding herself with both hands.

"Oh! Oh! quick! Somebody! Help! Get the midwife—please, somebody—*any* midwife, but *hurry*—"

There was a flurry, and Vaniya said, looking up the slope, "She will be here in a minute, my precious, she will come to you here. . . ."

Miranda sighed with relief. She said, shakily, "It took a tidal wave to make my lazy daughter decide to be born—and wouldn't you know? I am the first woman to have her baby while visiting the sea!"

"Miranda!" said Vaniya in shock, "How can you make such a joke at a time like *this*—" for all the women around had burst into scandalized giggles.

Dal said plaintively to Cendri, "Will you please tell me what the hell is so funny about that?"

But Cendri knew that she could not explain it, in the presence of the women of Isis, to any man. Not for generations.

A portion of the Report submitted to the Mentor Lokshmann, of the College of Xeno-anthropology and Comparative Culture on University, by the Scholar Dame Cendri Owain, resident on Isis/ Cinderella:

. . . this season the great dam on the river Anahit has been completed, with earthquake-proof safeguards. The Inland Land Reclamation Project has absorbed most of the workmen from the dam construction site. Most of the men continue to live in the inland villages which they have colonized, and to hire out for wages. Few of them bother to exercise the legal franchise, saying that too much concern with politics serves to destroy a man's natural instincts.

Shortly after the great tsunami which destroyed the first construction site, the Council of Ariadne, under the advice of the Intelligences who have been designated pro tem *as Ruins A Culture, appointed the High Matriarch Vaniya to assume all the religious duties of High Priestess, while the High Matriarch Mahala was chosen to administer all secular matters within the City of Ariadne. A representative from the Men's Houses is chosen every Long Year, with the provision that he must be of what the Council calls a "sedate old age" and therefore, as they say, no longer at the mercy of his sexual drives, and capable of abstract thought. Thus the Council is headed by a tripartite authority, with an absolute provision that no matter shall be settled unless to the satisfaction of all three parties. This, as they say, assured that no majority can force the will* and conscience of a minority, and that no material considerations may override the spiritual needs of the people. The formal designation of the male appointed to the tripartite authority is Elder Brother, and the new custom states that a former Elder Brother shall retain for life his Council seat, without a vote, but shall advise and instruct his comrades and younger brothers in the Men's Houses of the city and countryside.

The archaeological expedition to We-were-guided has now had a full Long Year in the ruins at We-were-guided. This preliminary team of a hundred and nineteen men and a hundred and twenty-four women have worked together admirably well with volunteer workers from the College of Ariadne, which is now known as the Women's College. After observing the work of the men and women from University, ninety-two men from the city of Ariadne have volunteered to enroll in the new Men's College built in the colony village of Anahit. The first class will graduate with the status of Scholar, two Long Years from now.

There is little social mingling between men and women, except among the relatively enlightened women of the college of Ariadne, and a few of the men working with the Unity team in We-were-guided. However, it has been noticed that over thirty women, a full half of them still of reproductive age, have applied for a license to take a Companion. Most women, however, still prefer a life-partnership with another woman, and the status of a Companion is very low. A new insult is in use among children in Ariadne; "Companion's-child." This word is considered too gross for use among grown women.

Twenty-nine women of the University team have formed a Household in Ariadne, and although I have entered the household only on formal terms as a guest, I have noticed that a few of the women have *chose life-partners, although as yet there are no cross-partnerships between women of Isis/ Cinderella and the Unity.*

Enclosed in this report are several applications, passed on through the Embassy and approved by the Council, of five women and two men who have applied for matriculation and residence permits on University, with provisional Student status. Two of the women are personally know to me; Laurina, of the household of the High Matriarch Mahala, and a full professor of History at the Women's College, assisted me competently during the preliminary mapping of the site at We-were-guided; she comes with the personal recommendation of the Master Scholar Dallard Malocq as well as my own. She has written a monograph on archaeology for the use of the two colleges here, and has requested that when she achieves Scholar's status she be reassigned to Isis/Cinderella to do her advanced work in the field of communication with nonhuman intelligences, among the people designated as Ruins A Culture.

The second applicant to bear my personal recommendation is Miranda, daughter of the High Matriarch Vaniya. She holds a degree in vocal and instrumental music from the Women's College, and is my close personal friend; she has appointed me guardian of her daughter Cendriya during the period of her absence.

The other applicants are not personally known to me, although one of the women bears the personal recommendation of the Scholar Dame Lurianna di Velo and holds a degree in Temporal Mathematics; both of the men bear the recommendation of the Master Scholar Dallard Malocq, and are advanced students and instructors at the Men's College.

At a later date I shall submit information as to the continuing cultural investigation of social organization among the Ruins A Culture, a project which is barely beginning.

I know that you and your colleagues are also interested in the progress of the study of the ruins at We-were-guided. May I direct your attention to the study forwarded under separate cover by the Master Scholar Dallard Malocq and the Scholar Dame di Velo. This is, of course, a preliminary study; it has not yet even determined whether or not the ruins were erected by the race designated as the Builders. The Scholar Dame Lurianna di Velo will forward an advanced report by the next ship from Isis. I enclose also her request, to be forwarded to the Mentors of the College of Archaeology, for an advance team of four hundred; I wish in my capacity of resident expert on matriarchal customs to remind the assigning committee of University that by the laws of the Matriarchate, the committee must number fewer men than women. The Scholar Dame has also requested that among the committee, at least half a dozen women be included who hold degrees in Temporal Mathematics. She is aware of the current Scholar's attitude toward the theory of Time stasis, which is why she asked me to forward this request informally instead of going through channels.

I thank you for your kind wishes, and the offer to grant me a maternity leave for the next season, and to delay the forwarding of my advanced reports and qualification data, but it is not the custom of women on Isis/Cinderella to take such leaves, and it would reflect poorly upon the women of University if I were to do so. Nevertheless, I am deeply grateful for your attempted consideration.

I shall be awaiting your reply, and your promised visit to the site of the Ruins A Culture.

> With respectful greetings,
> Cendri Owain Malocq
> Scholar Dame (qualified; Isis/Cinderella)